EVERY MOTHER'S SON

THE JACKALS

EVERY MOTHER'S SON

WILLIAM W. JOHNSTONE
AND J. A. JOHNSTONE

THORNDIKE PRESS
A part of Gale, a Cengage Company

Thorndike Press® Large Print Hardcover Western.
The text of this Large Print edition is unabridged.
Other aspects of the book may vary from the original edition.
Set in 16 pt. Plantin.

LIBRARY OF CONGRESS CIP DATA ON FILE.
CATALOGUING IN PUBLICATION FOR THIS BOOK
IS AVAILABLE FROM THE LIBRARY OF CONGRESS.

ISBN-13: 978-1-4328-9115-2 (hardcover alk. paper)

Published in 2021 by arrangement with Pinnacle Books, an imprint of
Kensington Publishing Corp.

Printed in Mexico
Print Number: 01   Print Year: 2022

EVERY MOTHER'S SON

PROLOGUE

Letter to Captain J.J.K. Hollister,
Texas Rangers, Purgatory City
Captain Hollister:

This letter was never written. If anything in this letter ever is mentioned publicly, by you, the press, your men, or by the biggest wastrel and drunk in West Texas or anywhere in Texas, Mexico, the Southwest, the United States and Her territories — or anywhere in this world, for that matter — your reputation, your career, your life are officially over.

This letter and envelope are to be burned immediately after you have finished reading it. The terms of the preceding paragraph apply to this order, too.

Having read your report to Austin on the 7th inst., I have met with Major McDonald, Attorney General Eubanks, and Brigadier General Marshall, commander of the Department of Texas, and we have reached this conclusion:

Leave Harry Holland alone.

While Holland is a notorious cutthroat, whose crimes rival those of the most desperate felons in the annals of Texas, as well as our nation, the fact is that Holland and those thirty banditti that ride with him confine most of their crimes south of the border. General Marshall and Major McDonald agree that harassing those greasers keeps them from raiding our ranchers and villages in the Great State of Texas. Everyone in Austin believes that the Mexicans would love to reclaim Texas as one of its provinces, or at the very least reset the international boundary at the Nueces River instead of the Rio Grande, and I will not let that happen on my watch, So Help Me GOD!

But as our lily-livered president in Washington, District of Columbia, does not want to provoke a war, we cannot send Army troops or Texas Rangers across the Rio Grande. So the consensus here is to let Harry Holland carry out the war for Texas and the U.S. Army.

Is that clear?

Yes, I know, Captain, that the Texas Rangers never shirk duty, that they, like those abysmal Mounties in that frozen tundra of Canada — which also should be part of our

United States — always get their man. By thunder, the Texas Rangers even caught that notorious evildoer John Wesley Hardin — by pursuing him all the way to the Florida Panhandle. Boundaries are not our concern. Justice is.

But let us face the facts, Captain. Holland and his men have built an impenetrable fortress in the Big Bend country. Your last pursuit of a band of Holland's hellish marauders was unsuccessful. Having read your report, allow me to point out how vain it was:

1. You led your entire battalion, except for ten men left to keep the peace in Purgatory City and the western-most extremes of our state, after six of Holland's men wounded one cowboy and made off with forty head of Lazy H beeves. (I suppose Holland and his men had grown tired of eating javelinas for supper.) This makes me ask why you thought a crime of rustling fewer than one hundred head was worth risking almost your entire command. Could the $12,500 reward the U.S. government and the state of Texas have put up for the capture or killing of

Harry Holland have motivated this campaign?

2. Three of your men had to turn back and walk — walk! — leading their horses all the way to Mr. Ben Madison's ranchero — as their mounts went lame riding over this harsh country. It was Mr. Madison's beeves that the raiders rustled, and now Mr. Madison had to loan your three Rangers horses so they could return to Purgatory City. Your commander, Major McDonald, has informed me that he just received a bill for those horses, since they have not been returned, for $150. You and your three footsore Rangers can only be relieved that the rancher did not swear out a complaint for horse theft.

3. Two civilian scouts, hired without authority for Major McDonald's office, apparently got lost in the rugged country. According to your report, after three days of searching, the scouts were given up for dead.

4. On the seventh day in the Big Bend, according to this report, having ridden into dead end after dead end,

and barely finding your way back to the main trail yourselves, this Ranger expeditionary force was attacked by what you call hostile Apaches. As Brigadier Marshall so succinctly put it: HOSTILE APACHES is redundant. Were you unaware that a band of Apache warriors is also holed up in the Big Bend? Colonel John Caxton at Fort Spalding near Purgatory City has had no luck flushing those Apaches out of that godforsaken country, either. But since the Apaches also seem to prefer raiding south of the Rio Grande, Colonel Caxton at least has the brains not to send his troops into the Big Bend Country on what amounts to a suicide mission.

5. The ambush by the Apaches cost you a mule laden with food stores and a mule laden with ammunition. Captain, I must commend you for giving arms and food to an enemy of the people of our state, and even an enemy of those peons below the Rio Grande. To your credit — and I remember how gallantly you served in the late Rebellion under General

Hastings, God remember his name and the glory he reaped at Fredericksburg — you suffered only four casualties, of which only one was killed. Killed, by your best estimation, by friendly fire.

6. Over the next two days, you sustained one more casualty when a young Ranger fell into a hot spring and was severely scalded. You said in this report that he is expected to recover, although his face will no longer be admired by his sweetheart, and that he still screams whenever he rolls over.

7. A rabid coyote ran off two more horses, leaving two more Rangers afoot. They were ordered to ride double, until one slipped off his horse and broke his left leg in three places after tumbling seventy-seven yards down a rocky slope. He had the good luck, I assume, to at least be able to ride in a travois with some comfort — once all the cactus spines had been removed from his body. This begs the question: I assume the whiskey rations you mentioned in your expense report might be the blame for a Texas Ranger

falling off his horse!

8. After two weeks without getting any closer to Harry Holland and his marauders than finding ancient tracks and horse droppings that were dried, you decided that you had "put a scare" into Holland as he must be hiding. Let me repeat that phrase — "put a scare" — into an outlaw who you never saw, not even dust from his ponies, and for all you know, neither Harry Holland or any of his nefarious associates ever knew you were in the general area of his hidden compound. The only ones that knew of your existence, in my estimation, were some Apaches and a coyote, and I can imagine the ravens circling over your heads laughing, CAW, CAW, CAW, CAW.

9. While figuring the way out from the maze that is Texas's Big Bend, you ran out of water at the time you found the main trail again, and headed north for Apache Springs. Apache Springs is twenty miles away, according to the Major, but the Rio Grande was probably a quarter mile south? Can we blame

this on sunstroke?

10. Luckily, a severe thunderstorm drenched you and your men that afternoon, bringing some comfort to your command but not to the pack mule that was struck by lightning.

11. Four days later, you returned to the Rangers headquarters in Purgatory City, having lost only one Ranger — so far, unless the two men who came down with pneumonia after the monsoon have succumbed by the time this letter reaches you. I assume you do not consider your guides left behind and presumed dead as part of your command since they were not sworn in as Texas Rangers.

Well, Captain, I think these facts sum up why you are to leave Harry Holland alone. Colonel Caxton, according to the Brigadier, believes the same. Unless Holland is foolish enough to attack Purgatory City or Fort Spalding en masse, forget he exists. Leave him to the foolish bounty hunters who think they can find his hideout and not be staked out beside an ant bed with honey poured over their faces by Apache Indians. If Holland is killed by Mexican Rurales or Apaches or by his own men, good riddance. As far as you are concerned, Harry Holland does not exist. You may send out a SMALL patrol every now and then, just to save face, but that patrol should not venture beyond the outskirts of the Big Bend.

If the press were to find out about this, the embarrassment would raise Sam Houston from the grave, and his wrath would be worse than that of Apaches and Holland's marauders combined.

Remember your orders. And remember that if you disobey my instructions, the points I made in this letter regarding your stupidity can be made to every newspaper in our glorious state.

Sincerely,
David X. Cumberland IV
Governor of Texas

P. S.: Speaking of nuisances and blights on Texas's Good Name, is there any word on "The Jackals?" You could start your return to my good graces if you were to inform me that Matt McCulloch, Sean Keegan, and Jed Breen are now dead.

CHAPTER ONE

Jed Breen damned well knew how much trouble he was in. Stuck in the middle of the salt fields, his horse dead a hundred yards away, buzzards circling, and those big black birds likely knew they'd have more than a roan gelding to feast on before too long. Two men had Breen pinned down. The baking sun beat him down, too. His canteen lay underneath the dead roan. So did Breen's Sharps rifle. The only thing Breen had to defend himself was a .38-caliber Colt Lightning revolver, and the two men who wanted him dead positioned themselves far, far away. Out of pistol range, they were, but Breen pulled the Colt from the holster, and cocked it anyway.

At least, he tried to cock it. The casehardened iron would not budge. The Lightning being a double-action, Breen tried to pull the trigger, which should have brought the hammer back, but no matter how hard

Breen squeezed, neither trigger nor hammer moved. He jostled the cylinder. Nothing. Not a movement, not a creak. He jammed it on the dead junk of juniper he hid behind, then worked hammer and trigger again. His end results? A string of silent curses.

Breen had yet to catch his breath after running for the nearest shelter he could find — this one dead juniper in the middle of a sea of white. His heart thundered, and Breen wet his tongue while he reevaluated his situation.

No rifle. No horse. No water. And a jammed revolver.

Well, he thought, if those two hombres get close enough, I can always blind them by throwing salt in their eyes.

Breen tested the Lightning once more, only to see the same results.

No rifle. No horse. No water. No revolver.

He sighed.

No chance.

He took off his hat, ran his fingers through his bone-white hair, and briefly checked the position of the sun. Dark was a long ways off. Mountains rose off to the northwest a ways, but Breen would have to run more than three-tenths of a mile before he reached the end of the salt flats in that direction. Southwest and west would take him another mile before he left the white desert for the tan one. It would also take him farther and farther from the water of the river to the east. And if he ran west, his back would provide an inviting target for the two assassins.

Never wanted to cash in my chips with a bullet in my back. Unless I was making love to a jealous husband's wife.

His smile didn't last long.

The only directions, heading east, would mean covering two hundred yards or more, and he would be moving straight to two men waiting for him. Two men who had already proved themselves to be pretty good shots with rifles.

Jim Kincaid. That's who brought Breen to this country. That's who got Breen in this fix. Kincaid. And that $400 price on his head.

Kincaid had made a name for himself robbing trains in the Indian Nations. Deputy United States marshals had been hunting him for two or three years with little to show for it except three wounded and one dead deputy. The KATY railroad had put up a $200 reward on Kincaid, the dead deputy's widow had offered another $100, and the state of Texas figured he was worth $100 for being a general nuisance and for the fact that the KATY — nickname for the Missouri-Kansas-Texas Railway — had finally reached Texas a few years back.

With the pressure and noose tightening, Jim Kincaid had left the Nations and had last been seen in El Paso. Breen saw the latest reward poster on Kincaid in Mesilla, New Mexico Territory, where he had just deposited a murderer for a $150 reward. Heading back to his home in Purgatory City, Texas, Breen stopped in at a saloon in El Paso, where he learned that Jim Kincaid had just moseyed out of town and was making his way to Lincoln in New Mexico Territory, where he figured he might as well sell his gun to the highest bidder in this range war going on up there.

This time of year, hot as things were getting in Texas, Breen figured that he might as well head to Lincoln, too. Pretty country, that part of Southern New Mexico Territory, and if a man like Jim Kincaid wanted in on the action, chances were other desperadoes would be joining the rival forces in Lincoln, too. Desperadoes with their descriptions on all sorts of wanted posters. If Breen could collect enough bounties, well, he might have enough money to last him till fall.

What Breen had not counted on was that Jim Kincaid would run in to John Murrell on the ride up to Lincoln.

Murrell was wanted for three murders, two assaults, one rape, and six or seven stagecoach robberies. The last poster on Murrell that Breen had seen said his bounty totaled $300, which did seem a tad low for a man who had killed three men and raped a woman, but Breen didn't think about that until he was trapped in the salt flats.

He saw where Murrell met Kincaid, just northeast of Howell's Tanks. Neither men had stopped at the roughshod station run by Lucius Howell — at least that's what rawboned, tightlipped Howell had told Breen, but most smart men knew better than to drink Howell's rotgut or play cards with any gambler operating there. That meant Murrell must have ridden in to Kincaid's camp, shared some coffee, then camped there for the night, and that morning, Murrell rode east, and Kincaid kept on the trail to Lincoln.

What Breen didn't figure on was that John Murrell had been in El Paso, too, and had seen Breen ride off after Kincaid. Probably the same barfly who confided Kincaid's plans to Breen — for $10 — took money from Murrell to learn of Breen's idea. Breen didn't even know Murrell and Kincaid knew each other. Maybe they didn't until then.

A few miles past Howell's Tanks, the trail went through the salt flats. Breen stopped to rest his horse, drink water from his canteen, and scan the country with his binoculars. The hoofprints left by Kicaid's horse revealed a man in no particular hurry still riding along at a leisurely pace, it being hot, and Lincoln County being a good distance away.

Satisfied, Breen rode through the country and made a careless mistake. He left his Sharps rifle with the fancy telescopic sight sheathed in the scabbard. Two rifle shots rang out, one punching a hole through the bedroll behind the cantle, another slamming into the roan's head. Breen barely managed to clear the stirrups. Landing in the sand, two other shots kicked up white dust a few feet from Breen, who climbed to his feet and felt a bullet tug on his bandana and another slug buzz past his left ear.

He took off running before the next two bullets sounded, seeing the juniper, and figuring that his luck would not hold. Yet it had. Breen dived to his right, as two bullets clipped the brittle branches of the dead tree, and that's where Breen pulled himself up into a ball and started figuring his options.

"Señor Kincaid," a voice called back from the rocks, "that *bouledogue* of a *chasseur*, he runs like a *pura sangre,* and is *uno hombre con suerte.*"

"Keep quiet, Murrell," Kincaid rang out from his position. "And if he raises his head, blow it off."

That was when Breen understood that the second gunman was John Murrell. He was the only outlaw in these parts who could not complete a sentence in one language. It always came about as a mix of English, French, and Spanish.

While he beat on the Lightning some more, Breen did some backtracking in his mind and came up with his theory about how Kincaid and Murrell met.

"Cazador, mi amigo," Murrell yelled, "you should have remained in that *salon pas cher* in the *ville* of El Paso."

"Shut up, Murrell. Keep your rifle sights on that mad-dog killer."

That exchange just confirmed Breen's theory.

"You should have kept running, bounty killer!" Kincaid yelled. "Might have made it. But not now. We've found our range, right, Murrell?"

A bullet shattered a limb on Breen's right, bathing the brim of his hat in bark.

"*Bueno,* my new friend. Now . . . *regarde ça.*"

The next shot thudded into the lower trunk. Had John Murrell carried something more powerful than his repeating rifle — like Breen's Sharps rifle — the slug probably would have torn through the juniper and punched a massive hole through Breen's back.

Once the echoes of the bullets drifted away over the white vastness, the two killers started laughing.

Breen wiped the salt off the palm of his left hand and used the right to try to get that Lightning to work again. All he needed was two shots. If he could somehow get close enough to the outlaws.

"Bounty killer!" Kincaid's voice thundered again. "I'm enjoying a cold sip of water from my canteen right now. I reckon your canteen is keeping your hoss company."

"And I, *mon nouvel ennemi,* I sip from this *bota* that contains *un excelente vino blanco.*"

"Come join us!" Kincaid yelled after another round of laughing. "Because that sun must be frying your head right about now. And I don't see a cloud in the sky."

The laughter continued, and Breen stared across the salt flats, saw the heat waves rippling across the white expanse of nothing.

Hell, he realized, *I never knew just how salt could make a body thirsty.*

CHAPTER TWO

Since his family had been wiped out by Apaches, Matt McCulloch conceded that he had not acted neighborly in years — well, his wife, killed in that raid, probably would have let him know that he had never been on friendly terms with anyone other than his family. And those years as a Texas Ranger had not made him popular with the general public around Purgatory City. He was hardheaded, a hard rock, and a hard man to get to know. Pretty much impossible to like.

Which is why he was surprised that morning when Abel Cook rode up to the horse ranch McCulloch was trying to rebuild. Cook was what McCulloch would have to consider a competitor. He raised and bred quarter horses a few sections over to the east. McCulloch preferred mustangs, but he conceded that Cook knew good horseflesh.

"Mornin'," Cook called out after reining

in his dun a few yards from McCulloch's dugout. He raised his right hand in a friendly greeting, or maybe it was a gesture from those olden times. When a man raised his hand or offered to shake — to show that he carried no weapon and meant no ill will.

I ain't that dislikable, McCulloch thought.

McCulloch eased his Winchester against the wall, nodded, and stepped out of the shadow.

"Cook," he said. "How are you?"

"Fine."

McCulloch couldn't help himself. He scanned the horizon but saw nothing, not a cloud of dust, not a sign that anyone was waiting out in the vastness of West Texas to ambush.

Lord A'mighty, you are getting far too suspicious in your old age.

"Nice day," Cook said.

McCulloch looked back at the visitor. Cook was middle-aged, in his late forties or early fifties, sat a saddle like he had been born to it. He wore chaps over blue trousers, well-beaten boots with a good set of spurs. McCulloch judged a man by his spurs, and these didn't sport the big rowels some cowboys fancied, rowels that could cut up a horse's sides. The vest, collarless paisley shirt, frayed bandana, and badly beaten hat spoke of a man who worked hard and did an honest day's work. His face was bronzed, scarred, the nose misshapen, and the sandy hair sweaty, with a mustache that would make many a Texan envious.

"Might rain," McCulloch said.

"Wishful thinking."

McCulloch couldn't help but smile. He stepped closer. "Light down, Cook," he said, for they had never been on a first-name basis. Gesturing toward the dugout, he said, "I got some coffee cooked. It tastes like iron, but there's a bottle of brandy that could help make it more palatable."

The saddle creaked as Cook leaned forward, but he made no move to dismount. "Not sure I got time for coffee, McCulloch." He pointed to the north. "Comanches run off with ten of my horses." He glanced at the corrals McCulloch had put up. "They bother you?"

He shook his head. "No horses for them to take, except the two I got. Sold what I had. Figured I'd make a ride out to the mountains when the weather cooled. See how many mustangs and ponies I could catch then." He wiped his brow. "This heat doesn't make a man want to catch and break horses."

"But you still drink coffee, hot as it is."

McCulloch grinned. "You know what they say: Coffee'll cool a body off."

"With brandy instead of milk or sugar." Cook laughed.

The ex-Ranger pointed at the water trough. "Water your horse. You going after your horses."

Now the horseman swung out of the saddle, and led his brown gelding to the trough. McCulloch admired the horse, with its shoulders deep and strong, the high withers, short back, long legs, and lean muscles. Sixteen hands high, maybe a thousand pounds, probably three years old. A horse like that could take a rider a long way — and run faster than the West Texas wind.

As McCulloch walked to the visitor and horse, he saw the extra canteens over the saddle horn, the well-packed saddlebags, and the rifle in the scabbard. The loops in Cook's gunbelt had been filled, and the smell of grease and oil remained prevalent. A glance told McCulloch that the holstered revolver was a Colt, and McCulloch figured it would fire the same cartridges as the Winchester.

"You going after the Comanches." It wasn't a question.

"Wouldn't you?"

"Not alone."

The horseman straightened, keeping his eyes locked on McCulloch's. Eventually he sighed, and shook his head. "The boys I'd hired quit this morning."

Cook was a bachelor. At least there was no woman in his life as far as McCulloch knew. Now that he stood close to his nearest neighbor, McCulloch could see the crow's-feet on Cook's face, the wrinkles, the worries, the redness in the eyes, too.

Sighing, Cook shook his head.

"Must've been some raid," McCulloch said.

"You know Comanches."

"I know Comanches." McCulloch looked north. "Unless they were taking those horses they got from you to sell to Comancheros, they'll be raising dust back to their lodges. Staked Plains."

Cook pointed northwest. "Trail was headed that way."

McCulloch frowned. "Comancheros."

The horse stopped drinking, raised its head, and snorted.

"I reckon so." Cook drew in a deep breath, exhaled, and swallowed down his pride. "I can pay you two dollars a day. And the pick of the best horse we get back."

McCulloch shook his head, then hooked his thumb toward his dugout. "I wouldn't take either. This is what neighbors do in this part of the world. But you best get that coffee and brandy. Fortify yourself while I saddle my black."

Winchester loaded and slid into the scabbard, canteens filled, the bottle of brandy wrapped in extra clothing and stuffed into a saddlebag, bedroll and rain slicker tied up behind the cantle, McCulloch looked over the black gelding's back and stared hard at Cook.

"If those Comanches are taking those horses to the Canyon of a Hundred Crying Women, we won't be able to catch them," McCulloch said.

"This isn't a quarter horse," Cook said. "Or your mustang. It's —"

"A Thoroughbred, I know. Damn good-looking horse. But no white man outrides a Comanche. Our one chance is to try to intercept them. With luck, they won't have someone watching their back trail. Hell, they're Comanches. Comanches want to be followed. Give them more scalps to bring back for the victory dance at their village."

Cook nodded slightly, understanding.

McCulloch stepped into the saddle. "That horse of yours can outrun mine in a long race. Don't let him do it. We pace ourselves.

Steady. Ride hard. But not too hard. Ride fast. But not too fast. It's rough country. And you've been in West Texas long enough to know that you get put afoot, you're as good as dead."

"I know."

"You could just let the Comanches go. It's worth considering. Are ten horses worth your life?"

"You wouldn't let them go."

"But I'm one of Purgatory City's Jackals."

"Which is why I came to you for help."

McCulloch shook his head, let out a mirthless chuckle, and turned the black's head. "Let's ride."

They made a cold camp that night, then rode out before daybreak. There was no trail to follow, but the men kept the horses at a steady pace, weaving around rocks and yucca. At length they could see the outline of the high country — high in this part of Texas. The Canyon of a Hundred Crying Women lay at the edge of the rugged, rocky slopes before the land flattened into a sea of nothingness that stretched to the salt lakes and beyond that more desert that led into New Mexico Territory.

As the sun dipped, they entered an arroyo and followed it in the gloaming, slowing their horses now, letting them breathe as they walked below the skyline. Cook pulled up one of his canteens, uncorked it, and drank greedily.

"Save the water," McCulloch said. "We're a long spell from the tanks."

Nodding, Cook wiped his mouth with a dirty shirtsleeve and held the canteen out toward McCulloch as they rounded a bend in the sandy, dry bed.

"Hell," McCulloch said, and reined in the black.

Cook, still holding the canteen, rode a few feet ahead before he saw what had stopped the former Ranger.

His horse stopped, snorted, and pawed the sand.

McCulloch wet his lips, and then let his reins drop over his gelding's neck.

"Buenos tardes," said the Mexican with the big black sombrero with bandolieers of ammunition crisscrossing his chest. "You ride good. Good horses you bring us."

The Comanche with the red and yellow stripes painted across his cheeks and forehead said nothing. The Mexican aimed his rifle at Cook and McCulloch. The Indian had an arrow nocked on a bow. It, too, was pointed at the two white men.

"You're a long way from the Canyon of a

Hundred Crying Women," McCulloch said.

The Mexican shrugged. "A day's ride. That would be my guess."

"Half a day," McCulloch said.

The Mexican grinned. "On good horses. You two ride good horses." He laughed. "Or rode good horses. I will take them."

So, the Comanches had someone watching their back trail after all. Indians were getting smarter. Or maybe the Comancheros had ridden with the Indians on the raid at Cook's ranch. That seemed to make more sense.

A third man appeared to McCulloch's left, another Comanchero, but this one much younger, and a white man. He stood on the rim of the arroyo, holding a double-barreled shotgun.

His shadow fell between the Mexican and Indian and Cook and McCulloch, and the Mexican shot a quick glance at the white man, started to say something, but shrugged. He lowered his rifle, reached into his shirt pocket, and withdrew a cigarette. "Well," he said. "We will take your horses. I will bring them to Reynaldo."

"You'd leave us afoot?" McCulloch said. "In this country?" He took a quick glance at Cook, who still held out the canteen, as in shock. This would have to be McCulloch's play.

"We will leave you here," the Mexican said, and fired up the cigarette. "Step down, and away from your horses."

"Why?" This was the first thing Cook said.

"So," the Mexican said, and paused to draw deeply on his smoke. "So we do not accidentally hurt the horses when we kill you."

McCulloch was diving off the black before the Mexican had finished his sentence, the Colt in McCulloch's hand, the hammer pulled back, and he triggered a round while in midair. The bullet struck the white kid in the center of his throat, toppling him backward as he pulled the trigger of the shotgun to send buckshot straight into the evening sky.

By the time the roar of the shotgun sounded, McCulloch had hit the ground. He raised his head just in time to see the Comanche send the arrow straight into Cook's chest. The canteen fell and the horseman somersaulted over the back of his horse.

McCulloch's second shot twisted the Comanche around and dropped him to his knees. The Mexican had his rifle halfway up now, and jerked the trigger, sending a puff of dust followed by the noise of a ricochet.

McCulloch flattened, aimed from the ground, cocked the Colt's hammer, and fired through dust. He couldn't hear anything now but a deafening roar, but he caught a glimpse of his black thundering straight ahead.

Another shot. Dust blinded him, but he saw the black rear, kicking hooves widely, then falling, falling, falling right toward McCulloch. He rolled away, saw dust fly again from another ricochet, saw the horse coming down. He tried to lunge, but the horse fell hard, and McCulloch screamed in agony from the weight of the horse as it fell on his left leg, pinning him underneath eight hundred pounds of deadweight. His head slammed into rocks and cactus. He tried to breathe.

When his eyes opened, he saw the Mexican smoking the cigarette, grinning widely.

"You shoot good," the Mexican said.

The wounded Comanche was limping toward him, nocking another arrow in his bow.

"But not good enough." The Comanchero lowered his rifle. "Maybe we'll leave you here to die."

The Comanche grunted what had to be a *hell, no* and when the Mexican turned to his comrade, McCulloch twisted as far as he could, screaming at the pain that almost blinded him from his injured left calf. He still held the Colt, and it boomed just as the Comanche loosed the arrow. Now pain shot through his right thigh, but the Mexican was toppling down, and the Comanche was dropping his bow and reaching for his knife. When the warrior lunged, McCulloch had just enough time to thumb back the hammer and pull the trigger once more.

His head dropped, he tried to breathe, tried to stop the pain, got ready for the sound of his scalp being taken.

Instead, he heard iron shoes on stones in the arroyo.

He turned his head, saw the Comanche dragging himself away. McCulloch tried to find his Colt, but knew he didn't have strength to lift the revolver. He turned back, grimaced at his left leg underneath the dead gelding. He frowned at the arrow in his right leg, the blood streaming.

He knew one thing:

He wouldn't have to worry about dying of thirst. Very soon, he would bleed to death.

CHAPTER THREE

"Now, now, now," Sean Keegan said, smiling across the card table at Howell's Tanks. "That is a mighty fine hand you have there, my friend. It certainly beats my queen-high flush."

The tinhorn let his left hand slide toward the cash and coin, but stopped when Keegan kept talking in that rich Irish brogue. "But do you mind telling me, laddie, how you happened to draw that ace of clubs to fill your full house?"

Hard gray eyes looked from the grizzled face of the gambler. "The gods of poker must have smiled upon me." The tinhorn tried to smile, but Keegan's eyes were not friendly, either. The old face rose slightly, and the gambler asked: "And how did you know that I drew the ace — if you don't mind my asking?"

Lucius Howell, standing behind the bar, began gathering the jugs and glasses and putting them beneath the stone bar. He didn't bother lowering the mirror, for that looking glass had been so shot up and cracked from brawls and gunfire, a person couldn't see his own reflection anyway. He just kept the mirror up to hide the myriad bullet holes. Few people stopped at the station these days. Most camped in the clearing and filled their canteens and horses' stomachs from the rainwater that the cracks and hollows in the igneous rock held. Stagecoach lines eventually bypassed the station because too many people got killed here. The only reason Lucius Howell kept the place open was because he made money selling dead men's traps and horses, taking gold fillings out of dead men's mouths, charging for the liquor he made himself, and collecting ten percent of the house gambler's winnings. The house gambler was Abel Koontz, the long-faced gent holding a Smith & Wesson in his right hand under the table.

"I don't mind you asking," Keegan said. "The ace of clubs hasn't come up in the four hours we've been playing."

"The cards roll that way sometimes." Koontz had yet to rake in the pot, or show his right hand, which was still below the table.

"Aye. Luck. It's with some people. And others." He shook his head, and called out to Howell. "I reckon it's time for another of whatever it is you've poured into that Jameson bottle, me lad."

As he rose from the table, Koontz relaxed and began to bring in his winnings. But as Keegan stood, he slammed the knife he had onto the table, sending three fingers on the gambler's left hand flying toward the leaky ceiling as the gunshot roared from underneath the table. Keegan felt the heat of the muzzle blast. Screaming in agony, Koontz hit the floor and kept pulling the trigger of the double-action revolver, more out of reflex than intent.

Keegan adjusted his grip, and as Koontz, frothing, screaming, began to shift the Smith & Wesson toward him, Keegan let the knife fly straight down into Koontz's chest. The gambler gasped, dropped the pistol, and brought both hands, one with all fingers and thumb, the other bloody and practically worthless, to the hilt of the big bowie knife. He tugged, but then both hands slipped to his side.

By that time, Keegan knelt over the dying tinhorn.

"Luck?" Keegan shook his head, and raised the gambler's left arm. Holding the wrist with his left hand, he used his right to reach down the bloody sleeve, and pulled out the king of spades. "Aye," Keegan said. "And here's another card that hasn't been seen in all our games." He flicked the card onto the gambler's chest and let the bloody arm drop onto the stone floor.

"Cheating at cards can get a man killed." When Keegan jerked the knife out of the man's chest, Koontz gasped, and tried to bring both hands to the hole to stop the rush of blood.

But he was dead before the hands got to his chest.

"Lucius," Keegan called out as he fingered the dead man's eyes closed, "methinks ye'll are in need of another gambler. Try to pick a better one next —" He stopped cold when he turned around to smile at the bartender and owner. "Oh, bloody hell."

Wiping the blood on the dead man's trousers, Keegan stood and walked to the bar, sheathing the blade in his tall cavalry boots. He couldn't tell if one of Koontz's wild shots from the Smith & Wesson hit the mirror, but at least two had drilled Lucius Howell. The skinflint, cheat, and liar sat on the floor, leaning against the stone bar, clutching a bottle with a fancy Scotch whisky label on it, although Keegan doubted

41

if the bottle had held any Scotch in years. Blood already soaked the man's dirty shirt and pooled around his hips and between his legs.

"I'm done fer," Howell whispered.

"Yeah."

The barkeep tried to smile. "Nobody . . . lives . . . forever," he said.

"Koontz found that out." Keegan pried the bottle from Howell's hands, sniffed the top, grimaced, and, with great regret, held the bottle toward the dying man. "Want a snort for the road?"

"Can't . . . swaller."

Keegan shook his head, held the bottle out as in toast, and took a mouthful. After turning his head, he sprayed the foul liquid onto the floor, spit, and wiped his mouth with his shirtsleeve.

Smiling, Howell whispered, "Gotta . . . know . . . how . . . to . . . drink it." He gasped, closed his eyes, and drew in a ragged breath that whistled and caused bubbles to appear from the bloody wounds in his chest.

"I . . . lied!" Howell sang out when his eyes opened.

"You never was known for speaking the gospel," Keegan said.

The barkeep's head shook violently. "No.

No. I lied . . . to . . . your pal . . . Breeeeeeen."

Keegan stiffened. "Jed Breen?"

The nod was barely perceptible.

Keegan tried to smile. "I've been lying to that dirty cur more times than I can remember."

The head shook again. "No . . . he was . . . after . . . Kincaid. I said . . . he didn't . . . stop . . . here. Murrell . . . neither."

The names meant nothing to Keegan, but he was just an old horse soldier, not a bounty hunter. Biting his lips, Keegan waited.

"Murrell . . . they . . . knew."

"Knew what?"

"Gonna lay ambush."

"What are you trying to tell me?"

Howell's head dropped to his chest, but his chest kept rising, the bloody bubbles kept popping, so he wasn't dead yet. With his free hand, Keegan slapped the dying man, not hard the first time, slightly harder the second, and the third blow caused Howell's deadening eyes to open. Blood seeped from the left corner of his mouth.

"Kincaid and Murrell. Who are they?"

"Outlaws."

"I figured that."

"Killers."

"And?"

Howell spit out a glob of bloody phlegm. "Breen . . . was . . . after . . . Kincaid. Trailing him . . . since . . . El Paser . . ." He coughed again, moaned, turned his head left and right. Keegan was surprised the barkeep could still be alive, but he had always been a mule-headed son of Satan. "Murrell . . ." Howell whispered. "They . . . were gonna . . . catch . . . kill . . . Breen." The eyes closed, and just when Keegan was prepared to slap the man again, they opened. "Salt . . . lakes."

After breathing in deeply and slowly exhaling, Keegan tried to put it all together. So Jed Breen had been trailing some owl-hoot named Kincaid from El Paso. Another bad man named Murrell appeared to know that. The two outlaws had happened to meet here at Howell's Tanks and plotted an ambush. Kincaid looked toward the door, trying to figure how far it was from here to the salt flats.

"When was this?" he asked.

There was no answer.

Keegan repeated the answer, louder. The dying man's eyes opened, and he spit again. "Yes-ter-day."

"Didn't want . . ." Howell said, the voice growing weaker with each word and every

44

ragged, ugly breath the barkeep could take. ". . . to . . . take a lie . . . with me."

He groaned, twisted, and this time coughed up a bloody mess that splattered against the stone bar. Turning back to Keegan, Howell said, "You reckon . . . God'll . . . forgive me . . . for . . . that lie?"

"I imagine. That's one less sin on your tally sheet."

Howell smiled. "Don't think . . . I . . . got . . . time to. . . ." He couldn't finish.

Keegan held out the bottle. "Can you swallow now?"

He tried to shake his head, but couldn't. "No," he said. "Drink one . . . for me."

"That's a damned dirty request to lay on a friend," Keegan said.

"Yeah." Howell grinned. "It is. Drink it. Drink . . ."

Seeing the man was about to die, Keegan raised the bottle and took a heavy pull. He had to summon up plenty of courage to swallow, and it took all the willpower he could muster not to gag or vomit as the rotgut ripped through his tonsils and down the throat, sending fire spreading throughout his chest and exploding in his stomach.

Howell's eyes beamed.

After sniffing his runny nose, Keegan set the bottle between Howell's legs. "Reckon a man could develop a taste for that once he gets used to it."

"Yeah," Howell said. "It's only three hundred and twenty proof." Those words came out clearly. And those were the last words Lucius Howell would ever speak.

Keegan picked up the bottle, held it in front of the dead man's eyes, and took another sip. This one he swished around his mouth before swallowing, and put the bottle beside Howell's right hand.

"In case you need a drink on your way to hell, old man," Keegan said and rose. He walked out the door, looked at the sun, and moved toward his horse. He told himself that if Jed Breen got himself into a pickle, it wasn't his concern, that Jed Breen knew the risks of his occupation. After swinging into the saddle, he looked back at the roughshod station. On the other hand, he thought, there had to be a reason Lucius Howell had lived long enough to spill his guts about the ambush these two ne'er-do-wells, Kincaid and Murrell, had planned.

It was like Howell said. Nobody lives forever.

Keegan turned his horse, and kicked the bay into a trot. He rode toward the salt flats.

CHAPTER FOUR

Stern Morgan had to be the worst stage-coach driver in Texas, if not the entire United States and its territories. The worthless galoot had to be hitting every rock and pothole on what passed for a road intentionally. That's the only way Newton S. Bainbridge could see things as he felt himself lifted off the hard bench in the Concord and came down hard, almost toppling over against his daughter, Virginia.

"Are you all right, Colonel?" asked Murry Holt, Virginia's betrothed, who sat across from Bainbridge and his daughter, next to the Widow Teitelbaum. They were the only people in the wagon as it tried to make its way to El Paso. Well, they were the only ones Bainbridge remembered loading into the Concord when it left Purgatory City. He couldn't see much because of the dust — and the heavy leather curtains to the windows and doors were closed. His brain had

47

been slammed against his skull so many times that he figured he had amnesia. It was a miracle he could remember anything.

"That driver is trying to murder me out of revenge," Bainbridge snapped. "For drumming him out of the service six years ago."

"How's that . . ." The next bump sent everyone flying. When he had righted himself and apologized to the Widow Teitelbaum, Murry Holt looked back at Bainbridge. "How's that, Colonel?"

"The fool was the worst soldier" — another bump caused Bainbridge to swear — "worst I ever . . . saw. Damnation!" Now Bainbridge pounded on the wooden frame. "Are you trying to kill us all, Morgan? There are women in his coach, sir!"

"He can't hear you, Colonel," Holt said.

"He hears everything," Bainbridge shot back. "And stop calling me Colonel. I am no longer an officer in the United States Army. I am" — he spit out the next words with pure disgust — "a civilian."

Blonde, beautiful Virginia, gripping the edge of the seat with her left hand, reached over with her right and patted her father's thigh. "Steady, Papa. Remember what the doctor says about apoplexies and all."

"Damn the doctors. Damn Stern Morgan.

Damn whoever created mules, stagecoaches, and jehus."

He had barely coughed out the last word when the stagecoach slid to a stop, throwing the widow and Virginia's betrothed onto the narrow floor that separated the two benches.

"Now what?" Bainbridge demanded as he leaned forward to help the widow off the dust-covered floor and back into the place.

The driver answered: "Everybody get out. Y'all gots some work to do."

Choking obscenities, retired Army Colonel Newton S. Bainbridge threw open the door, and leaped out of the rickety wagon, feeling his boots sink up to his ankles in mud. "What the hell?" he barked, then spotted his daughter and helped her out, although there was no way he could find a spot in the narrow pike that wasn't drenched in mud. The widow stood helplessly in the doorway, and Bainbridge stepped back, motioning for Mrs. Teitelbaum to stay where she was for the moment.

"Morgan!" Bainbridge called up. "Surely you don't mean for the ladies to step into this filth."

"You don't give no orders to me no more, Private Bainbridge." The tiny, bearded man leaned over the seat and sent a stream of brown tobacco juice perfectly placed between the retired officer's muddy boots. "This is my ship, boy, and I'm lord and master. Get out. Everybody's gotta push if you want to get up this infernal hill."

"These are women, you fool," Bainbridge thundered.

"Women's got muscles, too. And they also weigh more than a fly. So they's pushing."

Defeated, Bainbridge turned back and gently lowered the widow into the thick muck. "I am sorry, ma'am," Bainbridge said, finally in a whisper.

"It's all right," the old woman said. "Besides, I am not helpless."

Murry Holt stepped into the mud and quickly moved to Virginia's side. "What are we to do?" he called out to Morgan, who sat alone in the driver's box while cutting off another chaw from his plug with a pocketknife.

"Get in the back of the coach. Put your muscles into it when I say go. And try not to slip down and get all filthy. I try to keep my coach as shiny as a baby's bottom." He giggled and shoved the tobacco into his mouth.

As the two women and the young man moved as directed, Bainbridge stepped forward, staring up the muddy road.

"This is odd," he said.

"What's odd about a monsoon this time of year?" the jehu called out as he folded the blade of his knife and dropped it and his tobacco into a vest pocket.

"The mud is just on the road," Bainbridge said. "Right here. Nothing else is wet."

"Your forehead and your clothes are gonna be wet, old man," Morgan said. "With sweat. Now get back with them others and push. This hill's hard enough to manage when the road's dry as a bone."

When he reached the back of the Concord, Bainbridge looked down the slope where the water, now soaked into the earth, had pooled at the bottom. "This is odd," he said. "Damned odd."

"Oh, Pa," Virginia said as she found a place near the right wheel and leaned forward, bracing herself, getting ready for the driver's orders. "You know what everybody says about Texas weather. If you don't like it, it'll change in ten minutes."

He found a spot near the left wheel. Morgan barked something unintelligible, the mules brayed, and Bainbridge put his shoulder and muscle into pushing, moving his legs, reminding himself that he served in the infantry during the war in Mexico before being transferred to the cavalry during the Civil War, so he knew how to use his legs.

Morgan was right about one thing. Climbing this hill in any condition was never easy. Once the widow slipped, staining her skirt and burying her hands and forearms in the mud. After helping her up, Bainbridge tried to get her to sit on the rear boot, let the others do the hard work, but she insisted on helping.

"How . . . high . . . is this . . . hill?" Murry Holt gasped about forty minutes into the chore.

"Just . . . push," Bainbridge responded.

Mules strained. Harnesses creaked. The jehu's whip popped, punctuating Morgan's vile curses. Even Murry Holt once let an oath slip through his lips. The wheels turned, flinging mud onto Bainbridge's shoulder and pants. He growled, sweated, cursed, breathed hard, and ground his teeth. They moved, slowly, but at least they moved. Ten more minutes. Six more feet. Finally, the depth of the mud lessened, the ground grew firmer, though far from dry bedrock, and the wagon lurched forward to where the road bent along the side of the hill, and began its descent toward the flats that ran for miles before the next batch of hills east of El Paso.

"What the hell?" Morgan sang out from the driver's box.

"Stand and deliver!" called out another voice, followed by mocking laughter.

"It sure took y'all long enough to make it up here."

Releasing his grip on the boot, Bainbridge straightened and stepped around the wheel. From his spot on the road's edge, he spotted four men, unmasked, wearing linen dusters and pointing all types of weapons at the jehu and the passengers afoot.

The black-mustached man in the black hat waved a revolver, motioning Bainbridge forward. "You and the others, come up this way."

"What is it?" the widow gasped.

"Holdup," Bainbridge said, and spread his arms away from his sides, although he carried no weapon. Slowly, he led the way through damp earth, not thick mud, and kept walking until he stood next to the lead mules. The widow, his daughter, and his future son-in-law came up behind him.

"We ain't carryin' no payroll, no mail, just folks," Stern Morgan said, working his tobacco with his teeth. He motioned to his right. "That's how come we ain't got nobody ridin' shotgun on this run."

"But you're hauling a valuable commodity," the man in black said, and he nodded at Virginia Bainbridge.

The retired Army colonel stepped farther onto the shoulder and looked down over the cliff.

"Watch your step, Bainbridge," the man in black said. "It's a long ways down."

Bainbridge stared at the wreckage of wood scattered on the rocks below. He cursed. Rain? Monsoon? Freak of nature? No, no this was all carefully organized. Shaking his head, trying to hold in his temper, he stepped back, and stared at the leader of the gang of cutthroats. "What kind of man would empty a water wagon in this country? Then wreck it?"

The man laughed, but did not lower his revolver. "Easiest way to slow y'all down. Let us see what kind of passengers you might be hauling. Wouldn't want to stop the wrong coach."

"And," said another one of the bandits, "look a little closer, old-timer. That ain't just one water wagon. It's three." He and others laughed, and three of the men moved closer to the leader.

"You're Harry Holland," Bainbridge said.

The black-hatted man nodded, even bowed, and used his free hand to tip his hat. "At your service, ladies."

"Only the worst vermin in the world would wreck three water wagons in West Texas to hold up a worthless stagecoach hauling a widow and three poor passengers."

"You're far from worthless, Colonel Bainbridge." The man's pale eyes danced in the sun.

"But I am carrying less than a hundred dollars."

The outlaw laughed again. "I think you're carrying much more than that."

"Here!" cried out the sweating, flushing, wide-eyed Murry Holt. He reached inside his coat pocket with his left hand. "I have forty-seven —"

The first bullet, fired by a man in a Mexican sombrero, caught Holt in the abdomen and slammed him into the door of the coach. The second, fired by an outlaw with a brown patch over his right eyed, hit him higher up. The third, fired by the man wielding a Winchester carbine, hit him between the other two bullet holes.

The widow fainted. The wagon lurched as Morgan tried to control the mules. Virginia Bainbridge stepped away from the coach, and her father moved to stand in front of her, while Harry Holland took control and holstered his gun, bent over, and dragged Mrs. Teitelbaum away from the wagon in case the team broke loose in a run.

Holt stepped forward, withdrawing his billfold. "I was . . . I was . . . I was . . ." he tried, as blood seeped from the corners of his mouth. The outlaw with the Winchester reached up and took the wallet.

"Thank you," he said, "but it wasn't necessary."

And Murry Holt dropped dead onto the road.

"You swine," Newton Bainbridge said.

"Step over here, Miss Virginia," Holland demanded. Virginia took a step back.

"What?" the colonel demanded.

"Twenty thousand dollars, Colonel," Holland said, and the other two gunmen walked to take the blonde-haired beauty by each arm. "Twenty thousand dollars. I'll give you one week to raise the funds and get them to me."

"I . . ." Bainbridge couldn't find the words.

"Twenty thousand dollars, Colonel. If you want to see this lovely lass again."

Now, Bainbridge closed his mouth, felt blood rushing to his head, and charged toward Harry Holland, but the bandit with the Winchester clubbed the back of the retired officers' head, sending him into the rocks and cactus at the roadside.

Holland raised his Colt at Stern Morgan.

"Are we gonna have any trouble from you, driver?" Holland asked.

"Nope." The jehu spit over the far side of the stage.

"Good." Holland holstered the revolver. "Boys, load the poor, muddy lady in the coach. And strap the good colonel in the boot with the other luggage." He stepped back as his orders were carried out and looked at the driver. "You don't stop till you hit the next station. Savvy?"

"My ears work fine."

"That's good," Holland said and paused to smile. "You best make good time. Bainbridge's bank is in El Paso. Make good time on the ride back to Purgatory City. And you damned sure better not get held up on the return trip."

"What about the dead idiot?" one of the killers asked.

"Leave him for the buzzards," Holland said. "But take his watch." The outlaw kingpin did not take his eyes off the driver. "And if the colonel doesn't remember too well after that hit he taken to his noggin, you remind him," Holland said, keeping his voice steady, his face expressionless. "Twenty thousand dollars. Brought to me. In one week."

The jehu's head bobbed. "That don't give him much time."

"It doesn't give him time to try to rescue his daughter, either. Which would be a fool's errand anyway."

The jehu nodded.

"Git!" Holland snapped. The driver released the brake and found his whip, and the wagon began the treacherous descent down the hill.

Harry Holland then smiled and looked at Virginia Bainbridge. "Ma'am, we are going to have the pleasure of your company for a week." Smiling, he offered her his hand.

CHAPTER FIVE

If my body was as white as my hair, I could strip naked, crawl across this hot desert, and those two damned killers wouldn't even notice me — as long as I dragged myself very, very slowly. It would be perfect. Then I'd just sneak up behind those owlhoots, one at a time, and send their worthless souls to hell.

Closing his eyes, Jed Breen shook his head, tried to focus, not daydream. He realized that the longer he sat here, sweating, baking from the heat of the sun above him and the blistering salt he laid on, the more delusional he became. His tongue felt as though it had swollen three times its normal size, and his vision seemed cloudy.

"Hey Breen!" Kincaid called out from his cooler spot in the rocks. "Murrell and me is getting bored. Why don't you just stand up and get this over with? We promise to make it quick. We'll end your suffering and then we can make our way to New Mexico Territory. It's cooler, we figure, up in those mountains than it is in this hell."

Breen tried to swallow, but couldn't.

"*Oui!*" Murrell shouted out. "That would be *muy bueno.*"

If only the wind would blow. Just a slight breeze. That might cool him off a little. But the wind remained as dead as this country and as dead as his horse. He tried to wet his cracked lips, but the roughness even hurt his swollen tongue. Breen chanced a look at the sky. No clouds. Just turkey buzzards circling, waiting for Murrell and Kincaid to clear out, waiting for their chance to feast on Breen's dead horse for supper. Then having Jed Breen's corpse for dessert.

Breen made himself roll over. That exhausted him. He made himself blow the salt and sand off his revolver, which felt as heavy as the Sharps rifle still in the scabbard on the saddle. With his canteen.

Don't think about that, he warned himself. Again, he measured the distance to where those two killers were hidden. Then he thought of something. Not that it would work, but it might give him a chance. A slim chance. But those odds were better than what Breen kept looking at the longer he sat beneath this dead tree in the middle of hell.

He lowered the barrel of the Lightning just inches from the white ground at his side. But for his plan to work, he needed a pistol that actually worked, and the .38 was jammed. Anger at his poor luck had him lift the gun, and he started to throw it toward the two killers. That's when he noticed the pebble jammed inside the cylinder.

Pressing his finger against the hot metal, he felt the sharpness of the small bit of lava rock, which bit into his finger. That meant he wasn't hallucinating. He tried to pry it out with his fingers, and when that didn't work, he remembered his pocketknife. He drew it from his pocket, opened the smaller blade, and worked out the stone.

The Colt was a double-action revolver, meaning he didn't have to cock the hammer before it would fire. All he had to do was pull the trigger, and that was a good thing. Weak as Breen was after waiting hours out here in the sunbaked purgatory, he wasn't sure if he had enough strength to cock a weapon and pull a trigger. And he didn't want to get his hopes up in case the damned weapon still wouldn't work. It was hard enough just getting the muscles in his pointer finger to pull the hot metal. He saw the hammer moving back, heard the clicking of the cylinder, and he bit his miserable lips and closed his eyes. The gun barked, deafening — mainly because he still didn't think the .38 would actually fire. Salt sprayed with the gunsmoke, and Breen rolled over, stretching the Colt out in front of him.

He lay still.

The pungent smell of gunpowder reached his nostrils. The smoking revolver stretched out by the dead tree trunk. He breathed in and out. He did not move. All he did was watch the rocks.

He waited.

Most folks, trying to save a friend's life, would have ridden hell-bent for leather from Howell's Tanks to the salt country. Sean Keegan knew better than that. Well, some might also say that he was just one of Purgatory City's Jackals, and jackals didn't have friends, and they didn't risk their own necks to save anyone. And Sean Keegan couldn't quite reject such an argument, either.

Oh, Keegan had ridden hard at first, on a direct trail that led to the sea of white, but then he moved well off the path and made a wide loop to the east. Cross those flats, and he knew he could find himself in the same predicament Breen might have ridden into. Upon hitting the rocky country, he had also cut a wider loop until he approached what he figured would be the most likely place for two ruffians to set up an ambush.

Keegan might have been out of the United States Cavalry, but he hadn't forgotten what he had learned from grizzled old scouts, white, Indian, and Mexican, who had helped guided patrols in Indian country. After dismounting, he wrapped his horse's hooves in rawhide. That would deaden the noise the iron shoes made on the rocks. He drew the Springfield from the scabbard and walked the horse into the wind. That would also carry any noise the hooves made away from where two men might have set up an ambush.

Dread filled his throat like bad whiskey. Chances are, Jed Breen was already dead. The buzzards circling in the sky soured his stomach worse than the whiskey he had consumed at Howell's, but if those vermin kept flying, that meant something, or someone, was not dead yet. Or it meant wolves or coyotes were feasting, and the scavengers in the sky had to wait for leftovers.

Expecting to ride up to a dead man, Keegan at least could give Jed Breen a burial. Hell, it wouldn't be too hard to dig a grave in the salty ground, and maybe the killers had left behind Breen's Sharps rifle and saddle. Those would fetch a good trade for whiskey at Keegan's favorite watering holes in West Texas.

He guided the horse around a rocky point, dipped into an arroyo, stopped long enough to wipe sweat from his brow and settle the hat on his head, then let the bay gelding pick its own path up the embankment. There, he let the horse breathe, while he tried to figure out any words he might say over a dead bounty hunter's grave.

That's when the words started bouncing off the rocks. Shouts. Keegan wet his lips, dismounted, and walked the horse to the corner of the next ridge.

"It's cooler, we figure, up in those mountains than it is in this hell!" a voice sounded. He tried to estimate the distance.

Another voice called out. "*Oui!* That would be *muy bueno*!"

"Bloody hell," Keegan whispered. "Breen must still be living and kicking."

After securing the reins around a rock, Keegan walked to the bay's side, took the canteen, and drank. Next he filled his hat with water and let the horse slake its thirst. The wet hat felt cool, refreshing, when Keegan put it on his head. He opened the saddlebags, saw the flask of whiskey, and that refreshed him more than a wet hat or the canteen's tepid water. He had just returned the flask to the bottom of the saddlebag and pulled out a pouch of cartridges for the .45-70 when he heard the gunshot.

It barked like thunder.

The bay's ears went erect. "Easy, boy," Keegan whispered, as the echoes bounced across the rocky country. That hadn't come from the rocks, but off to the northwest, in the salt beds. Keegan frowned. It sounded like a pistol shot, and if Breen had pulled that trigger, it would've been a wasted round. Those two men were too far away for a pistol, especially a toy like Breen's Colt, to be effective.

Another thought crept into Keegan's mind, and then he smiled.

"Suicide," Keegan mouthed. "Not on that bounty killer's life." He sank onto his haunches and removed his spurs, leaving them on the rock that held his horse's reins.

He turned, slipped around the rocks, found a path up the slope, and made the climb, hearing the voices of the two-bit assassins.

"He ain't moving."

"Gutless coward. Killed himself. *Une bonne blague. Pero es el Diablo quien ríe.*"

"Jed Breen ain't one to take the coward's

way out, Murrell. He's trying to get us out into the open."

"If not for that damned tree, I could kill him easy. *Vamos a dejarlo. Donnez-lui une mort lente.*"

"Can you say something I can understand for once, Murrell?"

Keegan had found his spot. He saw the horses the two killers had staked. He saw the bottle of whiskey they had been sharing. He didn't know who the hell these two men were, other than one went by the handle Murrell, but he knew one thing. There was about to be just one of them.

Jim Kincaid was wiping his mouth and shifting his rifle in his other hand when the bullet hit him in the back of the head and blew blood, hair, and brain matter through the crown of his hat. Keegan then dropped the smoking carbine, and pulled out his Remington revolver, firing at the other man, the funny gent who spoke a mixture of languages. One bullet might have grazed the coward's arm as he ran. The horses danced in their hobbles from the gunshot, the carnage, and more echoes. Keegan fished out a brass cartridge and reloaded the Springfield, but by the time he got to the edge of the rocks and stepped over the corpse of the man whose head he had mostly taken off and aimed down the slope, he saw the smaller man running across the salt fields.

Frowning at the sight of the dead horse, Keegan spotted the dead tree in the center of the vast expanse of salt. He found a comfortable perch on the rocks, aimed the rifle, and tried to figure out the adjustments he needed to make. The wind. Shooting downhill. The shimmering of sun and blowing sand. How fast the coward was running.

That's when he saw something else. Movement behind the dead tree. Well, that didn't surprise him. He knew Jed Breen wouldn't take his own life. He knew Jed Breen would be a hard man to kill.

Breen didn't know what the hell was going on. He heard shots, screams, and now a man was running right toward him. Running like a crazy man. It wasn't Kincaid. No. Breen couldn't see that well, not after baking in this white misery for so long, but there was no way that man was Jim Kincaid.

"Murrell," he whispered and raised the Colt.

His first thought was to say something, call out for the man to stop, to give himself up, but Breen didn't have enough voice to say anything, and out of the corner of his eye, he saw the dead horse.

Holding the Lightning with both hands, Breen pulled the trigger. Once. Twice. Again.

The first shot made Murrell twist. The second one knocked him to his knees. The final shot put him on the ground.

"Mon Dieu," John Murrell gasped. *"¿Debo morir?"*

By the time Breen made his way to stand over the killer, John Murrell was staring at the buzzards, but he couldn't see them. Yet those birds, Breen thought with a smile, they damned sure could see John Murrell.

Then he saw something else. A man. A man in a tan hat standing high on the rocks, with sunlight reflecting off the rifle in the man's hands.

"Kincaid!" Breen tried to shout, though it sounded more like a cough. He brought the Colt up, still using both hands, and squeezed the trigger, hearing the gunshots, the echoes, and he kept pulling that trigger, until long after the echoes died and all he heard were metallic clicks.

The Colt slipped and fell into the sand.

The man in the rocks barely moved.

"Breen!" a voice boomed, and the bounty hunter tilted his head, trying to compre-

hend. "You owe me plenty, and I'll be collecting from you till the cows come home."

Breen blinked.

"Keegan?" he mouthed, before pitching
forward into the salt.

CHAPTER SIX

Grinding his teeth against the pain, McCulloch took his free leg and propped it against the dead horse that pinned his left leg to the ground. He could see blood spilling down the calf and coloring the feathers on the arrow's shaft. He screamed as he shoved against the horse but managed to get horse and saddle up just enough to drag his pinned leg from underneath the weight. The calf was torn. Pain rifled from his ankle all the way to his chest, and he fell back, breathing hard, half-blinded by tears.

"No!" he thundered, just to keep himself from passing out, and he sat up, focusing on the arrow now. Reaching down, he gripped the arrow, slippery with his own blood, and jerked hard. That agony dropped him back onto the ground, his chest heaving, but when he turned his head, he found some relief. The obsidian arrowhead was still secured to the arrow, which he flung away. At least it wasn't still inside his leg.

But the bleeding . . . He had to stop the bleeding.

He remembered the Mexican. McCulloch sucked in a deep breath and rolled over. The corpse remained a few yards away. Then, McCulloch reached forward, dug both hands deep into the earth, and pulled himself forward, yelling to dull the pain in both legs, yelling to keep himself awake. He dropped his face into the sand, breathed in again, and stretched his arms out closer to the dead Mexican. Drag.

Drag.

Drag.

Drag.

He saw the cigarette, grabbed it, and rolled over, putting the smoke to his mouth. He inhaled deeply, catching only a taste of smoke. "Come on," he whispered, and pulled hard on the cigarette again. This time, he filled his mouth with smoke. Keeping the cigarette in his mouth, he rose, saw the powder flask on the Mexican's belt, and grabbed it, shook it and heard the grains of gunpowder. Lucky. Most men used brass cartridges these days. Most cap-and-ball pistols had been converted to metallic cartridges, too, but the Mexican had carried one of the old-style revolvers. This fellow was so behind the times, he didn't even use ready-made paper cartridges, still filled his chambers with powder, then seated a lead ball, and set a percussion cap on the cylinder's nipple.

McCulloch thumbed the flask's brass release, dipped the spout close to the deep arrow wound, and watched the black grains fill. After dropping the flask, he grabbed the cigarette, dragged hard so that the tip was red with heat, and stuck the smoke to the powder.

The whoosh of flame intensified the agony in his right leg. He caught a brief odor of burning flesh. Then he felt nothing but the comfort of needed unconsciousness.

When he came to, he saw the turkey buzzards circling.

McCulloch sucked in a deep breath, closed his eyes, and after the longest while, found enough strength to push himself up into a seated position — though the pain in the right thigh and left calf almost sent him back into the dark void. Once he could breathe without pain, he looked at the arrow wound.

Nasty, he figured, but it wasn't bleeding. He found a plug of tobacco the Indian must have dropped, bit off a mouthful, and worked his teeth until he had softened the chaw. Bending forward, he spit brown juice onto the wound, kept chewing, and began unknotting the bandana around his neck. A few moments later and he had the ragged old piece of calico under his leg with the ends hanging near the burned flesh and burned trousers. He spit again, but this time grabbed the wet chaw and slapped it on top of the wound, holding it there as he tied the bandana against it.

He could have ripped the trousers near the hole in his thigh, but thought the cloth might add protection against infection or reopening the hole. Someone also had told him that chewing tobacco sucked out blood poison. McCulloch wasn't sure he believed it, but at this stage he was willing to try anything.

The left leg was another matter. Broken, but he had no way to set the break. That would have to wait.

Damn, he thought. The sun would bake a man forever here, and he felt thirsty. He dragged himself back to his horse, found the canteen, and drank just enough to fool most of his aching body. He tried to whistle, didn't get much sound, tried again with even feebler results. After another sip of water, he made sure the stopper was tight in the canteen and looked around.

All around him was death, and the dead began to smell. This would draw more than buzzards. Coyotes. Wolves. Badgers. Anything hungry. And Matt McCulloch would be even fresher meat. McCulloch wet his lips and glanced at the body of Abel Cook. He hated to leave a good horseman like that, but Cook would understand. There was nothing McCulloch could do for anyone here. He certainly couldn't bury anyone.

The easiest thing to do, McCulloch knew, would be to wait here to die. He could even hurry things up, take one of the weapons, put the barrel under his throat and pull the trigger. No one — not even God — would blame him for that. It would be quicker than the death that would come to him eventually.

The horses were gone. The Indian was likely dead and gone, too. McCulloch would be dead soon enough, but, damn it, his lungs and heart still worked right now. He looked around, trying to get his bearings.

Howell's Tanks, he mouthed.

Yes, that would be the closest place.

Howell's Tanks. It would take a man on a good horse a long time to ride there. It would take a healthy man all day to walk there.

McCulloch couldn't walk. Hell, he

couldn't even stand.

But, by thunder, he could crawl.

He scavenged the dead for what he could find. More chewing tobacco. Matches. He kept the Mexican's powder flask and Abel Cook's flask of whiskey. He had his canteen. Didn't want too carry too much weight, so he left most of the weapons except his holstered revolver. After grabbing his hat and seating it tightly on his head, McCulloch rolled onto his belly. Again, his hands stretched in front of him, and the pain shooting up both legs turned nauseating. Again, he sucked in as much air as his lungs could hold, and biting his bottom lip, he dug his fingers deep into the hot earth and pulled himself forward.

He caught his breath, closed his eyes, and dug deep inside himself, finding enough strength to reach forward again. Finding the will to live that had him pull himself forward. This time he did not wait, did not breathe, did nothing but moved those arms forward, dug those fingers deep, pulled himself, dragged his body.

Stretch those arms. Dig into that ground. Pull and drag. Stretch. Dig. Pull and drag. Stretch. Dig. Pull and drag.

Stretch.

Dig.

Pull.

Drag.

Stretch.

Dig.

Pull.

Drag.

Now he had to stop. Now he had to breathe. His mouth, tongue, and throat screamed for water, but McCulloch told himself to wait. Not yet. Fill those lungs with air and keep moving.

Keep moving.

Stretch those arms. Dig those fingers. Pull that body. Drag those worthless legs.

Keep moving. Keep moving. Keep moving.

Stretch. Dig. Pull. Drag. Stretch. Dig. Pull. Drag. Stretch. Dig. Pull. Drag.

Move. He had to keep moving. Moving gave him a chance to live. Stay put, he knew, and he'd die.

When he stopped again, he made the mistake of looking back, to see how far he had come from the ambush site. That would have killed most men, broken their hearts, reduced them to tears. At this rate, it would take him fifty years to reach Howell's Tanks. Again, he refused to drink water.

I will drink, he told himself, *at Howell's Tanks.*

He looked forward. He reached out with both arms, filling the tug of the canteen's canvas strap on his shoulder, feeling the weight of his Colt that felt like a battleship's anchor. McCulloch grimaced as he dragged his legs, one wounded, one broken, another agonizing yard. He kept dragging, kept moving. Eventually, he found a way to block out the pain.

An hour later, he made himself drink. Just one swallow, careful not to spill a drop. This time, he did not look back.

There was nothing for him behind him. His future, his life, lay ahead.

After tightening the stopper, he breathed in deeply, held the air in his lungs for a moment, and slowly exhaled.

Then, he started dragging himself again, moving with purpose, moving for his very life, unable to block out the pain in his legs or the tormenting in his arms and shoulders. Yet he remained acutely aware of what he had to do.

Two hours later, he thought about resting longer than just the time it took to sip water. Find some shade, he told himself, and then he had to chuckle just for a moment. Shade? In this furnace? Finding shade in West

Texas, especially at this time of year? Hell, a man could find shade in Hell quicker than he could find shade here.

The muscles in his forearms and shoulders burned with brutality. The arrow wound in his right thigh throbbed with each heartbeat, and the broken bone in his lower left leg felt like razors slicing into the bone, the muscle, the skin, even the hair on his legs.

Yet the pain kept McCulloch from passing out. The pain kept his focus. He wet his lips, breathed in and out, and continued the long, impossible trek to Howell's Tanks.

Stretch those arms. Dig into that ground. Pull and drag. Stretch. Dig. Pull and drag. Stretch. Dig. Pull and drag.

Stretch.

Dig.

Pull.

Drag.

Stretch.

Dig.

Pull.

Drag.

CHAPTER SEVEN

Murrell's horse carried the two dead bodies. Jed Breen rode the late Jim Kincaid's horse, although Breen had taken his own saddle and bridle off the great horse those ruffians had killed. Having eaten the outlaws' grub and consumed some of their liquor, Keegan and Breen rode easily away from the salt beds.

"Maybe we can stop at Howell's Tanks," Breen said. "Get some whiskey. I'll buy."

"Aye, you do owe me some whiskey, Jed," Keegan said. He then laughed. "I might even say you owe me whiskey for life."

"How about if I split the reward for these two killers?"

Keegan grinned. "Split?"

"All right, all right, all right." Breen shook his head. "You take all the reward. I guess I owe you that much."

A few yards farther up the trail, Breen amended his terms. "But you buy the liquor at Howell's Tanks."

Shaking his head, Keegan chuckled. "I fear no man shall have the chance to corrode his tongue, throat, stomach, and liver with that snake oil at Howell's Tanks again. But you can drink water till you've turned into a fish."

"Something happened at Howell's place?"

"Aye. And something happened to Howell, as well."

"What?"

"What would you expect?"

"Oh."

They rode a few more miles without speaking, just checking to make sure the load Murrell's horse carried did not shift or even fall off. They rode steadily, but not in a hurry, resting the horses in the heat of the day. They rode until Keegan reined in.

"Hell," he said.

Breen pulled up alongside him and stared at the canyon country, and the buzzards circling overhead.

"That's not Howell's Tanks," Keegan said.

"No."

"Could be anything," Breen said. "Dead deer."

"It could be."

"Not our business," Breen said.

"Nope. Not our business."

"Hell," Breen said, tugged on the lead rope, and headed toward the southeast.

The deafening roar and whistling bullet from Keegan's Springfield sent the buzzards scattering and squawking, their huge wings flapping like demons as the scavengers took flight.

Murrell's horse, already skittish from the stink of the corpses it was carrying, snorted, pawed the ground, and tugged hard on the rope. Keegan's horse had no interest in moving any closer to the carnage, so the old Army soldier swung out of the saddle, shoved his carbine into the scabbard, and handed Breen the reins.

"I got my hands full already," Breen said.

"Aye." Keegan waited. "But I saved your worthless hide."

Shaking his head, Breen took the reins in his left hand, holding the reins to his own animal, or what was his horse for the time being, and the lead rope to Murrell's gelding in the other. Keegan drew the Remington revolver from his holster and moved to the first dead body.

"Mexican," he called out.

Now he stopped, spit, and pulled the bandana over his nose and mouth. He squatted by the dead body, studied some tracks, and moved a few yards down the canyon. "Looks like another one dragged his bleeding self off that-away." He pointed with the revolver's barrel and looked up into the sky.

"He didn't get far," Breen called out. "At least that'd be my guess."

"Aye." Keegan saw most of the buzzards he had frightened away diving from the blue sky to the brown and bleak earth. Now he moved to the other corpse.

A minute later, he stood, faced Breen, and said, "I know this guy." He raised the kerchief from his mouth to spit out the gall. "Not his name. But he bred horses. Had a place outside of Purgatory City."

"It ain't Matt McCulloch is it?"

"Hell's fire, Breen," Keegan fired back, "if it was McCulloch, I'd have said it as McCulloch. That sun must have fried any sense you had left permanent like. No. It ain't Matt. Some other horseman." He turned, went to the dead horse, and paused.

"Hell," he whispered. Again, he had to spit out the bad taste, and he moved to the horse, which the buzzards had been feasting on. They hadn't gotten to the brand. Keegan stepped away from the sight, breathed in deeply a few times, and finally found enough voice to call out to Breen. "But this is McCulloch's horse."

Breen stiffened.

Keegan looked around, and followed the trail, talking as he moved. "He must've gotten pinned underneath the horse. Shot. No. No. Here's a bloody arrow." He picked it up, brushed off the ants dining on dried blood, and tossed it aside. "Guess a redskin was with the Mexican. Must've gotten Matt good with the arrow."

"Indian and Mexican." Breen yelled. "You know what that means."

"Aye. Comancheros." He followed the trail back to the dead Mexican, turned and walked thirty yards. "He's dragging himself. Must be bad hurt. Can't walk."

He stared at the sky, turned, and walked quickly toward Breen and the horses.

"Bad hurt. But how bad?" Breen asked as he handed Keegan the reins to his horse.

"He's alive. Or was alive."

"He's still alive," Breen said, and nodded at the pale blue horizon. "Those buzzards over that way are circling. That means they're waiting on something to bite the dust."

Keegan swung into the saddle. "Maybe." He brought down the yellow kerchief and spit again. "But it could be they're waiting for wolves, or maybe another flock of those black-winged vultures, to finish their meal before swooping down to eat a bunch of leftovers."

"Hell," Breen said. Now he dismounted, handed the reins to Keegan, and walked back to Murrell's horse.

"What are you doing?" Keegan called out. "Matt McCulloch's bad hurt over yonder way."

"I know that, you damned fool," Breen said, and dropped Murrell's body over the side. The horse danced, but Breen kept a firm hold on the rope, stepped back to the horse, and loosened the rope that held Jim Kincaid's body. That one plopped into the dust.

"That sun really baked you good," Keegan said, as Breen returned to Kincaid's horse. "You leaving bounty money for buzzards."

"Maybe." Breen swapped the lead rope for the reins to Kincaid's gelding. After swinging into the saddle, he nodded at the circling buzzards. "But there are limits to even what I'll do. That's Matt McCulloch out there. He doesn't have a horse, and he'll need one to get back to Purgatory City."

"And if he's dead."

"He'll need one then, too." Keegan was already guiding the gelding up the embankment, away from the gruesome battle scene. "To haul his body back to his ranch. Figure that's where he'd want to be buried. Don't you?"

"Aye." Keegan spit again, and followed Breen out of the death trap, pulling Murrell's horse behind him. Once both had reached the top, they put their mounts into a hard trot.

A quarter mile later, Breen dipped his horse back onto the trail and rode around until he found the trail McCulloch had left dragging his broken body through the desert.

"The hell do you think you're doing?" Keegan bellowed when he caught up. He had to stop to fight the mule-headed horse he was pulling.

"Following the trail Matt left for us to follow," Breen said, and put his horse into a fast walk.

"Follow the trail!" Keegan spit and pointed at the sky. "Those birds. That's the trail we gotta follow. Follow them vultures. Just make a beeline . . ."

Breen didn't look back. "It'll be faster to follow the trail than it will be to follow buzzards in the sky," he said. "Besides, what if those turkey buzzards are circling over a dead wolf?"

Keegan blinked repeatedly. Murrell's horse snorted and tried to back away, but Keegan jerked the rope with his left hand, and spurred his gelding after Breen.

"Hell's fire," he said when he caught up with Breen. "I reckon that sun and that salt didn't bake all the sense out of your bloody brains after all. But it sure must have scrambled some of mine."

They rode at a steady rate, pausing when they came to a rocky patch.

"That man's got guts," Keegan said, shaking his head. "Dragging himself across those rocks."

Breen pointed. "Not to mention that patch of prickly pear beyond it."

"I don't see what keeps him going," Keegan said a half-mile later.

"Sure, you do," Breen said. "You and me both. We've ridden with him before."

"Yeah. Never met nobody ornerier than him. Except, maybe . . . you."

They found McCulloch thirty minutes later, passed out in the middle of a patch of wasteland. Keegan swung down from the saddle, grabbed his canteen, and wrapped the lead rope around the horn of his saddle.

Breen was rolling McCulloch onto his back, holding his breath, and exhaling only when he saw the chest rise and fall. He dropped beside him, and slowly lifted Mc-Culloch's head.

The eyes opened, fluttered, and Keegan knelt and quickly brought the canteen to the former Texas Ranger's cracked, filthy lips.

"Matt?" Breen asked.

Keegan spilled some water over his fingers, and brushed those across Matt's mouth.

The eyes fluttered, focused, blinked, and Matt slowly forced a brief, ugly smile.

"You don't look so good, Matt," Keegan said.

McCulloch's voice could barely be heard, but it sure made Breen and Keegan smile.

"Better than you two jackasses."

CHAPTER EIGHT

"Tell me something," Keegan said. "Which leg hurts worse?"

"Go to hell," McCulloch whispered before closing his eyes.

"Matt?" Breen asked.

When McCulloch did not respond, Keegan leaned away from the battered, bruised, sunbaked horseman and scratched his nose.

"He's not riding any horse out of here," Breen said.

"Aye." Keegan looked around the bleak terrain. "My blessed Aunt Kathleen always wanted me to pursue a career in medicine, but being a sawbones never agreed with me." He wet his lips and stared at Breen. "You any hand at setting a broken leg?"

"I've had to put my shoulder back into its socket after a fight once, but that's about it," the bounty hunter said.

Keegan wet his lips. "I might be able to set a busted arm, but that leg?" He shook his head. "Aye, perhaps I should have listened to my auntie. A blessed saint she was. Gave me my first taste of Irish whiskey when I was but knee high to a leprechaun."

"We'll need to make a travois," Breen said.

"Aye, laddie, that is what we have to do." He stood and tilted his head toward the rise. "Let me ride up there and see if I can fetch a couple of limbs. Then we'll use one of those dead blokes' bedrolls and that saddle blanket for Matt's bed." He shook his head again. "That'll be a long spell before we get him to Purgatory City."

"Maybe I should go," Breen said.

"Noooooo." Keegan shook his head. "Your skin took a blistering in that salt field, me boy. Stay in the shade." He nodded at the sleeping McCulloch. "Keep an eye on him. I'll be back with a veritable ambulance before ye know it."

As soon as Keegan had disappeared, Breen brought his hand up to his cheek, feeling the heat. He wet his lips and touched his neck, flinching at the pain, and thinking that when the skin started blistering and the dead skin turned white, with his white hair he would look just like a ghost. The hand lowered and he frowned at how red the backs of both hands were. Well, he could lather himself with salve when he got to

Purgatory City. Salve on the outside. Whiskey on the inside. Just what the doctor ordered. The only problem was that Purgatory City was a damned long way from this inferno.

Keegan whistled a jaunty tune as he trimmed two thick, twisting juniper branches into something that would at least pass for the poles to a travois. It might not be the best-looking contraption he had ever fashioned, but it could get the job done. He was just thankful that it wouldn't be Sean Keegan that had to travel those countless miles in this thing.

After he got the smaller branches chopped off, he dragged the limbs closer to his horse, checked his measurements, and nodded in approval before slaking his thirst with a quick swallow from his canteen. Next, he lashed the two poles together with rawhide thongs and strapped one pole on each side of his horse. The gelding didn't care too much for it, but Keegan gave the animal a drink of water from his hat.

He climbed onto his horse and eased his way back toward McCulloch and Breen.

The blow to his right foot hurt, and Breen swore, dragging his right leg up toward him, opening his eyes, and swore again. This time, he cursed himself for falling asleep. Not that anyone could blame him after the hell he had gone through in that salt country for hours. He had figured it was Sean Keegan who had kicked him awake. That would be just like the Irishman, but as Breen stared up, his right hand started for his holster.

The man in the sugarloaf sombrero laughed as he held out his left hand, which held Breen's double-action Colt.

"You sleep like a baby," the Mexican said, spinning the weapon in his left hand. "Or Bernardo when he has had too much tequila. Isn't that right, Bernardo?"

To Breen's left, Bernardo, a wiry, bald-headed man with a white mustache, shook his head. "There has never been too much tequila for Bernardo, Juanito."

Juanito laughed briefly, before tossing the Lightning into the dirt, and palming his own weapon, an old Starr revolver in .44 caliber, a double-action just like Breen's Colt, but older, and that barrel looked like a howitzer as the Mexican aimed it at Breen's groin.

"There is a third man, amigo." Juanito's face lost its bemused countenance. "Where is he?"

Breen swallowed, looked over at Mc-

Culloch, still unconscious. "He rode over to Howell's Tanks," Breen lied. "See if he could get some medicine and a horse to bring this man to Purgatory City."

"This man will be going to Purgatory, *sí*," Juanito said. "We Comancheros do not like having two of our best men murdered." Bernardo moved away from McCulloch and followed the tracks left by Keegan's gelding, and finally turned and walked back until he stood next to the leader of the worst kind of outlaw in Texas and the Southwest. Comancheros. Men who'd sell guns or anything, including women, to Comanches. Breen would never cash in on a reward for any of that breed of men. He'd kill them as he would a cockroach — though right now he realized that these two Comancheros were likely to kill him.

"Señor," Bernardo said, and pointed at the tracks he had followed for twenty yards. "That is a strange direction to take to get to Howell's Tanks."

"I was thinking the same thing, mi amigo," Juanito said. The smile returned. "Do you think this gringo is lying to us?"

"I think he believes we are two fools," Bernardo said. He drew a machete from the long scabbard on his left hip.

"Do you wish to change your story?"

92

Juanito asked. "It would be shame for you to meet your Maker with a lie upon your lips."

"He went to Howell's Tanks," Breen said. "He knows a shorter way."

The two Comancheros glanced at each other.

"Why is it that you bring back this man?" Juanito asked. "You were not with him when this one" — he pointed at McCulloch — "killed our compadres. You both came from the salt country." He gestured. "Is he an amigo?"

"Never laid eyes on him before," Breen said, thinking: *Just keep them talking. As long as they're talking, you've got half a chance to live another minute. Just keep them talking.* "We were coming back, saw the buzzards, rode in to find him and the others."

"But you did not bother to help the others!" Bernardo barked.

"The others," Breen said, trying to summon up enough saliva in his mouth to swallow. "The others were dead. Nothing we could do for them."

"You could have at least buried them," Bernardo, said.

"Would you have?"

Juanito laughed, shook his head, and nodded with an evil grin as he looked down at

93

Breen. "You have a point, amigo. You have a point. In fact, we did not bury them, either, after we found their bodies. Well, Bernardo, he did take the scalp of the Indian your amigo killed."

"He's not my amigo," Breen said.

"Well, you are his amigo, mi amigo, for I would call anyone who kept me from dying in this country a very good friend indeed."

"Only he did not keep his amigo from dying after all," Bernardo said.

"No," Juanito said. "Instead he died, too. In fact, he died sooner than the man he tried to save."

Breen sucked in what he figured would be his last breath. He didn't have the strength to stand, but he filled both hands with sand. Juanito lowered the Starr. "You will have to kill him, Bernardo," the Comanchero said. "We do not want the third man to hear my gunshot. Chop his head off. Neatly if you can."

Sand flew from Breen's left hand into Bernardo's face, and as the old Mexican cursed in Spanish and twisted, Breen threw the sand in his right fist at Juanito. But the Mexican dropped his head, protecting his eyes with the big brim of the large hat. At the same time, Juanito raised his .44, and fired a quick shot that roared in the close confines. The bullet dug up sand where Breen had been lying. Now the bounty hunter rolled over and over, every inch a painful reminder of how hard this country was.

The next gunshot didn't come from a pistol.

Breen stopped rolling.

Sean Keegan ducked underneath the white smoke and saw the Mexican with the sombrero grabbing at his face — or what had been his face — the blood and gore pouring between the fingers as the man kept backpedaling until he finally tripped and fell to the ground, hands still covering the bloody mess that had once resembled a human head.

The other Comanchero, the old guy who shaved his head but kept a white mustache that most men would envy, stopped twisting, and began screaming in rage.

There was no time for Keegan to reload the Springfield, so he leaped over the edge of the arroyo and landed in front of Mc-Culloch, who appeared to be peacefully sleeping through all this hell. Keegan's knees bent, but he quickly forced himself up, gripping the carbine by the hot barrel and behind the trigger. He brought the weapon up as the machete came slamming down.

Sparks flew off the barrel as the sharp edge of the big knife slid down toward the front sight.

Keegan let go of the barrel, the blade sliced into the dirt, and the Mexican fell. The old man moved like he was still in his twenties, but a man in this profession had to be quick. Slow Comancheros got killed.

A quick glance told him that Breen had stopped rolling, and he had found his feet, and started weaving toward his Lightning or the .44 Starr the dead Comanchero had dropped. But Breen didn't move as fast as he usually did.

Keegan jumped out of the way as the machete came down. He felt the whistle of the blade, saw the old Comanchero fly past him. Keegan pivoted, raised the Springfield with his right hand, all the way up and over his shoulder. Then he brought his left hand up. His legs turned. The Mexican gathered himself, spun around, and raised the machete high over his head. The old man screamed vile Spanish curses and he charged, but Keegan was stepping toward him and swinging the carbine with both hands. The barrel caught the man full in the throat, and dropped him into a heap near McCulloch's boots.

The machete slipped from his grasp. Both hands rose and found his smashed throat. He struggled to breathe, but no breath found his lungs. Keegan stepped closer to the killer. He looked over at Breen, who was kneeling by the dead Comanchero's feet and palming the Starr. Breen froze, seeing that the danger had passed.

Keegan spit, turned his Spencer over until he gripped the hot barrel. The weapon rose again, and came down, the stock slamming into the forehead of the wheezing man, crushing the skull, ending the dying killer's suffering.

After that, Sean Keegan dragged the Springfield over and let the sand clean the mess off the walnut stock. He caught his breath, looked at McCulloch, who still slept, and turned toward Breen.

For a hardened killer, Breen's face turned whiter than his hair. His mouth remained open, and his chest heaved.

Keegan laughed. "Breen, me lad, that makes it twice I have saved your hide." He tilted his head slightly toward the sleeping Ranger. "And McCulloch's as well. That means the both of you owe me for two lives. Glory be, I'll be drinking free whiskey for the next fifty years!"

CHAPTER NINE

Holding the lantern in his left hand, retired Army Colonel Newton S. Bainbridge knocked on the door of the flea-bitten rat-trap that lay a hundred yards behind the privies out back of The Donnybrook Saloon in Purgatory City. The one-room shack was downwind of the privies, and the stink was awful. How a man could live in such squalor was beyond Bainbridge.

Inside the hovel came the curses of a man aroused out of a whiskey-induced sleep. A tin cup clattered onto the floor. More curses followed, and Bainbridge stepped away from the door and smiled at the memories the voice brought back.

"Who it the bloody hell . . . ? By thunder, it's not a fit time . . ." A match flamed to life, lighted a candle, and a boot must have kicked the tin cup across the small living quarters. That caused another curse.

"If the kids don't leave me alone, I shall

cut your throats, but only after I put a .44-caliber ball through your private parts." The door opened, and Bainbridge raised his lantern so that his own face was illuminated.

Sean Keegan squinted, snorted, spat, and stepped closer, raising the hand that held the Remington .44 to dull the dim glow from the lantern.

"Sergeant Keegan," Bainbridge said.

The .44 dropped to Keegan's side, and he came to about as close to attention as he could under the circumstances, the circumstances likely being two or three gallons of whiskey.

"Colonel Bainbridge, sir." Keegan slowly brought up a salute.

"It's not Colonel anymore, Sergeant."

The Irishman lowered his right hand. "Aye, sir. Ye retired." He turned to blow out the candle. "I wish I had the bloody sense you had." He flipped the candle inside his home. "Retired with you. For I am no longer a sergeant in the fine cavalry."

"I know. They forced me out. They drummed you out."

Keegan nodded. "Well." He forced a smile. "They could have sent me to do a long spell in Leavenworth." The grin widened without any force to it now. "Killed me a West Pointer, ye know."

"That's what I read in the newspapers."

"Aye. But the bloody papers did not say why I killed the yellow-livered coward."

"I heard the truth, Sergeant. The truth the Army would not want known to the public."

"Indeed. Did ye, Colonel? Aye, that's grand. It burned in my gut for many a night thinking that you might have thought I brought shame to your glorious command."

"As I say, Sean." He tested the first name. "It is no longer my command, and, from what I understand, the glory is a thing of the distant past."

Keegan smiled, sniffed, and wet his lips.

"Colonel Caxton loves his book. By the book. Always by the book. Ye . . ." Keegan shook his head. "Ye were a real fighting man, sir. A man who could lead a bunch of misfits through the gates of hell."

"You know men, Sergeant," Bainbridge said. "There were parts of the book that I never went by."

"Aye." Keegan grinned broadly.

"I guess we were two soldiers who just never went by that damned book."

"Indeed. Books, you always said, were made to be rewritten."

Now Bainbridge tried to equal the size of Keegan's smile.

A moment of silence followed, and Keegan must have smelled the stink from the latrines, so he held open the door. "Colonel, would you care to . . . ?" He let the door swing shut as he stepped outside. "Well, sir, maybe . . . well . . . my home isn't fit for . . . well, Colonel, what brings you to the salubrious climate of South Purgatory City?"

"I desire a few minutes of your time, Sergeant Keegan."

"Certainly, Colonel." He glanced again at what passed for a door in what few people would call a house.

"The Donnybrook appeared to be still serving customers when I passed on my way here, Sergeant," Bainbridge said. "Perhaps we can toast to the United States Army of olden times."

Keegan smiled. "That would be grand, sir. Grand indeed. Allow me to fetch me hat, and I shall lead the way."

"As you always led the men," Bainbridge said. He was glad Keegan agreed to his terms. The Donnybrook Saloon was one of the worst grogshops in West Texas, but it was upwind of the privies.

He waited until Keegan finished his second whiskey. Then Bainbridge leaned forward and whispered, "Sean, I need your help."

Keegan stopped reaching for the bottle of Irish whiskey, and leaned back, staring into his former commanding officer's hard eyes. "Aye, Colonel."

"Call me Newton, Sean."

The old soldier licked his lips, mouthed the first name, and shook his head. "I don't think I can do that, sir. Old habits, you know. And you a man of property. A man with a wife and a family. Why your ranch . . ." He stopped, leaned back.

"How about Bainbridge?"

Keegan mouthed that name, too, and sighed. "I just cannot see me, or hear meself, calling you anything other than Colonel, Colonel. But ye may call me Sean to your heart's content."

"I'm in trouble, Sean," Bainbridge said. "I need your help."

Keegan almost came straight out of his chair and attention. "Anything you say, Colonel. You give the word and —"

He stopped when Bainbridge raised his right hand. "Not so fast, Sergea—" Bainbridge forced his own smile, and shook his head. "I guess it's harder for me to call you anything but Sergeant. But don't go off half-cocked here, my gallant top soldier. You need to hear what I want of you. And I will not be angry if you decline."

"I'll never decline . . ." Again, Bainbridge stopped the old noncommissioned officer by merely raising his hand.

"It's my daughter," Bainbridge whispered, and Keegan leaned forward.

"Ginnie?" Keegan whispered. "Sweet little Ginnie. Is she sick?"

"No." Bainbridge shook his head. "You were the only one who called her Ginnie. She goes by Virginia now, which, well, is what we named her."

"Aye. A sweet little girlie. She made me laugh so at the fort."

"You were her favorite of the soldiers under my command."

"Must be ten years old by now," Keegan said. "I'd hardly recognize her, methinks."

"She's twenty-one, Sergeant."

The old soldier almost toppled over the back of his chair. When the front legs rested again on the warped plank floor of the saloon, Keegan reached for the bottle and refilled his glass. "Twenty-one," he whispered. He gulped down some amber liquid, and shook his head. "Twenty-one," he repeated. He sighed heavily. "The time goes by so fast."

"It does."

Keegan remembered something else. "Oh, Colonel, all these years I've been meaning to let you know how sorry I was to hear of . . . well . . . the passing of . . . your . . . missus."

"Thank you, Sergeant."

"Well, what problem has Ginnie gotten herself into?" He smiled. "She must have a company of suitors if she is as pretty as she was when she was six."

"She was engaged."

"Was!" Keegan shot down the rest of his whiskey. "Why, some no-account blackheart has . . ."

"Sean," Bainbridge said, "her intended was murdered. Shot down. Killed in cold blood on a stagecoach robbery to El Paso."

Keegan's shoulder's slouched. He breathed in and out, and the cold eyes turned deadly. "I heard of no robbery. No holdup." He studied the bottle of whiskey. "I drink too much, I know. Had I read the news, had someone told me, I would —"

"Nobody knows, Sergeant. I bribed the driver of the coach and a woman passenger that were with me."

"You were on the stage, too?"

"Yes. That's why they robbed us."

"And they took your money —"

"They took Virginia, Sean. They . . . took . . . my . . . little . . . baby."

Bainbridge buried his face in his hands.

Keegan snorted, spat, filled the two glasses with the last of the whiskey, and slid one of the glasses until it touched Bainbridge's left arm near the elbow. The retired Army officer lowered his arms, saw the liquor, and nodded his thanks at Keegan.

He sipped the whiskey, feeling the liquor burn his throat, drew in a deep breath, and sighed.

"Sergeant Keegan," he said as he set the tumbler back on the table. "They kidnapped my daughter. They want twenty thousand dollars. They say if they don't have the money in five days, they will kill her. They . . . will . . . murder . . . my . . . precious . . . baby . . ." This time he killed the rest of the Irish before slamming the empty tumbler on the table.

"Did you hear me? Did you hear what I said? They are going to murder my only girl in five days."

All Keegan could do was blink.

After wiping his face, Bainbridge steadied himself, ran his shirtsleeve across his mouth, and breathed in and out until he felt he had control.

"They want twenty thousand dollars. They want it delivered in five days, Sean. If they don't get the money, they're going to kill . . . Ginnie."

105

Keegan's eyes seemed to lose all trace of being bloodshot. He no longer looked like a roaring Irish drunk, but a steady, hard man. The leader that Colonel Bainbridge had depended on for years on the frontier, and even during the war before that, the horrible war in the East, the dreaded Civil War where both men, Bainbridge and Keegan, had learned how to survive warfare. Both men had been molded by those long, arduous, bloody years of the Civil War.

"I want you to deliver the money for me, Sean," Bainbridge said.

"Tell me where to go," Keegan said. "Ye know you can trust me. Twenty thousand dollars. I have no need of such fortune . . ."

"I know," Bainbridge whispered. "I know. I trust you. You're the only one I could trust."

"Then I am your man."

"Wait, Sergeant. There's one thing you must know."

Keegan waited.

"Virginia was kidnapped by Harry Holland."

CHAPTER TEN

Sean Keegan did not hear the name Harry Holland. Not at first. Right then, in The Donnybrook Saloon, all he heard were the cannons, cannons from two thousand miles and more than a dozen years ago.

The colonel was dead. The major was running away, screaming, "God help me! God help me! God preserve me! God, I don't want to die!" The coward yelled so loudly that his voice carried above the musketry and artillery.

Sean Keegan ran forward to pick up the colors. He forgot all about the colonel and the coward of a major. He tilted the pole left and right, left and right, letting the Johnny Rebs see the Stars and Stripes waving through the white smoke. Bullets whistled over his head. Another cannon roared and men screamed as grapeshot tore through their bodies. Keegan felt something slam into his waistline, but he still waved the flag. Later, when it was all over, he would see the lead ball flattened in the breast of the eagle on the brass plate of the belt.

He waved the American flag, while men, in uniforms of dark and baby blue, ran past him, their faces as white as the six stripes or thirty-four stars on the flag. They ran past him, ran as if they wanted to catch up with the cowardly major.

"Keep waving that flag, soldier!" a voice called.

Confederate cannons fired again. Solid shot cut down an oak tree as if it were a twig fifty yards to the left. Suddenly, an officer stepped in front of Keegan. The face turned around, and the man's cold eyes bored a hole through Keegan's soul.

"Follow me, soldier. Don't let that flag fall. Follow me!"

The man wore the insignia of a captain, but his uniform was not that of Keegan's Irish brigade. It didn't matter, though. When the man started marching toward the Johnny Rebs, pointing his shiny saber to the south, Keegan fell in behind him.

Other soldiers in blue kept running past them, ignoring the captain's orders, "Follow me, boys! Follow me! We'll drive these secessionist trash all the way back to Richmond. To Atlanta. To Tallahassee, by Jehovah."

Keegan didn't know where the blazes Tallahassee was, but, by Jehovah, hell, yes, he would follow this man there.

This man, he knew, was a born leader.

They kept on, marching against the tide, waving flag, waving saber, trudging over flattened grass and the dead.

Keegan waved the flag.

"Follow me, boys," the captain bellowed to men who likely heard nothing but their own screams, their own prayers to God for mercy, to spare their lives.

Once Keegan tripped over a dead Reb, dropped to his knees, but kept the flag waving. A man — no a boy, a drummer boy who had lost his drum — stopped to help. Then his left eye was blown out, bathing Keegan's cheek in blood. The boy fell, and Keegan rose, ignoring the gore on his face. Now he picked up the captain's commands.

"Follow us!" he yelled to the panicked, running soldiers. "Follow us. For the Union! For the Glory! For God!"

"Follow me, boys!" the leader said. "Follow me."

"Follow us, boys!" Keegan shouted. "For the Union."

One soldier stopped, considered, but a bullet dug into the sod a few yards past him, and he turned and continued his flight.

"Follow us!"

"Follow me!"

"For the Union!"

"For the Cause!"

Keegan could never exactly tell when he noticed the line of soldiers to his right. Men in blue, marching, firing, and reloading as they continued. Men dropped, only to be replaced by others. Keegan waved the flag, and looked to his left. There was another line of men, men in blue, screaming, shooting. One man held a pitchfork, jabbing it in the direction of the line of Confederates. The soldier closest to Keegan stumbled, gasped, "I am killed," and pitched his Enfield forward. Keegan stopped just long enough to pick it up, carrying the rifled musket in his left hand, the flag in his right, using the musket as a walking stick to help him push upward as they started climbing a small knoll.

"Follow us, boys! We've got them licked."

"You heard the captain!" yelled the man who had filled the spot of the dead soldier with the Enfield. Keegan didn't know who this man was, either. He wasn't infantry. He was artillery. He wasn't a private. He was a major.

On they marched, until the captain stopped, turned and said, "Ready!"

Keegan stopped, too, as did both lines on either side.

"Aim!"

The captain stepped back until he stood against the American flag.

"Fire!"

When the roar ceased and the white smoke rised, Keegan moved the flag and saw just how close they were to the wall of Confederate cannons.

"Charge!" the captain yelled.

And the mismatched soldiers let the Confederates hear the Yankee version of a Johnny Reb cry. Screaming, they ran, as the enemies tried to reload their cannons. But the Union soldiers had gotten too close. Revolvers cracked. Metal rang against metal. Bayonets tore into human flesh.

Keegan rammed the point of the flagpole into a Johnny Reb's gut, saw him fall against the wheel of a twelve-pounder. He planted the colors next to the wheel, grabbed the Enfield, and lunged at a gray-clad man with a red-trimmed kepi. The bayonet tore into the man's throat, and he fell into a sea of his own blood.

And that was all Keegan remembered, until his eyes opened. His head hurt like hell. He couldn't see out of his left eye. Blood felt caked on it, and his tongue located a hole where a molar should have been. His left arm felt numb.

His right eye saw the determined face of the captain.

The captain was carrying him.

Keegan wanted to tell the soldier to put him down, but his mouth wouldn't work. He didn't know how this man could keep at it. Bullets whistled around him, but the man did not stop until they had reached the white canvas tents that served as the corps' field hospital. The captain barged into one of the tents, and Keegan looked on in horror.

A body was rolled off onto the grass. An orderly tossed a bucket of water on what passed for a surgeon's table. And the next thing Keegan knew was he was on that very table. And a surgeon stood over him but did not look at him. The eyes must have locked on the captain who had carried Keegan from the Rebel row of cannon all the way to the Union hospital.

"By whose authority . . . ?" the surgeon demanded.

Now Keegan saw the Colt revolver in the

captain's hand, saw the thumb pull back the hammer, and saw the surgeon's eyes grow as his face paled.

"Doctor, if this man dies, our cause dies, our country dies, and you will not let this happen, sir. Because if this man dies, you, sir, will also die."

The man stepped back. The surgeon stepped forward, looked up at the captain and back at Keegan. The Adam's apple moved, and the surgeon said something, but Keegan could not hear the words. Soon, he heard himself screaming. But that was followed with blessed darkness.

And when Keegan's eyes opened, he was in a home — a Virginia plantation that had been converted into a Union hospital. He knew his head was bandaged, covering one eye. He knew he had never hurt this much since his first hangover. He drew in a deep breath, exhaled, and moved his right hand until he could see it.

Yes, it was still there. He remembered soldiers telling him of men whose hands or legs or feet or arms itched when those hands or legs or feet or arms had been sawed off in field hospitals. Keegan reached across his body and felt his left arm, moved down, and, breathed easier because his left hand remained where it should have been.

He could feel both thighs, but had to figure out a way to sit up to see if the rest of his legs were there. The first attempt landed him back on the pillow. He had to thank Virginia for one thing. Their pillows were a lot softer than Union Volunteer Army pillows. He tried again, only to feel his head slam into the downy pillow. Keegan sucked in a breath, which hurt.

Then he felt hands move beneath his shoulders. "Easy," a voice whispered, and Keegan felt himself being lifted, slowly, but not slowly enough, because he had to fight a wave of dizziness. For a moment, he thought he might turn and vomit all over the legs of this angel.

That, too, passed, and Keegan saw his legs. Bare legs, bare feet. He wiggled the toes on his left foot. Laughed softly. Did the same on his right foot.

The voice of the angel holding him said, "See anything you like, Sergeant?"

The voice did not sound like a lovely lass from County Cork, but a gravelly voice that had been barking orders and a throat that had been breathing in gunsmoke for hours.

"Aye," Keegan said. "It's as beautiful as a bottle of Irish whiskey."

He looked up and found a mirror on the far wall. He also saw the beds of men. He saw orderlies and doctors moving among the wounded, and then he looked at his own reflection. The gaze rose until he could see the face of the angel.

It was a face he recognized, only the sweat and the residue of gunpowder had been washed clean. It was the face, and the uniform, of the captain who had led the men on some wild charge. The man Keegan knew he had to follow.

"Did we win the battle?" Keegan asked.

The captain laughed. "You are quite the soldier, Sergeant." Gunfire sounded again, and the plantation home shook from the artillery. "It is yet to be determined, Sergeant. But we will win the day. If we do not carry this day, we will win the war. As long as we have soldiers like you."

"Captain. We'd be in New York City by now if not for you. You led the charge. You . . ."

"It's Colonel, Sergeant," the man said, and lowered Keegan gently. Keegan turned his head and smiled at his savior. "Colonel Newton S. Bainbridge." He laughed. "Well, they needed colonels. After this ugly day."

Keegan swallowed. "I'm not a sergeant, Colonel," he said, though he wasn't sure Bainbridge had heard him.

"You are today, Sergeant. This man's army

needs new sergeants, too."

Keegan tried to register all this. He sighed.

"What's your name, Sergeant?" the new colonel asked.

"Keegan, sir. Sean Keegan." He tried to salute, but the colonel grabbed the hand, and squeezed tightly. They shook.

"Sergeant, it is an honor."

"You saved my life," Keegan said and could not dam the tears.

"Sergeant, your life was worth saving."

CHAPTER ELEVEN

"Yeah," said the burly man in the tweed cap. "He sure is a white man. No mistakin' that."

The thin man smoking a cigarette while leaning against the empty hitching post grinned at his companion. "I think he's a ghost."

Ignoring the idlers, Jed Breen kept walking down the warped boardwalk. He didn't look at either man, possibly because Purgatory City's boardwalks were often death traps. If you didn't watch where you put your feet, chances are you'd step where there should be a plank but wasn't and wind up with a broken ankle. Breen didn't want to be wearing a cast like Matt McCulloch.

"You're right, Vern," the burly man said. "He is a ghost."

"Passed right through us," Vern said to Breen's back. "I didn't feel a thing, Hoss. Did you?"

"Just a whiff of air," Hoss said. "But it felt

cold, real cold, and it's a mite on the warm side this afternoon, don't you think?"

"It's a ghost," Vern said. "I was right. A white, spooky ol' ghost."

"With white hair."

The two laughed.

By then, Breen had reached Bonderoff's Gun Shop, and the bell chimed as the door opened and closed, and Breen removed his black hat and smiled at the lovely woman behind the counter. She straightened, her face contorting, and Breen remembered that she hadn't been working when he had dropped off his Sharps.

"What happened?" she gasped.

Breen planted on one of his smiles. "Sunburn, Ramona." He looked at his reflection in the mirror and sighed. The doc here in town said the salve would help the healing, because that was "one wicked sunburn." That was that old bone-cutter's diagnosis: "One wicked sunburn." And that would be two dollars. Another four bucks for the salve, which painted Breen's face, neck, and the backs of his hands and fingers. The salve hardened like paste after an hour, and while Breen had gotten used to the whiteness, he couldn't quite stomach the smell. Six dollars, including the visit to the doc's, to look like a ghost, be the butt of everyone's jokes in the whole damned county, and have to go around smelling like wild dandelions.

Ramona grinned. "Why, you look a fright, Jed, but you sure smell sweet."

Smiling cracked the hardened paste, which pinched the corner of Breen's lips.

"Is Bondy around?" Breen asked.

"He's in the back," Ramona said. "I think he's finished with your cannon. I'll fetch him for you."

"Thanks."

Breen watched her disappear behind the curtain, and then he focused on how he looked in the mirror. It was enough to strike fear into a bounty hunter, but the doc had said if he kept applying the salve three times a day, he would probably escape with sunburn scars and be able to just scratch away the dead flakes after three days. At least on the face. The backs of the hands and fingers might need protection with gloves for a week or two, but the neck. The neck was "fried like one of my wife's steaks." That was the sawbone's other diagnosis. "Fried like one of my wife's steaks." Everybody in Purgatory City had to crack a joke.

The chimes on the door rang again, and Breen watched Hoss and Vern come inside. When Hoss elbowed Vern's ribs, Breen knew another joke was about to be fired in his direction. He hoped maybe it would be funny.

"Hey, do you reckon he sees his own reflection?" Hoss asked.

Breen grinned. Well, that one was different at least. The curtains parted, and Ramona laid the Sharps on the counter.

"That's too big for a sweet honey like you to be packin', Ray-Moan-ey," Vern sang out.

Hoss just whistled.

Ramona ignored them, and smiled when Breen turned around. "Bondy said to tell you that he got all the salt cleaned out, and —"

Vern's hackles interrupted her. "Salt. Did you hear that, Hoss? She said salt."

"Salt. That's white as our friend the ghost."

"Maybe he's a salt ghost?"

"But I never smelled salt that smelled like wildflowers."

"Me, neither."

After clearing her throat, Ramona said, "Bondy said he replaced the mainspring, so you should be as good as new. He also sighted in the telescope. You're ready." She slid him the bill.

Breen looked at the paper and smiled. There was one good thing about living in Purgatory City. People in this remote part of the frontier just didn't know how much to charge for quality workmanship. Bondy was about the best gunsmith Breen had ever seen. On the other hand, considering as much business as Bondy got in a rawhide Sodom like Purgatory City, he probably earned as much money as a good bounty hunter, no matter how little he charged.

As he reached into his pocket to pull out some coins, the floorboards squeaked as the two idlers came to the counter. Breen dropped the money next to the Sharps and smiled at Ramona.

"I'll get you your change," she said, staring at the money so she wouldn't have to look up at Vern and Hoss.

"That's all right, Ramona," Breen said, pocketed the receipt, and started to lift the Sharps. "Keep the change."

"Well, that's mighty sweet of you, Ghost," Vern said.

"Course it's sweet, Vern," Hoss said. "He's a sweet-smellin' ghost."

"But sweetness won't get you inside Ramona's skirts, white boy," Vern said. "She's going to the dance with me and Hoss."

Ramona straightened. Breen felt his own face flushing underneath the white paste mask.

"I told you boys not to come in here unless you're buying something," she snapped. "And I told you I'm not going to the dance with either of you. I wouldn't be seen walking next to you on the boardwalk."

"You won't be seen, 'cause we won't be going to the dance, sweetheart," Hoss said.

"We'll be doing something much more fun than dancin', one after the other," Vern said.

"Or at the same time," Hoss giggled.

Ramona's face flushed, and tears welled in her eyes. That was all Breen had to see.

The butt of the Sharps came off the counter, knocked over the looking glass, and caught Vern hard in the stomach. He doubled over and vomited, while Hoss leaped back and brought up his fists in a pugilistic stance, but he didn't have time to block the barrel of the rifle as Breen swung around and slammed the heavy iron against Hoss's cauliflower ear.

"God a'mighty," Hoss roared as he went falling into Vern, who was trying to push himself up. Down they went into a heap. Breen shifted the Sharps to his left hand, and kicked Hoss's rear end, sending him to the floor. Then he dragged Vern to his feet and flung him across the room. The bell chimed when he slammed into the door. It chimed again when Breen rammed the Sharps barrel into Vern's groin, and now he screamed, fell to his knees, and began the dry heaves.

Again, music entered the gunsmith's shop as Breen opened the door. His right hand gripped Vern's collar, and he hoisted the gagging man to his feet, and shoved him out of the store. The man's left foot stepped into one of those holes in the boardwalk, and he twisted, screamed as the ankle broke, and fell into the street.

Breen stepped outside, looked up and down the boardwalk at the crowd of men, women, and boys on both sides, and as Vern rolled over and tried to lift his head, Breen slammed the Sharps's stock against his forehead, just enough to send the loud-mouthed idiot into a deep sleep for an hour or two. This time he ignored the crowd of gawkers as he returned to Bonderoff's Gun Shop.

Leaving the door open, Breen walked to Hoss, who was slowly standing. The stock of the Sharps busted the man's nose, blood spurted, and Breen slammed the barrel against the back of the man's head. Hoss crashed to the floor, and Breen grabbed the unconscious man, dragged him out, over the boardwalk, and rolled him over on the sobbing Vern. He went back inside the shop to pick up his hat that he had dropped when the ruction started. He also picked up the tweed cap and flung it outside.

Bonderoff was standing in the curtains. The mustache moved as the gunsmith laughed. "Nice fight. I would've paid six bits to have seen most of it."

Breen studied the floor, shook his head, and looked up at the gunsmith and his assistant. "Sorry about the mess. There's some vomit and blood on the floor."

"Like the last time you was in here," Bondy said.

"Well," Breen said. "That was different. That was Abel Jones trying to buy a Colt, and he was wanted for attempted murder in Eagle Rock with a two-hundred-dollar price on his head."

"I'll clean it up," Ramona said.

"No." Bonderoff moved out of the curtains and through the gate at the corner. "I'll do it, Ramona. You go back there and finish loading those .44-40s like I showed you."

"All right, Papa."

Bonderoff looked and listened, let a few seconds tick off the clock, and turned to Breen. "I've been meaning to teach them two blowhards a lesson for some time, now."

Breen smiled. "They have some bad manners."

"You might have cured them of that."

"If they were able to move, I'd have them clean up their mess," Breen said.

"That's all right. As soon as I'm done mopping up their mess, I'll use it to dump on them and revive them."

He held out his hand. Breen shook, fitted his hat tight on his head, shifted the Sharps under his arm, and walked outside. The bell chimed as he closed the door.

He glanced at the crowd gathering, and when one boy filled a cup with water from the nearest trough and started to splash it on one of the hoodlum's heads, Breen said, "Don't do that, boy. Mr. Bonderoff will take care of that chore."

Turning, Breen took a few steps and stopped.

"You must've been paying attention," Sean Keegan said, "to me after all, the way you handled yeself."

Breen merely stared.

Keegan sniffed. "What's that smell?"

"Me." Breen sighed.

"No, it smells like . . ."

"Dandelions."

"Yeah." Keegan nodded. "That's right."

"It's me. That's what started the fight."

Keegan laughed. "I thought it was your face and hands and neck."

"That's what smells."

"You look like a ghost."

"That's what also started the fight."

"Well, Jed, ye know, ye could dye that salve before putting it on. Make it more dirt colored. Tan. Ye wouldn't stand out as much."

Breen lowered the rifle, tilted his head, and studied the Irishman. "Hell," he said softly. "I never even thought about that. You think it'd work?"

"Worth a shot. And you could maybe add some bourbon or some hair tonic that ain't quite as . . . well . . . pungent. That'd cut down the smell of them wildflowers. I mean, it wouldn't make ye the most-handsomest man in this part of Texas, but it would help cut down you getting provoked into fisti-cuffs."

Breen laughed. "I wasn't provoked this time, Keegan. I was defending the honor of a gunsmith's daughter."

"Grand, simply grand. Now I wish I'd really seen the whole shebang."

"But I owe you." Breen brought the rifle back up. "How about if I buy you a drink?"

"I'll accept," Keegan said. "And that will square us for my medical advice. And then we can talk about ye repaying me for saving your hide on those salt fields, and from those low-down Comanchero dogs."

"Aw," Breen said with utter fatigue, "hell."

The old Irish trooper put his arm around Breen's shoulder, causing Breen to flinch when Keegan's coarse woolen shirt scratched through the hardened paste on the back of the bounty hunter's neck.

"That hurt?" Keegan asked, sounding almost sincere.

"Not as much as what I fear you're going to rope me into."

Keegan laughed. "Now, now, laddie, it's not as bad as ye might think. Bad enough to get us killed, certainly. But it could also make a man like you, with your skill with that big cannon you got there, rich."

Breen turned to look at the former soldier. "The rich part I like," he said.

CHAPTER TWELVE

Lying in the cot that served as his bed, Mc-Culloch stared at the tintype of his wife, gone all these years. The image was old and scratched, and the fellow who had charged them a dollar for four copies of the same photograph hadn't been the sharpest man of his particular trade. But the dark eyes of his wife always seemed so real.

He lifted the bottle of whiskey in his left hand and took another swallow. The sawbones in Purgatory City had charged Mc-Culloch a couple of dollars for laudanum to help ease the pain, but McCulloch didn't like the taste of that stuff — or the dreams he had after just a spoonful of the potion. The rye seemed a bit better and certainly dulled the pain in his leg.

"Hell," he whispered, slowly swinging his legs off the bunk, moving the busted one gingerly, and staring at the cast on the ankle. Sighing, he took another glance at the tintype and slipped it in his vest pocket. Then he studied the bottle of rye.

"Keep this up," he said aloud, "and you'll be like Sean Keegan." So he corked the bottle and tossed it next to the pillow.

The sod home he lived in smelled like dirt. What else would it smell like? He didn't like being crippled, unable to bust horses. Hell, he couldn't even climb into a saddle these days — and wouldn't, the doc said, for a good six weeks, maybe longer, depending on how the bones healed. He might even have a limp, but he'd keep the leg as long as he didn't do some damned fool stunt. He had six mustangs in the corral that he was readying for gentling, and his own three good horses and a mule. The brother of the late Abel Cook had sold the last of Cook's livestock to McCulloch — at prices even a stoved-up former Texas Ranger could afford. Now all he could do right now was just make sure they got food and water, maybe a brushing if his bum leg could take it.

He started reaching for the crutches when he heard the whinny of one of the mustangs, followed by another nervous whicker, then the hooves pounding the hard ground. He recognized something else, too, the sound of a human trying to be quiet. McCulloch left the crutches for the time being and slid over to where his gunbelt and Colt lay at the foot of the cot. He slid the long-barreled revolver from the holster, thumbed back the hammer, and used just one crutch. He hopped his way to the door, pushed it open, and stepped into the afternoon sun.

Two men stood by the corral, one holding four horses, the other watching a third man try to put a loop over the bay mustang, the best of the bunch, a good four-year-old with guts and brains.

"What the hell are you boys doing?" McCulloch barked, and used the crutch to step closer to the corral. It was a stupid question, he realized, and another reason not to drink whiskey in bed at this time of day. Anyone with half a brain knew what those boys were doing. They were rustling.

"Why don't you just lower that hogleg," a voice called behind him, and McCulloch felt the barrel of a pistol push against his spine.

And that's the last damned good reason a man shouldn't drink whiskey on an empty stomach when there is plenty of daylight left, he thought. Four horses usually meant four men.

The two men outside the corral turned around and laughed. One of them, the one by the gate, not holding the horses, pushed back the brim of his slouch hat and cackled. "He, Gimp. We heard you had good horse-flesh for the taking."

The man behind McCulloch said, "Lower the hammer, and pitch the iron into the dirt. Don't want it to go off accidental, you know."

McCulloch bit his bottom lip.

"Do it." The barrel pressed harder against McCulloch's backbone, and he let out a slow breath, eased down the hammer, and tossed the Colt about ten yards away.

The voice behind McCulloch exhaled. "That's smart, old man. We're just taking your horses, and then we'll be on our way." The voice then laughed. "You can go back to your drinking."

"Drinkin'?" called out the one by the gate. "He's got whiskey, Scott?"

"He might not have none left the way he smells," Scott, the man behind him, said.

"Well . . ." The man with the slouch hat stepped away from the corral and made straight for McCulloch's house. "I guess I'll take a look-see."

"The hell you going?" called the one holding the horses.

"I'll be back," the slouch hat said.

The one in the corral ducked underneath

the swinging head of the bay, fell to his knees, moved out of the way of hooves, and cried out, "I could use a hand in here."

He got up and retreated toward the corral's poles. "You said this would be easy, Scott." He wiped his face and eyes with a gloved hand, and then gathered up the length of rope.

The one with the slouch hat brushed past McCulloch and went inside. A moment later came a Rebel cry, only from someone who had never been a Confederate soldier, had just heard stories about Rebel yells and the War Between the States. "Rye whiskey, boys!" the voice called through the open door. "Rye whiskey and sixty dollars' worth of horseflesh."

"Sixty dollars my ass," said Scott. "These are McCulloch horses."

Cook horses, actually, but Cook horses were almost as good as McCulloch stock.

"You want me to help your boy?" McCulloch said.

The man called Scott laughed. "You gonna help us rustle your own horses?"

"If it'll get you out of here quicker," McCulloch said.

Scott laughed, and called out, "Hey, the old Ranger here wants to know if you need some help, Stevie?"

Stevie dodged the mean little roan mare. "I need somebody to help me."

Scott looked at Stevie, and then at McCulloch, then at the sod house before one of the horses jerked his arm that held the reins to two of the mounts.

"What the hell can a fellow on crutches do?" said the one in the slouch hat, now rustling through McCulloch's belongings for whatever else these boys planned to steal.

"You got a point there," Scott said, and McCulloch felt the barrel of the gun leave his spine.

McCulloch shifted the crutch underneath his busted leg.

"Jimmy Ray," Scott called to the man inside McCulloch's home. "Get out of there now and help Linwood in the corral. I want to be riding for Deep Water before I'm a graybeard."

Boots thudded, spurs jingled, and McCulloch saw the shadow of Jimmy Ray as he exited the hut and walked toward the corral. McCulloch swung the crutch as he turned, saw the end tripping Jimmy Ray's boots, and sending the man and the bottle of rye crashing to the dirt, while McCulloch kept spinning, bringing the crutch up as he turned completely around and let the crutch catch the wide-eyed Scott in the side of his head. He was bringing the gun barrel up when the crutch slammed him. The gun roared, kicked up dust that swallowed Scott as he crashed forward.

McCulloch fell, too, breaking his fall with his arms, dropping the crutch and feeling the blinding pain in his bad leg. He saw the pistol Scott had dropped, though, and now he grabbed it and started to sit up.

Scott was coming up, but McCulloch had the gun the punk had dropped, and slammed the barrel hard right across his forehead. Down he went backward, spread-eagled, blood seeping through the deep cut the revolver's sight had dug.

Now McCulloch thumbed back the hammer and watched Jimmy Ray roll over and try to pull his pistol from the holster. McCulloch felt Scott's Colt buck in his hand and saw Jimmy Ray spin around, dropping his weapon, unfired, and twist himself into a ball.

A horse raced past McCulloch, followed by another, and McCulloch looked through the dust at the corral. He wasn't concerned with the kid holding the four horses — no, just two horses now. That one had his hands full, but he made out Linwood climbing over the corral and reaching for a Winchester he had leaned against the outside of the corral before moving inside to gather the mustangs. Again, McCulloch cocked and fired Scott's pistol, and the bullet slammed into the fence post and sent shards of post oak into Linwood's right hand. The boy yelped and fell back against the fence rails, staring at the wood that stuck out of his palm like tree branches. The Winchester remained where he had left it.

As McCulloch turned to the last man, the horse holder, he saw the third mount, a big pinto, jerk the boy to the ground. It loped off toward Purgatory City, and the last horse dragged the kid about twenty yards before stopping. McCulloch thumbed back the hammer, and sighted down on the kid, who came to his knees and pulled the reins hard until he climbed to his feet. He was screaming like a crazy man, sending the mustangs in the corral circling like a whirlwind, before he leaped into the saddle and galloped through the dust.

McCulloch let that one ride free.

He caught his breath, found the crutch, and lifted himself off the ground. Moving awkwardly through the yard, he stopped and bent to a knee to pick up his own Colt. After blowing the dust off the barrel and cylinder, he shoved his revolver inside his waistband and looked over the scene.

Scott remained unconscious. Jimmy Ray sat in the dirt, his left hand clenched tight against the bullet hole in his shoulder. Linwood remained leaning against the fence rails, staring at his bloody, wood-wounded hand.

McCulloch waved the smoking gun barrel at the whiskey bottle in the dirt near Jimmy Ray.

"You might help yourself to that, boy," McCulloch said. "It'll ease your misery."

Then he pushed himself up and cocked the revolver again.

Horses were coming. Two men, who rode through the dust before reining up.

"How long you been watching?" McCulloch asked.

Sean Keegan leaned forward and just grinned.

Jed Breen shifted the Sharps off his thigh and said, "I guess you showed these boys just what hell a fellow on crutches can raise."

Keegan jutted his jaw at the dust the fleeing one had left. "Want us to go after that one?"

"No," McCulloch answered. "But you can help me gather these boys up. We can take them to Purgatory City, let the sheriff decide what to do with them."

"Why don't we just string these owlhoots up?" Breen said and laughed when Linwood started sobbing and fell to his knees, pleading not to be hanged, that this was all Scott's idea, that he had never done anything like this before, and that his pa would tan his hide if he found out.

"I reckon your hide's gonna get tanned then," McCulloch said.

"We'll be glad to help you, Matt." Keegan swung out of the saddle.

"You want me to try to round up those horses that got spooked off?" Breen asked.

"No."

Keegan straightened. "How you plan on getting these pathetic horse thieves to Sheriff Juan in Purgatory City?"

"They can walk."

"How you gonna get there?" Breen asked.

"I'll ride in my wagon." McCulloch said. "That's one thing I can do." He limped over to close the door to his house of dirt. When he turned around, he looked at the bounty hunter and ex-soldier. "What brought you here?"

"A business proposition, Matt," Keegan said. "But it can wait till we get these bad, bad boys in the calaboose, and find us a cool spot in a saloon to discuss."

CHAPTER THIRTEEN

The owner of the Rio Lobo Saloon stepped from behind the bar and held up his hands when the three men pushed through the batwing doors. "Sean," the mustached man called out in a panicked voice, "you're not busting up my place again. I barely got it —"

"Aw, calm down, you hussy in a petticoat," Keegan said and let his end of the door start banging away. "I'm here with me friends to have a cold beer, nothing stronger except a bottle of Irish, and that's all."

The owner was sweating, and only partly from the heat. "I know those two . . ." He swallowed down the word.

"Were you going to say *jackals,* ol' boy?" Breen asked.

The owner shook his head.

"Just bring us beers and a bottle." Keegan hooked his thumb toward McCulloch. "Hell, man, how much damage can a fellow on crutches cause?"

They found a seat in the quiet corner of the saloon, and McCulloch, once he settled into his seat, gently raised his bad leg and rested it on an empty chair. He leaned the crutches against the wall and waited until a buxom saloon girl came over with a tray holding six foaming mugs of beer, three shot glasses, and a bottle that was marked IRISH WHISKEY.

"There's only us, darling," Keegan said as the woman hurriedly emptied her tray and laid the glasses and bottle onto the table.

"Yes," she said, "but this will keep me from coming back for a while, and I hope to be out of here by the time you're finished with these before" — she wet her lips and stared at Keegan — "hell breaks loose."

"Oh, bother," Keegan said. "A man wrecks thirty-seven saloons in one town and they brand him for life."

"Sean." The woman gathered the tray and began a fast gait back to the bar. "You've wrecked this place thirty-seven times, and you don't come here that often."

McCulloch grabbed the handle of the nearest glass and sipped without bothering to toast anyone at the table. Breen did the same. Keegan uncorked the whiskey, drank about half of the first beer, and refilled the glass with the Irish, then guzzled about half of it down before wiping the suds off his mouth with his sleeve.

"What kind of hell have you gotten yourself into now, Keegan?" McCulloch asked as he set his beer down.

"It's the colonel, Matt." Keegan leaned forward.

"Bainbridge?" McCulloch asked.

"Aye. Or rather, it's his daughter."

McCulloch frowned.

Breen sipped beer and said, "You know Virginia, don't you?"

For a long while, McCulloch just stared. Finally, he breathed out, found his beer, and finished it with a few swallows. As he set the empty glass on the table, he shook his head. "I haven't seen her in years. She used to play with . . ." He could not say his daughter's name, the teenager who had been taken captive by the red devils who had laid waste to his ranch and his life.

"Ginnie was engaged to some dude," Keegan said. "Can't remember his name."

"Was?" McCulloch asked.

"He was murdered, Matt. On a stagecoach to El Paso." Keegan sighed. "Harry Holland took her, Matt. Killed her beau and took her."

"How come nobody has heard of this?"

McCulloch asked.

"Because Harry Holland told the colonel to keep his trap shut."

"When does Harry Holland give orders . . . especially to a ramrod-straight Yankee son of a . . . ?"

"If a man has your daughter, Matt —" Keegan stopped immediately, and looked at his drink. "Sorry, Matt."

A minute passed. McCulloch frowned and drank more beer. "Go on," he said after a long, uneasy silence.

"Holland wants twenty thousand dollars delivered to his hideout in four days," Keegan said.

McCulloch straightened. "Nobody has been able to find his hideout," he said. "Not the Army. Not the Rangers." He glanced at Breen. "Not any bounty hunters."

"Well," Breen said and drank more beer. "That's because I've never tried."

Setting his second glass on the table, McCulloch stared hard at the bounty killer. "And how come?"

Breen let a sheepish grin crack his white-painted face. "Because I don't fancy getting myself shot to pieces and left for ravens to pick at."

"Exactly." McCulloch shook his head. "That's a fool's errand, Sean. Did Bainbridge talk you into this?"

"He asked me to do him this favor," Keegan said.

Breen cleared his throat. "I told Sean he'd have more than Harry Holland and his thirty or forty gunmen to worry about, Matt. I told him that Rojo's renegade Apaches have holed up in the Big Bend country, and some of those bucks know the value of gold . . ."

"Gold?" McCulloch asked.

Keegan shrugged. "That's what Colonel Bainbridge brought back from El Paso. Twenty thousand dollars in double eagles."

"Greenbacks would be a whole lot easier to carry," McCulloch said.

"But that's what the bank had on hand. Twenty-dollar gold pieces."

"That's a lot of weight to be hauling," McCulloch said.

"Aye, the colonel, he said the two iron boxes weighed about a hundred and fifty pounds — more than half of that, or close to it, would be the weight of the two iron boxes. Including the padlocks."

"There's something else to consider," Breen said. "A man draws twenty thousand in gold coin out of a bank in El Paso . . . that doesn't stay secret for long. There will be others who'd like to get that money

142

before it falls into Harry Holland's hands."

McCulloch nodded, drank more from his glass, and looked at Breen: "But you've set your stick to float alongside this hell-raising fool." It wasn't a question.

With a chuckle, Breen raised his glass, finished his first beer, and reached for his second. "Well, the way Keegan tells things, all this Bainbridge fellow — I've never met the gent — wants is his daughter back."

"Aye, that's the truth, and the beauty of it all." Keegan just drank straight from the bottle now. "The colonel, he tells me that the twenty thousand can go to that no-account ruffian, murderer, and rapscallion Holland, for the ransom . . . or it can go to us. Payment for the return of his lovely daughter. All the colonel wants is his daughter returned."

McCulloch shook his head. "What the hell can I do?" He pointed at his broken leg. "With that? I can't ride a horse."

"You showed what you could do with those scalawags we left in the Purgatory City calaboose," Breen said with a smile.

"Four kids. Punks. Harry Holland doesn't have one punk riding for him. He has a couple of dozen — more than that — seasoned gunhands."

"And Holland wouldn't expect no trouble

from you, a poor old horse trader with a badly busted limb." Keegan smiled. "And you might not be forking a saddle anytime soon, but I daresay you can drive a wagon."

"Only so far." McCulloch slid his empty second glass away. "You've trailed Indians into the Big Bend, Sean. I know that much. You know that country. It's the hardest patch of earth in Texas . . . hell, in all these United States . . . and there's probably not a whole lot meaner places anywhere on this globe." He shook his head. "I can get the wagon only so far. How the hell are you supposed to get that ransom to Holland?"

Keegan shrugged again. "Me figures it'll be Holland who comes to us. He'll want to make sure we're not being followed, and when he figures it's just the three of us, he'll ride down, get the money, give us the girl, and we can go home."

"Or," Breen said, "we can follow him back to his hideout."

"And collect the reward money on Holland and his boys and collect the payment from that Yankee colonel." McCulloch leaned back in his chair, careful not to upset his busted leg resting on another chair. "You two fools have gone completely loco." He looked at Breen. "That sun fried your head, burned out any common sense you had left." Now he faced Keegan. "Whiskey has rotted your brain."

He reached again for his glass, only to realize it was empty, and shook his head. "Three men against thirty is a suicide mission." Yet he did not get up to leave. "You really think you can collect a bounty on Harry Holland? You really think you can get out of this alive? You don't know Holland."

"Aye," Keegan said. "But word in these parts is that you do."

McCulloch shook his head. "That was a long time ago. The man I know isn't the man who has been on the dodge all these years."

"You also know the Big Bend," Breen said. "That's what all the old Rangers and some of the scouts from the Army posts keep saying."

McCulloch nodded. "I know enough to keep my hide out of there unless I don't have any choice."

"Well." Keegan took another pull from the whiskey bottle and slid it toward McCulloch. "You've got a choice here, laddie. You can do something for yourself, for the colonel —"

"I don't even like the colonel, Sean," McCulloch fired back.

Keegan slammed the bottle on the table.

"Aye, but what about his daughter, Matt? Do ye think she deserves to be in the hands of thirty low-down rogues? Do ye? Do ye think good old Harry Holland will leave her alone? Do ye think anybody else has a chance of getting that girl out of that hellhole alive other than three jackals such as ourselves?"

After taking a short pull on the bottle, McCulloch frowned. He turned to Breen again.

"Bounty?"

"And my share of twenty thousand dollars." Breen grinned.

"I don't see much in it for me."

"Horses?" Breen asked.

McCulloch started to take another drink of whiskey, but instead passed the bottle to Breen. "Harry Holland was a good judge of horseflesh, even before the war and before he started his fight against Yankee authority and anything south of the border."

Keegan let his head bob. "And I hear he has a fortune in stolen stock in that fortress he has built for himself in the Big Bend."

"I've heard the same," McCulloch said, the words barely audible. "Mexican horses, mostly."

"Meaning free for the taking to anyone on this side of the Rio Grande," Keegan said with a grin.

"Or being honest and taking the horses into Old Mexico to turn them over to their rightful owners."

"For a nice reward," Breen said.

Yet again, McCulloch shook his head. "Boys, I thank you for considering me." He pointed at the cast on the lower part of his left leg. "But I'd just slow you down, get you killed. And you can get yourself killed without my help — especially if you go up against Holland."

"So be it," Keegan said. "You can bow out, too, Breen. I'll go this alone."

McCulloch cursed, spit, and leaned closer to the old Irish soldier. "Bainbridge is a horse's ass. Has been since he got out of your bluebelly Army. From what every soldier under his command has told me, nobody at the fort even liked the mad-dog martinet. So why are you risking your hide for him?"

"Because, Matt," Keegan said without a hint of anger. "Colonel Newton S. Bainbridge saved me life." He reached for his untouched beer. "I owe him, Matt."

Another silence stretched two minutes. McCulloch ended it by slowly pulling his leg off the chair and easing it ever so gently onto the floor. Reaching for his crutch, he said, "Well, Sean, I'm sorry, but Bainbridge

147

never saved my life."

"No." Keegan smiled, and sipped his beer. "No, Matt, he didn't save your life." He set the beer on the table, leaned forward, and grinned. "But I did. Twice."

CHAPTER FOURTEEN

Harry Holland stepped through the turret's door and onto the roof of his hacienda. Well, he called it a hacienda. And he called it a turret, although some smart aleck said turrets were usually in the corner of a structure, not just off center by the entryway. And Harry Holland had heard too many times people asking why anyone would call this a hacienda, stuck as it was in the middle of Texas's Big Bend of the Rio Grande, a hard, mean country unsuited for cattle, horses, crops — unsuited for anything except coyotes and savages.

More people called it a fortress, and from here he could see the rough hills and jagged rocks that helped make his compound impregnable. Turning around, he could see the patio where a bunch of his men lounged in the heat of the day, while others patched the water drain his laborers, a decade ago, had paved with rock. Water was precious in

Texas, and even more valuable in this country. Beyond the patio, past the eight-foot-high adobe wall, the corrals. Horses sought shade. Some rolled in the dirt. Smoke wafted from the bakery to his right, and the blacksmiths pounded away in the far corner.

Past the entryway, the heavy wooden door open now, but always closed at night, were three rooms for his best hands. Two more rooms housed more men next to his sprawling living quarters and office beneath the turret. These rooms faced the east. The cooking rooms were across from him, and two other thick-adobe- and rock-walled rooms housed his arsenal and gunpowder. That was closer than most people would want, which was why the heavy granite had been brought in and mortared against double-thick adobe — when the rest of the fortress's walls were twenty-four inches thick. Those made the last west-facing walls of the patio. To the north were supply rooms, and the watering hole where his men could get drunk, play cards, and do anything short of killing one another. On the south were more rooms, and the food stores, complete with a root cellar that had taken his men eighteen months to dig. The ground here, one could say, was harder than Harry

Holland's head.

Next to the smithy's shop, buttressed against the supply warehouse lay the saddle and tack room, and, of course, a small dungeon to punish the men whenever they got out of line. They only got out of line and tasted the snake-filled dungeon once. To err is human, Harry Holland said. To err twice is to die.

Next to the blacksmith shop, lining the rest of the southern wall were the gunsmith's operation and the storerooms for the horse's hay and grain, and on the rest of the west wall lay the wells. The privies were on the far corner of the corral.

It was a magnificent place, although many of his men wondered why he had spent so much time perfecting a place like this, when no man alive could ever find the way here. Well, they might, but Harry Holland had made that less likely by persuading the Apache Indians holed up here to kill anyone that got too close. In turn, Harry Holland supplied the Indians with Winchester repeaters and whatever else he could steal that he didn't fancy — the horses, on the other hand, even Apaches had to pay for in gold or silver. But these Apaches had turned into pretty good murdering thieves themselves. Well, Harry Holland had taught them well, too — just as he had his men.

Holland had hoped to find a breeze, but the wind refused to blow this afternoon, so he pulled a cheroot from his shirt pocket, struck a match, and soon enjoyed the taste of tobacco smoke in his mouth.

He felt a pang of regret now as he leaned against the hard wall of the turret. He had spent years, blood, sweat, and pain getting this place built, and now he had perfected his own world. A perfect world. A world where he could even find peace because no white man, no lawman, no one dared hunt for him in this remote corner of hell. Here, Harry Holland was God. Here, Harry Holland had carved his own paradise. A paradise in hell, but a paradise nonetheless. And in less than a week, he sighed, and blew a stream of smoke that vanished in the pale white sky, he would leave all of this behind.

Leave behind the fortress, the greatest building in West Texas, leave it and his fame and everything behind.

He pulled another drag on the cheroot and started to laugh. Started to laugh too soon, because he coughed and choked and spit and laughed even harder before tossing the cheroot onto the gravelly roof and smashing it with his boot.

"Well," he whispered and spit again to

clear his throat. "With twenty thousand dollars, I can soon buy myself another hacienda. But maybe this one will have some water that I can look at. An oceanfront view. Now that would be nice." He removed his boot from the cigar to make sure the fire was crushed out of the cheroot. Fires would be deadly. There wasn't much to burn here, but one knew better than to take needless chances.

Twenty thousand bucks. He shook his head.

"Or maybe . . . Paris."

Then he heard a woman's scream.

Pivoting, Holland leaped through the open doorway of the turret, rounded the corner, came down the winding stairs, his boots taking two steps at a time, then leaping over the last three, and barged through into his room. He knew who had screamed. There was only one woman in this place — except when he let some of the grizzled Apache women come or the Apaches had brought some Mexican captives in to pleasure his men — and Holland had given her the small living quarters that adjoined his sprawling place. There was no doorway separating Virginia Bainbridge's room from Holland's, just a curtain, and he moved through that to see the colonel's daughter

— the stunningly beautiful angel worth all that money in gold — lying on the settee, the shoulder of her French-made dress ripped down — the dress Harry Holland had presented her when they had arrived at his mansion — and he could see the whiteness of part of a breast, and the fear in her eyes.

He also saw Brute Ketchum — a fitting name for a savage man — turning around, clutching a purple piece of silk in his right hand.

"Boss!" Ketchum cried out, and only then did the big man notice the piece of damning evidence he held right out as though for Holland to inspect. He dropped the cloth as though it were a hot coal, and stepped back. "It ain't like it looks, Boss."

"You . . ." Virginia sobbed. "You . . . brute."

Which caused Ketchum to turn toward her, confused. The man was such a dunce, he didn't even know what brute meant, other than a handle someone had stuck on him years ago.

Virginia Bainbridge turned now to Holland. Her lips trembled. She sniffed. "He . . . he . . . he . . ."

"She was headed out the door, Boss!" Brute wailed as he spun back toward Bainbridge. "She was . . ."

"She was what, Ketchum?" Holland stepped forward. "She was going outside for a breath of fresh air?" Holland walked, ignoring the shivering daughter of a wealthy old soldier of blue, and Brute Ketchum stepped backward. "Do you think she was trying to escape?"

Ketchum stepped through the opening and into daylight. He was in the patio, and he took six more steps before stopping as Holland kept his distance and his composure.

"Look around you, Ketchum," Holland said, and waved his right arm toward the men lounging against the walls to the eastern rooms, while other men stood smoking and chewing and scratching and grinning now that some excitement might break up the monotony of another hot day. Those men lined the walls of the buildings before the corrals. Other men poured out of the cantina on the north side of the patio.

"Do you think she might have sneaked through these men?" Holland asked, and then gestured at the sally port. "Maybe even gotten out of my hacienda?"

Brute Ketchum swallowed.

Holland continued. "Then what on earth would we do? For she would be free, free to find the law and bring the wrath of Texas justice to us. This woman, this poor lovely woman, would have to crawl through rocks and cactus afoot, brave the wild animals and even wilder Apaches, find the right trail that would lead her to the wasteland that stretches from the Rio Grande all the way north till one eventually, luckily, might find the Davis Mountains. On foot! Is that why you ripped off a forty-five-dollar dress? To stop her from getting all of our necks stretched?"

The men on all sides began chuckling, elbowing one another. Some lit cigarettes. Only a few went back to their dice or cards. Most understood that the fun was just beginning.

"Boss," Brute Ketchum said, "I swear! I . . ." Maybe something in Holland's eyes told Brute Ketchum his fate, because he turned then. He did have brains enough not to draw the hogleg on his hip. That would have gotten him drilled with dozens of bullets. But running? All he had to do was make it through the sally port. Then do the same thing Holland had described that the prisoner would have had to face.

He made it only four steps before a bullet sent through the back of his right knee blew out the cap.

Screaming in agony, he fell into the shade of the entryway, and several men now cocked their revolvers or unsheathed their knives and started to join in on the fun. This was better than Spanish monte or craps or blackjack.

"No!" Holland yelled, and the men obeyed.

Brute Ketchum rolled over and over, whimpering, knowing he'd be crippled for life — and understanding that his life would not last much longer.

"Richie, Gonzalez," Holland said, and two men stopped forward. "Take him to Chief Rojo. Tell Chief Rojo to let his squaws do as they please. That should make our Apache brothers and sisters happy. Since we didn't deliver them much after our last excursion."

"No!" Ketchum shrieked and began frothing, spitting, sobbing, and Richie and the Mexican, grins stretching across their hardened faces, moved toward the bleeding, paling big cuss. "For the love of God, Boss . . . I swear . . . I didn't."

Richie silenced the big fool with a kick to the head.

Three of the men on the north wall made the sign of the cross before they returned to their drinks.

The fun was over. Well, at least for the

boys at Holland's hacienda. The fun for the Apaches, especially Rojo's squaws, would just be beginning.

"You know the rules, boys," Holland said. "That twenty thousand dollars is only good if this woman isn't harmed. Remember that." He lowered the hammer on his revolver and walked back through the door and into the room of Virginia Bainbridge. She still sat in the bed, still trying to cover her ripped dress, her face pale.

Holland started to pull the door closed, but left it open and said in a firm, loud voice, sure to carry across the patio. "I do not think you shall be bothered again during your stay with us, ma'am. If anyone even looks at you with a look you dislike, please tell me or my best men. They will keep the Apaches busy. I am a killer. I am a thief. I am a butcher. I am bound for hell. But I am also a gentleman. Let me go, ma'am, and bring you back a new dress. There's one we took off a fancy wagon sixty miles from Raymondville. I think it's from Madrid, Spain. And there are some lovely pearls that complement it perfectly."

"Thank you," Virginia Bainbridge said.

"I just want to make you as comfortable as can be during your stay with us, ma'am."

And then Holland pulled the door shut and slammed the bolt in hard.

CHAPTER FIFTEEN

McCulloch was standing outside the sheriff's office when Colonel Newton S. Bainbridge rode in the next morning just as dawn started to break. That early, hours before even the first café in Purgatory City opened for breakfast, the far side of the street and the balcony of the opera house and hotels were lined with people. So were some of the flat roofs of homes. Jed Breen had said that he heard some homeowners were charging a dollar for someone to sit on the roof and watch the spectacle.

The colonel rode a prancing gray Arabian stallion, and six riders with heavy rifles flanked a freight wagon that had four guards with shotguns and revolvers and a driver wearing a grim look on his face. The wagon squeaked as it pulled to a stop.

Only then did McCulloch, Winchester in his right hand along with the crutch, begin hobbling off the busted boardwalk before he stopped and looked up at Bainbridge.

"I appreciate you doing this for me . . . and my . . . girl," the colonel said.

"I'm not doing it for you," McCulloch said, tilting his head toward the jail. "It's for that son of a gun inside."

"Well . . ." The colonel shifted in the saddle. "Thank you anyway."

McCulloch stepped around the big horse, and nodded at the men in the wagon. "Move it to the back of that one." He gestured at the buckboard waiting in front of the water trough by the sheriff's office.

Bainbridge turned in his saddle and barked like a damn Yankee Army officer. "You heard the man, get moving, you lard asses. We're burning daylight."

The men in the back of the wagon lay down their weapons. McCulloch limped back and watched the cowboys strain and sweat, grunt and swear, as they dragged two heavy boxes from the back of the wagon. Each of four men used his left hand to carry a metal grip, kept his right hand on the butt of his Colt, and struggled to carry the pair of matching boxes to the wagon McCulloch had personally selected.

"You'll find the chains in the back," Mc-Culloch called out. "Thread those through the top holds of each box, and use the

161

padlocks to seal them tight. I don't want them rolling around in the bed across the country we'll be cutting through."

Bainbridge swore, spit, and sighed. "I don't think, heavy as those boxes are, that they'll be sliding anywhere."

"I'm not taking that chance," McCulloch said, and he followed the struggling men, keeping an eye on them — and the crowd in Purgatory City — all the while.

Bainbridge swung off his horse and led the Arabian behind him as he followed McCulloch.

"Big turnout," he said.

"It don't happen every day," McCulloch said.

"No." Bainbridge sighed. "Those are good horses you got hooked to that wagon." He hesitated, and then cleared his throat. "Wouldn't mules work better in the country you're going through?"

"We got four days, Newton," McCulloch said. "These horses go faster than mules."

"I see." The throat cleared again. "But even those six horses won't be able to cover all that . . ."

"I sent some good men — men I trust — with fresh teams ahead. That should get us close . . . if nothing goes wrong."

"Good." Bainbridge's head bobbed repeatedly. "Good. Good. Good. Very good. Damned good thinking. Good thing you're a horse man."

"They weren't my horses," McCulloch said. "My horses aren't good for pulling wagons, especially a wagon hauling all that gold coin. I breed and train riding horses."

"Right. Then whose . . . ?"

"Abel Cook's," McCulloch said, turned, and spit in the dirt. "He doesn't have any need for them anymore."

Bainbridge's men were done, and they walked back toward their wagon.

Again, McCulloch glanced at the door to the sheriff's office, and shook his head. The sheriff had picked the right day to be out of town. The sheriff, while a pretty good man and honest by Purgatory City's standards, knew when would be a good time to be out of town.

"Is there anything I can do?" Bainbridge asked.

"Just stay out of our way," McCulloch said. "And you might pray for your daughter's well-being."

The old Army soldier drew in a deep breath, held it, and slowly exhaled. "I never was much of a hand at praying."

"I wasn't, either," McCulloch said. "But I learned how when I needed to. Antietam.

163

Franklin."

"Yes," the old colonel said, nodding, even grinning slightly. "Yes, yes, indeed. Keegan and I . . . we were on the other side."

"Whose side are you on now?" McCulloch turned and stared hard at the colonel.

"Yours," the man barked out. "Yours, of course."

"Be on your daughter's side," McCulloch said. "Go back to your ranch and pray hard."

"Should we ride with you?" Bainbridge looked at the boardwalks and the roofs. "At least till you're out in the clear."

"These are just gawkers," McCulloch said. "Nothing to worry about. The worrying will come when Purgatory City is behind us, and the Big Bend country lies ahead."

Bainbridge must have sensed there was nothing left to talk about, and that the more he talked, the less time McCulloch and his crew had for getting into the Big Bend maze and finding Harry Holland, because he turned like a soldier, found the stirrup, settled into the saddle, and turned the gray stallion. His right hand raised, and he signaled, calling out, "All right, men. About face. Forward, ho-oa."

McCulloch did not watch the parade out of Purgatory City. He used his crutch to get him back to the doorway of the sheriff's office. Holding his Sharps with the brass telescope sight in his right hand, Breen stepped out, his face still painted with that white paste, and his left hand gripping six or seven canteens. He nodded, and carried the canteens to the wagon, which had already been loaded with two water barrels, foodstuffs, bedrolls, cooking gear, and boxes and boxes of ammunition. Keegan came out with the Springfield carbine in his left hand and two jugs of liquor in his right.

He studied the roofs and the boardwalks, too.

"You sure this is a good idea, Matt?" the sergeant said softly.

"No. It's a damned fool idea, Sean," McCulloch barked. "It's a damned suicide mission. You're going to get Breen, you, and me killed. That's what I'm sure about, you bullheaded Irish pig."

"Aye," Keegan said.

"You had to play that card. That I-saved-your-life card."

Now Keegan shook his head. "Quit fooling yourself, Matt. You know why you're doing this, and it's not because I saved your hide. You're doing this for your own daughter. And you damned well know that, my old friend."

"Let's get the hell out of here," McCulloch said, and using his one crutch — the other he had left earlier in the wagon's driver's box — he started making his way to the farm wagon. Breen swung into the saddle of his bay gelding, and Keegan shoved the Springfield into the scabbard on his brown horse. The men eased into their saddles, Breen still holding the Sharps across his thighs, and Keegan drawing the Remington, cocking it, and keeping it held high in his right hand, barrel pointing at the lightening sky.

Breen stopped his horse on the left side of the wagon.

Keegan reined to a halt on the right.

Both the bounty hunter and the old horse soldier wondered how Matt McCulloch would manage to get into the driver's seat with a busted left leg. Yet neither one of them asked if the old Ranger needed a hand. They had known him long enough not to make that sort of mistake.

The crowds — those on the roofs, on the balconies, and lining the boardwalks — watched in awed hush. McCulloch reached the back of the wagon and stopped. Leaning against the rear, he shoved his crutch across the rough wood toward the front — and the tightly chained Wells Fargo boxes.

He put both hands on the wagon bed and heaved himself up with a multitude of curses and groans, until his rear end was seated at the wagon's edge. Then he gradually pushed himself back, lifting the leg with the cast high enough to avoid getting banged up even more.

McCulloch found his crutch, dragged it forward, then pressed on it and began slowly, painfully, pushing himself until he stood. He had to wait after that agonizing exertion. As he panted and sweated — and the day was just beginning, with nowhere near the intolerable heat the sun would produce in the coming hours.

Breen shifted the Sharps and glanced at Keegan. "Four days?" he whispered.

"Don't ye worry, laddie boy," Keegan said with a smile. "He's just getting started. We'll get there . . . on time. Mark me words, and that stubborn son of Satan will be the man to get us there."

The men and women began talking among themselves, their voices carrying in the still morning air. Breen looked at the roofs, the windows, the building corners and the alleys. He wet his lips. "I still don't think this was the wisest way to leave this burg," he said. "Like we're asking for trouble. Showing everyone in this part of Texas that we're three men with a lot of double eagles."

"Nay, Breeney boy," Keegan said with a smile. "We're showing some poor fool just what he's up against. By now everybody this side of San Antone knows what we're doing, what we got in that box, and where we're going. We're just letting them know that we don't give a damn what the hell they know. You see, laddie —"

He stopped, swallowed, then held his breath. McCulloch was moving again.

McCulloch turned on the crutch and moved past the Wells Fargo boxes, his chest heaving, his face masked in pain. He reached the front of the bed and now turned around, eased his buttocks on the wood, and began pivoting carefully, moving, then sliding back inches at the time. At last, he moved the Winchester and the crutch to the driver's seat, inhaled, held his breath, and used both hands to raise his bad leg up and over the wood. Now he turned, keeping his left leg held out, brought his right leg over, and let the right foot drop to the bench.

"That man's got more guts than a pig farmer," said a burly-looking cuss in suspenders and rubber boots by the butcher shop.

No one else spoke.

After another pause for breath, McCulloch

slid over and gathered up the heavy leather lines, while sliding the crutch and Winchester to where he wanted them . . . within reach, just in case.

After pulling down the brim of his hat, he looked first at Breen and next at Keegan.

"You two think I can't hear you, talking across a wagon, Breen going through this ear, Keegan going through the other. You got anything else you want to say?"

"We're just waiting your orders, boss man," Breen said with a grin.

"I ain't giving orders." McCulloch let his eyes bore through Keegan. "He's the idiot that got us into this fix. You all ready?"

Keegan raised his pistol, and brought it down, the barrel pointed the way out of west, the way to the Big Bend Country, the way to certain death.

"Forward, let's ride," the Irishman bellowed.

McCulloch whipped the heavy leather, and the horses began moving. They were fine animals, McCulloch knew. He moved his busted leg to a more comfortable spot. It would take him a while to get the feel of handling a team. He rarely rode in wagons, but he knew horses. And he knew what was at stake here. Keegan was right, too, the damned old Irish dog. McCulloch wasn't doing this for Bainbridge or Keegan or for any stupid debt. It was for his own daughter. He wanted to save Virginia Bainbridge because he had never been able to save his own baby girl.

Suddenly, the damnedest noise reached his ears. He looked to his right, at the crowd, on the ground and on the rooftops, then to his left, along the boardwalk and on the balconies.

Men, women, boys, and girls, of all ages, all colors, jobs. They cheered. Some waved flags, Confederate and Stars and Stripes. Others saluted. And they all sang out.

"Good luck, you brave men!"

"Hurrah! Hurrah! Hurrah for these fine Texans."

"Three cheers for the Jackals. Hip, Hip, hurrah!"

"Hip, hip, hurrah!"

"Hip, hip, hurrah!"

CHAPTER SIXTEEN

The second switch of horses in harness and saddle mounts for Breen and Keegan came in Deep Flood, a misnamed town, ramshackle and dry as a Kansas buffalo bone. Bainbridge's men were ready — as they had been at the first switch ten miles out of Purgatory City. McCulloch liked the way these cowboys worked, fast and efficient. Some years back, they could've found work at a Pony Express station or handling Butterfield's Overland stagecoaches before the War Between the States moved that line out of Texas and farther north. What McCulloch didn't like was the sight of all these people.

"Where the hell did all these people come from?" McCulloch whispered to Breen, who was slugging down water from his canteen while one of Bainbridge's cowhands saddled and bridled his new horse.

"Word travels fast." Breen corked the canteen, dropped it beside the moneybox in the wagon bed, and wiped his mouth with his dusty shirtsleeve. "They come to see the show, just like they did up in Purgatory City."

McCulloch whispered a curse.

"Come to see another show, too," Bainbridge's young cowboy said, as he ducked underneath the big bay's head and handed the reins to Breen. The cowboy pointed across the street.

"I must be mad as a hatter," Sean Keegan said as he stepped away from the sorrel another Bainbridge man saddled. "I'm seeing and hearing things."

The fresh horses in harness snorted, stamped their feet, and McCulloch had to pull hard on the reins to keep them from bolting. While down Main Street — Deep Flood's only street, unless one counted the paths to the privies, trash heaps, and the one crib for the town's one prostitute — a three-piece band — fiddle, tuba, and banjo — marched from the old bank that had closed and become a church, across the dusty street to the hotel.

The tune the trio played was something McCulloch could not recognize, perhaps because he wasn't sure the three old coots were playing the same song. Thankfully, the eardrum-damaging clamor ended when they turned around in front of the hotel's open door. The tuba player looked like he was about to have a heart attack from lugging that big piece of brass across the street on such a hot day.

"Ladies and gentlemen," the banjo player called out, "I give you the Reverend Finbar Flinders Fletcher."

At that moment, a red-bearded man in black broadcloth stuck his head out of an open window on the second floor.

"Folks!" the man roared out, waving a black Bible in his left hand. "These three brave men —"

Keegan whispered a blasphemy.

Breen moved to his saddle and put his hand on the butt of the Sharps in the scabbard.

McCulloch seconded Keegan's curse.

". . . are doing yeoman's work here, risking their lives to save a poor girl from Lucifer's lieutenant. There's nothing in this venture for these three men, except the glory of God and the streets of gold when they go to their reward. But I'm not here to preach and pray for these fine men. I'm here to champion the cause of a great man, a soldier for our country, a cattleman and horseman and entrepreneur who is sending his entire life savings — fifty thousand dollars — to the notorious fiend, Lucifer's right-hand man, Harry Holland."

The band members leaned their instruments against the watering trough in front of the hotel, and picked up empty coffee buckets from behind the trough, then dispersed on both sides of the street.

"Won't you please pitch in to help poor Colonel Bainbridge. Whatever you can spare. Fifty thousand dollars is a fortune to you, but think of all that Colonel Bainbridge has done for this part of Texas, for this country, for you."

McCulloch looked at Breen.

"Fifty thousand dollars?" Breen whispered.

McCulloch shook his head. "Those strongboxes would be a lot heavier."

Keegan turned to the Bainbridge man who had saddled his horse. "You know what this is about?"

"Loco sky pilot," the cowboy said. "I hear he started in El Paso, hittin' up folks to repay the boss man for the ransom he's payin' out for his girl." The man spit tobacco juice into the street and wiped his mouth with the back of his hand. "Don't reckon he's got no fifty thousand bucks, though."

"He isn't likely to get more than fifteen cents in a place like Deep Flood," Keegan said and swung into the saddle.

"Yep," said the Bainbridge man as he moved to his horse on the far side of the street. "Damn sure ain't gettin' nothin' from me. Good luck to you boys."

"He should have stayed in El Paso if he wanted to fill his collection plate." Breen sighed and mounted his horse.

"Coffee cans," McCulloch corrected, nodded at the cowboys who backed away from the fresh horses.

"Ladies and gentlemen," the reverend began, "let us bow our heads and pray for these fine men, these God-fearing men, these knights of the Great State of Texas, noble heroes and —"

McCulloch lashed out with the whip and a blast of profanity and the wagon lurched forward. The dust and the din of the wagon and two riders did not appear to stop the Reverend Finbar Flinders Fletcher's collection of tithes.

"What do you make of that?" Keegan shouted over the pounding of hooves and the rattling of the wagon as the three men rode into the desert.

"Confidence man?" McCulloch called back.

"Why fifty thousand?" Breen yelled.

"Because it's more than twenty!" Mc-

Culloch yelled.

"I don't like it!" Keegan yelled.

"Well, there's nothing we can do about it now!" McCulloch whipped the heavy leather.

The conversation ended. Thick dust stopped any more talk. Bandanas offered only so much protection.

Two changes after that, they turned directly south. McCulloch conceded that everything had been going well, so far, and for that he had to credit Newton Bainbridge and his men. The horses were excellent. The cowboys knew what they were doing. In sixty miles — six more changes — they would reach the Big Bend country. But here the trail dipped into an arroyo, and the sand would make it hard hard to keep the heavy wagon going as fast as it had been. This was the troublesome part, but it was still the fastest way to get to the Big Bend.

And then what?

He rounded the bend and saw the rider standing in the middle of the path on a white horse. The man was dressed in black, with a black silk bandana covering his face. The only thing white about him, other than the horse he rode, was the handkerchief that whipped in the wind. It was tied to the barrel of a Winchester rifle in his right hand, but the barrel was pointed at the sky.

Breen and Keegan drew their revolvers as McCulloch pulled the team of horses to a stop.

"This had to be planned," McCulloch said. "By Holland."

"Well," Breen whispered, "I wish Harry Holland had let us in on the plan."

The masked man rode toward them.

" 'And I looked, and behold, a pale horse: and his name that sat on him was Death,' " Breen said.

"That preacher in Deep Flood get to you?" Keegan whispered.

McCulloch snapped, "Shut up."

The rider stopped his horse in front of the sweat-soaked lead horses in the harness.

"I'm from Holland," the masked rider said.

"All right," McCulloch said.

"You're making good time."

"We have a schedule to keep."

"I won't keep you long. When you get to the Big Bend, go straight to the river. Stay on the Texas side of the border. Find the hot springs."

Keegan said, "I know where they are."

"Good." The black-covered head bobbed. "You'll be met there."

"With the girl?" Breen asked.

The man did not answer. "Be there. On time."

"Then get out of our way," McCulloch said.

"One more thing." The man straightened in the saddle. "Right when you climb out of this sandbox, there are six men waiting for you. They don't ride for Harry. Don't let them take our money."

"Six against three," McCulloch said. "You could help even the odds."

"But Harry didn't tell me to help you. He just told me to give you the instructions. I figured letting you know about what's up the trail would be a good mark for St. Peter to consider after I get rubbed out."

"I appreciate the warning," McCulloch said.

A laugh escaped from the black bandana. "I appreciate the money. Make sure you get it to Harry on time. It would be a waste to kill such a pretty girl."

McCulloch waited, but the man did not move out of the way. "There's more you ought to know," the rider said. His head bent forward. "You're also being followed. And not by Harry's men."

"We figured that," McCulloch said, and they had. Someone would have trailed them out of Purgatory City, and maybe that preacher had stirred up some interest in El Paso, and maybe even Deep Flood. But most of these fortune-seekers would give up the closer they got to the Big Bend country. That place was mighty inhospitable, and not many men had enough courage to risk their hide and lives. Apaches and Harry Holland ruled that part of Texas, and those weren't the only things that could kill a man out there. The sun could bake a man to a crisp. Rattlesnakes. Rabid wolves or coyotes. Rockslides. Even cautious men had stumbled to their deaths in this country. So some would turn back. Most of them, actually. But a few?

Well, hell, nobody could live forever, and he had not been joking when he said this was nothing more than a suicide mission. He sure hoped Sean Keegan would at least say he was sorry right before they all got killed.

"I suppose that ain't your department either," McCulloch said. "Getting rid of anyone following us."

The man laughed. "Yeah, I don't get paid for that, either." But his eyes now moved past McCulloch and toward the wagon bed. His Adam's apple bobbed. The black silk moved and McCulloch figured the outlaw was wetting his lips. "Can I see the money?" he asked after a while.

Keegan and Breen raised their revolvers, and McCulloch smiled. "Something tells me that those weren't in Harry Holland's orders to you, either."

The man sank back deeper in his saddle. "Well, I'll see it directly — just make sure you get it to the hot springs. On time. The clock keeps ticking."

"Then get the hell out of our way," McCulloch said.

The man in black turned the horse, slammed the white-flagged rifle barrel against the pale horse's side, and galloped down the sandy arroyo.

McCulloch cursed and popped the whip. The wagon lurched forward. Keegan and Breen pushed their mounts into gallops. The man in black kept riding ahead.

McCulloch whispered to himself, " 'And Hell followed with him.' "

CHAPTER SEVENTEEN

They stopped at a bend in the arroyo, roughly a half mile before where the arroyo dumped into a seasonal stream, and where McCulloch, Breen, and Keegan figured the four bandits were waiting to relieve them of the $20,000 in the back of the buckboard.

Turkey buzzards circled ahead. Keegan could tell because of the V pattern their wings made as they soared. Big birds, nasty, despicable creatures, and this was their season. Fly in during the spring; leave come autumn for Mexico or South America. Nasty and despicable, but smart birds. This time of year, plenty of things died in West Texas, and buzzards preyed on the dead.

Keegan swung off his horse, handed the reins to McCulloch, and said, "I'll take a look." His spurs, military issue, didn't make noise, but he removed them anyway and stuck them in the saddlebags, from which he pulled out a pouch of ammunition —

shells for the heavy rifle and his Remington. Next, he pulled his hat down low, took a sip of water from his canteen, drew the Springfield from the scabbard, and slipped off to the east. After climbing out of the dried bed, he moved into the rocks. Crouching, he slipped off in a southerly direction.

He moved quietly and patiently, two traits one needed in this country, and especially on this job. He stopped often, listening and wiping his forehead. The last thing he needed was to be blinded by sweat. There was no wind. Just heat. At least he wasn't burned to a crisp like Breen — or temporarily crippled like McCulloch. Still no sound. He wet his lips, wishing he had taken another pull from that canteen — or, better yet, a sip of the Irish in the flask in the saddlebags.

Reaching the edge of the rocks, Keegan again surveyed the land before him. He muttered a curse, followed that with a prayer, and stretched out on his stomach, Springfield in his right hand, the revolver in his left, and he began belly crawling over pebbles, stones, and sand, glad that at least he didn't have any prickly pear or baby barrelhead cacti to contend with. He moved silently, feeling like a snake, as he inched his way into the dried creek bed — the dumping-off point of the arroyo he had left four hundred yards back.

Again, he stopped, half-expecting a bullet to shatter his spine or blow out his brains. Nothing. Still no sound. He waited until he had caught his breath, and then he moved to the far bank. Now he rose into a crouch, wet his lips with his tongue, and again wiped off the sweat with the back of his left sleeve.

Now came the ticklish part. Trying to get up this bank and over the rocks without sending a stone tumbling down, without making too much noise. He started to curse again, but stopped himself, and remembered a prayer from his youth. After that, he swallowed despite a lack of moisture in his throat, and began climbing, easily, gingerly, inches at a time.

Patience, me boy, he told himself. Down in the arroyo, McCulloch and Breen would be waiting, fighting that urge to move. But McCulloch and Breen were patient, too. Unless those owlhoots waiting to waylay them were smarter than Keegan figured — and had crept up behind the Ranger and bounty hunter and killed them.

Then he heard the flapping of wings. He looked up at the buzzards, saw one coming down, and Keegan felt his left boot slip, heard a rock tumbling. The sound was nothing more than a faint tap-tap-tapping, but to Keegan, it sounded like an avalanche. He tensed, left the Springfield on the rocks, and grabbed the .44 revolver with his right hand, waiting for a face to appear at the top of the rise.

But all he saw were the buzzards, coming down, and then Keegan understood.

Lifting the Springfield with his left hand, he rose, charged up the ridge, hearing more stones sliding toward the creek bed. At the top of the hill, he stopped, stared, and spit. He raised the revolver, almost fired a shot, but stopped and frowned. Instead, he shoved the pistol into the holster, brought his right hand near his mouth, raised his head, and howled like a coyote. He swallowed, repeated the cry, and moved down the hill toward where the arroyo turned to the dried creek, and where the sandy trail ended and a narrow path began.

The turkey buzzards looked fearless. They were no danger to him — as long as he was alive. They might flap their wings, they might vomit on him, but they had little to help them in the way of defense. Besides, they were busy for the time being.

He heard the jingling of harnesses and the clopping of hooves. McCulloch led the wagon around the bend, with Breen following, pulling Keegan's horse. The wagon climbed out of the arroyo and McCulloch pulled hard on the leather to stop the tired animals. McCulloch set the brake, reached into the driver's box, and pulled out a canteen, which he held out toward Keegan.

"Thanks." Keegan swapped his rifle for the canteen, and drank greedily, but not for too long. He wet his lips, took the Springfield from McCulloch's hand, and turned around.

Breen, still mounted on the other side of the wagon, started to curse, but Keegan's horse began pulling hard on the reins, and that commanded the bounty hunter's attention.

McCulloch cleared his throat and said in a voice that was difficult to hear. "Hell, that one's alive."

"Damn," Keegan said, and he walked away from the wagon and the horses and to the massacre site.

The first man was dead, and the buzzards hadn't gotten to him yet. Only the ants, and they were interested only in the pool of drying blood that covered his throat, and chest, and where his legs spread out. Apparently, the Apaches had gotten him first, slicing his throat from ear to ear, and stabbing him in the chest just to make sure. He leaned up against a black rock, eyes still open, with a look of complete and total surprise.

The next two men resembled porcupines, and they were pinned to the ground with maybe a dozen arrows each. Apparently, they had been running toward wherever they had picketed their horses. They lay facedown in the creek bed. A few buzzards were already working on their dinner. Maybe they would take the arrows and use those to reinforce their nests.

The next man must have put up a fight, maybe had even wounded or killed a couple of his would-be slayers, because there wasn't much left of him to feed to scavengers. Even the best coroner in New York City or Dublin would have had a difficult time pinpointing the cause of death. Gun-stocks, clubs, and stones had been used to pulverize his head, and then they had cut open his belly and pulled out his guts. The ants were enjoying those, too.

The fifth man lay spread-eagled a few yards away, also filled with arrows, and the buzzards were filling their stomachs on his remains. Keegan stopped to pull up his bandana to mask the smell of death, rot, and excrement. Finally, he reached the last man. His ears had been sawed off, and arrows had been put into his body at several painful places. The coals had died down, but the burning flesh was something even the bandana could not lessen. The man's eyelids had been sliced off, too, and by now the man had to be blind, but the lips still moved, and the chest still heaved slightly.

Keegan's shadow crossed the man's face. The eyes did not react, but the lips did. His fingers trembled, and perhaps he could still hear. Keegan would have to ask someone smarter if just because a man's ears had been sliced off with a knife, did that make a man deaf? It was something to ponder.

The lips formed a word, "Kill." Keegan waited. The lips moved again. "Me."

Keegan knelt next to the man.

"Laddie," he said. "You were here to do me in. To waylay my pards and me. The Apaches gave you what you were going to give to us. Maybe a little nastier, but me-thinks you got what you deserved. But, laddie, don't worry, if ye can still hear me, I don't think you're much longer for this world. Before the buzzards start working on you, your soul will be burning in hell with those others the Apaches killed. Have a nice life — may it be longer than what you want."

He turned, and left the dying, tortured bandit in the rocks.

When he reached McCulloch and Breen, Keegan slid his carbine into the scabbard. He took the reins to his horse, calmer now, and moved to the saddlebags. He did not bother putting on the spurs. That could wait the couple of miles they had to go before they reached the next station to change the horses. Instead, he found the flask and drank greedily, savoring the burn of the whiskey, the smoothness of good Irish, triple distilled, whatever that meant, letting the taste of peat return him from this harsh country to the beauty and the green of Ireland. He screwed on the lid, dropped the flask into the saddlebag, and swung into the saddle.

McCulloch was drinking water. "Any guess as to how many?"

"No more than eight," Keegan said. "Probably wanted their horses, which they got."

"Yeah." McCulloch set down the canteen and pulled his bandana up over his nose and mouth.

Breen looked back down the arroyo. "These men might help us out a bit." He looked back at Keegan and McCulloch. "When those boys following us get a sight of what the Apaches did to these fools, that should have them lighting out as fast as they can for Fort Spalding, El Paso, Fort Stockton, maybe all the way back to Austin or San Antone."

"It should discourage most of them," Keegan agreed. After shaking his head, he let a wide smile crease his face. "I guess we owe those Apache bucks our ever-loving thanks for what they've done to help us."

"I'm not sure of that." McCulloch raised a gloved hand and pointed south.

Keegan and Breen looked. More turkey buzzards — or maybe these were black buzzards. They were too far for Keegan to identify properly. Higher in the sky, they circled, the rising buttes of the Big Bend in the distant background. Keegan tried to estimate how far away those carrion birds might be. Two miles. Probably that. Certainly not farther than three.

"Hell," he said.

"The next relay station," Breen said, and added a curse for an exclamation point.

"You'd think the six horses they got here would be enough for those bucks," Keegan said. "Damn it all to hell, Apaches don't even like horses. They'd rather be afoot."

"We're wasting time," McCulloch said, and he released the brake.

"This is my turn," Breen said, as he eased his horse ahead of the horses. "I'll ride

189

ahead." He pulled his hat down tight.

"Don't run your horse to death, Breenie, me boy," Keegan said.

Breen nodded, gave his horse a hard kick, and took off at a lope. They watched him go, and Keegan pulled his horse alongside the wagon closer to the driver's side.

"How long do we give him?" Keegan asked.

"Five minutes," McCulloch said. "Then we'll have to slow these horses. They're already blowing hard, and if the Apaches got the horses at our next swing station, we have ten more miles to go across this furnace. I'm not sure these horses, good as they are, can get us ten more miles. Hell, I'm not sure they can get us five miles."

"Aye, and what happens if the Apaches are greedier than the tinhorn they strung up in Purgatory City three months back? And they got the next change of horses, too?"

"Then Bainbridge's daughter's good as dead," McCulloch said. "And so are we."

CHAPTER EIGHTEEN

The last thing Jed Breen wanted to do was hobble his horse, because if he needed to light out of this desert at a high lope, he damned sure wouldn't have time to loosen the hobbles on a frightened horse's forefeet. But the gelding kept fighting bit and rein like a catamount, and Breen certainly didn't want to be left afoot in this country, either.

Reluctantly, Breen swung out of the saddle, keeping a tight hold on the reins as he tied the horse up short to the branch of a mesquite. One thorn ripped into his sunburned hands, but he ignored that until he had the reins secure. Sucking the bloody cut, he spit, wiped his mouth, and pulled the hobbles out of his saddlebags. When the hobbles were secure, he let the horse sniff his hand, then found some corn in the saddlebags and let him eat some.

Breen smiled. "Still scared, eh?" The horse's eyes and ears revealed that the snack of corn hadn't eased any tension in the animal. "You aren't alone, boy. You sure aren't alone." He lifted the Sharps off the warm rocks, and moved in a crouch down the road about twenty or thirty yards.

He knew what he would find. He knew what scared the horse. The gelding could smell better than a human, but Breen knew that stench, and the buzzards had told him what he would discover. The truth did not make him feel any better, though. He wanted to fire a shot, but that would not be wise in this country. Not with Apaches around. So he picked up a stone in his left hand and hurled it toward the feasting black birds. Then he let out a few yips and hurrahs, but he did not stand. Standing up, waving his arms, they might frighten those black buzzards even more, but that would also give any hidden Apache one inviting target.

The buzzards' wings began beating, sounding like drums from hell, and they took off from their meal and slowly lifted their ugly bodies off the ground, leaving behind the remains of two of Newton Bainbridge's cowboys. The corpses didn't look any better than those of the dead men who had been planning to ambush Breen, McCulloch, and Keegan for the ransom money.

None had been tortured; and the arrows had probably killed them before they realized they were in trouble.

The horses were gone. These Apaches were making out like bandits. And without those horses, Breen understood, getting to the next string would be tough. Real tough. Even with nightfall coming. That's what gave Breen the idea. He looked at the buzzards circling overhead, smiled, and braced the Sharps across a rock, touched the trigger, and heard the cannon-like blast, and the echo of the roar. His horse snorted and pulled, but the reins held tight, and so did the hobbles. Breen drew his Colt, squeezing off three shots, and followed those echoes with a bunch of crazy cries.

Sound traveled far in this country, especially at this time of day. The smell of the blood told Breen that these two cowboys had been killed not all that long ago. With luck, the Apaches would hear the shots. Apaches weren't stupid, either. They knew those two cowboys were waiting for someone. They also knew those outlaws that they had killed had been waiting to ambush someone. And Apaches were like most men of all colors. They were greedy.

Breen shouted again, hearing his echoes, and began reloading his revolver and the heavy rifle. He wet his lips. Then he heard the sound of McCulloch and Keegan, the wagon filled with gold and the hooves of worn-out horses.

After wetting his lips, Breen scanned the terrain before turning back down the trail. He holstered the revolver, and waved his hat over his head. Keegan reined in his horse, and the wagon slowed to a stop.

"Horses are gone," Breen called out. "And the two men are dead. Apaches."

Both of his partners swore.

"What were those shots and shouts?" McCulloch asked.

"Me."

Keegan spit. "That spell in the salt country must have fried your head worse than I thought. You've gone loco. You want those red butchers to come back here?"

"That's exactly what I want," Breen answered.

Keegan and McCulloch exchanged glances. "Our horses won't be able to outrun those Indians," McCulloch said. "And this isn't a good place to defend ourselves."

Breen grinned. "Exactly."

The campfire was big and bright, and at least it kept the black buzzards from returning, and like in most deserts, the temperature substantially dropped once the sun disappeared. The smell of death died with the day, too. They drank hot coffee and ate salt pork with their fingers, wiping the grease on their legs and pitching the skin into the fire.

Breen checked his Sharps, decided against it, and left it leaning against his saddle. Keegan honed the blade of his knife, sheathed it, and took his Remington out of the holster, rotating the cylinder on his forearm and checking the loads in each of the six chambers. McCulloch, holding his Winchester, moved to the rock and looked into the darkness. He couldn't see anything in the distance, but he had been studying the terrain since Breen had revealed his plan.

"Well?" Breen whispered when he came up beside the old Texas Ranger.

"If the Apaches came back," McCulloch whispered, "my guess is that they'd set up right back yonder." His jaw pointed in the direction. "What do you think?"

Breen knew McCulloch wasn't asking him. Breen hunted white men, outlaws, murderers, thieves of all sorts. Keegan and McCulloch were the veteran Indian fighters in this trio.

"They're like anybody else," Keegan said quietly. "Once something works, they'll keep at it till it don't work anymore. And from the way I read things before it got dark, that's where they had to be when they sent those poor boys of the colonel's to their reward."

"If they came back." McCulloch turned to Keegan. The campfire cast shadows across his darkened face, but the flames reflected in his eyes like some phantasm in a penny dreadful.

"If they're not here," Breen whispered, "at least our horses got a rest. Maybe that'll help us get to the next station."

"Providing the Apaches haven't hit those boys, too," McCulloch said. "You better hope those bucks are here."

"They're here," Keegan said.

That made Breen feel better. Keegan, as an old horse soldier in this country, had even more experience fighting Indians than McCulloch. "Listen. Don't hear no night-hawks, no bullbats, no coyotes, nothing moving around here except our horses. No sound except our whispers. They're here. Waiting for daybreak to kill us."

"Good thing Apaches don't attack at night," Breen said.

"You better hope these warriors haven't been educated in the ways of Colonel Bainbridge's warfare," Keegan said.

"How do we play this?" Breen asked.

"We'll move across the road." Again, Mc-Culloch used his jaw to point the way. "There's a deer trail that cuts up that hill. Wait there till the moon rises. Then we'll find their camp. Eight men, right?"

"That's our best guess," Keegan said.

"Handguns only," McCulloch said. "We light the torches, hold them high. Kill them before they wake up and kill us."

"A cold, nasty business," Keegan said, "one that's fit only for jackals like us to see it done. But it's the only way to do this."

"There will be a sentry," Breen said.

"Aye," Keegan said. "He's your problem."

"Why me?" Breen asked.

"Because," McCulloch answered, "this is your damn fool idea."

He crept through the night like a thief, but not just like one of the thieves Breen had tracked down for the price on their heads. Jed Breen became the slowest, most cautious thief the world had ever known. Breen stepped, stopped, listened. He waited before taking another step. He wet his lips, wondering if the Apache could hear his heart pounding against his chest. The moon was barely a crescent, good in that it gave off just a little light, mostly letting Breen have a halfway decent idea about where to put his foot next.

For more than an hour, Breen had been moving in the darkness, making his way around the most likely location for the Apache camp, now coming up from the front. Keegan, if he hadn't been killed, would be moving in from the rear. McCulloch, if he hadn't decided this was a fool's play and had turned back for Purgatory City, would be moving in from the east. The west was nothing but a forest of ocotillo. But if any Apache tried to run through that, the moonlight would be just enough to line his back up through the gun sights of these three jackals.

Breen stopped, jerked his head toward the noise. He smiled grimly. A horse had nickered. A hoof suddenly kicked a rock. He had guessed right. The Apaches had heard his gunshots and had rushed back to add to their wealth. Now all Breen had to do was find that damned sentry.

About thirty feet to his right, a stone tumbled, followed by a sigh and a guttural grunt, probably a curse in Apache. Breen's luck still held. That had to be the sentry. His left hand reached down till it touched the cold stag-horn handle of the bowie knife, and he slipped it out of the sheath.

Biting his bottom lip, Breen moved in a crouch up the hill, hoping that his boot did not send some stone bouncing its way to the bottom. When he reached the crest, he paused. Below he saw the horses milling as best they could. They had hobbled their horses, too, even those they had stolen from the men who had planned to ambush them, and the fresh livestock, and the horses of the cowboys that they had stolen from the Bainbridge men they had killed.

That told Breen that these bucks weren't seasoned veterans, but young braves hoping to get power and wealth from this raid. Veterans of these raids would have kept their horses with them where they slept, the hackamore wrapped around their wrists.

A second later, Breen saw the outline of the sentry.

Rising, Breen took quiet steps, stopped, and looked at the herd, then decided where the Apaches must be camping. Keegan had made a good guess, and the Apache guard had found a perfect spot. Here he could watch the horses, and he could see the camp. Breen held his breath. The big bowie felt like a guillotine in his hand. His other hand clutched the torch.

I'm sorry to have to do this, kid, he thought, and moved like a cougar. The left arm came up and back, crushing the brave's throat, while the right rammed the ten-inch blade through the sentry's back, all the way to the hilt. The Apache's cry was nothing more than a gasp, but the rifle he had, probably stolen off one of the bodies of the men the war party had killed, hit the ground hard, rattling, the suddenness of the sound ringing so loud Breen feared his eardrums would rupture. He eased the corpse to the ground, wiped the blood off the blade of his bowie on the deerskin leggings, and heard the horses.

The knife returned to the sheath, and Breen stepped over the man he had killed and moved to his position. Now the horses began dancing and whickering, excited, but Breen knew he had to reach the best place he could quickly.

He reached the rock at the same time another figure stepped right in front of him. Had they not been slowing down, they would have run into each other. Breen could only see the outline of the Apache, and he did what came instinctively. He slammed the torch into the man's face. The Apache yelled and went tumbling back over rocks and cactus.

That's when Breen saw the light, a blinding flash of orange not far away. Another torch flared, and gunshots roared. Breen tossed his torch away. There was no time to light it. The ball had started.

Breen shot the Apache he had knocked down as the warrior tried to rise and draw a revolver from his waistband.

Behind him, the horses snorted, whinnied, pounded the ground with their hobbled feet. Breen stepped over the second Indian he had killed this night, and saw the flashes of gunfire as Keegan's Remington and Mc-Culloch's single-action Colt sounded like artillery. The noise echoed across the land. Another figure spun around, came up, and began singing — the death song, maybe, but Breen couldn't be sure. The man kept running for the horses, and when he looked up, he saw Breen.

Who shot him in the face.

The night quieted. The echoes of gunfire faded. Breen could see only wild colors, but that would go away. He closed his eyes, shook his head, and heard a voice call from below.

"Breen? Are you dead?"

McCulloch. Breen laughed. "You're out of luck!" he shouted back.

"There was an Apache headed your way," McCulloch shouted.

"Maybe two," Keegan called from the

other orange glow. "But I think I hit him."

"They're both dead!" Breen yelled. "And the sentry, too."

The voices bounced across the darkness. Breen holstered the Colt.

"How about the horses?" McCulloch said.

"They're here," Breen said. "And they're not going anywhere till we get them saddled and hitched to that buckboard."

Another gunshot popped. Either McCulloch or Keegan had finished off a wounded Apache.

"We're burning daylight," McCulloch said.

Like it was high noon. Breen shook his head.

"Let's get out of this slaughtering ground and make for the Big Bend!" McCulloch shouted. The two torches began heading toward Breen.

"Where the hell are you?" Keegan shouted.

Breen went back to the second Indian he had killed, fumbled in the darkness, and finally found the torch. "Give me a minute!" he shouted. Standing, he fished the match out of his vest pocket, struck it against the buckle on his gunbelt, and set the pitch aflame. He waved this back and forth, back and forth, and waited for the approaching light. Finally, they were close enough for Breen to make out the faces.

Grim warriors those two, he thought, seeing how both had blackened their faces with grease from the wagon. So had Breen — and he had even slicked back his white hair.

The men stopped a few feet below Breen, who pointed his torch toward the horses.

"Now I know why Apaches don't like to fight at night," Keegan said and spit. "It's a damned good way to get killed."

"Anybody hit?" McCulloch asked.

"No," Breen and Keegan replied simultaneously.

"Then let's get those horses saddled and harnessed and let's get the hell out of here in case our little ruckus brings back more night raiders."

CHAPTER NINETEEN

"We can pull out, boss," the gunman said as he squatted by the fire and helped himself to the coffee. "Soon as the moon rises."

Retired Army Colonel Newton S. Bainbridge lowered his steaming tin mug and shook his head. "We'll wait till daybreak."

The gunman set the pot back on the stone resting on the hot coals. "They won't be stopping."

"I know," Bainbridge said. "But I don't want us to get too close to them. We'll follow. Gradually."

"They'll be harder to find, maybe, when they get into that Big Bend country." The killer brought the coffee cup to his lips.

"I got two Tonkawa scouts working ahead of us." Bainbridge rose. He heard the hoofbeats coming from the direction of Deep Flood.

"Tonks. Comanches hate Tonks. Reckon the Apaches don't like 'em, neither."

"Everybody hates Tonks. They're cannibals. They'll eat you if they kill you. But they can find a trail better than any white man."

The hired gun started to say something, but then he heard the approaching rider. Setting his cup on the ground, he rose quickly from his squat and drew the Smith & Wesson from the holster.

"Don't shoot unless I tell you to," Bainbridge said, and he walked to the sound of the rider.

The other gunmen he had hired, along with a few of his loyal riders, were spreading out, away from the flames and coals, disappearing in the darkness.

The clopping of hooves stilled, and that meant the rider wasn't completely a damned fool.

"Hallooo," a voice called out. "I'm just a lay preacher, my fine Christian friends, and I can preach you a sermon for nothing more than a cup of that delicious coffee I smell in this county of perdition. Maybe I can save your soul or just comfort you on your journey. I carry nothing with me but the Good Book in my right hand and the love of the Heavenly Father in my heart."

"Ride in," Bainbridge said, "and welcome." He nodded at the gunman standing just behind him, and the man cocked his revolver. "Remember what I said," Bainbridge said. "Don't kill him unless I say so."

Two minutes later, the Reverend Finbar Flinders Fletcher rode in on a jackass and smiled. Indeed, he held a Bible in his right hand. His left clutched the hackamore, and his white wooden teeth reflected the campfire as his red beard and mustache parted like the Red Sea.

"I preach the Word," the reverend said, lowering the horsehair hackamore and holding the Bible higher. "And I am a man of the Word."

"Where's your band?" Bainbridge said.

The preacher slid off the ass's back, dropping the hackamore to rub his buttocks and the insides of his calves. "I've garnered contributions to reimburse you of all that money you're sending for the soul, life, and legacy of your lovely daughter," he said. "From El Paso to Purgatory City to Deep Flood. But I fear unless I dared attempt the journey to Fort Stockton, I have run out of settlements that might generate a farthing. So I dispersed my disciples, instructing them to spread the word of that nefarious woman-napping fiend Harry Holland and perhaps send them south with the Lord's vengeance and His might on their side."

"Jimmie," Bainbridge called to his foreman, "pour Finbar a cup of coffee." He looked back at the night rider. "How do you take it?"

"Black," Finbar F. Fletcher said. "Like my heart."

"You have no heart, Finnie," Bainbridge said.

The man's grin spread. "Then my soul?"

"I don't think you have one of those, either."

Fletcher laughed and accepted the cup from the cook. The cook wore two belted guns on his hips. He sipped the brew and said, losing the attitude and the pompousness, and focusing on the facts. "Bert went back to El Paso. He'll play the part of the *St. Louis Weekly* scribe, working on the story of the kidnapping. Hodges is off for San Antonio, maybe Austin. He'll be the traveling troubadour telling about what he heard was going on at Purgatory City."

"And Duvall?" Bainbridge asked.

"I sent him with Hodges. By now, Duvall is deader than dirt, buried in some badger hole. He never could play that tuba worth a damn, as well you know from his days in the regimental band at Fort Spalding."

"He never could keep his mouth shut, either," Bainbridge said.

"Handy for a tuba player." Fletcher brought the tin cup to his lips and drank more. "Not so handy for a man in our business."

The man finished his coffee and looked at the insides of the tin cup. "My compliments to your cook," Fletcher said, "but might you have something stronger on your back bar?"

"No," Bainbridge said. "Everyone has taken the oath on this journey."

"Damn," the fake preacher said. "Had I know that, I gladly would have taken Hodges's place, killed Duvall, and taken a ride in the next coach for the city of the Alamo."

Bainbridge let out a mirthless laugh. He looked at the men gathering closer to the fire.

"Boys," he said, "this is . . . well . . . let's just call him the Reverend Fletcher. He'll be riding with us for the rest of the way. Don't expect him to save you from the fires of hell, and don't turn your back on him for longer than two seconds. Don't leave any money in his sight, and if he accidentally stumbles into you and begs his pardon, check your money pouch. His fingers aren't like his mouth. His fingers work real quiet."

Fletcher bowed and smiled.

"Ain't he the one who was preaching up a

storm in Purgatory City?" the head gun-fighter said.

"And the one we heard about in Deep Flood?" asked one of Bainbridge's men.

"He's the one," Bainbridge said.

Fletcher walked to the fire and refilled his cup with coffee. "I'm hired just like you folks," he said as he poured. He looked up from the fire and smiled at Bainbridge. "And let me guess that you don't have milk or sugar for my coffee."

"You like it black," Bainbridge said. "Like your heart and soul."

"Indeed. I must have forgotten." He drank more before rising and bowed. "My performance as the preacher was not to raise the fifty thousand dollars from the good, God-fearing citizens of Purgatory City and all of West Texas to help the fine, upstanding retired colonel." He drank more coffee and looked at Bainbridge. "Should I explain?"

Bainbridge said, "Go ahead."

The confidence man and killer, wanted in Dallas and New Orleans, sipped more of the bitter but hot liquid. "I spread the word . . . not of God and God's forgiveness and wrath, but the word of our leader's poor daughter."

"Which will send a few damned fools looking for her," one of the gunmen said.

"Exactly," Fletcher said. "And West Texas is populated with plenty of fools."

"Amateurs," Bainbridge explained, and now he moved until he stood next to the faux preacher. He turned so that he could look at most of his men. "If I kept the kidnapping a secret, Holland would become suspicious of anyone following Sergeant Keegan. And if you know Keegan the way I do — or the reputations of Matt McCulloch and Jed Breen — you know they wouldn't want anyone trailing them. But a bunch of greedy fools? They won't worry too much about us."

One of the gunmen shook his head, spit out tobacco juice, and said, "From what I've heard about Matt McCulloch, he don't want nobody trailin' him."

Bainbridge nodded. "You're right. But they have a tight deadline. They can't worry too much about men following them. And after the Reverend Fletcher's performances — they heard his preaching in Deep Flood, remember — they will think it's likely fools who'll quit once they hit the Big Bend."

"And if they don't?" said another hired killer.

"Then you'll have to kill them," Bainbridge said. "That's why you're getting well-paid." He turned back to the confidence man. "Why did you tell them Holland wants fifty thousand dollars? He's only demanding twenty thousand."

Fletcher shrugged. "Well, I figured if I could raise more than twenty thousand bucks, you'd be a tad happier. Shoot for the moon, my ma always said."

Bainbridge shook his head. "All right," he said as he turned away from Fletcher and looked at his men. "Four men on watch. Spelled in four hours. We ride out of here at daybreak." He looked back at Fletcher and said. "You expect to keep up with us on that ass?"

"You won't be riding fast," the con man said. "Especially once you reach the Big Bend. And I'll have plenty of horses to pick from after we've killed Holland and all his men."

Bainbridge turned away and headed for his bedroll, but he stopped after covering fewer than thirty feet, turned, and looked back at Fletcher. "Just out of curiosity," the retired Army officer said, "how much money did you collect from the good Samaritans of West Texas for Virginia's ransom?"

Fletcher laughed. "Three dollars and seventeen cents. Two dollars and thirty-seven cents of that came from El Paso. They are much more generous in El Paso than the rest of this hellhole."

"I'll take that three dollars out of your pay when this is all over," Bainbridge said, "but you can keep the seventeen cents."

"You are a most generous soul," Fletcher said.

Five seconds later, they heard the gunfire far off to the south, faint pops that carried a long way in the desert night.

The men all stared into the blackness beneath the rising moon.

"That could be your ransom money saying, *'Vaya con Dios,'* " Fletcher said.

"It could be," Bainbridge said. "Life is nothing but a gamble, as my pa always said. But my money is on Sergeant Keegan and his two jackal friends."

He disappeared in the darkness beyond the glow of the campfire, heading for his bedroll.

CHAPTER TWENTY

The moon and stars lighted up the desert floor enough to travel, but not enough to run hell-bent for leather. When they pulled into the next swing station, the skies off to the east were showing the gray warmth of dawn. A cigar glowed red in the faint darkness, and then sparks flew as the cowboy tossed it onto the hard ground. McCulloch slowed the wagon. A match flared, and a kerosene lamp bathed this wide spot in an endless starkness with light. That light cast far enough for Matt McCulloch to breathe easier.

He saw a cowboy leading the harnessed team, ready to hitch it up to the wagon.

"What the hell took you fellows so long?" the first cowboy said.

"Ran into trouble at the last station," McCulloch explained, and spit. *Station?* A designated place on the trail, like this one. This wasn't the Butterfield stagecoach line or the old Pony Express. It was a raw piece of lawless frontier where men risked their lives for a wealthy rancher and the safety of his daughter. "Apaches hit the last place."

Keegan and Breen reined in, and immediately went to work unsaddling their sweat-soaked mounts before tossing fresh blankets and their well-used saddles on the two fresh saddle horses.

The first cowboy went to help his pard with harnessing the fresh horses to the wagon. McCulloch started to step down, find a coffeepot — even though the coffee would be cold since there was no glow of a campfire — and maybe even relieve himself, but he knew he had no time. Not with that busted leg. His stomach groaned; his tongue felt six times too big for his mouth. He wanted to wash his face — with plenty of soap — and he remembered those times so many lifetimes ago when his beautiful wife would scrub his back as he sat in a horse trough, and wash his hair with shampoo she created from some kind of cactus.

Hell, he thought, *here you go again, McCulloch, daydreaming.*

Now he cleared his throat. "Afraid to tell you, your pards back there are dead. Apaches got them."

The Bainbridge hired men stopped just

briefly, looked at McCulloch to make sure he wasn't joking — as though anyone but a fool would attempt some disrespectful witticism about such a tragedy in this part of Texas. Next, they eyed each other, and then went back to positioning the horses.

The silk-headed youngster on McCulloch's left shrugged, spit out tobacco juice, and said in a Texas drawl that was barely audible. "They knew the risks. Same as we did."

Said the other Bainbridge man: "The things fools like us'll do for thirty dollars a month, a hard bunk, and a bedroll with six dozen holes in it."

McCulloch liked that attitude. He almost said, "At least you boys are getting paid," but didn't.

Keegan eased up beside the wagon on a fine-looking claybank. Breen, looking plumb sick with that sunburned face and neck, reined in his pinto of most black but with a neck almost entirely white.

"We hit the Apaches that led the ambush," Breen said. "So I guess you can say we avenged your pards."

"Weren't our pards," said the tobacco-chewing kid. "But thanks for ridding the country of more of those fiends in red skin."

"If we hadn't killed them and gotten those

horses back," Keegan said, "we wouldn't be here. And the colonel's sweet girl would be done for."

"Sweet girl?" The silk-headed thin man sprayed a beetle with tobacco juice. "Shameless hussy is —"

"Ingram," the other one said, and just that word stopped the young Bainbridge rider from saying anything else.

McCulloch stared at the kid, then looked over at Keegan, now on McCulloch's right. The old soldier sat ramrod straight in his saddle, holding the tin cup inches from his mouth, his eyes flaming in fury at the audacity of some young whippersnapper slandering the daughter of Keegan's idol and commanding officer.

The Bainbridge hired cowboys had finished. They stepped away, picked up fresh canteens and tin cups of cold coffee, giving one of each to the three jackals.

"You cook good coffee, boys," McCulloch said, and held the cup up toward each cowhand, hoping that might ease Keegan's fury. He sipped, smiled, and managed to swallow this god-awful brew. It tasted more like warmed-over tobacco juice than actual coffee, but it sure did its job of waking a fellow up. McCulloch kept drinking, finished his while watching Keegan drink without making a face. McCulloch pitched his can toward the bedrolls of the riders. Keegan simply threw his on the other side of the narrow trail. Breen dropped his near McCulloch's.

The older of the cowboys held out his right hand toward McCulloch. "Luck," he said.

The handshake was brief. "Thanks, boys," McCulloch said. "You boys watch your back. There are Apaches and probably six groups of wannabe heroes back there."

"We will," the cowboy said, and he stepped back toward the saddle horses and the bone-tired team that had hauled the ransom money to this junction in hell. "But you boys watch your backs and what's ahead of you."

"Yeah." McCulloch released the brake, cracked the whip, and felt pain slice up from his busted leg to the back of his head.

The gray of dawn would soon give way to the brightness of the sun, and the sun would bring down all the wrath of the hottest flames in hell.

Long before they reached the next place to exchange horses, McCulloch could see the reddish and black peaks of the Big Bend, named for where the Rio Grande bent sharply south and then began a gradual northwesterly ascent toward El Paso. Sometimes, McCulloch wondered why the devil the leaders of Texas wanted this patch of misery for their own. The Mexican government for years — and many Mexicans still to this day — had insisted on making the Texas/United States boundary with Mexico at the Nueces River. Had the old hands of Texas not been so adamant about acreage, Texas wouldn't be as big, but it would have been a hell of a lot safer. Rangers often had a saying that nothing good had ever been found south of the Nueces River — and when the Good Lord and the devil had been negotiating a treaty and tried to carve out Hell, the Lord had offered Texas's Big Bend. Satan had shook his head and cried, "No deal." That land was too hot, too dry, too full of misery, and too damned mean to be his hell. So he left it to Texans to tame.

McCulloch worked the leather reins and the whip, feeling stiff all over, but he ignored the pain in his leg and looked over at Keegan, riding hard alongside like the horse trooper he was.

"You all right?" McCulloch yelled. He had to shout the inquiry again before Keegan heard and looked over.

"Yeah."

When Matt McCulloch gave a person a one-word answer, folks would wonder when the old Ranger and horse trader had become such a conversationalist. When Sean Keegan answered directly, soberly and with no side trips, lies, or ancient memories, one knew to prepare for an eruption on the scale of Mount Vesuvius. Or something like that.

"We'll make up the time we lost!" Mc-Culloch shouted.

Keegan said nothing.

"We have fresh horses and the next stops aren't tough terrain. Just hard, hot, and dust-choking miles. We'll get Virginia back to your colonel."

Keegan stared ahead for about a hundred yards. Finally, he turned his head and said, "I'll rip that waddie's head off, pin his ears back, and stomp him till he resembles . . ."

The wagon bounced hard after the left front wheel hit a giant hole. That jarred Mc-Culloch's busted leg so much he cried out in pain, but at least that stopped him from hearing Keegan's descriptively gory details of what he planned to do the next time he met up with a Bainbridge hired man who had dared to insult the colonel's daughter's honor.

They rode. The Big Bend was drawing

closer, but still a long, long way from where they were.

They rode. Sun warming. Dust thickening. Horses already beginning to falter.

They rode. Sweating. Stinking. Hurting. Bones aching, teeth jarring, eyes burning, muscles stiffening, stomachs growling.

They rode. Farther and farther from what passed for civilization in West Texas, closer and closer into what Shakespeare called the undiscovered country, a country most people — wise people — never wanted to discover.

They rode. Closer to the deepest pits of hell.

He knew the spot, when Colonel Bainbridge had been explaining the details of where each change of horses would be located, McCulloch knew this spot. The top of the hill, or what the Mexicans had first called The Highest Point in Hell. From here, one had a good look at all that was behind and all that lay ahead, at least till the Big Bend ridges obscured one's vision.

It was a treeless rise, where not even one cactus could be found. Like God had decided to dump all the leftover sand and gravel from the earth. No, not God. God did not want anything to do with this

220

country. Anything to be found here, well, that was the handiwork of Lucifer.

Now they came to the beginning of the incline. It wasn't steep. But it was gradual, and, when McCulloch had to compare it to climbing a trail in the Davis Mountains, or the rugged Guadalupes over on the Texas–New Mexico Territory border, it wasn't even all that high. But with tired horses and bone-weary men moving a wagon filled with $20,000 in gold coins, it wasn't an easy climb at all.

McCulloch had slowed the horses for about two miles, saving them for this last stretch. Once they reached the peak, these horses would be spelled. The cowboys of Newton Bainbridge would be waiting with fresh mounts. And from there on out, till they entered the Big Bend, the ride would be a whole lot easier.

Now, two hundred yards from the beginning of the incline, McCulloch found the whip and popped it over the lead horse's ear. McCulloch called out to Breen and Keegan. "You boys ready?" He did not wait for an answer, but popped the whip twice. The bad leg wouldn't let him stand, but he whipped the heavy leather reins hard as he could.

The animals lowered their heads and

began a hard pace. When they hit the beginning of the incline, they hardly slowed. But McCulloch knew this would not last.

On the animals pushed, and the momentum for that hard run before the horses had to start climbing helped, at least for the first third of the way up.

By the next third, they had slowed, breathing hard, trying their best, and McCulloch, hard man that he was, could not bring himself to lash out at these valiant champions with whip or curse words again. Instead, he offered praise, "Onward, onward, you're better than any horses I ever owned!"

With the wagon moving slower now, McCulloch turned and shouted, "Breen, ride on up. Let those cowboys know we're coming." He hadn't seen a figure, just the rising smoke of a campfire. McCulloch blinked.

Neither Jed Breen nor his horse could be seen.

CHAPTER TWENTY-ONE

McCulloch swore savagely, twisted in his seat, feeling more numbing pain from that busted leg, and looked back. Keegan also had slowed, but he rode alongside the rear wheel of the wagon, and the old army trooper stared down the ridge road.

Through the dust, McCulloch made out Breen swinging off his horse. The bounty hunter waved his hat, "Go on!" he appeared to be calling out. "He's gone lame. I'll catch up."

Again, Breen waved urgently before turning his attention to removing his saddle.

After letting yet another oath fly, McCulloch turned back, swallowed as best he could with a throat so dry, and lashed out at the horses with words, not whip.

With the ridge crest less than three hundred yards ahead, McCulloch did something he rarely did. He prayed. The horses snorted, wheezed, and he could almost feel their hearts bursting, but they kept going. A man in a big sugarloaf sombrero appeared. So did a cowboy in worn chaps and a tall Texas hat. They waved, yelled for them to hurry, to keep at it. This time McCulloch lifted the whip, started to let it fly, but again he just couldn't do it.

How those inkslingers and gossips back in Purgatory City would have loved to have seen that! The leader of the Jackals . . . showing compassion for work animals.

The last few yards slid past him, and then he was pulling hard, ramming the brake, and sliding the heavy wagon to a stop at the top of the ridge. The wind blew hard here, and below him he saw nothing but dust.

Finding his crutch, McCulloch pushed himself to a stop. "Boys," he said, "I don't have the time to climb off this wagon, so while you're changing the teams, I'm gonna loosen my bladder of some extra weight. Good thing the wind's blowing downhill."

He was about to make a joke about Jed Breen — until he saw the man with the sugarloaf sombrero. The Mexican held a big shotgun, the twin barrels sawed off, and that cannon was pointed straight at McCulloch.

"Where's the other rider?"

McCulloch turned to find the man in the big brown Texas hat holding a shotgun at

Keegan, who had raised his hands over his head.

"Where's that damned bounty hunter?" the tall Texan yelled.

Keegan jerked his head down the incline. "Horse went lame just before we hit the rise. He's running up here to catch up."

"Lawson!" the Texas cowboy called out. "Check it out."

Now McCulloch saw two other cowhands coming up. This one was mounted on a black quarter horse that wore a Bainbridge brand. The cowboy reined up behind the wagon and stared downhill. "Damned wind's raising too much damned dust."

Lawson sat up in his saddle. "No, no. Here he comes." He rode over to the leader of these thieves. "If he lost his hoss at the bottom of this ridge, he's got wings on his feet."

"How far back?" The leader in the tall brown hat barked orders that drowned out Lawson's reply. Two more men came up and began switching out the teams to pull the wagon.

Lawson stepped off his horse and into the buckboard alongside McCulloch.

He knew this man. McCulloch had a way of remembering a man's face. That came in handy when he was working for the Texas Rangers. He remembered faces and voices.

Jed Breen remembered faces and likenesses on wanted dodgers. Sean Keegan remembered . . . hell . . . whiskey bottles. This man . . . McCulloch remembered. He rode for Colonel Newton S. Bainbridge's brand, and now McCulloch remembered the one in the tall brown hat. Yes, another Bainbridge rider.

Bainbridge had said he had confided in only the most loyal riders he had, men he could trust. Well, that old hardheaded martinet would soon learn that loyalty had its limits. You rode for the brand, cowboys liked to say, but once you left that ranch, everything was fair game.

Looking at all the men on the rise, McCulloch counted. Five men. He wasn't sure the Mexican or the other two had worked for Bainbridge, but it didn't matter. He just hoped that some of these men hadn't been part of the next place where they were to change horses. Not that it mattered. The way things looked, Virginia Bainbridge would soon be a corpse, but Jed Breen, Sean Keegan and Matt McCulloch would be in hell long before her body had grown cold.

"Boys, let me tell you that sure is a beautiful sight," Dawson said. The man's eyes stared down into the rear of the wagon. "What does that gold look like?" asked one of the men harnessing the fresh team.

"Like two damned strongboxes," Dawson said. "Chained up like a virgin's undergarments." He let out with a Rebel war cry.

"Shut up, Lawson," the leader said. "I don't fancy getting killed up here by that bounty hunter."

Lawson nodded, turned back to McCulloch, and said, "We're relieving you of your wagon and your gold. We're damn sorry about Miss Virginia, but she never lifted her skirts for none of us boys."

"Bainbridge will track you down and kill you all," McCulloch said.

"That old miser should have paid us more," the Mexican in the sombrero said. He moved to the edge of the ridge. "If I had a rifle, I could kill him now," he said.

"You couldn't hit him on flat ground with a cannon," one of the men working on the harnessed horses said. "Shooting downhill takes some skill."

The leader snapped, "Someone might hear a shot. No gunfire. But let's be damned quick."

"Right-oh," called another of the men working the harness. "Mexico's a-callin', and we'll have us gold galore to spend on pretty wimmen."

The weathered horses were drifting off the

road searching for water or grass to lay down on or even eat, finding nothing but a campfire that didn't even have coffee cooking.

McCulloch wet his lips, and he saw the one called Lawson reach over, grip the Colt in McCulloch's holster, and fling it about a hundred feet down the hill. "You heard the man," he said with a gap-toothed grin. "Can't risk nobody hearing the shot." Again, he looked back at the strongboxes, but not long enough to give McCulloch any advantage.

He grinned again at McCulloch. "I don't think I can risk bending down to lift that Winchester off the floor here, now can I? You might stove in my head with that crutch."

Dawson lunged forward, the pistol in his right hand and the palm of his left slamming hard into McCulloch's chest, and McCulloch felt himself off balance. The crutch fell away, and McCulloch cursed as he went over the side of the wagon. His shoulders slammed into the hard road, and he cried out in pain that almost knocked the breath out of him, and jammed his neck, and he saw his legs, the good one and the one with that, by now, dust- and dirt-covered cast, coming for the ground. The legs hit, and

McCulloch saw only flashes of orange, red, and white light.

He rolled over, tried to sit up, couldn't, because the intensity of the pain dropped him down. His chest heaved. Rough hands grabbed his shoulders, dragged him out of the way. McCulloch's chest heaved, and he felt the wetness in his crotch.

"Hey, boss!"

McCulloch managed to see through the blinding tears of pain the fifth man, the punk who had dragged Bainbridge out of the road. "Never knowed a Texas Ranger to wet his britches," the punk said.

His four companions joined him in laughter, but the laughter did not last long.

"Boss," the Mexican said.

The wind, unpredictable like every other part of weather in Texas, had changed directions, and the dust had settled.

"Is Breen getting closer?"

"Not lugging that saddle and that cannon of a rifle I hear he carries," the Mexican said, "but I got a clear view maybe all the way back to Purgatory City."

"Then why don't you make a sketch of it and mail it to the editors of *The Austin Monthly Magazine*?" The man in the tall brown Texas hat had cursed his men to hurry up.

"I mean," the Mexican said, "I see about six or eight dust trails. And they all appear to be moving this way."

The Texan swung into his saddle and eased to the rim's edge, and, after a vile curse, turned the horse and rode to Mc-Culloch. By that time, Sean Keegan, also disarmed but not in jarring pain, knelt beside McCulloch.

"Are you being followed?" the leader of the traitors demanded.

"Aye." McCulloch could have kissed Keegan for answering. The question had been directed to McCulloch, who damn well couldn't say anything right now. His leg — his entire body — hurt like blazes.

"Aye," Keegan repeated.

"Who's trailing you?" the cowboy barked.

"Well, laddie, I don't know who all got the invitations we sent out or who all read the advertisement I put in *The Austin Monthly Magazine.*"

The boot slipped out of the stirrup and the toe caught Keegan a glancing blow that sent him to the ground. "Get smart with me and I'll blow your damned head off!" the boss man barked. "Who the hell is following you?"

"Don't shoot him, boss man," the Mexican said. "They will ride faster if they hear a gunshot."

"Who?" the boss yelled. "Who is following you?"

"How in hell" — McCulloch had found strength to beat back the pain that now tormented just his broken leg — "do we know?"

The boss in the brown hat turned away from McCulloch.

"How far away are they?" he demanded.

The Mexican shrugged. "Spread out. Some maybe as far back as Deep Flood."

"And the closest one?"

"Not close. It's hard to tell from this distance. But that bounty hunter, he runs good for a man carrying a saddle."

"We're ready." One of the men harnessing the new horses to the wagon climbed aboard. The others, including the Mexican, began moving to their saddle horses.

"What about these two?" called out Dawson, who pointed at Keegan and McCulloch.

The man in the brown hat looked down at the two men. His right hand went down to the revolver he had shoved into his holster. He scratched the palm of his right hand with the hammer on the big Colt.

"I could slit their throats," the Mexican said. "No shot. And I can cut deep, so they

231

could not scream, either."

"Get on your horse," the leader said, then he turned to Dawson, who sat at McCulloch's place, released the brake, and grabbed the whip.

The Mexican brought the leader's horse over, and the man in the brown hat stepped easily into the saddle. "How far back is that bounty hunter?"

"He tires," the Mexican answered with a wide grin. "We will be down this rise before he gets here." He looked down from the horse at Keegan and McCulloch. "Are you sure you do not wish for me to kill these two men?"

"We don't need to." The man in the brown hat looked at Dawson. "Rojo's renegade 'Paches will likely do the job. Or them comin' after the gold we just got. Or the desert herself. Get going. Fast as you can."

The whip cracked, and the new team of fresh horses exploded down the rise.

CHAPTER TWENTY-TWO

Sean Keegan took just a moment's glance at McCulloch before he sprinted toward the road and started running for the Springfield rifle one of those owlhoots had flung down the ridge. Gunfire rang out, and bullets from a Winchester carbine whined off the rocks near him. Keegan dived to his belly, rolled off into the side of the path, and covered his head.

As if my hams for hands will stop a .44-40 slug.

Another bullet whistled over his head.

He made himself look up and saw the smoke from the rifle, heard the report of that lever-action repeater, and saw the bullet kick up dust thirty yards in front of him.

"You all right?" McCulloch's voice boomed from the top of the hill.

"Yeah!" Keegan drew in a deep breath. He had underestimated those brigands. One of the hands was laying in the back of the wagon, which kept kicking up dust that the wind carried away to the west.

The Winchester spoke again, and Keegan came to his feet and hightailed it back to the safety of the ridgetop, diving the last five feet, landing on his chest, feeling the bits of gravel rip into his blouse, then he crawled past McCulloch until he figured he was safe from any lucky shot. Keegan crawled until he came to the northern edge of the hill, and he waved his hands over his head.

"Breen!" he shouted. "Get your bloody arse up here now."

Breen stopped, panting like a hydrophobic dog, and gasped, "What . . . is . . . ?"

"Drop the damned saddle, Breen, and get that Sharps up here. We've been robbed."

The saddle dropped, the bounty hunter turned, and a moment later Breen was weaving like a drunkard, climbing the last fifty or so yards to the top. Keegan ran back to McCulloch.

Hell, he had to catch his breath, and he hadn't climbed nearly as far as Breen. "You all right, Matt?"

"That's a damned fool question."

Keegan had to grin. Yeah, Matt Mc-Culloch would be fine.

"Those shots will carry," Keegan said.

"Whoever is trailing us will come faster."

"Probably why they fired those shots," McCulloch said. "They figure whoever gets here first will kill us."

Keegan shrugged. "Well, they also had to keep me from getting my Springfield."

"You could've kept trying for that long gun," McCulloch said. "Chances of them hitting you weren't good."

Keegan spit. "For a man lying flat in the back of a wagon heading downhill at breakneck speed, that fellow's shots came a mite too bloody close for comfort. There's a reason those fellows let him ride in the back of the wagon. He's a damned good shot."

Then Jed Breen staggered to the top of the ridge.

"But then" — Keegan grinned — "so is this jackal."

McCulloch turned as Breen used the Sharps as a walking stick to get closer to his two partners.

"He don't look so good," McCulloch said.

Indeed, the sunburned face and all the salve, now mixed with sweat, had been caked with dust. Breen wheezed as he moved, mouth open, barely moving.

"What . . ." he began, "the . . . hell . . . ha- . . ." He couldn't finish.

"Five traitors is what happened," Keegan

barked. "The colonel's hired men waylaid us. But lucky for us your horse went lame." He pointed at the edge of the hill. "They're getting away. With all that damned ransom money!"

Breen managed to swallow. Then he struggled forward, no longer using the heavy Sharps as a crutch. He fished out an extra shell from his vest pocket and moved with intense purpose — tired, yes, but moving like a man possessed. When he reached the edge, he moved off toward the east, away from the road, kept moving. Keegan wondered if the bounty hunter suffered from sunstroke, but fifteen yards away, he sat down. The wagon was halfway down the ridge. The three riders were about two hundred yards ahead.

Breen waved his left hand. "Get down here, Keegan."

Still sprawled on the roadside, sitting up, but making no effort to stand, McCulloch barked out, "You heard him. Move!"

When Keegan reached Breen, he squatted beside the gunman. "I'll spot for you," Keegan said. He figured that's why Breen had called him down.

"If I need . . . spotting." Breen still breathed like a man gasping for his last breath. He removed his hat, and used it as a cushion as he sat down, and took his bandana to wipe both ends of the telescopic sight.

"I could . . . use . . . some . . . shooting sticks."

"There's not a limb up here," Keegan told him.

"Let me use your shoulder," Breen said.

Now Keegan sighed, but he moved in front of Breen. The sharpshooter in the wagon didn't fire, perhaps because shooting uphill was just as difficult as shooting downhill, perhaps because he figured at this distance, they were safe. If Breen had asked Keegan to guess the chances of hitting anything, hell, Keegan would have agreed with those boys.

"Here."

Keegan turned back to find Breen holding his double-action Colt. "When I stop that wagon," Breen said, "you'll have to charge down that hill. I'll cover you from up here, but Matt won't be able to help. It'll be just you and me."

Keegan lifted the Colt and shook his head. "You've got a snowball's chance in hell of stopping that wagon."

"Don't I know it! Turn around and don't flinch."

Keegan felt the weight of the heavy rifle

on his shoulder, the barrel pressing against his neck.

The wagon was almost to the bottom by now.

"How in hell do you plan on stopping that wagon?" Keegan whispered.

He heard the heavy hammer click into place on the big Sharps.

"You have a single-shot rifle," Keegan said.

"All I need is one shot," Breen whispered. "Which . . . I'll make . . ." He still struggled for breath. "If you'll . . ."

Keegan finished the sentence for him. "Shut the bloody hell up."

"Hold your breath, Keegan, and don't move," Breen whispered.

The ex–cavalry trooper wished he had stuck some cotton or something inside his ear. He drew his breath, held it, and tried not to move. A second went by. He watched the wagon.

It sounded as though nitroglycerin had been detonated right against the side of his head. The heat was likewise intense, and the barrel came up as the kick slammed Breen back. Keegan felt the brass telescope clip the side of his ear. He fell to the ground, cursing, but unable to hear the curse in his right ear. His right hand tried to clasp the ear, but Keegan had forgotten that his right hand held Breen's revolver. That flattened his ringing ear, and for a moment, Keegan was back in Ireland, and his mother was trying to cure him of his earache, telling him that this medicine wouldn't hurt a bit, and Keegan knew she was lying and that the medicine would burn like flaming alcohol.

"Get . . . up!" his father was saying. "Get . . . up!"

Only now Keegan realized that it wasn't his father shouting, but one bastard of a bounty hunter who might have ruptured Keegan's right eardrum. He heard only in his left ear.

"Get down there!" Breen shouted as he fought for breath and struggled to reload the Sharps. "Move, damn you . . . Move."

Keegan stopped twisting and turning. All that did was tear more holes in his britches and blouse. He rose, wet his lips, cursed, almost cried, and saw the dust below. What he saw through that massive white cloud near the bottom of the hill brought him to his feet. Then he began running, bending forward, feeling his legs move like he was a Thoroughbred running in that race he had read about somewhere in Kentucky. He didn't have the challenge facing Jed Breen.

Sean Keegan was running downhill. He just had to keep himself from tripping and rolling down the incline toward the wagon.

He took in all that was happening. The wagon lay on its side, off on the eastern edge of the trail. One horse lay dead in the center of the road, still in harness. Its mate in that span was trying to get up. The other horses drifted as though dazed over to the western side of the road. At the bottom of the trail, the three riders had reined up. They appeared to be staring up at the ridge, at the wreckage, trying to figure out what had happened.

Keegan kept running. Not bad, he thought, for an old horse soldier. He was back in the infantry. Charging. As he had done for Colonel Bainbridge. Charging like hell.

He saw the body of the driver. Maybe he was dead, or perhaps he just had been knocked cold, but he wasn't moving. When the lead left horse went down with Breen's bullet to the head, the wagon had split apart with the rest of the team staggering one way, and the wagon lurching to the side of the road, where it had tipped over, catapulting the driver to the center of the road. Probably he had not been able to drop the heavy leather reins, and he had been jerked forward. The wagon must have rolled over at least twice.

Now Keegan had to find out what had happened to the man in the back of the wagon with the Winchester. He couldn't see him. The dust cloud caused by the wreck was being blown away. Most likely, from the looks of the Bainbridge wagon, that man was dead. He could have been thrown halfway to El Paso.

What about the strongboxes? Keegan wondered. Then he understood he had more pressing concerns than the ransom money for sweet Ginnie Bainbridge.

The three horsemen were galloping back up the hill.

The Mexican had the best horse, probably was the best rider, and maybe he had reacted first. Whatever the reason, he galloped up the hill. Keegan knew that he could never reach the wreck before the Mexican. But he kept right on running.

A pistol shot rang out, fired by the Mexican, but Keegan never heard the bullet's whine or felt it anywhere close. The man couldn't hit a running target. Riding uphill on a fast-moving horse? Aiming at a man running downhill? He had wasted a shot. But the Mexican did not stop when he reached the wrecked wagon and surviving horses. He galloped past, put the reins in his left hand, and kept his revolver in his right.

The pistol fired again, with the bullet kicking up dirt a few feet in front of Keegan, who kept running and brought up Breen's double-action pistol. Keegan fired and cursed himself for burning powder. Keegan was used to his big, heaving Remington .44. That was a man's gun, not a toy like Breen's short-barreled .38. Keegan had not taken into consideration that pulling the trigger on a double-action could pull the shot wide right. He was used to cocking the hammer, then firing. Not only that, he was running downhill.

The Mexican kept galloping toward Keegan.

The wind took the sugarloaf sombrero off the Mexican's head.

Jed Breen's next shot took off the top of the Mexican's head.

Keegan, his right ear numbed from Breen's first shot, didn't even hear the roar of the big Sharps up on the ridge. He just saw a pink mist spray in the wind, the Mexican's boots slip out of the stirrups, and the Mexican fly off the horse, hit the side of the road, and roll down about forty more feet.

The horse kept running, but Keegan stopped running down, and began waving his hands over his head, trying to stop the horse. He spoke what he thought might have been soothing words, though he still couldn't hear anything in his right ear. He waved his hands, tried cooing, tried to look like someone not completely desperate.

None of that likely worked to his advantage, but something worked in Keegan's favor.

That horse had been running hard down this infernal hill, running hard on the flatland below, and running even harder up the hill, past at least one dead horse, running at this steep incline. And now that it had no rider spurring its sides, it wanted to slow down, turn around, and find some good grass to eat — which was damned hard to find in this country.

By the time the riderless mount had reached Keegan, it was slowing, breathing hard. Keegan already saw the salty lather on the horse's neck.

His left hand found a rein, reached over to take the next rein. The horse blew heavily, snorted.

"Easy, boy," Keegan whispered. He looked over the saddle and saw the man in the brown hat and the other man. Both men had slid their horses to a stop by the wrecked wagon. One of them had even gotten off his horse and was looking for either the man in the back or, more likely, the strongboxes of gold. They had likely figured that their Mexican compadre would have dispatched Keegan.

Now, the man in the brown hat yelled something, and his partner in crime returned to the saddle.

That gave Keegan hope. Not that two men would be riding up to shoot him dead, but that he had heard something. Maybe he wasn't deaf. What gave him more hope, and, indeed, pleasure, was when he swung up into the saddle of the dead Mexican's horse, turned the animal around, and spurred the mount down the hill.

The two surviving bandits rode hard. Smoke and the report of two pistols made Keegan grin. This was more like it. He was back in the saddle. Charging to meet the enemy. And his hearing wasn't great, but he could hear the pounding of hooves, the pops from revolvers, and his own curses.

The stirrups were too short, the saddle too small, and the horse smaller than the ones Keegan like to ride, and he was firing an unfamiliar revolver. But, by damn, he was like a soldier again.

He saw the muzzle flashes from two revolvers. He raised the gun in his right hand, and this time cocked the hammer. They were riding past him, one on either side. He decided to kill the leader. The Colt popped, and he was close enough to see the look of surprise on the brown-hatted man's face before the villain slipped off the right side of the horse. Keegan also felt the burning of the remaining cowhand's bullet as it carved through the back of his blouse.

Keegan turned the horse to the left, off the side of the road, then back. He heard the cannon that had to be Jed Breen's Sharps. But this time the bounty hunter missed.

The last man rode downhill. Keegan got the Mexican's pony back on the road and galloped uphill.

The cowhand's gun jerked without the sound or flash of a gunshot, and he cursed, threw the gun at Keegan as he charged past. Keegan had fired, too, but his shot must have missed. Or maybe he had fired more than once. Hell, in all of this excitement, he wasn't certain about anything.

But he turned his horse around and saw the cowboy doing the same. Keegan urged the Mexican's pony back down the hill. The

cowboy turned his big Texas cow horse.
They prepared to duel one more time.

Chapter Twenty-Three

"That damned fool," Breen said. He had moved back to the road, hoping to get a better shot at the remaining road agent, only Sergeant Sean Keegan had to play hero, lead the charge.

"What is it?" McCulloch demanded.

"Keegan's right in the line of fire," Breen answered. "There's only one left." He heard the pop of a pistol. Breen lowered the heavy rifle. "Keegan will have to take him himself."

Another gunshot sounded. Breen saw the trace of white smoke briefly before the wind obliterated it. "Son of a gun," he said softly, and set the stock of the Sharps on the ground and used the support of the .45-70-caliber weapon to push himself to his feet.

"He got him," Breen said.

"Figures," McCulloch said. "How's the wagon?"

Breen looked down the road, and did not answer. "Looks like Keegan's rounding up some horses." He turned away from the scene and slowly moved toward McCulloch.

"Their riders won't need them anymore," the ex-Ranger said.

"Reckon not." A moment later, Breen stood over the injured Ranger. "How bad are you hurt?"

"No worse than before." He nodded toward the southern tip of the ridgeline. "You mind seeing how far away those dust trails might be."

When Breen stood at the edge, he saw just how far he had run up this damned hill, saw where he had dropped the saddle, saw his lame horse slowly moving down the slope. It was a miracle the three of these . . . good Samaritans . . . yeah, that's what Breen, McCulloch, and Keegan had become. Good Samaritans . . . Damned fools. But whatever you called them, they had been extremely lucky to still be breathing Texas air.

"At least we still got horses," McCulloch said. "And our wagon."

Breen frowned. Maybe they weren't all that lucky.

He loosened his bandana and wiped the sweat off his face.

"You see dust?" McCulloch asked.

"Yeah," Breen answered.

"How many parties do you make out?"

"Hard to tell from here. Some of those could be caused by the wind, dust devils, and they're too far away for me to make a guess at how many riders might be coming after either Harry Holland or a wagon filled with gold."

"They won't get the wagon or the gold," McCulloch said. "And I don't think they're any match for Harry Holland."

"I'm not sure we're a match for Harry Holland," Breen whispered. He turned around and slowly moved back to McCulloch. "We got some time," he lied. Oh, they had plenty of time . . . to get away . . . if they took the dead men's horses, left the gold in the wreckage of the wagon, and whipped their horses into a lather to make way for the Mexico border. Yes, sir, they had a right good chance of making it to Mexico.

He moved to the worn-out horse Keegan had been riding before their exchange of mounts went wrong. Finding the canteen, he shook it, heard the splash of water, and walked back to McCulloch, where he squatted, loosened the stopper, and handed the cavalry canteen to the onetime Ranger.

McCulloch drank just a couple of swallows. "Thanks," he said. Clopping hooves sounded, and Sean Keegan appeared, bringing two horses with him. McCulloch handed the canteen to Breen.

"Drink," McCulloch ordered.

"I'm all right," Breen said.

"The hell you are. You just ran up this death climb. It's hotter than hell's hottest hinges and we've got work to do. Drink."

Breen obeyed, but he took only a couple of swallows.

"How do you know Holland, Matt?" Breen asked.

McCulloch frowned. "He served with the Rangers. Briefly. Then decided the other side paid more." The ex-Ranger shook his head. "He was right about that."

"Were y'all friends?"

McCulloch shook his head. "He didn't stick with the Rangers long enough. Took to the owlhoot trail. And after I killed his brother, who wanted to be just like his big brother, well, that ended any chance of me and Harry becoming pals."

Keegan swung out of the saddle. "We've got a lot of work to do, laddie boys," he said and took the canteen from Breen. "The first thing we have to do is get ol' Matt down to the wagon. That's why I brought this horse."

At least, Breen thought, Keegan had brought the smallest of the mounts.

McCulloch shook his head. "You think I

can ride down that hill to our wagon?"

"Nay," Keegan said, "but we don't have time for you to walk or crawl down. So you're gonna get in that saddle, and I'll lead you down to the wagon."

"You've been drinking whiskey," Mc-Culloch said. "Just bring that wagon back up here, and we'll be on our way."

"Aye, Matt, me boy, that would be a grand plan indeed, but there's one little problem with your plan."

Keegan and Breen moved to McCulloch's sides.

"Hell," McCulloch whispered, "how bad is the wagon?"

"It ain't good," Keegan said.

Breen said softly, "We're going to lift you up, Matt. We'll get the smallest horse, let you get on from the high ground. Then Sean will lead you down to the wreck." He glanced to the south. "We might have some time, see if we can fix it, put together a team." He looked at the half-dead horses that had brought the wagon this far. "Maybe those can get us to the next change."

"They'll have to get us farther than that," McCulloch said. "There were five men. One of them I didn't recognize. But I'm betting the boys from our next designated swing station were in on this holdup. So instead of getting us one leg, they'll have to get us two."

"Aye," Keegan said, "and time's running out for sweet Ginnie."

"Let's stop beating around the bush and dragging our arses," McCulloch barked. "Get me on that damned nag."

"Brace yourself," Keegan said as they lifted Matt from the ground and eased him to the small cow pony.

"I know," McCulloch said through a tight jaw. "This is gonna hurt you more than it'll hurt me."

"No," Breen said. "This won't hurt me at all."

After McCulloch had cut loose with every curse word that Jed Breen had heard, and even a couple that he knew but had never verbalized, and screamed and spit and groaned, Breen helped ease the horseman's good foot into the stirrup. Keegan grabbed the reins to McCulloch's horse, and Breen walked to the mount he had been left with. Not a McCulloch horse, but it would do till the next change of mounts.

Breen swung onto his horse and called out to his pards, "I'm riding back down to my saddle."

"We don't have time for you to change saddles, damn it," McCulloch barked.

"This Sharps doesn't work so well without much ammunition," Breen barked back.

McCulloch did not respond. It was the pain in his leg, Breen figured, and the head, and the hopelessness of this mission.

He reached where he had dropped the saddle, grabbed the saddlebags, and tied them on behind the cowboy saddle, which he did not like at all, but McCulloch was right. There was no time to change saddles, for the nearest dust devil was moving at a high lope. Breen loaded the Sharps, looked sadly at the lame horse he had to leave behind, and loped back up the hill. On the way down toward the wrecked wagon, he gathered up the weapons, those McCulloch and Keegan had been forced to surrender, as well as the guns of the men who had no use for firearms anymore, sticking those in his saddlebags or waistband, and carrying the long guns — the Winchester of the Ranger and the Springfield of the old horse trooper — and moved down the hill, past dead men, and to what once had been a mighty fine wagon.

The wreck had been worse than Breen had figured.

McCulloch stood again on his crutches, moving from piece to piece. Keegan was dragging the second strongbox to the side

253

of the road where he had managed to drag the first one. The heavy iron boxes had fared well in the wreck. The chains securing them had not. The wagon wasn't going to take anyone anywhere, but might come in handy for firewood.

Both axles were broken, the front wheels had been pulled off from the bottom, and at least half the spokes were broken on both wheels. The rear wheels had rolled or been thrown about twenty yards into the road, along with the man who had been shooting from the back of the wagon. At first, Breen thought only the horse he had shot with the Sharps had been killed, but now he saw two other animals dead. One's throat had been cut, to put the poor beast out of his misery, and Breen figured Matt McCulloch had done that unpleasant task. But it had to be done.

McCulloch turned and looked up at Breen.

"Sorry," Breen whispered.

"Don't be." McCulloch hobbled back to the road. "You stopped the wagon. That was the only way to do it."

"Aye," Keegan agreed, "but how do we get that twenty thousand to Holland on time? No wagon."

"We got horses." Breen nodded at the

riderless mounts and the survivors of the wagon wreck. He even gestured back to the horses up on the hillside, the team from the wagon and Keegan's mount.

"Those strongboxes aren't going to be comfortable on a horse's back," Keegan said.

"Saddlebags," Breen said. "We divide up the coin, stuff them in the saddlebags, spread them evenly among the horses."

McCulloch picked up the idea. "Put the horses on a string . . . Switch the riders who are pulling the string every few miles."

"No," Keegan said, "we each carry a string of horses."

"Not Matt," Breen said.

"I can —" McCulloch began, but Keegan cut him off.

"Aye, laddie, aye. He's right, Matt, me boy. You'll play hell just trying to keep up with us."

"You're right," McCulloch agreed. "You'll do better leaving me behind. I'll hold off the boys behind us for as long as I can."

Breen shook his head. "I don't think so, Matt. You're coming with us."

"I can't make it all the way to those hot springs," McCulloch bellowed. "Not on the back of a horse."

"You don't have to," Breen said. "The last

255

stop is at Dead Damn Fool's Station. They'll have a wagon there."

"And do you know how much money Harvey Plimpton will charge for the worst wagon he might have on hand?" McCulloch demanded. "He'll want an arm and a leg . . ."

"Which," Breen said, "he will collect from Colonel Newton S. Bainbridge."

"Lariats?" McCulloch asked after a minute.

"We're in luck there," Breen said, and let his hand drift to the coiled rope on the horn of the saddle. "Good thing it was a bunch of cowboys who tried to waylay us."

"We ought to get moving," Keegan said, "before we realize how hopeless this entire plan is."

"No," McCulloch said, and Breen echoed the Ranger's bark.

"We'll rest the horses," Breen said. "They'll have to carry us twice the distance we were planning, and they're already tired and nervous from the hard rides and gunshots, not to mention savage horse- and man-killing wagon wrecks. We wait here till just about dusk."

"We wait that long," Keegan said, shaking his head, "we might have company." He jerked his thumb toward the hill behind him.

"Good," McCulloch said. "You two boys have gotten a fine tally of kills for the day. I'm mad as hell, and I wouldn't mind putting lead through any low-down snake who thinks he can steal from three damned jackals."

CHAPTER TWENTY-FOUR

Outside the adobe fortress in the canyons of the Big Bend country, birds took flight from the trees. Coyotes and javelinas looked on with curiosity and alarm before disappearing in the brush. The Apaches scouting for Chief Rojo forgot about looking for a weakness that no Apache had yet found and began nodding with appreciation that their enemy, and sometimes ally, would be a worthy white man to kill one of these days, for he was as savage, strong, and ruthless as the Apaches themselves. This Harry Holland would make even a Comanche flinch.

Inside, that impregnable flat-roofed bastion of blood, horses, and mules began circling and neighing nervously in the sprawling corrals. Cattle lost interest in eating stolen grain or drinking tepid water. And the men, white, black, brown, red — renegades all — stopped cleaning their guns, mending their clothes or tack, drinking, eating, gambling, cursing, laughing, dozing, or answering to the call of nature. The men gazed at the sounds coming from the upstairs quarters of Harry Holland. The worst of the lot grinned. The rest stared in silence, some with disgust, others with disappointment. They listened. A few flinched. None spoke. Some of them barely breathed.

The whip popped from inside the sprawling room where few men, or women, were allowed to enter. It sang out relentlessly, a savagery uncommon even for this vicious land. And after each sound of the blacksnake tearing into its target, the woman screamed.

Screams like those would break even the blackest of hearts.

Pop!

"Pu-lleeezzeeee."

Pop!

"Nooo. Ohhhhh. Don't."

Pop!

"For . . . merc-"

Pop!

Silence. A brief respite. Then, the voice of Harry Holland: "Turn over, you shameless hussy."

"No, no, no, no, no. . . ." The woman's voice started out as a scream, but quickly lessened so sobs.

That followed with another damning sound of the whip in Harry Holland's hand.

The woman no longer shouted. She did not beg. She cried out in pain, and then blubbered words neither man nor beast could understand.

From then on, came just six more savage, furious, unforgivable pops.

"I told your father I'd return you if he pays us the ransom!" Holland yelled. "I never told him what condition you would be in, you damned harlot!"

The whip cracked with furious finality.

The woman sobbed, which at least let the men in the compound below know that she was, at least, alive. For now.

"And now," Holland yelled from inside his room. "Now I don't have to worry about you using your feminine charm and your harlot's wiles to coax one of my men into saving your soul and your life and helping you escape." Holland laughed like a mad wolf. "No one will dare even look at you again, you hussy. No one. Not even the great Colonel Newton S. Bainbridge." The laugh rang out again. "Hell, woman, I doubt if you'll ever leave without a scarf to hide your face. I've turned you into a leper."

Sobbing. The men did not hear Virginia Bainbridge's weeping, not through those thick walls, but they to a man imagined her agony and her tears. They tried not to picture just had badly Harry Holland had brutalized her.

For a few minutes, they waited, silently, still not doing what they had been doing. They felt the heat of the waning sun. Some felt revulsion, others felt empty, and most of them wanted strong drink. The door opened, and Harry Holland stepped outside into the compound. He tossed the whip to the nearest man.

"There. Now you men know what kind of man I am. And now I know that you won't be staring at that wench the way you have been, that you won't think about how much her rich pa would pay you to return this sweet virgin to her pa. She's nothing to you anymore, boys. Remember that." He laughed, and grabbed a bottle of tequila from the nearest man, who rolled over and scurried away like a dog that had been kicked. "She's not worth looking at. And when I called her a leper, I was being courteous. So stay away from her."

He turned, slugged down a swallow of the liquor, disappeared inside, but quickly popped out. "And don't think about sending her any medicine for the lashes. They aren't that deep, but they'll definitely leave their scars forever. I'll tend to her wounds." He laughed, and held up the bottle of one hundred and fifty proof. "With this!"

Holland was laughing as he slammed the door to his room. The savage sound of the securing of the bolt jarred some men, but not as bad as the heavy thumps of Holland's boots as he ascended the stairs. A moment of wonderful silence passed.

Only to end with the earsplitting cries of Virginia Bainbridge's screams.

The men turned their heads at that, even those who had laughed when the torture began, as they pictured the clear tequila splashing over the woman's back and face, probably her entire body, burning like acid. She screamed and wailed pitifully until she must have passed out from the brutality.

The horses, which had stopped raising dust in the corral after Virginia Bainbridge's screams had ceased, now thundered until the dust rose skyward like smoke from the worst of all prairie fires.

Inside the upstairs bedchambers of Harry Holland, the killer and bandit splashed the tequila into a second tumbler, which he handed to Virginia Bainbridge, who took the glass and clinked hers against the one Harry Holland held toward her.

"Cheers," she said and gave him a wicked smile. She sipped the tequila without making a face, touched his glass with hers once more, and tossed her head back, her lovely hair bouncing over her flawless shoulders and naked back.

Then she giggled. "How did they look?"

Holland finished his drink in a gulp and refilled it with the wretched tequila. He would open the bottle of brandy later.

"I'm sure you have seen that look before," Holland said.

Lowering the glass, Virginia studied him. "How do you mean, Handsome Harry?"

Holland took a smaller sip, and, looking over the glass, he said, "You know."

"I don't know," she said.

He let the glass slide to his side, and then he sat beside her on the bed. "It's the look you've seen so many times you can't count. The look of a boy whose heart has just been broken because you said you couldn't go to the dance or the recital or the opera or the picnic with them. Virginia the Heart Breaker. Isn't that what they called you in school?"

She drank and set the glass on the side table. "No, Handsome Harry. They called me far worse than that."

He drank again and put his glass beside hers.

She brought a hand up and touched his cheek.

"Do you plan on breaking my heart?" Holland asked.

Virginia giggled. "That would be a challenge, Harry Holland," she said. "I'd have to find your heart to break, and I don't know if I can live that long — and, Handsome Harry, you know as well as I do that I plan to live a very long, long, long time."

Holland ran his calloused fingers through her recently shampooed hair. Damn did she smell just like a woman ought to smell. She looked like a woman ought to look, too, without a scar on her body, not one blemish. The leather trunk he had stolen from a wealthy Mexican rancho two years ago, on the other hand, had taken a brutal beating with the whip, and that had left Holland sweating and breathing heavily. Whipping a trunk, pretending to be some brilliant thespian treading the boards, screaming curses while Virginia screamed and cried.

Even now, both of them wanted to break out in laughter.

And they probably could have. Thick as these walls were, Holland figured, no one would hear what was being said, or done, from the outside. But Holland would wait until the men began drinking to forget what they had heard, and imagined, and when the laughter resumed in the cantina, and maybe a couple of the more talented man-killers brought out fiddle, mouth harp, and banjo, things would return to normal here at the fort Harry Holland had built.

He picked up both glasses, put one in Virginia's hands, and raised the other in another toast.

"Larsen got back. He says McCulloch, Breen, and Keegan are bringing two strong-boxes filled with your daddy's money." Holland drank.

"The Jackals?" Virginia did not drink.

"That's what they are called," Holland said. He did drink.

She shook her head and snorted. "That would be just like that old coward. Too gutless to bring the money himself."

"Well, I think they have a better chance of getting that money here than he would have."

"Maybe." Now Virginia drank. She finished the tequila and set the empty glass down.

Holland tossed his down and threw the empty glass on a pile of laundry.

He looked at Virginia, up and down, and smiled.

"Call me that again," he said.

"Call you what?"

"Handsome Harry."

She gave him a wicked grin. "I've got better things to do with my mouth," she said, then leaned into him, wrapped her arms around his head, and drew him to her, her mouth hungry and open.

CHAPTER TWENTY-FIVE

Holding the Winchester, Matt McCulloch hobbled with his crutch a few yards back up the road while Breen and Keegan began getting the horses ready and transferring the gold coins from strongboxes to saddlebags. He heard the clopping of hooves on the far side of the hill. He knew that noise could mean anything. Wild horses running free. A cavalry patrol from Fort Spalding or Fort Bliss. People minding their own business. Apaches heading for Chief Rojo's camp. Warriors who had jumped the reservation and were moving down the Great Comanche War Trail for Mexico. More than likely, though, the noise forewarned a bunch of owlhoots who wanted to get rich and had no qualms about killing.

Twenty yards from the wreckage, he moved off the road to his left, settled into the deepest part of the ditch, groaning, sweating, biting back the pain in his leg, which he stretched out before him. The crutch lay at his side. He worked the lever on the carbine, wet his lips, and laid the weapon across his lap. The hat he took off, and then he wiped his brow with a forearm. Finally, he picked up the cocked and ready .44-40 and waited.

Four riders crested the ridge and reined up, their horses sweating, blowing hard. The riders stared down, taking in the dead and the living, both human and animal, and the wrecked wagon. They knew exactly what that meant. Two of them reached down and drew rifles from the saddle scabbards. One put the reins into his mouth and palmed two revolvers. The last one was carrying a shotgun that saws had turned into maybe the ugliest-looking handgun known in the West, the barrels cut down and the stock carved into a pistol grip. Their spurs touched their mounts, and they bolted down the hill.

"Here they come," McCulloch called out, set his jaw, braced the stock of the Winchester against his shoulder.

"They're all yours, laddie," Keegan said from behind him.

"Unless they kill you," Breen added with a grunt as he hefted one of the pouches.

"I hate killing damned fools," McCulloch

said grimly and leaned into the rifle, calibrating the range, wind, and how much to allow for shooting uphill at moving targets.

"That's four more horses we might need," Breen reminded him.

The Winchester roared. The pinto horse, the one on the far left, lost its rider, one of the pair that had pulled a rifle. The man closest to him looked back, and he might have called out a name, but McCulloch couldn't hear with the rattling of hooves and the popping of the road agent who was firing one of the pistols. The other rifleman also cut loose. That bullet kicked up dust and pebbles at the tip of McCulloch's crutch.

Which meant he was the man McCulloch needed to kill next. Obviously, he posed the biggest threat.

McCulloch found the bouncing figure, let out a breath, and touched the hair trigger. He was already jacking another cartridge into the Winchester, moving the barrel, and finding the man with the two pistols. He fired, missed, worked the lever again, and this time made sure not to rush his shot. The bullet struck, but the man did not go down. Instead, he swayed in the saddle, dropping both pistols but clutching the horn on the saddle with one hand. Dismissing that man as no longer a threat, McCulloch levered in a fresh round. The man with the shotgun was raising his weapon, but before McCulloch could fire, he heard the horse and man scream, saw the horse tumbling, and the man flying over its head. The shotgun flew over the ditch and into the cactus, and the man slammed hard onto the road, bounced up, landed again, and somehow retained enough sense to scramble off to his side, rolling into the ditch, and lying still, as the horse, a fine-looking black, rolled over, twisted, and rolled over again.

McCulloch held his breath and turned to the last man, the wounded warrior holding on to the saddle horn. After a quick glance at the shotgun-toter and his horse, Mc-Culloch breathed easier — the black had risen to its feet, and was snorting, the saddle twisted onto its side. The horse wasn't going anywhere, but it was standing on all four legs, so McCulloch figured that horse would be all right. When McCulloch looked back at the last man, he saw only the horse, still running past the dead and the living, reaching the bottom and whickering as it made straight for Mexico.

The rider lay spread-eagled on the ground.

McCulloch lowered the hammer on the carbine, grabbed the crutch, and struggled to push himself to his feet.

"You all right, Matt?" Keegan said.

"Yeah." McCulloch moved toward the man who had carried the shotgun for that one was closer to his weapon than the one who had fallen off his horse.

When McCulloch's shadow crossed the bandit's face, the eyes fluttered. His nose had been flattened to a bloody pulp, and the face was scratched as though he had been in a tangle with a mountain lion. The lips opened to reveal busted teeth, and he groaned as the eyes finally opened and focused first on McCulloch's face, then on the barrel of the rifle a few feet from his chest.

"Get up," McCulloch ordered.

"I . . ." The man spit out blood and saliva, and perhaps some teeth that he hadn't swallowed. "Can't . . . move."

"If you can't move, you're no good to us." McCulloch leaned on his crutch, and took the rifle with both hands. The barrel stopped moving. McCulloch sighted down on the bloody, dust-covered figure.

"Don't . . ." He spoke louder now and used both hands to push himself to his feet. When the man was standing, weaving, McCulloch lowered his aim. He wouldn't take any bets on how long that fellow could stay upright, but he figured this one was licked. "Go check on your pard down there," Mc-Culloch said, nodding at the two-gun man. "If you try something stupid, you'll be dead."

The man walked away, none too steady, and McCulloch, who wouldn't call his own movements anything short of rickety, headed up the hill to the two men who had been armed with rifles. The first was dead, the bullet having slammed into his throat and broken the fool's neck. Lucky shot, Mc-Culloch told himself. Could have — likely should have — missed him completely. He remembered what he had been taught, and what he had always taught, when it came to shooting. Aim low. Always aim low.

The next man, a younger kid, hardly old enough to shave, was whimpering, holding both hands to his chest, trying to keep the blood from pumping out. He saw Mc-Culloch and wet his lips.

"My legs . . ." he said. "My legs. I can't feel 'em."

McCulloch saw how twisted both legs were, and he knew the punk's back had been broken.

"What's your name, boy?" McCulloch asked. "I can send word to your family."

The kid just blinked.

"Where you from?" McCulloch asked.

The hands slipped from the bloody hole McCulloch had put just below his sternum. He spit out blood, and opened his mouth as if to speak. But no words came out, and the eyes stopped blinking, just staring up and seeing not one damned thing except the cloudless, pale sky.

"Hell." McCulloch turned away and walked to the boy's horse, which had not gone far after losing its rider, probably too tired from all the hard riding these four men had done over the past few hours, or maybe, days. The scabbard, of course, was empty since the boy had been shooting a Winchester, so McCulloch slid his own carbine into the leather, grabbed the reins, and rubbed the horse's lathered neck.

He limped down, sometimes stopping to lean against the horse. His broken leg hurt like hell, and now the thought of climbing into a saddle and moving like a galloper bringing word of the fall of the Alamo to Sam Houston made him hurt even more. His wisdom he had to doubt. But as he looked again at the crumpled remnants of the wagon, he knew that was the only choice they had.

Unless they wanted to forget the whole deal and take the money for themselves.

Hell, it wasn't like they had much of a chance to get to those hot springs in time to keep Virginia Bainbridge alive.

"Hey," McCulloch called out to the ugly-faced bandit. The man was leaning against a dead horse, but seeing McCulloch he rose quickly and let his Adam's apple bob up and down. McCulloch pulled the rifle from the scabbard and pointed the barrel. "Your pard?"

The man's bloody face shook, but McCulloch went to the body anyway. The bullet must have hit an artery. There wasn't that much blood on his body, but he sure as hell was dead. Bled out. Probably inside, which would explain the bloated corpse.

"I'm getting too damned old for this," McCulloch whispered. Everybody called him the old man, and he felt those years — all thirty-seven of them.

Looking back at the wounded man, McCulloch spit out orders. "Gather up all those horses. Picket them on the side of the road near the wagon. Or what's left of the wagon. And don't drag your ass. You do that and your ass will look like your face, and your face won't look as good as it does now. And if you try to run or you try to pull some double-cross, you'll be deader than all your pards."

"You mean . . ." The man looked up the road. "Billy's dead?"

"Which one was Billy?" McCulloch asked.

"The sixteen-year-old. Billy Shirley." He pointed in the general direction of the whimpering corpse with the bullet in his chest and the broken back. "Douglas's boy."

"Doug Shirley?" McCulloch said, and looked up the hill himself, frowning. "Up Tascosa way?"

"Yeah," said the wounded outlaw.

"Hell." McCulloch spit. Doug Shirley was a good man. A damned good man. He had ridden in the Texas Rangers for a year back when no one wanted to be riding for the Rangers, especially along the Nueces Strip. McCulloch spit the bitterness out of his mouth and hobbled toward Breen and Keegan, who had rigged up a sort of packsaddle.

"What's this?" McCulloch asked.

"We got to thinking," Keegan said, and McCulloch rolled his eyes.

"That can be dangerous," McCulloch said.

"Aye," Keegan said, "but maybe not this time. We put the strongboxes on this, one on each side."

"You'll need a damned big horse and a damned strong horse to carry that weight," McCulloch said.

"We have draft horses that pull stage-coaches," Breen said. "And we just have to get them to the Big Bend and the Rio Grande."

"Just," McCulloch emphasized. "It's not a ride to any church social or picnic on the Guadalupe."

"Dead Damn Fool's Station," Keegan said. "Then we get a wagon."

"If Harvey Plimpton has a wagon," McCulloch said.

"Harvey Plimpton has everything to sell," Breen said, "except his soul."

"Aye," Keegan agreed. "He sold that years ago."

McCulloch looked back at the busted-face man who kept gathering horses. "We'll keep the saddlebags," he said, nodding. "In case this doesn't work, and in case Plimpton isn't selling wagons."

"Plimpton —" Keegan started.

"Could be dead," McCulloch said. "I'm just thinking ahead. Planning for what might happen."

Keegan chuckled. "Which is why I picked you for this job."

"That's just one reason." He smiled. "But I like the idea."

"We figured you'd pull our packhorse," Breen said. "Keegan and I'll pull the string of spare mounts."

McCulloch nodded.

"It still won't be easy for you," Breen went on, "but it's just one horse you have to control."

"Two," McCulloch corrected. "The other one I'll be riding."

Now it was the bounty hunter who grinned.

"What about him?" Keegan gestured to the wounded man.

"I have plans for him," McCulloch said and tried to find a spot in the shade. "I'd like to help you boys, but, well, I am crippled."

When they had selected the best horses of the lot, and after they had, with the help of the flat-faced, bloody outlaw, lined up a good string of remounts, McCulloch dispatched Breen to find that sawed-off shotgun in the brush. The bounty hunter returned with it, dusting it off and checking the shells in the breech, then handed it to McCulloch.

"What the hell do you want with this thing?" he asked.

The old Ranger took the weapon, pulled back both hammers, and turned it on the lone surviving outlaw. "This being yours," McCulloch said, "you know what it'll do to a person, I suspect."

The man's Adam's apple still worked. The blood looked much darker on his face as the color drained quicker than a whiskey bottle in Sean Keegan's hand.

"You see the horses we've left behind," McCulloch said. He did not wait for the man to acknowledge. "You'll take two or four, I don't care. Go easy with them, and they'll get you out of the state of Texas."

He seemed to breathe easier now, and some color might have returned to his ugly face.

"You'll be taking Billy Shirley's body back to his pa, up near Tascosa."

The man paled again. His mouth moved, but he could not speak.

"You'll tell him that Billy got killed by outlaws. You won't tell him how Billy really bought it. Doug doesn't need to know that. But you will tell him, and you will get his body to Tascosa so Doug can bury him."

Now the man had enough courage to say, "But that's better than five hundred miles."

McCulloch raised the sawed-off, double-barreled pistol. "That's right. And if you don't get this job done, I'll track you down. And you know damned well I'll do it."

They watched the man ride off, moving east, per Keegan's instruction, so he might avoid the rest of those damned fools trailing Nathan Bainbridge's ransom money.

Breen then swung into the saddle and looked back at his string of horses. Keegan glanced at the shotgun-pistol still in McCulloch's hands.

"You keeping that thing?" he asked.

McCulloch looked at it, sighed, and rammed it into the saddlebag on his horse. "I might find some use for it."

The Irish trooper looked off at the man carrying the body of a young outlaw. "You've got a streak of decency running through you, Matt. So much I'm almost sorry I got you into this damned fix."

"Not half as sorry as I am," McCulloch said. "Now help me get onto this big damned horse you picked out for me, you jackal."

CHAPTER TWENTY-SIX

At first, they rode easy, letting the horses they pulled get used to the lead rope and the rhythm. They also did this because they were worn out, burned by the heat, drained by what some people might consider an impossible journey on which many people would have bet with confidence that they would not have gotten half the distance they had covered. Matt McCulloch did not complain. He ground his teeth. The crutches he had strapped on behind the saddle and his broken leg stayed out of the stirrup.

But every step the horse made sent needles of pain from Matt's ankle to the bottom of his spine.

Yet he rode. He had to ride, had to keep going. It wasn't so much because he felt the desire to be a hero or to be loyal to the man, Sean Keegan — damn his black heart — who had saved his life. At this point, having covered all those miles, McCulloch had no other choice. If he turned back, there was no guarantee he'd live to see his hardscrabble land. There was no guarantee he would make it even up that damned hill. Going back would mean likely running into the bands of men who were trailing them — if they were still at it. Or Indians. Going back would be a long, hot, dry ride. If he had to dismount, he knew he never would be able to pull himself back into the saddle.

Mostly, going back would mean failure. Matt McCulloch had consumed too much failure in his life. He would keep on riding. He just hoped like hell Plimpton had a wagon he'd be willing to sell when they reached that ramshackle adobe and stone hut in the middle of nowhere. Maybe a surrey, with leather seats, plush and comfortable, with a roof you could pull up over your head to block out the sun, and lanterns on both sides to bathe the road ahead in kerosene-fueled light. That beat the blazes out of using the moon and stars for light.

He glanced to the west, saw the yellow ball begin to dip. The air began to cool, but he still mopped his face. The drop in temperature would not mean relief. McCulloch knew that all too well. All that sweat, the dampness of his clothing, and when the night winds kicked in, he would start to shiver. Some men had been known to catch their death, pneumonia, or whatever some sawbones felt like calling it, but McCulloch always figured many of those men and women had simply frozen to death. Frozen to death in a desert in the worst months of summer.

Yeah. This part of Texas was just like hell, but then most people would say that about all of Texas. Hell. But it was also home, and if Harry Holland had, as many people guessed, a fortune of stolen horses in his compound, then he would be set for quite a while. Well, providing that he was not planted six feet under, or probably only two or three, hard as the earth was in these parts.

And also providing that no sawbones had sawed off his leg by then.

The only good thing about the sun going down, Jed Breen figured, was that his face and neck and the backs of his fried hands wouldn't burn so much, although he had to admit that that salve had worked wonders. His face might not look too hideous, like some of those shriveled-up old prunes he had seen from West Texas to Southern California.

Of course, Breen had other ailments. His butt was bruised, and the insides of his thighs and calves felt like all the skin had been flayed off. Breen had always considered himself a pretty good horseman — not like he'd ever be asked to be a jockey in some match race in Purgatory City or Prescott, but he had made some hard rides in pursuit of some notorious outlaws, sometimes for as little as fifty bucks.

A Mexican wolf bolted out of a depression off to the right of the road, gave the three riders a quick look, and then ran like lightning toward the hills off to the east. That was the first wildlife Breen had spotted for some time. Had the riders been maybe a half hour later, he never would have spotted the critter.

You might not have gotten heat stroke trapped by those ruffians in the salt fields, Breen thought, *but now you know your brain has been cooked to a crisp. You're thinking about dumb predators and chicken thieves instead of the most important matters.*

Like how much reward money would he collect if he lived through this harebrained scheme of some idiot colonel that he didn't know and a hard-drinking, rock-hard Irish soldier and bruiser Breen knew all too well.

He tried to think about his injuries, the cuts, the bruises, the sore joints. The horses he pulled on his string practically jerked his

283

left arm out of the socket. His right kept a firm grip on the reins.

He looked back to make sure McCulloch was still behind them, still pulling the horse carrying all that money. He looked across the road at Sean Keegan, who looked like he had been born to that arse-bounding, backbone-numbing McClellan saddle the bluecoats issued its cavalry boys. On the other hand, the slickfork that Breen had been bouncing in for the past few miles would not compare to the comfort of one of those beds at Margie's den in Tucson, when he had spent most of his reward for Trevor Blue four years ago. He tried to recall the scent of Margie's perfume, but all he smelled was dust, sweating horseflesh, and the stink of his own miserable body.

It was almost enough to make him draw his double-action Colt and shoot Sean Keegan dead out of his saddle. For this was all Keegan's fault. That Irish blowhard. That glory-hunting fiend. Had he let those two murderers gun him down northeast of Howell's Tanks, Breen wouldn't be in this situation.

On the other hand, if he could collect just a small percentage of those rewards for Harry Holland's bunch, Breen could go back to Tucson, find Margie's den, buy

Margie some of that sweet-smelling stuff in that fancy little bottle, and, damn it, Breen wouldn't have to ride a horse all that backbreaking way. He could ride in the comfort of a stagecoach.

That thought made him look back at McCulloch.

"He's falling behind," Sean Keegan said when Breen looked back.

Keegan tugged on the reins and glanced at the bounty hunter to his right.

"Yeah," Breen said, barely audible.

"Slow down just a tad," Keegan ordered. "We'll let him catch up a wee little bit."

Inside, fury burned inside Keegan's gut. Slowing down. Hell's bells, they were already far behind schedule, and they had a long way yet to ride. Darkness would be over them before they reached the fork, and Keegan felt damned sure no fresh horses would be waiting for them there. They had horses on this string, but none of those animals were close to fresh. Keegan's own mount was lathered up and snorting hard.

Inside, he cursed Matt McCulloch. Horseman? What kind of horseman would be going at such a pace as he had his horse crawling? And Jed Breen? The man who looked like a damned ghost had trouble keeping that string of horses he was leading from jerking him out of the saddle. Keegan swore again, wishing he might have a dram of good Irish porter instead of just saliva to swallow.

He figured he had been a damned fool to ask McCulloch to join him. McCulloch, a horseman with a broken leg. He ought to be back in that hovel he called a home, eating his sorry beans and drinking what he thought was coffee or good whiskey. And Breen? Breen who almost baked to death in the white salt lands, Breen who knew nothing but how to collect rewards, and how to put men down so they don't get back up with that cannon he carried. Well, the bounty killer was also a fair hand at killing with his puny little revolver.

But had Keegan been smart enough to take the job on his own, hell, he would probably be all the way to those hot springs on the Texas side of the Rio Grande. He could have freed Colonel Bainbridge's beautiful Ginnie and delivered her to the best soldier in this man's, or any man's, army.

Instead, he was creeping along, trying to keep a Ranger with a busted leg from . . .

Keegan stopped and looked back. By now, the light had faded so much that Keegan could not make out the Ranger's face. The ex-Ranger's face. No, no, that wasn't right. Once you pinned on one of those little stars, you were always a Ranger — even if some glory-hunting martinet chased you out of the corps. Keegan couldn't see McCulloch's face, but he didn't have to. He knew that man was suffering pain that would have floored giants. Yet he still rode, despite one tough, angry draft horse that wanted to go somewhere else. And that man, well, he just had no quit in him. Yet here he rode. He didn't have to be here, and he rode with Sean Keegan, not because Keegan played that card of, *I saved your life, pard, and you owe me.*

McCulloch rode with Sean Keegan because that was McCulloch's way.

The saliva Keegan swallowed this time had the taste of bile. He looked over at the bounty hunter.

That man had spent hours baking in the heat, heat that would have driven most men mad. Then he had stuck with Keegan after they had found McCulloch. Yeah, Keegan had played that same hand on Breen. *I saved your life, so I'm calling in that I.O.U., pard.* Oh, sure, Breen had ulterior motives for tagging along. There was a fortune, and not a small fortune, to be had if he survived this adventure.

But that's not the only reason Jed Breen rode when he ought to be playing poker in some upper-class saloon that one might find in San Antonio or Fort Worth — certainly not Purgatory City. He rode on Keegan's right because he was a good man, if he didn't want many people to believe that.

He rode because this was the right thing to do.

And, hell, Keegan would not have gotten this far had he been traveling alone. Breen had saved his hide. So had McCulloch.

A man's blessed to have one friend, Keegan remembered his pa telling him.

"Well, Father," Keegan said aloud. "I've been blessed twice."

He stopped thinking, stopped complaining, and realized he ached all over himself. And he was an old horse soldier, used to going forty miles a day on beans and hay.

For the longest while, he rode until the darkness settled over him and the rest.

"Keegan."

Keegan looked over at Breen, or where he heard Breen riding. The moon had yet to rise, and while it wasn't pitch black yet, it still proved hard to see.

"Yeah," Keegan called back.

"I hate to say it," Breen said, "but we need

to be putting some miles behind us."

"Aye," Keegan said and let out a sigh. He twisted in the saddle and looked back. The clopping of hooves and the bouncing of those damned strongboxes on that rigged-up packsaddle told him that Matt McCulloch had yet to give up the ghost.

"Matt!" Keegan shouted over the hooves and rattling.

"I ain't dead yet!" McCulloch's voice boomed with pain but strength. "And I haven't quit on you."

Keegan grinned. For a moment, he thought this threesome might actually stand a chance of surviving this suicidal mission.

"You think you can put that horse into a lope a few miles?" Keegan called out.

"You don't watch out," McCulloch said, "me and this old nag will be galloping over your miserable bodies."

Keegan laughed. He called out to Breen, "What do you think, Jed?"

"It's a fine night for a good, hard ride," Breen answered.

"All right," Keegan said. "Let's see what these horses can do now that we've rested them a ways."

His spurs touched his horse. They rode. In the dark. Bound for who knew what.

They rode, and Keegan knew he was blessed.

Because he rode with men. Good men. Strong men. Loyal men. He rode with good friends, too.

CHAPTER TWENTY-SEVEN

By the time McCulloch, Breen, and Keegan reached the fork in the road, the sliver of a moon had risen. No Newton S. Bainbridge riders and no Newton S. Bainbridge saddle horses and no Newton S. Bainbridge Percherons waited for them. But the three men had expected this.

Keegan and Breen swung out of their saddles, letting the reins fall to the ground for they knew that the horses that had carried them these long miles would not run off, but they kept a firm grip on the lead ropes.

"Here." Breen handed the Irishman the rope that had chafed his gloved left palm. Without questioning the bounty hunter, Keegan accepted the rope, wrapping it around his hand once and watching Breen hurry — as fast as those worn, raw legs could move — to McCulloch, slumped in the saddle, both hands gripping the horn.

The exhausted Ranger had dropped reins and the lead rope, but neither his horse nor the big animal carrying the strongboxes would be moving anywhere for the rest of the night, and likely well into the next morning.

"Matt," Breen said.

The head barely turned, but the eyes were open.

"Let me help you down."

"Hell," McCulloch whispered. "I'm a damned nuisance."

Breen tried a joke. "That's not exactly news." He moved closer to the saddle, trying to avoid the busted leg.

To Breen's surprise, McCulloch did not scream as he slid his good leg out of the saddle and over the cantle, and Breen struggled to support the big Ranger's weight. Then he let McCulloch lean against him.

"We'll move about fifteen feet this way." Breen let his head point. "There's a rock you can sit on."

Once he saw that goal realized, he eased McCulloch onto the boulder, and hurried back to the horse McCulloch had been riding. Breen returned with crutches and the canteen. The former he leaned against the rock, and the canteen he put in McCulloch's hands. After examining the tough rancher briefly, Breen limped back to Keegan and the horses.

The horse trooper had already unsaddled his mount, had picked a fresh mount, and had bridled the new horse in the time it had taken Breen to get McCulloch off his horse and onto that resting place.

"What do we do with the horses we rode in on?" Breen asked.

"Leave them." Keegan tossed the saddle blanket on the back of a brown gelding that had some Thoroughbred blood flowing through its veins.

Glancing back at McCulloch, Breen frowned. "He won't like that."

"He's out of his head from pain," Keegan said, but he sighed and shook his head. "I don't like it, either, Breenie, me boy, but it's not humane to drag these laddies any farther. They'll drift off to find some water." He put the light cavalry saddle over the blanket. "If the wolves don't get 'em."

"Wolves might end up getting us, too," Breen said.

"Aye. There's no guarantee of nothing in this life except that you won't live forever. But here's the good news."

Breen waited.

"Those boys that have been following us,

well, they don't have spare mounts, most likely, and that means they'll be quitting now that it's night . . ."

"Enjoying hot coffee and sourdough biscuits," Breen interrupted.

"Don't think about such pleasures, laddie," Keegan said as he ducked to cinch the saddle into place. "That'll just drive you mad. But while they are resting and sleeping, we'll be moving farther ahead of those boys. They shall not catch up with us."

"Yeah," Breen said, "because by then we'll be in Harry Holland's kingdom." He shook his head. "That doesn't quite strike me as comforting, Sean."

"Then begone with you and your negative attitude," Keegan said. "And saddle your own bloody beast."

Breen drew in a breath, exhaled, and moved toward his horse and string.

"Jed," Keegan called out softly.

Turning, Breen waited.

"Hold the buckskin in your string till daylight. Pick a dark horse. Less chance someone might see us in the night if you're riding a dark horse. That bay with just the sliver of white on his forehead, that'd be my choice."

Breen started to go, but stopped, and asked, "In case you're wrong about those men trailing us?"

"Maybe so," Keegan said. "But there's also Apaches, Mexican bandits, white bandits, Comanches, scouts for Harry Holland, and all sorts of other scoundrels. Just playing things safe."

"And lightning."

Both Keegan and Breen turned toward the voice.

In the darkness, McCulloch said, "Every Texas waddie knows that a light-colored horse is sure to draw lightning."

"That man has the ears of an elephant," Keegan whispered, spit, and called out in a booming voice. "Lightning, Mr. Ranger. Do ye see any sort of cloud in this night sky, you bloody fool?"

"You know what they say about Texas weather," McCulloch said. "If you don't like it, stick around for fifteen minutes because it damn well will change."

"He's feeling better," Breen said and moved off into the darkness to pick his horse.

"I'll saddle one for Matt," Keegan said.

It took both men to transfer the packsaddle and the heavy strongboxes to the new horse. The temperature had dropped, the cold biting them down to their sore bones, but they

295

knew the ride would warm them up, and before long — from the position of the moon — night would be over and the furnace of daylight would bring back misery of the hot, sweaty kind.

Once they had the boxes firmly secured, Breen and Keegan eyed each other briefly, nodded, and both men walked toward the rock. Matt McCulloch still sat on the rock, the canteen on the dirt, his crutches within reach along with the Winchester. Breen put his hand on Matt's shoulder, calling out before he made contact, "Matt, it's Jed."

The soft snoring ceased, McCulloch's eyes widened, and his right hand reached for the rifle. Breen repeated, "It's me, Matt. Jed Breen."

McCulloch froze in mid-movement, his head turned, eyes straining to focus in the pale light and find the bounty hunter.

"Damn," he said, relaxing and letting his hand fall to his side. "Must have fallen asleep."

Breen looked over at Keegan, whose face — at least from what Breen could see — remained impassive. When Breen turned back to the Ranger, he asked, "We all need sleep. Maybe you'd like —"

"You got my horse saddled?" All of that weariness had left McCulloch's voice.

"Aye," Keegan called out. "A temperamental mustang with hell showing in his eyes. It wears a Bainbridge brand, but by my reckoning, it's a McCulloch horse."

"Yankee bastard probably stole it from me," McCulloch muttered.

Breen chuckled, and Keegan replied, "If that were the case, laddie, he'd be dead and buried."

Breen grabbed the crutches. "Here." He held them out for McCulloch.

Once those were secure under McCulloch's armpits, the old Ranger nodded at the canteen. "Grab that for me, will you, Jed?" He started hobbling in the dark toward where Keegan held the reins to a wiry black mustang.

"Hell," McCulloch said. "He's small even for a mustang."

"Aye," Keegan said, taking the crutches after McCulloch grabbed the horn. "Breen and me have a bet as to if your feet will be dragging the ground, tall as you are." The soldier began strapping the crutches on behind the saddle.

McCulloch pulled down his hat tight on his head before looking at the night sky. "Be dawn before we get to Plimpton's place."

"Indeed." Breen moved to McCulloch's

left, careful not to brush against the busted leg.

"Bainbridge's men might have given up on us," McCulloch said. "We were supposed to be there by now."

"They'll give us some time," Keegan said, securing the last knot before he stepped near McCulloch.

McCulloch reached inside his vest pocket and pulled out a handkerchief, which he wadded up and stuck inside his mouth, clamping his teeth down.

Neither Breen nor Keegan had to ask McCulloch to explain his reasoning. The piece of cotton would help keep McCulloch from screaming when they put him back into the saddle.

Drained, Breen stepped back as McCulloch brought the reins up and steadied the nervous mustang. That man had to be suffering pain that would floor practically everyone Breen had ever met — even Jed Breen himself — but McCulloch gritted his teeth and urged the mustang to calm down. "Easy, boy," he said, the words hardly audible, and kept the reins tight until the horse snorted and settled down.

"Quit burning daylight," McCulloch barked once he knew the horse wasn't going to bolt.

Daylight. Breen shook his head and smiled as he moved to his horse. Daylight would not show for several more hours. He found the reins and the lead rope, took both, and swung into the saddle a hell of a lot easier than McCulloch had done, but still not easy. Not as hard as they had been riding, for so long.

Keegan was shoving tobacco into his mouth, having already mounted. The animals on both strings snorted and stamped their feet, nervous.

Breen glanced over his shoulder toward the north, finding four new stars he had not seen earlier in the evening. Stars that looked closer . . . maybe planets . . . Mars? No, Mars had that reddish tent. These stars, maybe part of a constellation, glowed more yellow than white.

He blinked and then swore.

"Sean."

The former cavalry sergeant wiped his mouth and shoved the pouch of tobacco into his blouse pocket.

Keegan pointed.

Four lights moving lower than the horizon should be. Breen knew that. He knew these were no stars.

"Torches." That came from McCulloch,

not Keegan, and Breen looked at the outline of the Ranger turned horseman.

"Aye," Keegan agreed. "Night riders."

"None too smart," Breen said. "Torches? And four of them?"

"Maybe they're blind," McCulloch said.

"Aye." Keegan spit. After wiping his mouth, he turned toward Breen. "Blind or not, lost or whatever, you make south. I'll stay back and see if they just want to light my Daniel Webster cigar."

Breen and McCulloch started to protest, but Keegan cut them off. "All those years in the saddle, I know how to ride, and I've got good mounts left in my string. I'll catch up with ye laddies before ye reach Plimpton's miserable outfit. Now ride. I have to find me a place to tether these fine mounts, and see what kind of fools are on our trail, lighting the path for any damned fool to see."

Breen didn't like it, but he nodded as though he approved. Pulling the string of remounts with his left hand, he nudged his horse alongside McCulloch's mustang.

"Ready, Matt?" he asked.

A hoarse laugh that lacked any humor came as McCulloch's answer. "How about you?"

Breen didn't have an honest answer, so he

kept silent. He kicked his horse into a walk, and when the horses he pulled behind him passed McCulloch, the former Texas Ranger began following, pulling the big draft horse with those two noisy and damned heavy strongboxes.

I wonder who's the bigger fool, Breen thought as he rode into the darkness of West Texas, *four idiots lighting a path in hostile territory, or Matt and me, bringing a fortune in coin that is making enough noise to wake the dead?*

Chapter Twenty-Eight

Darkness made it impossible for Keegan to make out the distance, always deceiving in this vast country, but he figured he had enough time to get ready. The riders did not move fast, so he found a dip in the desert, a place that held rain — not at this particular minute — so that there was enough grass to keep the animals content for a while. He hobbled his mount, and used a lariat to make sure his spares would not wander off. At last he sprinkled grain from one of the pouches in his saddlebags to give the horses more to eat.

It was black as the ace of spades, even with the stars, and the horses had to be tired from the hard travels.

They wouldn't run off, Keegan figured. Might not whinny if they caught the scent of the horses heading this way, which from the slight breeze, Keegan found unlikely. He checked his knife and shoved extra cartridges for the Springfield carbine into the deep pocket of his trousers for easy access. Then he checked the loads, by feel of his fingers, in the .44 Remington. Four torches did not necessarily mean four men.

Leaving the horses, he moved out of the slight depression, hoping he could remember how to find this place in the dark, and moved to the edge of the trail. Not too close. He settled into a comfortable place, pointed the barrel of the Springfield in the direction where the riders would be appearing, and then he waited.

He counted time by watching the moon. His muscles tightened, stiffened, hurt, and he listened in the night but heard nothing except the wind. The night chilled him. He remembered back during the war.

Sean Keegan despised guard duty. Marching back and forth with a heavy musket on the shoulder, counting the paces, listening, and all those commands. "Corporal of the guard, post number four!" . . . "Halt, who goes there?" . . . Signs and countersigns. Serving in this man's army sometimes didn't really make a whole lot of sense.

A foot scraped on a Confederate rock, and Keegan tensed, bringing his musket ready, the long bayonet pointing at the dark green pine trees of a Southern forest. He worked his lips, moved his tongue, and called out the signal.

"How about some coffee, Reb?"

He waited for the countersign, hoping he would remember it correctly.

"Trade for Georgia tobaccy, Yank?"

Keegan let out a long sigh. "Come ahead."

The figure stepped out of the woods, and the half-moon provided enough light to see a dark uniform with enough trim on the sleeves and collar to reveal this man was an officer. A match flamed to life, and Keegan saw the face of Bainbridge as he stopped to light a cigar. He breathed easier.

Then another match flared, and the officer began puffing on a new cigar until the tip glowed red. The boots traveled over Southern pine needles and stopped a few paces in front of Keegan. Both hands held cigars. The left one reached out toward Keegan.

"How about a smoke, Sergeant?" Bainbridge said. "The South isn't much good for anything, but damn their treason souls, they grow good tobacco and can make a damned good cigar."

Keegan took the cigar, leaned his musket against a pine tree, and relaxed. He drew in a mouthful of delicious smoke and nodded his approval.

"Where are your stripes, Sergeant Keegan?" the major asked.

"Well . . ."

"We lost General Allison in our latest disaster," Bainbridge said.

"Aye, sir. I saw the brave man fall in that last charge." He shook his head, remembering the general spearing his kepi with his saber and marching into the Confederate guns, yelling, "Follow me, boys, follow me." Most of the men followed Allison . . . all the way to the grave. Keegan had been lucky. He had been with the platoon fifty yards to the right, the platoon that has suffered only sixty percent casualties.

"I asked about your stripes, Sergeant," Bainbridge said and flicked ash on this hallowed ground.

Keegan sighed and tried not to let Bainbridge see his Irish grin. "Well, sir, you see sir, I had a wee bit of a disagreement with the lieutenant, and he protested to the captain, and the captain, being an Englishman and with no common sense or decency in his soul, he ripped the stripes off my sleeve and told me if he had his way, he'd line me up in front of a firing squad but figured it would be better to save Union powder and lead and let the Johnny Rebs kill me today."

"What a damned idiot," Bainbridge said.

"Well, sir, me fine mother told me never to argue with an officer and a gentleman."

Bainbridge laughed just for a moment and turned around. "I hate the nights. Before the battle. And even after the battle."

"Aye." Keegan didn't know what else to say.

After Bainbridge let out a heavy sigh, he smoked his cigar for a moment in silence, then dropped the Southern-made cigar on the ground and crushed it with his heel. "I hear some of the savage Indians do not like to fight at night."

Keegan nodded as if he had heard the same bloody thing, but he knew nothing about Indians.

"I'm not partial to it, meself, sir."

Bainbridge chuckled. "Do you like guard duty?"

"It takes away from me drinking, sir, begging your pardon, sir."

"I see."

Keegan smoked and looked down the path of straw that he was supposed to be walking. "Well, sir, I thank ye for this spoil of war confiscated from the enemy, but I should be continuing my guard duty. Corporal Marcus thinks he is Napoleon."

"Tell Corporal Marcus that he answers to you now, Sergeant," Bainbridge said.

The cigar dropped to the ground. "I'm sorry, sir." He figured Bainbridge had said something else.

"I told you three months ago that we needed fighting man like you in charge. Hell, I likely could get you promoted to captain now."

"Sergeant will do me just fine, sir."

"I'd like to be general now that Allison is six feet under." He paused, lost in thought, before looking again at Keegan. "Rip two of the stripes off this Corporal Marcus's sleeves, and I'll give you another at first light. You're a sergeant, Sergeant, from now till kingdom come." He walked away.

Keegan picked up the cigar and began drawing hard, trying to bring life back to the confiscated Confederate smoke. Then he shouldered his musket and walked down the straw-lined path to find Marcus. The night, at least this night, no longer frightened him.

Keegan's eyes shot open. *Bloody idiot,* he thought, falling asleep on guard duty. *Colonel Bainbridge will bust ye —.* He stopped, remembering where he was, knowing that he had been daydreaming and then likely

307

had drifted off to sleep. But not for long. Something had wakened him.

He raised the Springfield, aimed in the direction of the road, and carefully pulled back the heavy hammer, keeping the noise to a minimum. Then he heard the clopping of the hooves. And he saw the light.

Just one torch now. The others might have burned out, or maybe the riders had become a little more cautious. More cautious, perhaps, but they hadn't gotten any smarter. They boys were drunk. He heard one laughing and another humming.

"How much further, Billy?"

"How the hell should I know?"

Hooves hammered the ground. The horses were walking slowly. The glow of the lantern shone on four men. Four.

"This is ridiculous," said a third voice. "I never should have left Deep Flood."

"Well, you're here," Billy's voice called out. "And we ain't turning back till we catch them bad boys and get all that cash. Seventy thousand dollars."

"Hot damn!" That would have been the fourth man. He let loose with a cheer and sent a whiskey bottle — presumably empty — smashing against Texas ground.

"Shut the hell up!" Billy's voice demanded. "We don't know where them boys are. Could be anywhere."

"Then," the third voice said, "that torch you're still carrying isn't the smartest thing to be showing in the dark."

"Well," Billy said, "we gotta see the road, don't we?"

Keegan shook his head. These treasure-hunting fools were idiots. Children in a man's world. And how in blazes had stories upped that ransom from twenty thousand to seventy thousand dollars? Keegan could likely kill all four men without effort, just shoot them out of the saddles with his Remington revolver when they crossed past him. But even Apaches did not believe in killing men with mush for brains.

Then he decided he'd just surprise them. They were likely so drunk they'd give up or turn tail. Most likely, he could send these morons back to Deep Flood without firing a shot.

The thought had barely run through Keegan's head when the first shot cut through the night, sounding like a cannon in all that still, dark quiet.

"Arggh." The torch fell, sending sparks into the night.

"What the . . . ?" Maybe that was the first voice. Keegan wasn't sure. He flattened himself on the earth as muzzle flashes popped all around. Horses screamed. Men died. And the war whoops followed, yipping, howling, echoing in the nothingness of black sky.

"Apaches!" screamed one of the men from Deep Flood.

Far too many horses pounded on the earth, and Sean Keegan had learned many things during all the battles he had seen. Including when to run like hell and retreat so you can fight another day.

Crouching, he hurried, glad he had left his horses a half mile back, far, far away. The rifles and the war whoops, and the horses running and dying — all those noises would drown out Keegan's boots as he flew over the harsh Texas dirt. He ran sideways, just in case those savages heard him and started taking pot shots as he fled.

Somewhere in the darkness the last of the four fools was screaming. "NO. No. Please . . . don't . . . Please. I'm too young . . . I don't . . . Nooooooooo!" The shots no longer fired, but in his imagination, Keegan heard the knives doing their work on the unfortunate fool who had been found wounded, not dead.

Keegan cursed the Apaches. And he kept right on running.

He almost fell into the pit. One of the

horses snorted.

"Thank God," Keegan whispered and tried to remember how a good Irish Catholic crossed himself. He shoved the Springfield in the scabbard, more from feel than sight, and moved to the remounts to remove the makeshift hobbles. After taking the lead rope, he hurried to his mount, took off the hobbles there, wondering if he had been a fool to hobble all of these horses. That would be his luck, to get killed by murdering Apaches who caught him because he had taken the precaution to keep those mounts from leaving him afoot.

He swung in the saddle. The screams and gunshots had faded. The Apaches would spend a while looting the dead and doing unspeakable things to the dead.

Still, when Keegan rode out of the dip in the earth, he rode wide to the west. It would be a longer way, but he had plenty of horses to carry him to Dead Damn Fool's Station.

The cold of the night felt good now against his face and body as he galloped away from the slaughter.

He rode hard, and fast, but only for a while. Then he slowed the horses. He had to save them. Damn, he thought, and thanked all the saints for getting him through this ambush. Falling asleep might have saved his life. The Apaches could have found him first, killed him while he slept.

"While I slept." Keegan repeated that though aloud, testing it.

He looked back toward the northeast.

"When?" he said, again aloud, if just a whisper. And he thought back to that night during the Civil War, the first time Colonel Bainbridge had brought up the savage Indians and the night. In the years since, Keegan had learned that what the dashing colonel had said that night wasn't made-up hogwash. The years on the frontier in the regular cavalry had taught Keegan a lot.

"When do Apache Indians fight at night?"

CHAPTER TWENTY-NINE

"If it's all right with you," the Reverend Finbar Flinders Fletcher said as he slid off his jackass, "I'd like to read over the dearly departed."

He did not wait for an answer but moved to the first dead man, pinned underneath his dead horse. Colonel Newton S. Bainbridge did not look at the murderous preacher, but stared off toward the east.

"I thought I heard something," he said when his foreman, Jimmie, rode up alongside him. Bainbridge pointed in the direction.

The foreman snorted and stared into the blackness, wet his lips, and turned to one of the hired gunmen. "Ace, did you hear anything."

Ace spit between his teeth. "Just the sound of men dyin'."

Bainbridge kept looking, but the only sound came from where he was, with horses stamping and wanting to get away from the stink of death and blood and gunsmoke.

"Might have been a coyot'," Jimmie offered. "Or a wolf."

"Maybe so," Bainbridge said.

"If it was a man, he wasn't with these idiots."

Bainbridge nodded. He had not planned on murdering any of the men chasing, foolishly, after Keegan and his companions, but these dunces had been moving too fast. With all the trouble Keegan, the bounty killer, and the onetime Texas Ranger had run into, even those oafs might have caught up with the moneyboxes. Keegan was already well behind schedule, and Bainbridge didn't know how much extra time — if any — Harry Holland would give to get all that precious money.

"I still can't believe some of our boys tried to pull a damned double-cross on us . . . on you, I mean, boss," Jimmie said, and he reached into his saddlebag and pulled out a bottle, using his teeth to remove the cork, then fingered the stopper and took a swig of rotgut whiskey.

Bainbridge shrugged and stopped staring into the dark as though he could see something or someone running from this slaughter pen. "Keegan and his crew just saved me payroll for the month," he said and reached out for the bottle in Jimmie's hand.

The foreman wiped the lip of the bottle and let his boss take it.

"Those Jackals have a way of getting luckier than anyone I've ever known," Jimmie said.

The liquor burned a fiery path down Bainbridge's throat, searing tongue and tonsils and scalding his esophagus before detonating in his stomach. But Newton Bainbridge had tasted worse liquor, and it did warm him a mite as the wind continued to turn cooler. Before he raised the bottle to his lips again, he said absently, "Luck has nothing to do with it. Those men are professionals. Maybe the best there are, certainly in West Texas, probably the whole state, and I wouldn't doubt if the entire Western states and territories of our United States." He drank and returned the bottle to the foreman. "Remember that. You and these men will have to be at their very best when the time comes."

Jimmie drank, corked the bottle, and slipped it back into the leather bag behind the cantle. He wiped his lips and asked, "Now that we've eliminated the only men between us and that Irishman and his man-killing friends, should we send the Tonks ahead?"

Bainbridge shook his head, and he looked in the darkness as the reverend and a few of his other men searched the dead, to make sure they were, indeed, dead, and to pick their pockets for anything of value. Seeing as how these four had come from Deep Flood, Bainbridge figured the pickings would be very, very slim. Tiny flames flickered as the preacher and other men held matches out, cupped in their hands to keep the wind from blowing out the light.

"Watch those matches," Bainbridge barked. "That's how come those men you're robbing are deader than dirt and burning in hell."

"Boss," said one of the younger gunmen he had found in El Paso, "those idiots had torches."

"And Apaches have damned good eyes," Bainbridge said. "Especially Chief Rojo's renegades."

"They won't attack us at night," the preacher said.

"Harry Holland's killers will."

The killing field turned black again, but Bainbridge figured the preacher would lack the willpower not to strike another match.

They had caught up with the Tonkawa

scouts because of the delays that had stopped his ransom deliverymen. Jimmie was right. Even Bainbridge didn't think the men who rode for his brand would have tried to double-cross him, but all that money tempted the best of men. The Tonks, like most Indians, had grunted and refused to take part in the ambush of the four men, which had been ridiculously easy. "Like shooting fish in a barrel," one of the killers had whispered after the carnage had been completed.

Then Bainbridge had heard the noise, just faint steps. He had been blessed with good ears all his life. Even all the deafening volleys of cannon fire and musketry during the War of the Rebellion had not lessened his hearing. He had heard everything he had ever needed to hear, including Harry Holland in the upstairs room of his own house, with Bainbridge's own daughter.

"I think you're trying to get me killed, precious," Harry Holland had whispered.

"My fine, upstanding daddy had far too much Madeira tonight, sweetheart," Virginia had said. "But I wouldn't overstay your welcome."

"I'm just glad that tree is close to your window."

She had giggled. "And I'm just glad Papa likes to sleep in the library, not upstairs. He hasn't slept in a bed in years."

"All those years soldiering, I guess."

Virginia had let out a mocking laugh. "No. He's scared of heights."

Kids were such damned fools. Talking in hushed whispers before getting to their lovemaking, thinking that their voices would not carry through the thick walls and heavy doors and down the stairs and through the sliding door that led from the foyer to the library and into those old ears of an old man who had consumed two bottles of wine. Fools not realizing that their voices, even whispers, could be heard as clear as anything when they came down the fireplace in Virginia's room straight below to the fireplace in the library, flues open.

He had started to rise, but the wine sent him back onto the couch, and he had to be thankful that he had opened that second bottle of Madeira. Because as he lay there, he heard Virginia and Harry Holland start whispering about arranging a kidnapping. So they could milk richer-than-God Newton S. Bainbridge for most of his fortune and make off to Mexico to live happily ever after.

Most of his fortune. Twenty thousand dollars. Kids today had no idea about money. Newton S. Bainbridge could lose forty grand in a poker game and make it up in six months.

And when he heard that conspiracy, Bainbridge had smiled. Suddenly, he had a plan. He'd let Harry Holland and that witch of a daughter — she took after her late mother — think they were getting the best of him. Only he would get his own revenge.

He could kill them both, and wipe out the Harry Holland gang, grab all that reward money for himself, and live out the rest of his days with all the glory that had eluded him during the Civil War and all those years fighting Indians out in this remote wasteland.

That also meant that Bainbridge would not have to climb those stairs. He had never been upstairs in all the years he had lived in this house. His damned fool wife had insisted on a two-story home, so she could have a view. A view of nothing.

Virginia was right about one thing, though. Newton S. Bainbridge could not stand high places. That's why he lived in Texas.

"Glory be," the reverend called out.

Bainbridge turned, frowning, seeing the

glow of another match as Finbar Flinders Fletcher checked another dead man.

"Bless you, my good man, bless you for your generosity." The match was shaken out, and the next sound Bainbridge heard was the unfolding of a knife. "Lord, we thank you for sending this man to our church. We thank him for seeing fit to give us a generous tithe. Gold fillings. Two of them. Glory, glory, hallelujah."

CHAPTER THIRTY

Keegan rode the first horse hard, knowing it wouldn't get him as far as he had planned. When the horse gave out, Keegan reined him up, dismounted, and somehow managed to get the next horse in the string bridled and saddled. With a firm hold on the lead rope, he leaped into the saddle, touched spurs to the blood bay's sides, and galloped toward Dead Damn Fool's Station.

As dawn began to break, he caught up with Breen and McCulloch. The Ranger stood leaning on his crutches and holding the ropes that held the last of their remounts. That's all McCulloch could do, leaving Breen with the chore of unsaddling and saddling the horses. That white-haired man was a lot stronger than he looked, for he had gotten those strongboxes off the packsaddle, although from the looks of things, they had fallen more than been eased to the earth. But the packsaddle was already on another horse, and two saddle mounts, a dun and a gray, were saddled and ready to ride.

" 'Bout time you showed up," Breen said, stepping back and wiping his palms on the front of his britches.

"Heard what sounded to be quite the fracas," McCulloch said, not moving on those crutches. "Figured you were dead."

"Yeah." Keegan swung out of the McClellan and realized he might as well saddle a fresh horse. "I didn't fire a shot." He stopped long enough to drink water from his canteen, and realized it was practically empty. He wrapped the canvas onto the horn, knowing he could refill at Plimpton's place, and took the spare canteen and drank just a swallow before returning it.

As he put the saddle on the fresh horse, he told the Ranger and the bounty hunter what he had heard a few hours back, the slaughter of the four idiots with the torches traveling from Deep Flood, Texas.

"Comanches?" Breen frowned. "Apaches?"

"That's what I thought at first, too," Keegan said. "Way those were yelling and acting up. For about five seconds." Actually, it had been quite a lot longer than five seconds, but the night, the lack of sleep, and the pressure of a suicidal mission could make a man lose most of his reason. For a little bitty bit.

"So you know it wasn't Indians," McCulloch said. "Who do you figure?"

Keegan didn't like the way the cinch felt, so he loosened it and tried again. "Holland's boys? I don't know. But they took care of our problem."

McCulloch stared north. "Holland's boys, maybe," he said.

"Competition," Breen said. "Some other greedy fools. There were quite a few boys coming after us, at least from the dust trails."

"Could be a band of night riders, too," Keegan said, tugging on the saddle, and now satisfied with the fit. "This country isn't known for a population of God-fearing, hardworking farmers, Quakers, and preachers."

McCulloch shook his head. "Whoever it was, they gunned down four men. By ambush. Now we had been thinking that most of those dullards would have turned back long before now. If we're being trailed, the closest ones behind us are hard-bitten murderers, scoundrels, and back-shooting bastards who do their dirty work in the dead of night and without giving a man a chance."

"And they call us Jackals," Keegan said. He adjusted his hat and started to remind his pards, but Breen must have been reading Keegan's mind.

"Figuring out who is behind us isn't the most pressing concern we have right now, boys." The bounty hunter tugged on the wooden supports of the makeshift packsaddle. "We're supposed to be at Dead Damn Fool's Station by now, and we've got a hard ride to get there. There's a woman's life in danger if we don't get to those hot springs. If those murderers behind us want to catch up with us, we'll fight that fight when we have to. But right now . . ."

"Right," McCulloch said. He pointed at the strongboxes. "Sean, you best lend Jed a hand with that fortune. Get those boxes on and make sure they won't fall off. Then you brutes have to get me on my horse, and this time, try not to break my good leg like you did the last damned time."

Taking advantage of the last of the cool morning, they rode hard for the first several miles. Breen and Keegan frequently glanced back to make sure McCulloch was still in the saddle. Somehow, he managed to stay upright. It was hard not to feel the pain that tough hombre kept enduring. His busted leg kept bouncing off the horse's belly and the tough leather of the saddle.

That, Keegan and Breen knew, was a man.

They rode through agave and sotol, yucca and prickly pear, watching the mountains rise forebodingly as they neared the Big Bend. Once they reached those mountains, the shade would protect them from the blistering heat, but at that point, the terrain would turn brutal. They'd have to slip through a rough trail to reach the Rio Grande, and after that follow the river downstream till they found the hot springs.

Before that, they had to find that skinflint who ran Dead Damn Fool's Station.

Century plants stretched toward the pale blue sky, the green and red of the mountains became clearer.

They neared the rock-walled compound, riding into Dead Damn Fool's Station through what Harvey Plimpton called his "gate," just the sprouts of two desert candle plants. Plimpton was too cheap to put up an actual gate.

The peg-legged skinflint stepped through the doorway, holding a Greener twelve-gauge in his left hand and a Walker Colt in his right. He sniffed, spit, and leaned against the rocky wall.

Keegan nudged his horse ahead, reining in a few yards before the stationmaster.

"Where are Bainbridge's men?"

"Who the hell's Bainbridge?" Plimpton snarled.

Breen dismounted and stepped between his horse and McCulloch's, and began talking to the Ranger, who looked like he was about to fall out of the saddle. Keegan wanted to go assist his pards, but he needed to figure out if they had remounts here.

Everything Plimpton built came from red and black rocks from the Big Bend. That's why nobody had been able to burn him out. The station, which also served as Plimpton's home, was rock. The barn was rock. Even the two-seat privy was rock. The corrals were made of rock — except for the wooden slats for the gate — and, damn it all to hell, there wasn't a horse in either the square corral or the round pen. Just two oxen, and two mules — and none of those looked good enough to have come from Newton S. Bainbridge.

"You know Colonel Bainbridge," Keegan said. "He was here enough times, haggling with you for water, when we were pursing Comanches on the prod or Apaches before Rojo's boys took root in this country."

"Well, my memory ain't so damned good,

you Yankee Irish pig," the one-legged man snapped. "And there ain't been no body, not no horse, and not no man set foot on this place in a month of Sundays." He brought up the shotgun. "So you might as well get the hell off my property and get out of my sight before I add to my cemetery." He pointed the barrel of the Walker Colt at the cemetery. The graves were numerous, bodies covered with rocks. Three of the crosses looked brand new.

"Git!" Plimpton snapped.

The sound reached him. He froze, keeping the shotgun trained on Keegan, but his eyes turning toward Breen and McCulloch. Keegan had heard the metal clicking, too, and he knew — as did Harvey Plimpton — what that sound meant. Keegan did not look away from Plimpton. He had heard Jed Breen cock that big Sharps rifle of his many times.

The trader's Adam's apple bobbed. His face was too burned and too hidden by a thick, wiry brush of gray and black beard crawling with lice to pale too much, but his eyes widened as he looked at Breen.

"Nobody's been here in how long?" Breen said.

"Weeks."

"Well, how do you explain all these fresh

horse apples on your place?"

"It's wolf dung."

A horse whickered from the barn. Another answered.

"And what's that?" Breen demanded.

"Termites."

"You worthless piece of crap," Keegan said. "You murdered Bainbridge's men for their horses. That's just like you. That's who's under those new graves of yours."

At that moment, no one, except Plimpton out of the corner of his left eye, saw the upper door to the barn push open just a hair, just enough for a rifle barrel to slip out a couple of inches in the direction of Jed Breen.

"Bounty-killing man," the one-legged cheat and killer said with a grin, "you got yourself in a no-win situation. You kill me, I touch both of these triggers and your friend the Yankee-loving sergeant sees his brains — if he has any — splattered all the way back to his home in . . . Liverpool."

Keegan frowned, and tried to figure out a play.

Ten seconds passed, but that small passage of time felt like twenty years to Keegan. Breen frowned, waiting for Keegan to make some play.

"Breen!" McCulloch barked. "Keegan!"

Another lifetime passed in a matter of seconds.

"Put the gun down, Jed. We got ourselves a Mexican standoff. Sean, take your hand off that hogleg in your holster. Just lower the hammers, boys, and we'll talk this thing through."

Plimpton smiled a black-toothed grin. At the second he relaxed, McCulloch palmed the shotgun pistol he had confiscated from the strap on his bedroll, bringing it up, thumbing back the hammer, and squeezing off a shot before anyone saw him move. The buckshot zipped through the opening, and a man cried out. The Winchester tumbled out through the loft door, and a second later the Bainbridge rider pushed open the door and followed the Winchester on the twenty-foot drop to the hard earth.

Harvey Plimpton made the fatal decision of turning the barrel toward McCulloch and cutting loose with one of the sawed-off barrels of the Greener. He quickly realized his mistake and turned around in a futile attempt to shoot Sean Keegan out of the saddle, but all he saw was the massive barrel of Keegan's Remington .44 less than a foot away from his face. He might have felt the muzzle blast that burned and blackened his sunburned face, but he never felt the bullet that blew the brains out of the back of his head.

That tired horse Keegan had ridden into the Dead Damn Fool's Station yard felt a burst of energy and bolted. Kicking free of the stirrups, Keegan dived off the mount, hit the dirt with his left forearm, and pushed himself over the quivering corpse of Harvey Plimpton.

That's when the second Bainbridge rider jumped up from behind the rock wall of the bigger corral, the rectangular one, but he turned his repeating rifle toward the spooked horse that Keegan had ridden in on, realized his mistake, and tried to find Jed Breen in his gun sights. Instead, he saw the flash from the large-caliber cannon and felt the bullet rip through his chest and blow a fist-sized hole out of his back.

He hit the ground on horse apples, fresh dung, just like that in the yard of the station, swallowed, and cried out, "Mama." Not that he knew who his mother was, and not that it mattered. He blinked once, stared at the sky, and wondered how something so far away could look so cool and peaceful and blue.

The last man raced out of the ground-level opening to the barn, holding double-action Smith & Wesson .32s in both hands, squeezing the trigger, and cutting loose with a Johnny Reb yell as he ran, spurs jingling, straight for McCulloch, who was lying on his back. He had underestimated that massive weapon's kick. The recoil had knocked him out of the saddle, letting his horse scamper to the watering trough.

The gunman's first four shots went high and wide. The fifth, coming out of the barrel of the sawed-off pocket pistol in his left hand, came closer to a cactus than McCulloch. The sixth shot dug up dirt only ten yards in front of him. The seventh came close — McCulloch felt the heat of the bullet as it zipped past his right ear. The eighth hit the dirt. The ninth ricocheted off the rock wall of the round pen.

Then he dropped to his buttocks, legs outstretched before him, and squeezed both triggers again. One bullet slammed through his right foot, ruining the five-dollar boots he had bought in Purgatory City three weeks earlier. The eleventh shot carved a furrow down his thigh.

He looked at his chest, saw the blood pumping from the several tiny holes that had drilled through him, then looked up at McCulloch, sitting upright, holding the damnedest-looking gun the killer had ever seen — holding the smoking cannon with both hands. The dying man raised his Smith & Wesson again, and blew a hole through the brim of his hat.

Both guns were empty.

He tilted to his side, coughed once, and died.

The gunsmoke cleared. Breen looked at Keegan, who was leaning against a wagon that the bounty hunter had not noticed when they had first ridden into Dead Damn Fool's Station, brushing the gore and grime off his clothes.

Then he looked at McCulloch, who stared at the shotgun pistol, and tossed it aside. "That damned thing's more dangerous to the man who shoots it than to them that it shoots," he said.

Breen ejected the brass casing from the breech of his Sharps and reloaded the rifle. Without looking up from his task, he said, "The men you just blew to hell and back might disagree, Matt."

Eventually, Keegan and Breen made their way to the Ranger, who looked up helplessly.

"I guess I owe ye a wee bit of thanks," the Irishman said.

McCulloch frowned. "Get me out of this sun without killing me, and I'll call it even."

CHAPTER THIRTY-ONE

After carrying McCulloch to the shade of the wagon, Breen and Keegan hurried to the barn. Every stall had a guest, and most of the guests wore the Bainbridge brand. Others wore something that resembled Harvey Plimpton's brand.

"Plimpton was no hand with a running iron, was he?" Breen said as he reached the last stall.

"He didn't have to be," Keegan answered. "No lawman and no rancher wanted to risk coming to the Big Bend for a forty-dollar horse and wind up getting killed by renegade Apaches or Holland's bad boys. And most men raising dust for Old Mexico weren't too particular about brands or bills of sale that old peg-legged miscreant would give them."

Three of the Bainbridge mounts they saddled in the barn, and they brought out the Percherons to pull the wagon. As they led the team out of the barn and passed the bodies of two of the Bainbridge deserters, Breen said, "That's close to half of the men your colonel hired to help who wound up deserting him. No, not just deserting, turning against him."

"Money's a temptation, Breen," the soldier said.

"You're not tempted?"

He chuckled. "All that money? For me? As much as I like to sample the Irish, I'd drink myself to death in a week. Nay, laddie, I prefer the slow death of a poor drunkard."

Breen looked at the dead, and the graves, and decided he liked the theory he had come up with, though he did not waste breath explaining it to Keegan or McCulloch. The three cowboys had piled up fresh stones and new grave markers so that Colonel Newton S. Bainbridge would think that bandits had killed the cowboys and stolen the ransom money. Likely, they and Harvey Plimpton would have ridden hard and crossed the Rio Grande into Mexico, split up the loot, and gone their separate ways, richer than they had ever imagined. Keegan was right. Money — especially the sum of $20,000 — could tempt even the strongest man with the morality flowing through his veins. Plimpton probably would have sold out for a fifth of what his split had been.

Yes, that's the way Jed Breen figured things. And seeing the dead bodies, he knew he would get no argument from the only men who had known the true reasons behind their poor choice of their last criminal act.

They stopped near the wagon and really stared at it for the first time.

Now it was Breen's turn to let out a hollow laugh. "Fitting," he said, "I guess."

"Aye."

Then they pulled the horses past McCulloch and lined them up to be harnessed to the hearse. When they had completed that, they stood over McCulloch.

The Ranger looked up, his face pale, grim, and while the temperature remained hot, even for West Texas standards, he was sweating a lot. Breen had seen corpses with more color.

"You ready to drive?" Keegan asked.

McCulloch just stared.

"We saddled an extra mount," Breen said, "if you prefer that torture instead."

"I'll have to ride it eventually," McCulloch said, his voice weak, strained. Breen had to strain to hear the words.

"Once we hit the river . . ." McCulloch tilted his head toward the hearse. "No wagon's getting us to those hot springs."

"Aye," Keegan said. "We also have a couple of spare horses to carry the money the rest of the way."

McCulloch looked at the body of the dead stationmaster. "What do we do with these bodies?"

"Coyotes and buzzards have to eat," Breen said.

The laugh that came out of McCulloch's mouth sounded more like a cough, maybe even a death rattle.

"Matt?" Keegan tried.

The head gave a quick, grim nod, and McCulloch said. "Boys, before you put me into this death wagon, you have to do something for me."

"What's that?" Breen asked.

"Get this contraption off my leg, and reset the damned thing."

They had to get his chaps and pants off first. After that, Keegan picked up the Springfield and walked over to the bloody body of Harvey Plimpton. Gripping the carbine's forestock with both hands, he raised the heavy rifle and brought the walnut stock down on the thin bottom of the dead man's wooden leg, snapping it off. He picked it up in his left hand, wiping it on his trousers as he returned to the Ranger, who was shaking with pain as Breen tore off the wrappings of the busted leg.

"You keep this up," Breen said, "you might be dead."

"Not likely," McCulloch said.

"No way you won't have a limp," Breen said. "And you might not even have a leg, just a stump like that owlhoot whose head I blew off."

"We'll see."

Keegan spit, knelt, and thrust the wooden stick toward McCulloch's face. "Here, Matt. Have a taste of what your future might be."

McCulloch took it, stared.

"In your mouth, pard," Keegan ordered. "Because this is gonna hurt worse than anything you've ever felt."

"Like hell," McCulloch said. He put the bit of foultasting wood in his mouth and bit down. It was a big piece of wood, and the wood was hard, but McCulloch had good, strong teeth. He knew Keegan was wrong. Hurt worse than anything he had felt? That soldier and the bounty hunter had endured much, but they had never come home to see their families butchered, their hopes and dreams shattered, and one daughter abducted, stolen, disappeared, probably dead by now. Hurt? Some men — the luckiest ones — would never know what true pain felt like.

Breen moved to the foot with the black, disgusting sock. Keegan gripped higher, just below the kneecap. The soldier looked at the bounty hunter, who looked into the horseman's eyes. McCulloch nodded, and closed his eyes.

"Now," Keegan whispered.

McCulloch's head slammed against the dust-caked side of the hearse, his eyes squeezing tightly. Breen thought the thick piece of wood from the dead man's peg leg might snap in half. The Ranger never cried out, though part of that was because he passed out.

They splinted the leg — not with pieces from Harvey Plimpton — and wrapped it as best they could with muslin cloth they found inside the trading post. They also found a bottle of Kentucky bourbon, which Breen said they should let McCulloch take a few sips of once he regained consciousness.

Keegan and Breen then helped themselves to two shots of tequila and javelina jerky they found underneath the bar. That had to fortify them as they returned to the misery of afternoon and hauled the strongboxes into the back of the hearse.

It was one of those fine funeral carriages that you never saw west of San Antonio. Black paint with gold trim, though the deep black had faded a lot, and if it baked for another few months it would be gray. The dust coated the sides, which lightened the color even more. And glass windows took up most of the sides and the rear door, so folks could get a good look at the casket as the dearly departed traveled to his final resting place on this earth. Well, glass had been there a while back. A few shards remained in the back window, but just the faded curtains, moth-eaten, ripped in places, hung partly from the top. The lanterns on both sides were long gone, too, and the cushion for the driver had been pried off. Keegan replaced it by spreading out the bedrolls of the dead Bainbridge riders. The silver-plated side rails on the inside had been pried out, probably sold for scrap, but the wooden flooring, although not hard as walnut, wasn't rotting. It could support the weight of the strongboxes and all the ammunition and extra guns Keegan and Breen could throw inside, along with water and food.

But the axles were well-greased, the suspension seemed solid, and the horses put in the harness were fresh, well fed, and well-watered. Once it had been the pride of some undertaker, and now it was going to do one final job before it was left on the banks of the Rio Grande to turn into dust, like all the bodies it had carried to some boot hill or fancy boneyard.

Buzzards, braver than most scavengers in this country, now perched on the roof of the barn and on the top walls of the rock corrals, waiting.

Those ugly black birds knew it was time for the survivors to ride out.

So did the three jackals.

"How do you feel?" Breen asked.

"The bourbon helps." McCulloch held the bottle toward the bounty killer.

"You better keep it," Breen said. "There won't be any refills once we pull out of here."

"Which," said Sean Keegan, squatting across from Breen, "we need to be doing real soon."

"You better both have a drink," McCulloch said.

"Why?" Keegan asked,

"Because both of you have to get me into this death wagon."

When McCulloch wiped the sweat off his forehead with his shirtsleeve, then pulled on his hat, Breen handed him the bottle of bourbon.

"We had to take the doors off the back," he said, "and hitch the spare mounts." They had tied the lead ropes on the corners. "Latch was gone, lock broken, they would have slammed open and shut all the way." They had positioned the strongboxes in front of that opening, Breen said. "So most of what we're hauling won't fall out."

"I'll be careful," McCulloch said. He removed the cork and swallowed a mouthful. "This isn't bourbon, you know?"

Breen nodded. "I wouldn't call what we found in the bar tequila, either, but . . . you sure you up for this?"

"Ain't like I have a choice." He grabbed the reins to the team of Percherons. "Let's get this funeral procession moving."

CHAPTER THIRTY-TWO

By the time they reached the beginnings of what Texans called the Big Bend, darkness had settled, and no one would go through this dark, foreboding country without light, so they waited for the moon to rise.

None of the three jackals spoke. They rested their horses, sipped from their canteens, and chewed on the hardtack and jerky they had taken from their last stop in civilization, if anyone could consider Dead Damn Fool's Station civilization.

They moved tentatively through the darkness. The myth about Texas was that it was all dust and flat and vast. Well, the vast wasn't myth at all, but Texas was not flat, especially in the Big Bend, which had its share of flats — Tornillo and Dagger, to begin with — and dust, but its vastness could chill the nerviest scout, and all around the rough desert country rose mountains that had the appearance of tombstones.

Even the names of the ranges spoke of death, danger.

By the time the sun rose, they found themselves in the middle of the Big Bend.

"There are the Sierra del Caballo Muerto," McCulloch called out, nodding to the ugly range to the east.

Caballo Muerto. Spanish for Dead Horse.

Dead horse, McCulloch thought, dead Virginia Bainbridge, for they would never reach the hot springs by the deadline Harry Holland had given them.

But the three men kept moving, raising dust behind them, moving deeper into the most savage part of Texas. They kept their eyes alert, scanning for signs of Apaches or raiders from Mexico who had crossed the river separating the two countries. Buttes rose, landmarks for one wasteland to another, three thousand feet, some a thousand feet higher, while off to the west, the reddish towers climbed even higher, more than seven thousand feet in many cases, surrounding the Chisos Basin.

Luckily for the three men, McCulloch thought, the journey would not take them into that violent land. The Chisos Basin was where Chief Rojo and his renegade Apaches were likely holed up. That was a country no white man cared to enter. If McCulloch had to make a wild stab in the dark, he would have figured that would be the best hiding spot for Harry Holland and his bunch of owlhoots. In fact, McCulloch would figure it was even money that's where Holland held court. The problem was . . . the basin was big and rugged with about as many likely hiding spots as there were coyotes and rattlesnakes in this part of the country.

As if waiting for his cue, a coyote bolted out of the brush and sprinted about fifty yards in front of the hearse and the two riders. The coyote never stopped running, though he quickly slowed into a trot when he became aware that the white men had no interest in him, although he kept glancing backward to make sure the men were not after him.

That was the only animal they saw. Not even buzzards circled, not at this time of day, not in this country, but one might say they had found plenty of dead animals — sometimes dead men — to keep them from flying. There was no need to circle over things waiting to die when a country this harsh, this brutal, this barren was filled with the dead.

Texans might not love the Big Bend, and God might not like it, and the Devil himself might not think it fitting, but for any animal that preyed on the dead to live, this damned place had to be something close to paradise.

He recognized Elephant Tusk, roughly a mile high in elevation, off to the west in the middle of the Chisos range, and they passed Glenn Spring, and followed the dry bed of some old stream or creek or perhaps just a sandy road to hell that would empty into the Rio Grande.

Upon reaching the river east of Mariscal Canyon, they kept their horses hobbled to keep them from drinking until they had cooled off, while they walked to the flowing water, and drank, splashing water over their faces, running wet fingers through their hair, bathing their necks with water, and looking across the border at the Sierra de San Vincente, before Keegan and Breen walked eastward and looked at the trail that led to the hot springs.

"How far would you say it is to the springs from here?" Breen called out to McCulloch, who was just now getting to his feet on his crutches.

"Nine miles," he said. "Ten maybe."

Keegan had walked a ways head, stopped, shook his head, and returned. "Still no trail to that hot water?"

"Not on our side of the river," McCulloch said. "You can swing southeast, skirt through the San Vincente range, pick up a trail that heads to San Vicente, ford the river there, then it's an easy skip or hop to the springs."

Breen whispered to Keegan, "Matt won't be skipping or hopping for some time."

"Aye," Keegan said softly in reply, "and that would cost us another day or two." He frowned.

"They'll give us extra time," Breen said, though his voice did not sound as convincing as his words.

"They bloody well better, or there will be hell to pay."

"That hearse won't get fifty yards down that pike," Breen said.

Staring back down the rocky landscape, Breen nodded. "We have the packsaddles. That's what we had planned."

"Even the best horse or best mule would likely break a leg or his bloody neck." Keegan swore, sighed, and shook his head. "If only we hadn't run into so much trouble. Dirty, greedy scum of the earth, looking for easy coin and risking the life of a sweet young gal." His hard eyes turned to the bounty hunter. "Breenie, laddie, ye've done a yeoman's job here, you and that hard-headed Texican, but I cannot let you risk any more hide or hair. I'll take the gold to

346

the springs meself. Ol' pal, ye'll need to get Matt to a doctor. Maybe you can make for that quicksilver-mining town due east of here, or keep going up the river to Presidio. It'll be an easier, if longer, trip back home for ye that way, but it'll get ye there. Alive and well if the Lord has his eye on ye." He extended his hand. "I've been honored to ride alongside with ye for the past year or two. A delight. More than ye'll ever know."

"Save it for your funeral." Breen ignored the extended hand and walked back to the hearse and the crippled Texas Ranger.

"How do you feel, Matt?" Breen asked when he reached the dusty, battered funeral carriage.

"How the hell do you think I feel?" Mc-Culloch answered. "Like a guy with a leg busted in two or three places who has been forced to travel halfway to hell on horseback at a high lope and in wagons that aren't fit to haul garbage. And if you want to count the shooting scrapes . . ."

Breen laughed. "Well, I think this is where we part company." He hooked a thumb toward Keegan behind him. "Sean and I'll get that gold to the ransom site. I'm thinking you can take that wagon and move upstream along the riverbank. Make it to Presidio. There ought to be a doctor there who can look over your leg, patch you up, get you all fixed up, and after that you can just ride back north to Purgatory City, taking it easy."

McCulloch stared. Breen waited. Keegan joined the two.

"You mean," McCulloch drawled, "you want me to trust the two of you, a bounty hunter who'd shoot his mama for a reward, and an Irish Yankee horse soldier who'd jump at the chance to drink twenty thousand dollars' worth of whiskey?" He rocked back and forth on his crutches, shaking his head the whole time. "You must think I busted my skull, not my lower left leg. I'm not addled, boys. I'm mad as hell and tired and pretty much at my wit's end, but I'm not stupid." He jutted his jaw out toward Keegan. "You brought me into this deal, and it's not like you gave me much of a chance to say no to you, you dumb Irish pig. So you're stuck with me." He tilted his head at Breen. "Just as you're stuck with this white-haired, heartless, money-grabbing man-killer."

Breen and Keegan both opened their mouths as if to argue, but McCulloch had not stopped and barely slowed down to provide either of them with an opening.

McCulloch kept going, still looking at

Breen. "Just ride in that hearse down the river, easy as pie, take a nice little trip to Presidio." His thumb hooked back toward the river. "Upstream. Do you know what's upstream of here, Jed? Have you ever heard of Santa Elena Canyon? The Rio Grande cuts through that gorge, and there are no banks at all. I've never seen that Grand Canyon that Powell cuss talks so much about, but I have seen this piece of hell, granite, and water, and you don't just take a wagon up that river."

He looked again at Keegan. "You're stuck with me. Both of you. And it's getting late in the day, we're already behind, there's a fair-to-middling chance they've already murdered that hostage, but we still have to do our best. Because we're Texans. And jackals or no, we have always done one thing pretty damned good. And that's keep our word."

Keegan turned and took a few steps back to the east. "That trail won't support the hearse," he said.

"I told you that some time ago," Mc-Culloch said.

"It'll be hell on horses, especially carrying that load," Keegan continued.

"We knew that before we pulled out of Purgatory City," McCulloch said.

Breen walked to the banks of the river and stared downstream.

"Could we ford the river here, cross downstream on the Mexican side?"

"Trail's no better south of the border than it is here," McCulloch said. "And if we got caught by Rurales on that side of the border . . ." He shook his head and spit.

"Or Yaqui Indians," Keegan added.

"Right." McCulloch nodded.

"Well . . ." Keegan shook his head and turned around. "How do you see us getting those two strongboxes to those springs?"

"We wait," McCulloch said.

"Wait?" Breen and Keegan exclaimed in unison.

The Ranger nodded, and he moved to what passed for shade, found a rock on the bank, let the limbs and leaves of a tree cool him, and he stuck his busted foot in the flowing, cold waters of the Rio Grande.

Keegan turned, cursed, but when he saw the horses, his shoulders slouched. "Aye." He sighed again and looked at Breen. "Matt is right, damn his smart brain. We can't keep these horses going. Let's water them. They've cooled off for now. Rest them an hour or so. Figure out a way to get to the springs."

Breen's head moved up and down. "And

pray Holland's men don't have a watch or a calendar."

As the first hour passed, McCulloch began thinking of another plan. His first one had been a long shot to begin with, but it would give him a chance to rest, and the horses certainly could not go farther without rest, grain, and water.

Yeah, he said as the second hour ended, it had been a gamble, and once again, Matt McCulloch had lost. He used his crutches to push himself to his feet and looked at Breen and Keegan.

"I guess we've rested the horses long enough," McCulloch said, and began hobbling his way back to that damned hearse.

"Ye have an idea, Matt?" Keegan said as he pulled on his hat and followed the gimp Ranger.

McCulloch started, "We'll have to —"

Then Breen, standing in the edge of the river and looking upstream, said, "What the hell is *that*?"

He palmed his Colt.

Chapter Thirty-Three

The knocking on the door came while Harry Holland was filling two glasses with Madeira. "Boss," the voice of his segundo came from behind the thick wood.

Sighing, Holland glanced at the bed and let his eyes do the talking. Virginia Bainbridge sighed and gave Holland the most unpleasant look, but she still managed to throw off the covers, toss the pillow aside, and grab the pillowcase off the headboard, which she held over her head. Wearing only a camisole and the pillowcase with the slits cut out so she could see, she crossed barefooted to the corner and slid down onto the floor, pulled up her knees, wrapped her arms around them, and began shivering and sobbing, broken up with the occasional, "Why . . . me? Oh, why me?"

Holland sipped from his glass, picked up the one he had poured for Virginia, and walked to the door. "Don't overplay your scene, darling," he whispered.

Virginia sniffed.

After setting one of the glasses on the top of the dresser next to the door, Holland slid back the bolt and pulled open the heavy door.

"Yeah?" he asked Fatty, and stepped back.

"Rojo's at the front gate," the steely-eyed graybeard said.

"I figured," Holland said.

"Oh, God, please kill me," Virginia moaned.

Fatty — who was leaner than a starving coyote — could not help but glance at the woman shivering in the corner.

"You want a turn at her?" Holland asked.

The gunman's head jerked back to his boss. "No, suh," he said with a heavy Southern accent, and Holland could read what his segundo was thinking: *I like a woman I can look at without cringing.*

Holland had to smile. *Keep right on thinking that, old man. And spread the word.*

"How many Apaches did the chief bring with him?" Holland asked.

"That we can see? Two. One on either side of him."

"How many you figure you can't see?"

"As many as he has able to ride, kill, pillage, torture, and scalp."

Holland's grin widened. "Did you put men up at the towers?"

"Yeah. Them bucks can see they'll get cut down if they try to attack us." He grinned. "Even injuns know what a Gatlin' gun'll do to a body."

"All right." Holland sipped from his glass, and tilted his head toward the dresser. "I poured some wine for our friendly Apache cutthroat. Take it downstairs. Open the gate, let Rojo and his two braves in, then close the gate, and have the boys stay up top, keeping an eye on things. Offer the glass of Madeira to Rojo. Tell him I'll be down in a minute." He looked down at Virginia. "You reckon Rojo and his bucks would like a pass at this wench? I'm getting sick of her."

Fatty frowned. "I don't think no white gal deserves that, boss." His tone was icy, deadly.

"Yeah." Holland killed his wine and tossed the empty glass on the bed. "And I wouldn't want to insult our guests by offering them something not fit for the trash heap. Not now, anyway." He pointed at the wine. "Take it, Fatty. Don't drink too much before you get back downstairs."

Fatty backed out with the glass of wine.

"And Fatty?"

The gunman turned.

"Make sure Rojo and his two pals are the only ones that get inside."

"Yeah, boss."

The door shut. Holland bolted it and grabbed the bottle while Virginia pulled off the pillowcase. Her eyes seemed to be hardening just like Fatty's.

"What if that piece of Alabama dung had taken you up on your offer?"

Holland extended his hand, pulled Virginia to her feet, and handed her the bottle.

"Damn," he said with a grin, "you are sinister but beautiful when you get riled."

She drank from the bottle.

"But not ladylike."

"What do you expect from someone not fit for a trash heap?"

He laughed. "I need to see what that Apache moron has to say. With luck, it's good news, and things will go just the way we planned."

"They damned well better go like we planned." She grabbed his glass off the bed and filled it with the Madeira. "And remember, I'm not some whore who drinks wine from a bottle, you pig."

"Like I say, darling, you're even more beautiful when you're madder than an Apache." He moved to the door, but checked the cylinder in his revolver before opening it. "If someone knocks, wail like a banshee and do your acting again." He pointed upstairs. "If someone comes down from the roof and tries to break in, put your pillowcase on." He nodded at the side table. "There's a Remington .44 in the drawer there, you know. Kill whoever comes in that way."

"Maybe I'll kill you when you come in the other way."

"Yeah." He opened the door. "And how would you be able to find your way back home? Remember, darling. We're going to Paris as soon as we play out this hand. Instead of Madeira, we'll be taking our baths in champagne with all that money your dear, sweet daddy's bringing us."

He stepped outside. "Bolt the door behind me. I'll give three hard raps when I'm back, count five, three more raps. Then you can let me in."

The door shut.

The wine had not been touched, not by Fatty, not by Chief Rojo or his two grim-faced warriors. Holland looked at the floor, frowned, and found the decanter of tequila. He splashed a couple of fingers into the glass, sipped, and walked to the Apache renegade, keeping the liquor in his left hand

and his right on the butt of his holstered pistol.

"Where's my money?" Holland asked.

Rojo smiled grimly. "Our money. That is what we agreed." For an Apache renegade, he spoke good English.

"I figured you had already taken your share," Holland lied. "Where's the money?"

"With the three white men."

"You didn't kill them?"

"They did not want to die."

"And you didn't get the money?"

"They did not want to give it up. They must want to give it to you."

"Hell." Holland killed the tequila and tossed the glass onto a leather-cushioned couch.

"You let three white men, one of them crippled, one of them drunk, and one of them worthless unless he has a Sharps in his hands, beat you."

"They did not beat us. They beat the white eyes who tried to take *our* money."

Holland frowned. The Apache explained that many of the white eyes who were supposed to help the men bringing the money had turned against that threesome. They had paid dearly for their choices.

"Where are the three . . . jackals?" Holland wanted to get another bracer of tequila, but he knew he needed to keep a clear head. The plan was simple or had seemed so easy when he and Virginia had concocted the scheme. They would fake her kidnapping and have her father bring the ransom money to the Big Bend. Alone. But an Army officer like that high-handed Newton Bainbridge could not lower himself to run some errand unbefitting an officer and a gentleman, so he had hired Purgatory City's lowest scum of the earth, those jackals — Breen, McCulloch, and Keegan — to do his dirty work.

Fine, Holland figured. The Apaches could just wipe out those three men. Holland and Virginia would have to figure out another way to put the devious girl's father six feet under. But then Holland got wise. A man like Bainbridge wouldn't be likely to give in, pay all that hard-stolen loot for even his only girl. Too bad Old Iron Britches hadn't had a son. He would have paid dearly for a boy. And a man like Bainbridge wouldn't trust Holland.

That thought irked Holland even more. He wouldn't trust Holland, but he would trust three low-down jackals with all that money. That was a hell of a thing. A hell of a thing. An insult to Harry Holland.

Which meant that Bainbridge would be

trailing the three men, hoping to get close enough to get his money back. Yeah, Bainbridge would not care for his daughter's safety. But money . . . money meant more than flesh and blood, when that flesh and blood came covered with a petticoat.

So it would still work to Holland's and Virginia's favor. The Apaches would kill the Jackals and Bainbridge and his riders. Then Holland would kill the Apaches — and his own men. And Holland and Virginia would ride off into the sunrise — heading east, to Paris, France — to live happily ever after — until Holland got sick of the hussy and found a way to kill Virginia, too.

"What of the Stern Blue Coat?" Holland asked, using the phrase the Apaches knew the miserable colonel by.

"He comes, too."

"With how many men?"

"His men are worthless, but are more than these fingers." He spread out the digits on both hands. "But he has two of the flesh-eating Indians with him."

"Tonkawas." Holland spit onto his rug.

Chief Rojo made no response, but said, "Good scouts and trackers."

"Yeah." Holland drew in a deep breath and let it go. A setback. That was all. A minor setback. He could still get his money and his freedom and that chateau in Paris.

"Why did you not kill the Jackals and take the money?"

Rojo gave the Apache version of a smile. "They fight good. And they bring money to you. White eyes money is very heavy. Too much trouble."

"All right." Holland had understood how lucky, and how good, Breen, Keegan, and McCulloch were. That's why he had given them instructions to make it to the hot springs on the Rio Grande. If they managed to make it that far, he had a crazy-as-a-loon river pirate as an ally, and he could have men waiting for the Jackals there. He already had that as a contingency plan. "Where are the jackals and *our* money?"

"On their way to the river. Maybe there by now."

"All right. We will still have our money — and you won't have to face the three Jackals again. I'll let my men take care of that trash myself. But I want you to kill Stern Blue Coat, the man-eating Tonks, and all his men. My men will take care of the Jackals. We will get the money and meet here. In two days."

Rojo nodded once.

"I need Stern Blue Coat dead."

"It can be done," Rojo said. "But what of

those jackals?"

"I'll have them exterminated," Holland said. He smiled and stepped back, a signal that the meeting was over, and that the three Apaches could leave the white-eyes fort in the middle of Rojo's land. Holland did not let his hand rise from the butt of his revolver until the Apaches had ridden through the gate and the heavy bars were back in place that would make it practically impossible for a herd of elephants to push that gate open.

Fatty followed Holland back into the meeting room after the visitors had ridden out of rifle range.

"Take half the men," Holland said, "to the hot springs. Bring a couple of wagons for the supplies that crazy greaser who thinks he's a pirate has brought. Then kill the three men delivering the ransom."

"A pleasure. We'll bring the money back to our shelter."

Shelter. What a joke. It kept Holland's men safe from the Apaches, but once they were beyond these walls, no white man's hair was safe. Rojo and his bucks would wipe them out if they made the slightest mistake. It had been a good bargain for a while, but now that the Army had declared the Big Bend no-man's-land, it was, indeed,

just that. No-man's-land. That was when
Harry Holland had figured it was time to
cut loose, to reinvent himself as a vintner in
France. To get out of Texas while the getting was good.

Years ago, Holland thought he was building a fortress. It turned out to be a prison
— a prison that could become a morgue. If
the Apaches had one brain, they could sur-
round the compound, starve and sweat
them out. But Apaches had this flaw that
was known as honor. They didn't fight that
way. They didn't fight like Harry Holland.

"Kill the three men," Holland said. "Let
the pirate be. He's with me." He didn't
think Rojo's red devils would harm the
crazed river man. Apaches held the insane
in high regard, or they were just scared of
crazy folks. "And bring that money back,
but keep it far, far ahead of the wagon
bringing us our nitro."

"All right." Fatty turned to leave.

"Fatty."

The gunman stopped. "You can't get out
of the Big Bend alive with just fifteen men.
Not carrying all that loot."

"I know, boss. Rojo would cut us down."

"That's right. But when Rojo shows up to
get his cut of the money." Holland raised
his glass of tequila. "We'll cut him down.

Split up the money. And get out . . . while the getting's good."

Chapter Thirty-Four

Sean Keegan slowly drew the Remington .44 from his holster, but the sight of the . . . whatever the hell it was . . . left him frozen, mouth open, thumb on the hammer of the revolver, but his brain could not send the message to his hand to cock the damned gun.

A pirate ship. A pirate ship sailing down the Rio Grande. He blinked. Surely, he was suffering sunstroke.

Yet there it was, rounding the bend, the black flag with the skull and crossbones flying in that West Texas wind that never dies down.

"I'll be damned." Matt McCulloch's Texas drawl sang out behind Keegan.

All right, the Irishman thought, reconsidering his diagnosis of sunstroke. And Jed Breen had his double-action pistol pointed at the floating Man of War. So they saw the pirate ship, too, or they were all characters in the weirdest dream Keegan had ever dreamt.

> So I gives ye fair warnin' afore we belay,
> Don't never take heed of what pretty
>   whores say.
> A bonnie good mate and a pirate too,
> A bonnie good ship and a rapscallion
>   crew!

If Keegan were seeing things, now his big ears were hearing the loudest, worst song he had heard — and for an old Army trooper, that was saying a great deal.

Suddenly the pirate captain, with a black scarf covering his head, seemed to notice the three landlubbers on the American side of the river.

"Shiver me damned wooden leg," he cried out, and began moving to the stern, the clump, clump, clump and the man's uneven gait assuring Keegan that this pirate had a wooden leg. Keegan wondered if the captain who flew the black flag was kin to the late Plimpton.

Then sanity and reason returned to Sean Keegan.

"Son of a . . ." He let the curse die in his throat, and the thumb pulled the Remington in his right hand to full cock. He raised the handgun and watched the . . . pirate ship.

"My Irish arse," Keegan whispered.

The one-legged thin man with black hair past his shoulders reached the tiller, and slowly steered the ramshackle raft to the shore.

"Pirate ship." Keegan shook his head.

It was a big raft, twenty feet in length and six or eight feet across, with a mast and a sail made up of stitched longjohns and saddle blankets and a purple shirt and what appeared to be muslin and Mexican denim. The wind happened to be blowing from the west, so the sail was speeding the boat with the current, but now it turned.

The bow slid into the sand, and the one-legged man moved back to the front of the boat.

"Pirate ship," Keegan repeated. The captain had no crew. Yet he bent down, calling out, "Secure the line and hold 'er fast till I come out." Still leaning down, his left hand brought up a length of stout rope, and he tossed it ashore.

A few of the horses snorted and stared, ears alert.

"Those mounts hobbled?" McCulloch asked quietly.

"Yeah," Breen said. "What the hell is . . . ?"

The pirate came up now, and in his hands

he held a blunderbuss, an old shotgun that had to be at least a hundred and fifty years old, a flintlock, maybe thirty inches in length with that flared barrel.

"Now," said the captain, bracing the old weapon against the purple sash across his waist. "Ye fiends with Her Majesty's Navy, what say he, do ye dare to try to board my ship, and do ye care to die or, worse, be captured? I'll have ye walk the plank and to Davy Jones's locker you will rest till eternity."

"Captain Long Juan, sir," McCulloch called out. "We've been waiting for you, but not to do you any harm. We'd like to sail a ways with you. On your ship."

"And how might ye know me name, you talk drink of water?"

"I chased you long enough, Captain Long Juan," McCulloch said. "Back when I wore the cinco pesos star of the Texas Rangers."

The massive barrel of the antiquated shotgun did not move, but the pirate captain's frown, tucked between a black mustache and long goatee, transformed into a smile. "A Ranger, say ye." He let out a belly laugh, but the blunderbuss did not move. And Keegan knew that any kind of load in that old weapon would do serious damage to Keegan and his two pards, not to mention the horses behind them. "Ye see ye have never stopped me. I rule the seven seas, or at least this patch of ocean between El Paso and Laredo."

"Indeed, Captain Long Juan," McCulloch said. "Let's talk. Boys, holster your irons. You don't have anything to worry about. Captain Long Juan Sacristán y Santo Seyjó is going to help us out."

"For a price, amigo," the pirate said, his accent shifting from something out of a Robert Louis Stevenson story to a cantina south of that river. "A good price. A price befitting the last — the only — pirate of the Rio Grande."

"Lower the guns," McCulloch said. "This is Captain Long Juan Sacristán y Santo Seyjó."

"If it's the Captain Long Juan Sacristán y Santo Seyjó I've read about," Breen whispered, "I'll keep my iron out till he's dead or gone."

"If he touches that trigger on that thunder gun," McCulloch said, "there won't be enough of all three of us to feed one ant."

Reluctantly, Breen slid the double-action Colt into his holster. Keegan lowered the hammer on his Remington and leathered his weapon. "Who the hell is Captain Long Juan Sacristán y Santo Seyjó?" he asked.

McCulloch smiled. "You wouldn't know it now, but for a while he was the terror of the border."

Keegan listened as he helped secure the . . . well, some might call it a *ship* . . . to the shore. McCulloch did the explaining while the captain, who now looked more pathetic than pirate-like and struggled with his wooden leg to find a spot in the shade.

Before the War Between the States, Juan Sacristán y Santo Seyjó had been a fisherman somewhere on the western coast of Mexico. He was a simple man, with no cares in the world, until some of Maximilian's boys murdered Juan Sacristán y Santo Seyjó's family, his wife, his parents, his two sons. And when Juan Sacristán y Santo Seyjó tried to stop them, they shot him in his leg, but the Austrian captain of the Army patrol ordered his men not to kill him. The captain had laughed and said, "Gangrene will do that for us. But maybe he can dig a grave for his loved ones. He won't have a ship to take him out to fish anymore." With a nod, the captain dispatched four of his men to scuttle the fisherman's boat.

That captain made a bad mistake. He should have slit the throat of Juan Sacristán y Santo Seyjó. Sure, Juan Sacristán y Santo

Seyjó lost his right leg, but when he could walk with the wooden leg, he set out for revenge. Benito Juarez did not want a man like Juan Sacristán y Santo Seyjó to fight with him for the freedom of Mexico, to drive out Maximilian, for he needed men who could ride fast, march fast, and he wanted soldiers, not sailors.

So Juan Sacristán y Santo Seyjó set out alone. The fourteen butchers who had ridden with that Austrian were soon dead. The captain was the last to die. By then one of Juarez's lieutenants had taken notice of the phantom now called Long Juan. Juan Sacristán y Santo Seyjó and the lieutenant talked, and after that Captain Long Juan Sacristán y Santo Seyjó was rafting down the Rio Grande.

The United States government officially did not support the Juarista rebellion, but for some reason, after the war had ended between North and South and Texas fell under Yankee Reconstruction rule, many U.S. Army patrols along the border lost crates of rifles and barrels of gunpowder. Which somehow wound up on the raft captained by Long Juan Sacristán y Santo Seyjó. And when Confederates tried to cross the river to join up to fight for Maximilian, who promised them cotton plantations and a free rein, more than a few wound up at the bottom of the river.

"Which," McCulloch said, "did not make Long Juan Sacristán y Santo Seyjó a popular man with those of us who wore the gray."

He wasn't too popular with the Mexican population in the northern part of the country, either. Juan Sacristán y Santo Seyjó was no longer the peaceful fisherman.

"He became a pirate," McCulloch said. "He flew under no flag. He set up ambushes against American soldiers, the state police. He organized raids on small ranches, even led a sack, they say, on a village near Del Rio. And that was just in Texas. Across the river, he hit Juaristas and Maximilian's forces. He plundered. He pillaged. He was, in every sense of the word, a pirate."

"Straight down to his wooden leg," Breen said with a slight chuckle.

Keegan stared at the thin man, seeing him move a whole lot easier than McCulloch was doing with his left leg wrapped up and likely looking real ugly underneath those pants and bandages.

"Men and boys soon joined him," Mc-Culloch continued. "Most of them were for Juárez, and by then you could see the writing on the wall for Maximilian. A number of the Texans and other Confederates who had fled Yankee rule grew tired of Maximilian's lies and treachery, or they just got homesick. Juan Sacristán y Santo Seyjó hit some of them as they tried to return home, too."

"And before you know it," Breen said, "Captain Long Juan Sacristán y Santo Seyjó had a price on his head."

McCulloch nodded. "In both countries."

So Maximilian was dead by the late 1860s, and peace returned — in small doses — to Mexico and southwestern Texas. Only a handful of "pirates" remained with Juan Sacristán y Santo Seyjó, and eventually Rurales, U.S. troops, and Texans killed most of those. When the Texas Rangers were formed in 1874, they chased Juan Sacristán y Santo Seyjó up and down the Rio Grande.

"It was more for fun," McCulloch said. "By then, that old pirate was just a shell of who, or what, he had been. We'd ride along our shore, whooping, hollering, firing pistols in the air. He'd cut loose with that blunderbuss and whatever weapons he had. We sunk his boat two or three times, but we always let him swim across the river — as long as he was swimming for the Mexican shore. Then we'd let him terrorize his own people for a while."

McCulloch sighed. "Can't say I'm proud

of it now. But I was young and foolish in those couple of years."

"I cannot believe I never heard of this rapscallion before," Keegan said.

"You're army," McCulloch said. "He's navy. I hear those kind never mixed well."

"Aye."

Breen sipped from his canteen. "But I thought Long Juan Sacristán y Santo Seyjó died years ago."

"Otherwise," Keegan said, "you'd have been after the price on his head?" He let out a loud Irish laugh.

"I don't know if there are any papers on him," McCulloch said. "At least not in Texas. Not anymore. He's become some fantasy, some figure, the kind parents tell their kids, 'Don't be a bad boy, or Captain Long Juan Sacristán y Santo Seyjó will get you.' "

"I can't believe he's still alive," Breen said.

"To tell you the truth," McCulloch said, "I figured him dead, too. But maybe a year ago, I read in a Laredo newspaper I happened to find that a saloon was broken into on a Sunday morning, and six kegs of Kentucky bourbon had been stolen. Then someone tells me that he was in Piedras Negras, across the border from Eagle Pass, and a gun store has been broken into. No weapons stolen, but plenty of powder and lead. In Del Rio, a butcher's store and a general store are robbed of salted pork and tins of sardines, flour, sugar, honey. Similar thing happens at a doctor's store in that little settlement near Seminole Canyon."

McCulloch shook his head, still staring as the pirate finished his chores. "Taken individually, just random thefts. Not enough to warrant the attention of a town marshal. But when you look at a map, all river towns, all heading upstream. Downstream's one thing. You're flowing with the current. But upstream . . . well . . . maybe if you had a sail, and maybe if you knew how to handle a boat like . . ."

"A bloody fisherman," Keegan said.

"There was another report in that Laredo newspaper," McCulloch said. "The writer of the piece thought it was dang funny, and said the town drunk saw a ship sailing away . . . north, up the river, not down it, and the writer laughed him off and suggested that perhaps the saloon was robbed by the ghost of Captain Long Juan Sacristán y Santo Seyjó."

CHAPTER THIRTY-FIVE

"How'd you know he'd be here?" Keegan asked.

McCulloch chuckled. "I didn't. But I read in the Purgatory City paper that a patrol out of Fort Spalding scouting in the Sierra Vieja near the river reported seeing a raft of some sort floating downstream. That and another small item about a couple of robberies — liquor from a saloon and food and ammunition from a trading post — at Quitman Crossing made me think that perhaps there was something to this new career of Captain Long Juan Sacristán y Santo Seyjó. There was also some missing military stores at Fort Murray on the river."

Keegan shook his head. "I never would have thought . . ."

"You should read the newspapers," Breen said, "instead of just labels on whiskey bottles."

Keegan chuckled. "Laddie, I don't even

read those."

Still staring at the river pirate, Breen shook his head. "It was still a long shot."

"Like I said, I didn't really expect to find that old one-legged reprobate here, but I did think riding our horses downstream would be easier than crossing to the hot springs by land."

"We're still behind schedule," Keegan said.

"I know." McCulloch nodded in agreement before jutting his jaw toward Sacristán y Santo Seyjó. "But it stands to reason that Harry Holland has to get supplies to his compound. The money they steal doesn't do them much good when there's no place to buy anything except at Dead Damn Fool's Station — and now we've put that out of business. He could send some of his boys to the settlements upstream, downstream, or in Old Mexico, but with wanted dodgers on all his men peppering walls in every town in this region, that posed danger. Burglary of a store or saloon or trading post is sure to make the owners of those establishments madder than a wet hen, but it's not likely to see a posse on the trail. Hell, they probably just chalk those crimes up to kids, misguided cowboys, or town drunks."

"And?" Keegan asked.

"And Holland is likely waiting on our ransom money." This time McCulloch pointed at the one-legged pirate. "And supplies to lay in."

Captain Long Juan Sacristán y Santo Seyjó turned away and raised his blunderbuss again. "Now, mateys, what is yer business with a pirate like me?"

"You're not deaf," McCulloch said. "You heard everything we've said."

"Aye," the crazed man said, "enough to know that I believe you're carrying all the plunder Blackbeard ever buried on some isle in the Gulf of Mexico."

The horses began pulling on their tethers, stamping their hobbled feet, but the river pirate did not look away from the three Jackals, who kept their eyes locked on Captain Long Juan Sacristán y Santo Seyjó.

"And you'd like all that plunder for yourself," McCulloch said.

The pirate let the wide barrel of the blunderbuss move slightly. "One touch of the trigger and it is all mine. The load this pal of mine is packing will send all three of you landlubbers to Davy Jones's locker."

"You'll be with us," McCulloch said. "There's a rattlesnake at your feet."

"Ha!" Sacristán y Santo Seyjó shook his head. "You think I would fall for —"

There are certain sounds in the desert, or practically anywhere in the United States, that are unmistakable. In Texas, the most certain sound is the blood-stopping whirl of a rattlesnake's warning, and that is what everyone heard.

That's what caused Captain Long Juan Sacristán y Santo Seyjó to spin on his peg leg and scream like a frightened schoolgirl. He lowered the barrel of the blunderbuss and touched the trigger. The explosion sent a fury of smoke and dust that swallowed the pirate and the rattlesnake.

Breen and Keegan already had their revolvers drawn and cocked, but through the smoke and dust they saw Captain Long Juan Sacristán y Santo Seyjó lying on his backside. Quickly, they holstered their revolvers and hurried to the bucking, stamping horses.

Using his crutches, McCulloch limped over to the stunned Mexican, who reached for the old shotgun, but stopped when McCulloch's shadow covered him. Then he tried for the sheathed broadsword, but by the time his hand grasped the hilt, McCulloch's Colt revolver was aiming at his head. The Mexican's right hand moved away from the weapon and reached for one of the golden hoops that dangled from his earlobes.

McCulloch looked at the massive hole in the desert floor, then faced Captain Long Juan Sacristán y Santo Seyjó again. "I don't think you have to worry about that rattlesnake anymore," McCulloch said.

"I didn't have to worry about him to begin with," Captain Long Juan Sacristán y Santo Seyjó said and spit into the dirt. "It would have sunk its fangs into kiln-dried willow wood." He patted the wooden leg stretched out before him, then interjected, *"¡Ay, caramba!"* He raised his eyes. "Kill me quick, gringo. And bury me at sea."

"I have a better plan," McCulloch said. By now, Breen and Keegan had rejoined him, having quieted the horses. "You get us to Harry Holland's rendezvous site. I'm guessing that's at the hot springs ten miles downstream."

"If I get you to that butcher, I'll be dead, same as you."

McCulloch shook his head. "I don't think so. He's expecting us." He nodded at the two strongboxes. "And Holland's also expecting that. Which you planned on taking for yourself."

The pirate accent disappeared. *"No comprende,"* the long-haired bandit said.

"Oh, you comprende real good, Capt'n,"

McCulloch said, "but if you play your cards right, some of what's in those heavy boxes could be yours. It'll just depend on how this hand plays out for all of us. And for starters . . ." McCulloch reached into his vest pocket and tossed a double eagle between the pirate's good leg and his artificial leg.

"That's all?" the pirate said.

"Hell." Breen threw in a half-eagle.

Keegan tossed down a nickel, and then he pulled the pirate to a standing position.

After Breen handed the empty blunderbuss to the pirate, Captain Long Juan Sacristán y Santo Seyjó walked to the strongboxes, shoved one with his good leg, then the other, and turned to the three Jackals.

"When do you have to be at the hot springs?" he asked.

"We're gonna be late," McCulloch said.

The pirate grinned. "So am I." He approached the three men, looked each one up and down, and then pressed the barrel of the blunderbuss into Keegan's chest and shoved him a little.

"What the . . ." Keegan began, but by then the barrel was in the Ranger's gut, and McCulloch felt the shove.

When the pirate turned to Breen, the bounty hunter grabbed the barrel with his left hand before it could jam his innards. "I weigh one hundred and seventy pounds." He smiled. "And that includes the Colt on my hip."

Nodding, Captain Long Juan Sacristán y Santo Seyjó stepped back. He pointed the barrel at McCulloch, then at Keegan. "You two," he said. "Just you two." The barrel of the old weapon then went to the strong-boxes. "And those, of course. That is all." He smiled at Breen. "You do not come. Not on my ship."

"And why not?" Breen demanded.

"For I am captain. And there is just so much weight my ship can carry. Those are my terms." He spun fast for a man with one leg, and stared hard at Keegan. "You will work the pole. If we need it." He licked a finger and held it above his head. "The wind blows for now, but in this country." He smiled. *"¿Quién sabe?"*

"Matt can't work any poles," Keegan barked back. "Not with his left leg busted to pieces."

"If I were only so lucky," the pirate said, and his fingers on his left hand dribbled a tune on his wooden leg. "That is why he goes instead of this white-haired man who . . ." He looked again at Breen. "What happened to your face, hands, and neck, gringo?" Without waiting for an answer, he turned again to McCulloch.

"What say you, Texas gringo?" the pirate demanded. "Is this a deal?"

"I'm not ramrodding this outfit," McCulloch said. "It's this landlubber who's in charge." His head tilted toward Keegan.

"Let's get 'er done," Keegan said, and he walked to the strongboxes. "Help me with these, Breenie, me lad. Then you'll wait for us here."

Breen grabbed one end of the first strongbox and Keegan the other. Both men grunted as they lifted the heavy box. "Where do we put it, capt'n?" Keegan called out.

"In the middle of the ship," the river pirate said, and he began reloading the blunderbuss.

"You're lucky," Keegan said to Breen. "You get to wait for us here while we risk hide and hair for glory." As they neared the docked raft, Keegan lowered his voice. "You know what you'll have to do?"

Breen nodded. "Find the nearest border town on the Mexican side and get good and drunk."

"Aye. And have two drinks on me."

Breen whispered. "Take the horses across the lava rocks and holes and rattlesnakes. Find my way to the hot springs I've never seen or heard of before."

"Keep the river near you, you won't get lost," Keegan said.

"I'm not worried about getting lost," Breen said. "It's the getting killed that troubles me a bit."

"You get killed," Keegan said, "it means we're pretty much done for, too."

"There's no way I can beat Captain Kidd's man-of-war to those springs," Breen said.

"Aye. We'll wait for you if we can. And if we can't, you'll have to follow our trail. We'll be going to find Miss Ginnie . . . if I'm guessing that Holland's bunch won't have the darling angel with them."

"They might," Breen said, but he could muster up no conviction in his voice.

"They might, but the way I figure Holland to operate, he'll want to kill us and take the money and then do the dirty deeds he and his ill lot . . . well . . . it's best not to think about such things."

They boarded the pirate's raft, and as they moved to the middle, near the mast, the craft began rocking. "Now I know why I never became a sailor," Keegan said.

"Don't get seasick," Breen chided.

"Hey, mateys!" Captain Long Juan Sacristán y Santo Seyjó shouted. "Don't put that box near that blanket. Don't even touch that blanket. Put it on the other side. For ballast."

The crazed old fool grinned. "And the next box goes starboard. Keep us from sinking or capsizing. The river is not always deep, but she is always deadly. Like me!" He laughed.

"He's deadly," Breen said, "but I don't know about deep."

Keegan just stared at the blanket, and Breen looked at it, too. It was heavy wool, gray, but it was on top of a multicolored plaid blanket, and there might have been another blanket underneath.

"It's covering something," Breen said.

"Aye, laddie. Rum would be my guess."

They lowered the strongbox on the port side of the mast, and left the ship for the second strongbox. Captain Long Juan Sacristán y Santo Seyjó was standing beside McCulloch, talking in a mix of border Spanish and border English.

Hefting the final container of ransom money, they moved back to the pirate's craft.

"The way that river's flowing and the wind's blowing, you'll beat me to the springs by maybe a full day," Breen said.

"Just watch for holes and watch for snakes. I'll be watching for that crazed fool's thunder gun."

Breen shook his head. "I wish you had joined the navy."

"Why?"

"Then you never would have met Colonel Bainbridge." They lowered the strongbox on the starboard side of the mast. "What's your plan?" Breen asked.

"Kill the men waiting at the springs to kill us, dispatch that pirate if we have to, follow the trail those vermin left back to Holland's stronghold, avoiding Chief Rojo's Apaches, and rescue sweet Ginnie. That should give you time to catch up with us to save our hides by killing the last of those vermin with that Big Fifty of yours."

"It's .45-70," Breen said. "Not .50 caliber." He let out a sigh. "Easy as pie," he whispered. "Your plan." He looked at the blankets again, curious as to what that crazy old pirate might be hiding.

"Get off my ship, mateys!" Captain Long Juan Sacristán y Santo Seyjó called out.

As he was captain of this ship, Keegan and Breen obeyed.

CHAPTER THIRTY-SIX

Bring the horses with you, McCulloch said. Let your horse pick his own path, McCulloch had coached. Those eyes of yours have to stay open, McCulloch warned, because if you break a leg or lose those horses, we'll all be dead. Keegan and I will stall for as long as we can, McCulloch had said.

Riding slowly, his left hand tightly gripping the lead rope that pulled those fine Bainbridge horses behind him, Jed Breen kept his eyes focused on the pockmarked ground of the rough trail, and now he whispered all those other things Matt McCulloch had tried to hammer through his brain.

" 'I don't know how long we'll be able to stall them, but it likely won't be long enough for you to reach us.' " Breen shook his head. " 'Well, Matt, let's say they don't kill you and Sean and Blackbeard's ghost over yonder.' "

" 'Yeah, Jed, let's say that.' " He couldn't shake that image of Matt McCulloch, his face hardening and eyes turning so savage. Breen could picture that toughnut whipping about a dozen men with his crutches.

" 'If they don't have that woman with you, you'll have to find Holland's hideout.' "

" 'That's where you'll find us, most likely.' " Matt McCulloch made everything sound simple.

" 'So how do I find you and Holland's hideout?' "

" 'You follow the damned bread crumbs Keegan and I'll leave for you, of course.' " That busted leg just made the Ranger/ horseman even ornerier. " 'You've trailed wanted men, savage desperados half your life, Jed. You can find a trail.' "

"And I say, 'In some country, but this isn't just any country.' And Matt says, 'Well, it's not like this was your idea, and it's not like it was mine, either. If you've got any complaints, take it up with the Yankee sergeant.' "

Breen laughed and thought about spitting, but decided he might need that moisture, even if he could still hear and sometimes see the bubbling, flowing Rio Grande. He wet his lips, twisted in the saddle, and turned back to make sure he still had the whole string of horses.

" 'Why do I have to bring all the horses?' I ask. Matt says, 'Because we don't know how many we'll need.' 'What about that pirate?' I ask, and Keegan chimes in, 'Have you ever seen a pirate horseback?' "

He wasn't exactly sure what Keegan had meant by that. The sun must have baked the Irishman's head, for he seemed to be as crazy as Captain Long Juan Sacristán y Santo Seyjó.

Breen removed his hat and wiped his forehead with his sleeve. The sun was behind him now and soon would be slipping behind the mountains to the west. Then he'd have to wait for the moon to rise, and moving through this field of holes, some small, many deep, in the dark, would really test his skills as a horseman.

"Horseman." Breen chuckled without humor and pulled the hat back on his head. His idea of a horseman was the liveryman who charged him two bits or a dollar, depending on the town and the stables, and had the horse ready when he came out in the morning, or afternoon, or evening. Oh, Breen could ride pretty well — but certainly not to the standards of a Texas Ranger or an Irish horse trooper.

He stopped for a drink from his canteen, though he would rather have had a good rye, or even a bad bourbon, and he drank, just two swallows, though the river lay just a few yards to the south. Securing the stopper, he returned the canteen strap to the horn. Then he heard the splashes.

The problem with this country, he realized, is that the river here was neither wide nor deep, and it was all too easy for Mexican bandits to come galloping across. Breen cursed his luck. He figured the four bandits had just been riding beyond the brush, probably for some peon's farm to raid or a cantina to cut the dust, and they had spotted him. Well, they had eyed the string of horses he carried. Of course, Breen did not have time to confirm his theory with the four bandits. He barely had time to let go of the lead rope and palm his Lightning .38.

His first shot took the fastest rider in the throat — which had to be the luckiest shot Breen figured he had made since he first learned how to shoot. His second round didn't come close to punching a hole into anything but air — but Breen could make an excuse for that. He was leaping out of the saddle at the time, and that was a good thing because one of the bandit's shots tore a hole through his hat.

Breen hit the rough ground hard, and fell back onto the hard rocks, seeing his horse and those he had been leading sprint off to the east. He had no chance to yell or curse, for he was too busy trying to stay alive. Of course, if by some miracle he made it out of this fix still among the living, Matt McCulloch would kill him for letting those horses get away. And if McCulloch were dead, Keegan would see that job done.

"Boys," Harry Holland said with a smile as he entered the cantina. He held two bottles of champagne in his hands. "I figure it's time to celebrate."

The men eyed him just briefly. Mostly, they stared at the bottles, which Holland set on the bar. They had already been opened, and the outlaws might have preferred rotgut liquor, but all of them wanted to know how champagne tasted. "Set 'em up, Joey," the outlaw leader said. "Because in a day or two, we'll be richer than the Almighty himself."

Joey and a thin, silver-headed Mexican brought out cups and glasses, and Holland went down the bar, filling each container till it overflowed, emptying both bottles, which he then flung into the fireplace, turned behind the bar, and fetched a bottle of tequila. This he held out to all of his men, except the three on guard duty. But he had already paid those men their bonus.

"A toast!" Holland said after pulling out the cork of the tequilla with his teeth, and spitting it onto the floor. "To Paris, France!"

They raised their champagne and drank. No one paid much attention to the toast. Paris, France, just as well could have been Paris, Texas, or Dead Damn Fool's Station. It was the novelty of the champagne that the men wanted to experience.

"It fizzes like a dynamite fuse!" Joey sniggered. "Don't it?"

Holland laughed as he swallowed a mouthful of the wretched liquor. "Drink it down, boys," he said. "Drink it down. More money than you've ever dreamed of will be coming here in a day or so."

He raised the rotgut bottle. The men polished off their champagne, and most of them stared and sniffed, not used to fine sparkling wine.

Holland set the rotgut bottle on the bar and slid it down to the Joey, who caught it.

"Maybe this is more to your liking, boys," he said. "Drink up. Enjoy the night. Now I've got to go upstairs and put that wench in her place . . . again."

■ ■ ■ ■

A bullet whined off the hardened lava in front of him, and Breen turned to the sound of the bullet. He saw the bandit with the crossed bandoliers, on a white stallion, triggering a big pistol. The next bullet clipped Breen's white hair, which was cut pretty close already. Breen aimed, but stopped short of pulling the trigger, for the stallion started rearing, and the rider's next shot went straight into the air as he grabbed a tighter hold on the reins to keep from being tossed.

Quickly, Breen whirled, found the rider with the tan sombrero. He controlled that survivalist urge to keep pulling the trigger, but Breen knew he had only four shots left. The Sharps was in the scabbard on his horse, wherever that horse was by now. Breen waited, calmed himself down, and thumbed back the hammer rather than just pulling the trigger on the double-action revolver. His patience and professionalism paid off. The bullet hit the man in the center of the chest, and down he went, and away went the horse, dragging the dead man behind him, over the rocks and brush, through the river, and across the

Mexican border.

Breen stood, seeing a boulder that might offer enough cover. But his foot slipped into one of the holes he had been watching for since leaving his partners and Captain Long Juan Sacristán y Santo Seyjó. Down he went, hard, splitting his chin, loosening a couple of molars, and bruising his knees. He pulled his foot free, rolled over, and tried to crawl to the rock.

The pressure of a barrel against the back of his neck stopped him, and Jed Breen knew he was about to become a corpse.

"Enrique!" the voice above him called out and fired off something in rapid Spanish that Breen guessed was directed at the rider who was trying to get his horse under control.

The horse soon stopped snorting, and Breen heard metal horseshoes on the rock. The rider said something. The man with the big rifle that had not moved from Breen's neck said something.

Breen understood part of the conversation.

"The horses, Manuel, they get away."

"We can catch them, Enrique. But first . . . vengeance." Maybe it wasn't vengeance. It could have been murder or this son of a strumpet or let's have some fun first. But the intention seemed clear. The barrel came off of Breen's neck, and the voice said, this time in English, "Roll over, my ghost-haired friend, but do not move your hands."

Breen obeyed.

By then, Enrique had dismounted and tethered his horse to a rock. Grinning, the Mexican bent over and took the Lightning without resistance from Breen. He studied the gun, hefting it, checking the trigger and hammer, aiming it across the river, nodding with satisfaction, and then shoved it into his waistband.

"How does it shoot, gringo?" Enrique asked.

"Ask your dead friends," Breen said.

Manuel laughed, and exchanged a rapid-fire but brief conversation with his surviving partner.

"Where do you take these horses?" Manuel asked.

"El Paso."

Both of the bandits laughed. "Gringo. You ride the wrong way."

"Not the wrong way," Breen said, for as long as he talked, he stayed alive. It would be dark soon. Not that Breen had much hope of living to see the sunset, and now he wished he had the gift of gab like Sean Keegan. "The *long* way." He stressed the long.

"El Paso. By way of Florida."

The bandits eyed one another.

"Take a ship from Tampa. Sail around the horn. Dock in San Francisco. Take the old Butterfield line. El Paso. There I am."

"No, gringo," Manuel said. "Here you are. And here you will be . . ."

Enrique finished the sentence in Spanish. Breen thought he caught the word for crow, and figured the bandit was saying here Jed Breen would lay until the crows picked his bones clean.

But Breen had a stone in his left hand. He wasn't that good with his left hand, but his right couldn't find anything big enough to hurt a beetle. He would hit Manuel in the head, roll over, and knock Enrique to the ground. Then he would have . . . not a chance in hell.

Still, he would die game.

CHAPTER THIRTY-SEVEN

For all his life, Sean Keegan had figured sailors lived the life of Riley. Just sit in a boat, let the wind fill the sails, and bask in the glory of sun, salt mist, and rum. Hell, sailors weren't a notch above foot soldiers.

Captain Long Juan Sacristán y Santo Seyjó, the laziest pirate Keegan had ever heard tell of, just rested at the front of this barely river-worthy raft, barking orders, telling Keegan to keep moving, or watch for the rocks on the port side, or starboard, whatever sides those were to an Irishman from County Cork who had spent most of his days on the backside of a U.S. Cavalry pony. Yet here he went, pushing a long pole into the rippling water till it hit bottom and then pushing hard. All the while he marched back and forth, steadily though, because it wouldn't take much more than a feather to turn this ship into either the *Monitor* or whatever that other ironclad had been called during the late War of the Rebellion.

Doesn't the wind push this thing with that ratty-looking sail? Keegan thought to himself, pulled up the long rod, and moved again, sinking the rod, pushing, keeping this damned little ship going.

Matt McCulloch rested. But Keegan had to concede that that tough-hided man needed some rest. He'd let his hand drag over the raft's side and come up and bathed his head with river water. And Captain Long Juan Sacristán y Santo Seyjó? He just kept barking orders. Man was a martinet. Maybe less than just a hair of that blue-coated miser who had helped drum Sean Keegan out of this man's army. That man sure wasn't any Nathan Bainbridge.

"You hear that?"

Keegan stopped. Matt McCulloch pushed himself up and looked off westward on the American side of the river. Captain Long Juan Sacristán y Santo Seyjó rose and moved back a ways, resting his left hand on the pole that kept up that flimsy sail and the flag of the dreaded pirate ship.

"Gunfire." Keegan's voice came as a whisper. He frowned.

"Where would you figure Jed would be right about now?" McCulloch asked.

Keegan frowned and decided to lie.

"Couldn't tell. Pulling a string of horses? In that rough land? He wouldn't be as far as you'd be. That's for damned sure."

A few more shots, then nothing but the water and the captain's peg leg tapping out a beat on the raft's leaky deck.

Another shot came faintly from Texas.

Keegan cursed.

"Mateys," Captain Long Juan Sacristán y Santo Seyjó said after a snigger. "Whatever plan you boys came up with, aye, well, me hopes is that you have another plan to fall back on."

"Apaches?" McCulloch asked. He picked up an empty tin of peaches that the pirate had given his crew for their dinner. He drank the last of the juice, and Keegan knew he was doing that just to do something. Something other than think about what might have just happened to Jed Breen.

"Nay," the pirate said. "Not Apaches. Too noisy."

Keegan feared the crazy old coot was right about that. Two of those shots had been fired quickly, from the same gun. Too soft to be from a rifle or shotgun, and too fast to have come from a pistol that you had to cock first before you could squeeze off a round. That kind of noise meant a double-action pistol. Like the .38 Colt Lightning

Breen favored.

"Could have been hunters after coyot' pelts," McCulloch said, just to offer some kind of hope. At length, he cursed, and threw the tin across the boat. The tin hit the blanket in the center of the boat, and that caused the pirate to curse up a storm.

"Watch what you do there!" Captain Long Juan Sacristán y Santo Seyjó bellowed after using about every curse a pirate, a blacksmith, a cowboy, and a horse-soldiering sergeant could use in a week. The old man hobbled over to the blanket — or whatever the blanket covered and, quite possibly, protected — grabbed the tin, and waved it in McCulloch's direction.

"Trash does not belong on my ship, sailor. Remember that." He pitched the empty peach tin into the river, which promptly dragged it to the shallow depths below. "And be careful around my blankets."

Turning, the pirate hobbled back to the front of the boat. "We shall pull to the shore around the next twist in this snaking stream," he said. "And wait out the night."

"You don't want to keep going to those springs?" Keegan asked.

"Not as black as the night gets here. Not if you want to live to see those hot springs, mateys." He grabbed his blunderbuss and moved to the bow, but looked back and stared in the direction of those gunshots.

"How much farther to the springs?" Keegan asked.

"We'll be there early in the morning," the ship's insane captain answered.

"Why not get there tonight? Be ready to greet the day and —"

"I can still have you walk the plank, mateys. Remember that."

A short while later, they were on the Texas shore, the pirate and Keegan tying ropes to keep the raft in place. On the shore, they got a fire going, using wood that would leave no trace of smoke, and quickly heated up coffee and soup. The fire went out when the darkness began, and Captain Long Juan Sacristán y Santo Seyjó moved back to the boat. He found a blanket, and rested beside the mound of blankets that covered the mystery of the ship.

"How about one of those blankets for us?" Keegan called out. "It will be cold in a few hours."

"You touch one of those blankets, matey," the crazed pirate said, "and you will feel the heat of rapier and lead shot."

Keegan sighed and swirled the dregs of coffee in his tin cup. He looked at Mc-Culloch. "Don't worry about Jed, Matt," he whispered. "That white-haired fool is like a cat. Nine lives. Hell, he's like ten cats. Ninety lives." He drank the rest of the coffee. "And he's only used up sixty or seventy of them."

Matt said, "Yeah. Maybe so." The Ranger raised his own cup to his lips but stopped.

Keegan felt his stomach turn over. Off in the darkness, on the Texas side, about where they had heard the gunfire earlier that day, came the horrifying scream of something like neither McCulloch nor Keegan had ever heard.

When the faint noise faded, Captain Long Juan Sacristán y Santo Seyjó let out a rough laugh. "Mateys, that is the sound of the Big Bend. And another reason we dare not travel till dawn breaks."

When it had happened, Jed Breen had not had time to think. Not at first. Things moved too quickly. Now that he had been captive, and especially now that it was dark, he had far too much time to think. He had told himself when the ambush started that, hell, he'd die like a man. Now he felt as though he might start blubbering at any minute. He had also told himself that he had never been much of a praying man, but for the past hours, when he had figured out

401

what was likely to happen to him and Manuel, he had been whispering nothing but prayers.

Not that his soul was worth saving. But nobody needed to die like that.

Enrique. He had been the lucky one. As Breen had rolled over and started to throw that stone in his left hand, Enrique had died and Breen had frozen — not sure of what had happened. One minute the Mexican bandit was just staring down at him. The next minute his eyes were gone. Replaced by feathered shafts. And two more hit him in each breast, and another in the center of his throat, right about at the Adam's apple.

And then Manuel was screaming and running, but he ran right into a bunch of copper-faced, black-headed men wearing little more than deerskin and headbands.

Apaches.

And just when Jed Breen's brain told him to stand up and run like hell, moccasins were pinning his arms to the ground, and two other grinning, mean-looking Indians were down on his legs, pinning him. Breen managed to swallow, and then managed to choke back his own screams. Hell, he figured, Manuel was screaming enough for the both of them now.

The Indians bound both men and dragged

them to a series of boulders. Dumped them on the ground and left them there. Two of the riders took off, and returned a short while later with the horses — the string and the one Jed Breen had been riding. One of them pointed off to the river. The leader stepped up and listened, then shook his head. Breen couldn't take his eyes off the leader, a man wearing a red coat — something that looked like it had been part of some Brit's uniform during the Revolution all those decades ago but likely had come from one of Maximilian's officers or some other Mexican government official.

His headband was red, too, probably silk, and he wore a garnet stone hanging over his bare chest tied with a piece of leather that had been dyed red.

Red. Spanish for red was *rojo.*

My God, Breen thought, *I'm a prisoner of Chief Rojo* — leader of the Apache renegades who had been holed up in the Big Bend.

And that's when Breen knew he was dead.

Only Breen wasn't dead. Not yet. And the flames the Apaches built kept growing higher, almost blinding him as the darkness thickened.

Manuel mumbled something in Spanish, kept calling out for Enrique and the two others Breen had killed. Then he must have realized that he was alone, except for Breen, and he cried out in anguish, then after a bit of peaceful silence, he called to Breen: "Amigo, they will not burn us at the stake, will they?"

Breen didn't answer, but that was exactly was he was thinking.

Turns out, being burned at the stake would not have been so bad.

Because before the moon rose, four of the Apaches came over to them. Breen whispered, "Well, Texas, this is good-bye." But the Indians picked up Manuel instead and carried the babbling man out of sight. Breen just looked into the blackness. He heard the Mexican bandit's pleas, and his prayers, and he figured from the noise that they had staked the killer out on that hard rock.

Some of the warriors started singing. Then Breen heard something that sounded like a shovel scraping across the rocks. That noise came from the flames. And Breen saw fire moving about waist high in the dark.

No. That's when he knew. A warrior was carrying a shovel full of hot coals from the fiery pit.

Manuel shrieked.

Then Breen felt something cool over him. Not wetness. Not a cloth. Just a presence. For a second, he thought it was Death, ready to take him away. But it was worse than death.

"*Tejano,*" a guttural voice said. "Do you know who I am?"

Breen swallowed. "Rojo." How he managed to say that, he wasn't sure.

"Sí. And I think you are one of those they call the Jackals."

"My name is Breen. Jed Breen."

"Answer me quick, Tejano, for your answer determines if you live or . . ."

That's when Manuel screamed.

"We dump coals into his thighs. Into the slits we have carved in his thighs. But that is just the beginning. Do you understand?"

Somehow, over those horrible wails of pain, Breen understood.

"I understand," he said, and each syllable hurt like hell.

"Bueno. Good. Do not lie. Are you one of those known as the Jackals?"

"Yes."

"We do his arms now," Rojo said above the shrieks. "Then his groin. And his belly — if he is still breathing. Most do not breathe after his belly has been burned."

Breen tried to swallow down the bile, but couldn't.

"I have need of a jackal, Jackal," Rojo said. "And I think you have need of the Apache.

I have had a truce with an invader in my country. I no like this invader. But you do not like this invader, either. So you help Apache, and I let you live. But if you ever return to my country, I will kill you and your two Jackal friends."

Breen tried to comprehend what was being said.

"Your next answer also means you live, you die. Do we have a . . . truce?"

Manuel's final scream drowned out Breen's answer.

CHAPTER THIRTY-EIGHT

When Keegan felt the cold hardness against his neck, he came full awake. His right arm came up in a flash — not encumbered by any blanket since that damned miser of a pirate had refused to allow him to borrow one from his raft. His knuckles grazed the side of his neck, and his forearm, just below the wrist, caught whatever it was that had brought him out of a lousy night of sleep.

Whatever it was against his neck, it was hard as iron, and the pain shot down to Keegan's fingertips and up to his shoulder. He didn't stop, though, just kept the arm moving, and the resistance vanished. Whatever had awaked Keegan was human. He knew that much. Even though as his eyes opened, he saw nothing but an inky blackness salted with flickering stars. But he heard the yelp of a man surprised. Then a thud. And a loud "damn."

By that time, Keegan had brought himself

up, used the right hand to boost him toward his attacker. His left hand found a stone and raised it above his head, as the former soldier kept moving. To his knees in an instant, his hearing made out the sound of his attacker. Keegan lurched forward, found the assailant's throat, and brought his left hand high above his head, ready to bring that stone down hard and drive it through this man's face.

"Keegan!"

He stopped, drew in a deep breath, and managed to recognize Matt McCulloch's voice. But that voice came from behind Keegan.

Staring down, he let his eyes adjust to the darkness, let the stars reveal his assailant, which Matt McCulloch also did.

"Our captain's just waking you up, pard."

Captain Long Juan Sacristán y Santo Seyjó growled. Keegan let his left arm come down, and dropped the stone beside the pirate's blunderbuss. After rising to his feet, Keegan bent down and offered his hand. The Mexican river bandit took it, and Keegan pulled the captain to his one foot and one peg leg. Then Keegan felt the pain just below his wrist, and he rubbed it.

"You ought to know better than to wake a man up that way," Keegan said.

Captain Long Juan Sacristán y Santo Seyjó cursed in Spanish, managed to pick up his blunderbuss, at which point Keegan found his revolver's butt and waited. He didn't like crazy people. Well, he didn't like most people, but the insane bothered Keegan even more, especially the criminally insane.

"I could have you run through, drawn and quartered, and sunk into the depths of the seas with stones in your belly, sailor," the captain said.

"I told you to call out his name softly," Matt McCulloch said calmly.

"Nay," the pirate said, "he could not have heard me, snoring, stiff as a battering ram he was."

"I don't snore." Keegan stopped rubbing his wrist. You were trained as a soldier not to snore in enemy country. Apaches, Comanches, and Kiowas had been known to sneak into a camp, called by a loud snore, and slit the man's throat, take his scalp, and leave him to greet the other soldiers on patrol — just for the fun of it. To let the white men realize just how easy they were to kill. And maybe keep them awake so long that when it came time to fight, the white men would be worthless in battle.

No one argued, and Keegan looked

around. No campfire. That meant no breakfast. He detested cold camps, but the pirate
was offering him a jug that he reached down
to pick up. And McCulloch hobbled over
with a piece of jerky extended in his right
hand. Peace offerings. Or leading the lamb
to slaughter.

"I thought we were shoving off at first
light," Keegan said.

"We are," McCulloch said and found
another piece of jerky after Keegan accepted
his breakfast.

"Hell." Keegan lifted the jug and stared at
the stars and moon. "It's four in the morn,
by my reckoning."

"Aye," Captain Long Juan Sacristán y
Santo Seyjó said. "We will be sailing at first
light. But you . . ." Now the crazed fool
sniggered. "You must leave now."

The rum burned Keegan's throat as he
lowered the jug, which the pirate snatched
away quickly.

"You remember what we talked about,"
McCulloch said.

"I remember," Keegan said. "And you
likely recollect that I said that was a damned
fool idea."

"This whole plan has been a damned fool
idea," McCulloch said.

Keegan bristled. He wanted another rum

wakeup, but damned if he'd grovel to a Mexican who thought he was Blackbeard's ghost.

"You want me to run in the darkness, somehow not break my neck or leg, get into position so that when you" — he gestured toward McCulloch, then followed that by nodding at the river pirate — "and this old hoss that has been chewing on loco weed for twenty years or so float downstream to the landing at the hot springs. If and when those Holland boys open fire, I'll surprise them by sending some to hell."

"Aye."

McCulloch sipped from his canteen and grinned over the woolen covering.

"Matt," Keegan again pleaded as he had after sunset the previous evening, "what is there to keep this mad rapscallion from shoving you into the river, after giving you the working end of his blunderbuss, and sailing off to Laredo or whatever port he chooses? Leaving me afoot in this godforsaken country?"

"Well, he might be able to leave you afoot, but he'd find it tough to give me a bath when it's not Saturday," McCulloch said.

"For all I know, it is Saturday," Keegan said.

"Sean." Now Keegan frowned, because he

411

hated it when that Ranger started calling him by his first name. "I can't run those miles. Hell, by the time this is all over, I might not even be able to walk. But we need something to surprise those boys who'll be waiting at the landing."

"They'll want to make sure you've got the ransom," Keegan argued.

McCulloch nodded. "Which'll give you more time."

"What if it ain't like we've figured? What if all we have to do is turn those boxes over and we ride off with Ginnie?"

"You know damned well that's not what'll happen. For all we know, they've already killed that girl." Keegan waited. "If Jed hadn't gotten himself killed . . ."

There it was. Turning over that last card. Keegan bent over and grabbed his Springfield, then pulled on his hat and picked up a canteen. He looked at the single-shot carbine, and raised his head and found Mc-Culloch.

"You any good with a Springfield?" Keegan asked.

The horseman nodded, and hobbled back to his bedroll. When he returned, he carried the Winchester.

"You any good with a fast-shooting gun?" McCulloch asked.

"Army didn't care much for repeaters, though a passel of officers had 'em handy. Some quartermaster must have thought we'd spread lead, not aim before we shot, which, hell, most of us would've."

"More than likely a general thought that, or the Secretary of War," McCulloch said, and smiled, "but the Rangers thought the same . . . for a while."

"Winchester will be handier for what we're planning in my hands," Keegan said. "Don't you think?"

"I wasn't going to suggest it," McCulloch said, "but it crossed my mind."

They tossed the long guns at that instant, catching their replacement carbines as though they had been practicing the move for days. The Winchester felt like a toy in Keegan's hand, but at least it would be lighter when he started running.

"Bueno," the Mexican lunatic said. "Now go. Run. *Vamanos.* The sun will be here and you will still be chattering like an old Tejano woman."

And that soured Keegan's mood again. He looked at Captain Long Juan Sacristán y Santo Seyjó and felt those doubts, the craziness of this plan, and faced McCulloch once more. "I'm supposed to trust this . . . pirate?"

Out of the corner of his eye, Keegan saw Captain Long Juan Sacristán y Santo Seyjó bow. "Gringo," the pirate said, and Keegan turned to face the damned fool. "I give you my word of honor. We are no longer captain and mates. We are partners. My word, señor." He bowed.

But Keegan could be a hard man to move. "Your word? I'm supposed to take the word of a riverboat pirate?"

Captain Long Juan Sacristán y Santo Seyjó gave a smile like none Keegan had seen. "I give you my word," the pirate repeated, "and the soul of Lucia Maria, my wife. On the souls of, *mí madre,* Mencía Constanza, and on the soul of *mí padre,* Antón González. And I give you my word, mí amigo, on the souls of my sons, Mateo y Javier." His right hand raised, his head bowed, and he made the sign of the cross.

Keegan could not look into the pirate's face when the captain lifted his head. Instead, he turned and saw McCulloch, whose head remained bowed, probably because McCulloch kept thinking about his own butchered family. Of course, that horrendous massacre had not driven Matt McCulloch insane. Well . . . Keegan considered another line of thought. Maybe it had. Just a different kind of madness. A hardness. A hole where a heart had been.

"Hell," Keegan said. "I'm burning daylight." And he started sprinting into the night, running to the banks of the Rio Grande, and moving east.

As he ran, Keegan remembered. He could hear the shouts of Newton S. Bainbridge, and others, as they charged against Rebel forces. Infantry.

"Follow me, boys." ". . . Follow us." ". . . Hurrah. Hurrah. For the Union!" ". . . Give them hell! And give us Glory!" ". . . Follow me, boys!" ". . . The Union forever!"

He kept hearing the words, the words spoken by that brave soldier. And hearing those words, spoken by the gallant and grand Newton S. Bainbridge, made Keegan's legs feel young again. They made his lungs feel like this was just a stroll from the Keegan farm to St. Patrick's Cathedral in Skibbereen or Youghal, where the Blackwater dumped into the sea. He remembered the words the newly promoted colonel told Keegan after returning the stripes of a sergeant to that poor, wounded soldier who knew nothing about war and soldiering until he had seen Newton S. Bainbridge, as grand a man, a fine as hero since Lugh and Manannán mac Lir.

"You saved my life."

"Sergeant, your life was worth saving."

Newton S. Bainbridge, a grand man, gallant soldier, who had never gotten promoted to general during the late war, then was shuffled off to the remotest region of Texas in the regular cavalry, and finally forced into retirement, forgotten. Keegan had never had a chance to repay that debt he owed the colonel. He had never saved Colonel Bainbridge's life — but if he could only save Ginnie's life . . . Now, Keegan turned away from the river's edge, moving through the brambles until he reached the rough, hard lava rock. But the sky began to gray and he could see his way.

He ran. He stopped, drank water from the canteen, shifted the Winchester to another hand, walked, breathed, and started running again, never going too fast, just keeping the right pace.

He had paused for breath and water again when he heard the bubbling of the outer springs. Keegan recalled that time, drunker than a skunk, he and old Titus Bedwell had spent two whole dollars apiece to try this Turkish bath. Damnedest bath he had ever taken, Bedwell said later, God bless that fine soldier's soul. But right now, as sore as Keegan was from that hell of a journey, he sure felt like stripping off his stinking clothes and slipping into one of those holes of hot water.

The canteen raised to his lips as though by automatic response. Keegan didn't even remember thinking that he was thirsty, and he wasn't exactly sure how he thumbed the stopper out before the cool water cascaded over his tongue and down this throat.

Sometimes water could be as reviving as Irish whiskey.

Then he heard the horses ahead of him. He also heard a spur jingle behind him.

CHAPTER THIRTY-NINE

Leaning against the mast, McCulloch saw the black-hatted man with his boots in the Rio Grande turn and see them sailing toward the landing for the hot springs. The fellow had two guns on his hips, and he seemed shocked to see what Captain Long Juan Sacristán y Santo Seyjó called a pirate ship. Must be one of Harry Holland's new men, McCulloch figured, as the average-sized man hurried out of the water and moved inland toward the springs.

"We'll be landing here," the captain said, and started to move the rudder.

"No," McCulloch said. "Go down farther, to the edge of the springs."

The dark-skinned man turned, his eyes narrowing. "Since when did ye become captain of my ship, matey?"

McCulloch's head tilted forward. "Sun's coming up," he said. "We'll get there first, and when they reach us, the sun will be shining in their eyes, not ours."

The pirate's eyes became slits, then one winked, and the crazed old survivor grinned. "Aye. Ye'll be me first mate if you keep your noggin working that way." He turned around, corrected his steering, and the raft moved to the center of the narrow river.

Six, maybe seven, men were coming to the riverbank when the raft shot by them. A lean, leathery man shouted in a Southern accent: "Ya danged fool. Where in Sam Hill is you a-goin'?"

"A new landing!" the pirate said. "This place be watched by Rurales and bandits!"

One of the men jacked the lever of his Winchester, but the Southern busman used his left hand to lower the barrel. "Don't be a gol-derned fool."

"But Fatty!" the rifleman said. "It's a double-cross."

"To the horses!" Fatty shouted. And the men left McCulloch's view.

"Matey," the captain said, "ye'll need to be fast on those wooden crutches of yourn, and I shall need to move faster with me wooden leg when we weigh our anchor."

McCulloch drew a backup pistol and checked the cylinder. "Horses will just slow them down," he said, rolling the cylinder across his forearm with the loading gate open. "The terrain here is worse, and the bubbling springs will make the horses even more nervous."

"Aye," the pirate said, "but we won't have much time to get ready."

"We'll have just enough time."

"They outnumber us two to one."

"More than that," McCulloch said, snapped the loading gate shut, and shoved the pistol into his waistband. "That wasn't all of the boys." He looked at the blankets that covered Captain Long Juan Sacristán y Santo Seyjó's precious cargo. "Wonder why they didn't cut loose on us. They could have cut us down — tried to anyhow — and caught the raft before we got too far."

"We surprised 'em, matey. They be land-lubbers, and we are pirates of the seven seas."

"Yeah," McCulloch said. "And I got a notion as to how we might surprise them again."

"You mean that mad-dog Irishman?"

"Partly. But I got another plan, too."

Keegan's left forearm pulled tightly against the throat of the gunfighter, smashing down to cut off any scream the man could yell out as he rammed the knife deep into the man's back, twisted the blade, and felt the

420

killer shudder, empty his bladder and bowels, and die without a word. Slowly, quietly, Keegan lowered the corpse to the hard ground near the bubbling spring.

He withdrew the blade, wiped the blood off the Damascus steel on the dead man's trousers, and slid the knife into its sheath.

That makes two, Keegan mouthed silently, drew the corpse's big Schofield from the holster, and shoved that into his waistband. The first man he had killed before daybreak, letting the fool with the loud spurs with jingle bobs come up to his left. Keegan had exploded upward, driving the man to the ground, and holding his head in the hot water, drowning him in the springs most people, Mexican, white, and Indian, came to for their healing powers. He had shoved the rest of the man's body into the water, figuring if he were discovered before the real party started, his cohorts might think he had slipped into the spring in the dark, hit his head, drowned a fool's death. But he had not disposed of the body until he had taken the man's rifle, a Spencer.

Now he had his Remington, a Schofield, another backup pistol, McCulloch's Winchester, and that Spencer repeater. That should give him enough lead to whittle down Holland's men.

He hoped.

Beyond the rocks where he hid, he spotted the horses tethered to brush, saddled, not hobbled, ready to ride. He couldn't count the number of men, but he could figure out how many horses were here. Eleven saddle mounts. But three wagons. And the wagons were still hitched to mules. All right. So that meant at least fourteen men. Maybe seventeen, if two men rode in each wagon. And if the wagons carried more men? Hell, Holland was said to have thirty men with him. A thin, wiry, mean-looking cuss stood where a handful of men played early-morning poker. That's when Keegan heard the splashing of a horse riding in the shallow water of the river.

Four other card players rose, drawing their guns, but the leathery gent waved those guns to be leathered. "Easy, boys," he said in a Southern accent. "It's Raymond."

And Raymond, a puny man with a big Texas hat, rode a pinto pony into the camp, swinging down out of the saddle before the horse had completely stopped, and gesturing upstream. "That loco pirate is sailing down here. Should be here shortly."

Twelve horses. Keegan recalculated his arithmetic. "Maybe fifteen men. Or more. Minus two."

"All right," the Southern-talking leader said. He called out some names and pointed downstream, and several men gathered their repeating guns and disappeared into the brush. Then he looked into the general direction, but instead of shouting orders, he cupped his hand and made several turkey calls. A signal. But to how many men? Two of them, Keegan knew, wouldn't be hearing any of those gobbles.

"Rest of ya boys," the man said, "follow me. Except you Milt. Wait over yonder in the brush."

Six men followed the lean bit of Southern trash and disappeared as the terrain dipped toward the river.

He looked east, saw how the sun, nothing more than a big white, hot, blinding globe, was rising. The men who had found cover beyond the landing in that rough country would be hard to see. But Keegan figured he could pick off the men by the landing.

Slowly, to keep the metal clicks quiet, he eared back the hammer of the Winchester. The Spencer leaned against the rock.

From Keegan's makeshift redoubt, he couldn't see the river or the landing, just the rising desert on the Mexican side of the boundary. He wet his lips, waiting patiently, while keeping one eye open for someone else who might be on this side of the camp.

Suddenly, the black flag of the pirate flashed by. Keegan saw that much, and part of the makeshift sail. The wind and the current had that raft of a ship moving surprisingly fast. It hadn't felt like they were moving at that speed while Keegan had been serving as one of Captain Long Juan Sacristán y Santo Seyjó's sailors.

The Southern accent cried out: "Ya danged fool. Where in Sam Hill is you a-goin'?"

"A new landing!" That was the insane Mexican pirate's voice. "This place be watched by Rurales and bandits!"

No, Keegan knew. That wasn't true. The only bandits watching this place were Harry Holland's boys. Rurales kept their attention on the regular crossings, since only a foot trail led from the Mexican side to the springs, and few bandits believed in soaking in hot water when tequila was available to cure their ills.

Some argument ensued between Holland's killers, but those came too fast, practically on top of each other, for Keegan to make out the words.

It didn't matter, though. "To the horses!" Keegan heard that just fine, and those seven men suddenly appeared running for the saddled horses.

"Ross! You others!" The Southern leader shouted, looking at the east. "Take off east to the edge of the springs! They're moving that way!"

Keegan thought about cutting loose with the repeating rifle, but then he guessed why the pirate and McCulloch had not landed here. The sun. That damned sun.

Keegan's smile widened when the leathery leader turned west and shouted, "Klink! Masterson! Pinto! Come on. Now!"

By then the men were gathering reins to their mounts, pulling them away from the line. Horses whickered, reared. Keegan wet his lips and watched a man in a plaid shirt emerge about forty feet closer to the river. The man wore moccasins and now tugged on his hat as he hurried to join his companions as they tried to mount their horses.

That Southerner had already mounted his bay. He whirled the horse around, looking right over Keegan's rock, and shouted. "Masterson! Klink! Get the lead out of your behinds, boy!" No response.

Keegan smiled. "Klink, you damned Hun! Masterson. Move, damn you, move!"

Dead men don't answer, Southern boy, Keegan thought.

That fellow couldn't wait. One man bolted

his horse off the sandy camp and Keegan saw him galloping about twenty yards before the horse screamed, and the rider went sailing and landed out of Keegan's view.

"Easy!" the Southerner shouted. "Damn it all to hell!"

Then he was riding, but not at a gallop, and the other men on horseback slowed their mounts, too.

About five men were still trying to get their horses ready when someone — not the Southerner — called back. "Joey. Leave those horses. Come afoot. This land is hell."

Keegan watched the men — those who had managed to get mounted — swing down. Their horses were secured back to the picket rope, and they started. But one of the men stopped. "Joey," he said, and pushed out his right hand. "You best stay here. Wait for Klink and Masterson. And keep an eye on things in case this is some kind of double cross."

And there came Joey, pouting like a schoolboy, kicking a stone and walking right toward Keegan. He kept yelling, "Klink. Hurry up, damn you. Masterson! What's keeping you turds?"

That was a problem. Keegan didn't want to shoot the sentry, give away his location. But he couldn't very well stand up and get shot. Lot of good that would do Matt Mc-Culloch and that river-bound madman.

"Klink!" The outlaw swore. He had to be on the other side of the big rock. "Masterson!" Another string of curses followed.

That's when Keegan smiled. He moved his right hand away from the Winchester and called out in a feeble voice, "Jo-ey . . ."

No response.

"Jo-ey."

"Masterson?"

"Jo-ey . . . help . . . meeeee."

"Hell's bells." A stone kicked, a piece of driftwood crunched, and Joey rushed around the rock. He gasped when he saw that gleeful expression on Keegan's face, and reached for his belted six-shooter. His right hand gripped the hogleg's butt, drew it partly out of the leather, then slammed the revolver back into its place. That hand came up along with his left hand. Both gripped the handle of Keegan's knife, which stuck out just below Joey's rib cage.

He staggered back, groaned, and his face, reddened from all that shouting, lost its color. Keegan was standing by then, and he put his left hand on the bandit's shoulder.

"Laddie," he whispered, "let me help you with that." He jerked the blade out. Joey gasped in pain, and his eyes widened as

Keegan sliced the blade across Joey's throat and pushed him to the ground.

"Ye'll be seeing Masterson and Klink directly, boy," Keegan said, and picked up the Winchester and the Spencer. Briefly, he considered taking Joel's Colt from its holster, but decided too much iron would just slow him down.

He ran across the landing camp, past the picketed horses, and onto the rough land of rocks and hot springs.

CHAPTER FORTY

When the raft struck the weedy bank, Mc-Culloch lunged off the wobbling craft. The crutches jarred his armpits, the jolt sent razors carving up and down the bones in his foot and lower left leg, and it took every ounce of strength and luck to keep from falling flat on his face, but he managed to straighten and suck in a deep breath. His head raised and he exhaled.

"Matey," the crazy pirate said. "Help me secure —"

"You do it yourself, skipper," McCulloch said, and started hobbling up the bank, through the brush — there was no real landing at this point — then stopped when he heard Captain Long Juan Sacristán y Santo Seyjó's savage curse.

"Ye will feel the taste of lead that will rip you to pieces, my friend," the pirate captain said after his lengthy and bilingual curses.

McCulloch turned and waved away the

gnats and flies that buzzed around his face.

"With that blunderbuss?" McCulloch laughed. "It's on the bottom of the river, twenty yards upstream."

The pirate spun, looked on the deck, then hobbled back onto his ship, looking behind the boxes, and then toward the blanket-covered cargo.

"If you want to get out of this fix alive," McCulloch said. "We might have use of what you've got bundled up there."

"Argghh!" Captain Long Juan Sacristán y Santo Seyjó said.

McCulloch laughed again and shoved his way through the thick grass and weeds. "It took you a long time to say that, Capt'n, sir."

A blunderbuss would be useless in a fight like this, McCulloch told himself. That one-legged old fool would have time for one shot, then the Holland men would cut him down before Captain Long Juan Sacristán y Santo Seyjó could reload. McCulloch just hoped he had guessed right about what the pirate was transporting underneath those thick woolen blankets.

The crutches carried him to the springs, about six of them here close together. He wondered if that hot mineral water would soothe the pain in his left leg. Hell, the pain in his whole body after these past several numbing, backbreaking, butt-bruising days.

He looked east, saw the sun, and found the perfect spot, then he turned, leaned on the crutches, and waited.

From the top of the ridge, Breen looked down through the scope of his Sharps. It was cooler up here, but when the sun crept higher, it wouldn't be cool for long.

"Do you see them?" Chief Rojo asked. The Apache crouched over Breen's left shoulder. Breen lay flat on his belly. Finally, he saw one of the men. Indian. No horse, but the Indian wore white-man britches and white-man boots. With Army spurs. Probably an old scout. And if he wore spurs, that meant he had a horse. And if he wasn't riding a horse, that meant there was someone with him, keeping his horse nearby.

"There's one," Breen whispered. "Ten o'clock." He closed his eyes and let out a sigh. Like an Indian knew how to . . .

"I have seen what your kind need to tell the time," he said. "And I knew where he is already."

"Yeah." Breen shrugged. "But there's another one with him."

Rojo grunted. "You are not the fool white man I took you for."

"I'm not altogether certain about that." Breen looked back to the southwest, biting his lower lip, trying to figure out where the other scout would be.

He shook his head in admiration. Rojo had seen the scout from up here with his bare eyes, and Rojo was a good twenty years older than Breen. Jed Breen had needed a fancy telescopic sight to find that Indian.

"There he is." Breen said after another two minutes of scanning through the telescope. "That clump of ocotillo between here and the river." He used his Sharps to point in the direction.

"Good." Rojo rose. "Could you kill them?"

Breen pushed himself to a seated position. There were some men worse than jackals, some men who would shoot an Indian dead without a call or a chance just because they were Indian. Breen wouldn't even do that to the worst killer on the frontier. He'd give the man — any man — a chance. Just not much of one.

"You want me to kill an Apache for following you?"

Rojo smiled, and raised two fingers between his nose, the tips pointing to those dark black eyes. "I see better than you. Those two men are not Apaches."

Breen looked back, not through the telescope on the Sharps, but with his own eyes, not bad at all, and now that he knew where the two trackers were, he spotted the first one quickly. It wasn't a Comanche, Breen figured, and probably not Kiowa. He didn't know enough about the Yaqui.

"Tonkawa," Rojo said. "They eat the flesh of those they kill." The chief spit and the wind carried it away. "I would eat a fish before I would eat any man."

"Tonks." Breen nodded. The Army had used some of those as scouts. He had seen a few around Fort Spalding, but never paid that much attention to them. Yet he had heard those stories about how they liked to eat the flesh of those enemies they killed.

"Maybe," Breen said, "they're working for scalp-hunters. How far back is that party they're working for?"

"Three miles. They stink up my country."

Again Breen looked at the first Indian, then the second. Long range. Cold-blooded murder. He shook his head. "Chief, I have no quarrel with those men. I'm willing to help you so much, but if they're following you, this is your fight. Not mine."

Rojo nodded. Breen let out a sigh. He figured the chief would just shove him over the edge of the cliff, and he'd be feeding buzzards on the rocks below.

"You are true. Mostly." Rojo looked at the two Tonks, then back at Breen. "Not mostly. Only partly. Those flesh eaters, they do not follow me, my brother. They — and the men who pay them for their eyes and noses — have been following you. For a long, long time."

"Howdy."

McCulloch kept slouching, feeling the heat of the sun on his neck. That reminded him of Jed Breen, suffering all that sunburn, now out of his misery, dead, feeding buzzards somewhere back in this god-awful country.

The men stopped in front of the springs. Some were limping. A few of the men pulled no horses behind him.

"Took you long enough," McCulloch said.

"My name's Fatty," the Southerner said, though he was about as fat as any lunger McCulloch had ever seen. "And I'm here to collect the cargo from that greaser."

"Captain Long Juan Sacristán y Santo Seyjó is unloading your supplies as we speak." McCulloch let a finger on his left hand point toward the Rio Grande. "Soon as you pay us for our trouble, the nitro is all yours."

Fatty and a few others straightened.

"Nitro?" one of the men closest to the Southerner called Fatty said. "What's he mean . . . nitro?"

"Nitroglycerin," McCulloch said. "One small bottle, close as you boys have gathered around, should blow you boys all to pieces." He raised his voice. "Isn't that right, Captain?"

From beyond the brambles and high weeds and rocks, the voice of Captain Long Juan Sacristán y Santo Seyjó rang out: "Nitro? *Nitroglycerin? Mon Dieu. Nada.* No. I have whiskey and wine. Salt pork. Black powder, lead, bullet molds. I have tins of sardines and peaches and flour. Nitro. Only a fool would transport such a nasty and dangerous — loco — nitro? Even the river is too treacherous to carry such danger."

McCulloch wet his lips and smiled. "Hell," he said. He thought: *Maybe I guessed wrong.*

Both crutches fell away from McCulloch's sides, and his arms raised. Only then did any of the Holland men notice the revolvers he held in his hands, and both spoke at the same time, and lead tore through both of Fatty's lungs and knocked him four feet back where he landed spread-eagled, and quite dead, between two of the hot springs.

The next shot from the revolver in his left

435

hand punched a hole in the ear of a fat man with a big sombrero, and the slug from Mc-Culloch's Colt slammed the mustached two-gun man on Fatty's left through the belly. By then lead started ripping through the air, and McCulloch was diving. He hit the hot water, touched the bottom, pushed himself up, and felt and heard bullets whining off the rocks. He had dropped the gun in his left hand, but his right was ready. With four shots left.

A killer dressed in black appeared on Mc-Culloch's left. He blinked away the hot water, and tried to twist around, get off a clean shot, but he knew he was too slow, knew the gunman had him dead to rights.

Then the man's face exploded in crimson gore, and he fell forward, deadweight, and landed with a sickening thud. The booming echo of a Springfield carbine made Mc-Culloch smile. Good old Captain Long Juan Sacristán y Santo Seyjó. For a crazy old fool with a wooden leg, that pirate was a good man. Now, McCulloch thought, as he dipped below the water to retrieve the second revolver, hoping that the hot water hadn't fouled up the powder in the chambers. Now . . . if only Sean Keegan can get his Irish arse moving.

Keegan moved on the northern edge of the springs, crouching, and had hoped to get maybe a hundred yards farther, find a good position there in the rocks. But Matt Mc-Culloch, damn his ornery Texas hide, started the ball about fifty yards too soon.

Horses scattered, and men dropped or charged, and one turned and saw Keegan. The man blinked — well, he might have been too far for Keegan to see if he actually blinked, but that's the way he imagined it, and then brought up his repeating rifle. He opened his mouth as though to shout out a warning, and Keegan put a .44-40 bullet through his mouth and blew out his brains.

As fine a shot as any Irishman had made, Keegan figured, one handed, with the stock of the carbine braced against his hip. Let Jed Breen make a shot like that.

Then Keegan had to dive into the brush.

He levered a fresh round into the breech and saw two men getting closer to Matt Mc-Culloch. He couldn't chance that shot with a Winchester, so he laid down McCulloch's fast-shooting gun and brought up the Spencer. He remembered these rifles from the end of the Rebellion. After wetting his thumb, he brushed the moisture on the front sight, and raised the weapon to his shoulder. Apparently, the only person in Holland's bunch who had seen Keegan was the man with a bullet through his mouth and head, and he wasn't telling anyone anything ever again.

Keegan waited . . . waited . . . waited . . . and waited more, a damned hard chore for an Irishman, but his patience paid off. The second man stepped into perfect position, and Keegan touched the trigger.

The bullet took the first man through the back, blew out a fist-sized chunk of this chest, and then punched the second man in the lower back and blew out a hole in his belly. The men twisted, stared, and toppled into the rocks.

Keegan wet his lips. Horses ran toward the river. Holland's men — those still breathing and not ripped to pieces by lead — found cover behind a boulder. And then Keegan's eyes spotted the damnedest thing. A whiskey bottle was flying over the brush by the river, twisting end over end. Jameson? Keegan wondered. Bourbon? Rye? Even tequila would do a fine job right about now.

It sailed in the white sky reached the top of its arc, and came down, silently, twisting, heading right for that big rock. What a waste, Keegan thought. Good whiskey, maybe bad whiskey, but whiskey nonetheless . . . slamming into a rock. Damn, that pirate must be mad, out of bullets and throwing whiskey bottles at these cutthroats.

He hoped that fool Captain Long Juan Sacristán y Santo Seyjó was at least throwing empty bottles.

A moment later, Keegan felt the heat that felt as if it came from the pit of hell.

CHAPTER FORTY-ONE

It was damned hot, this close to the river. So miserable, even the buzzards weren't flying, and if it hadn't been for the stink, Newton S. Bainbridge and his hired killers might have completely missed the two dead Tonks. No, he decided, that would have been impossible. Those scouts were left behind — to be found. Staked out. Stripped naked. Heads bent down over hot coals. The ants and flies were happy.

Even Bainbridge's toughest men lost their breakfast.

"Hell," was all Bainbridge could say. At first. He found the last of his liquor in the saddlebag and somehow managed to get that awful taste out of his mouth.

"Your Jackals didn't do this," one of the men said, after wiping the vomit from his lips with his shirtsleeve.

Another looked up at the ridgeline. "Rojo's bastards might be watchin' us this very minute."

"They might be 'bout to spring an ambush," said the greenest of the bunch.

The parson, Finbar Flinders Fletcher, now riding a good stud horse, giggled. "Why the poor soul doesn't even have good teeth to make a Christian burial fittin' — but then, savage that he was, he likely wasn't a true believer."

"Shut up, Preacher," Bainbridge said and regretted it. His hardened men suddenly saw fear in Bainbridge's eyes and heard uncertainty in his voice.

Thirty minutes later, Bainbridge realized that if nothing had happened at that moment, these men would have deserted him right then and there — a close look at what could happen to a white man or Mexican in Apache country turned a lot of brave men yellow — and everything Bainbridge had planned would have been ruined. But something did happen.

It was the preacher who saw the smoke balloon from off to the southeast. He opened his mouth in awe, but at that moment the ground rocked — two horses whinnied and pulled loose, and Bainbridge no longer saw Fletcher. Bainbridge felt his legs fly out from under him. He had the presence of mind to wrap the reins around his right hand so he would not be afoot. Even when he landed with a crunching jolt on the hard-packed rocks, his upper teeth slamming against the bottoms so hard he wondered how none had been broken — he kept hold of the leather. The last thing he needed was to be caught afoot out here.

About the time pain jarred him from tailbone to neck, he heard the muffled roar.

For minutes, the men — except the two who had lost their mounts — struggled to keep from being stranded. Horses fought. Men cursed. The preacher prayed, legitimately. Then a second explosion rocked the land. A new cloud of smoke, dust, and debris rose in the horizon. Newton S. Bainbridge had not seen smoke like that since the War of the Rebellion. Tightening his grip on the reins in his gloved hand, Bainbridge waited for another roar and plume of smoke, but all he heard was hooves pounding hard rock, men's curses, and the ringing in his ears.

No roar came. The ground stopped quivering, and the smoke began to disappear in the wind. Eventually, his own men stopped cursing, but most of them, keeping their horses close, stared at the dissipating clouds.

"That's from the springs, my flock," Fletcher said, "most like'."

Bainbridge nodded and rose to his feet.

"That ain't no Apache," another hired killer said.

"No." Bainbridge adjusted his hold on the reins and swung into the saddle. "Mount up," Bainbridge ordered. "We're riding to the landing."

"What about us?" asked one of the fools who had lost his mount.

Bainbridge did not even look at the man or the other idiot. "Catch up your horses. You're no good to me afoot." He kicked the skittish horse into a walk and rode toward the hot springs of the Rio Grande. He heard the two men begging to let them ride double, but no one in his right mind would give any thought to carrying extra weight. Not after what they had seen here, with the butchered Tonkawas, and not at what they were riding into ahead at the landing.

"Newton Bainbridge." Jed Breen lifted his right eye above the brass telescope and lowered the Sharps. From his perch, he watched the men ride off. Except for two. When those men finally gave up hope of finding a human being with a shred of human decency among their colleagues, one bolted in the direction of the runaway horses. The other made for the river, probably to swim across, and find shelter in Mexico. The latter, Breen figured, might have a chance.

"Stern Blue Coat," Rojo said, first in Spanish, then in his guttural English.

"Why would he be following us?" Breen asked.

But the Apaches are not ones to guess. When the two men afoot and the men on horses were out of sight, Breen rose to his feet, wet his lips, would have paid a double eagle for a lukewarm glass of beer, and looked into that hard face, and those unreadable eyes of Chief Rojo.

"What do you want from me?"

The Apache must have been expecting that question. "To help us drive the white man in the soldier fort from my land."

"Holland."

"Is how you call him."

Breen found his horse, and shoved the Sharps into the scabbard. "Again, Chief, you could starve him out."

"We are Apaches," Rojo said. "We do not toy with our enemy the way one of your sorry cats toy with a mouse."

"I've never owed a damned cat, Chief." He found his canteen, and drank, and remembered that he had not yet seen one of Rojo's Apaches drink water. After secur-

ing the canteen to his saddle horn, he nod-
ded in the direction of Bainbridge's men.
"What has Bain- . . . What has Stern Blue
Coat been doing?"

"He follow you long time," the Apache
chief said. "Others follow you. He no like.
So he kill them, too."

"Protecting us." Breen didn't like the way
those two words sounded. He shook his
head. "Protecting his daughter?" He let out
a long breath. Rojo wasn't going to offer
any opinion, and none of that mattered now.
He did not know what had caused those
two explosions at the landing. Well, actually,
he did.

He pointed at the remnants of smoke.
"That's nitroglycerin, Chief. Or a hell of a
lot of dynamite. And that's coming from
where the river pirate and my pards are.
And Holland's men might have just blown
my pards to bits because we weren't carrying any . . ." He looked again, and slowly
whispered. "That damned pirate."

Somewhere underneath that choking cloud
of dust, smoke, and gore, Matt McCulloch
cursed savagely, and that made Sean Keegan happy. Stunned, his head spun a mite,
but he was happy.

He could hear.

And McCulloch wasn't dead.

After picking up the Ranger's carbine and the appropriated Spencer, he moved forward, a mite uneasily, but he kept walking. He saw a twisted Henry repeating rifle, smoking like it had been put inside a liveryman's fire and banged into some sort of pretzel. Next he found an arm, the hand still clutching an old cap-and-ball Colt.

From the bank, he saw that crazy old pirate. The one-legged idiot must have waded into the river and fetched his blunderbuss because he carried that in his left hand. His right was empty, and Sean Keegan thanked all the Irish saints for that. It meant old Captain Long Juan wasn't carrying any more of the most volatile explosives known on earth for the time being.

"Matey!" the captain roared. "Come help me get my ship. She's going downstream!"

The explosions must have loosened the moorings.

"Get that sinking tub yourself, blast ye," Keegan shot back, then looked at the sky and shook his head. Blast ye. He was even sounding like the river pirate now.

The Mexican lunatic started shouting, but Keegan, his ears still not completely recovered from the deafening din, managed to drown him out. He looked into one of the

446

steaming springs. McCulloch sat on a stone. Only his head broke the surface of the hot water.

"Comfortable, me lad?" Keegan asked.

McCulloch's head tilted toward Captain Long Juan Sacristán y Santo Seyjó. "You best help our pirate get that raft back here," the Ranger said.

"And why in bloody hell . . . ?"

"Unless Captain Long Juan managed to get that crate of nitro off his ship, it's heading downstream. And if that hits some rapids or runs aground, who knows what kind of hell will be turned loose."

Keegan frowned. He looked around the battlefield. "We might," he conceded, "need that raft to get out of here. Those horses that ain't been blown to bits are running like hell." Then he remembered something. "The freight wagons." Maybe they still had those back where Holland's men had left them at the regular landing. Maybe . . .

"We might need that nitro," McCulloch said. "To finish your damned job."

Keegan nodded and stared again at the former Ranger, sweating in that hot water underneath that hot morning sun. "Want me to pull you out of that misery, Matt?"

To his surprise, McCulloch shook his head. "Actually . . . this doesn't feel too bad. About as good as I've felt since before that damned horse pinned me to the ground." He almost laughed. "I used to think all those folks who bragged about healing waters, the power of the springs, all that stuff that sounded like a grafter trying to sucker someone was . . . you know . . . horse apples. But you should try it."

Keegan snorted. "Maybe if it were a hot toddy." He left McCulloch's Winchester and the extra Spencer within the wet Ranger's reach. "Might take a while to get that raft back. Have to bring it upstream and all."

"It's not like I've got anywhere to go."

Harry Holland pushed open the door to his quarters, picked up the two cups of coffee he had set on the floor, and entered. He did not bother to close the door.

Peering around the corner, Virginia smiled and stepped out, pulling the robe over her body. Holland handed her a cup and sipped his.

"I'll close the door," she said, "in case . . ."

"Don't bother." Holland sipped, turned, and gave her a different sort of smile. "Why don't we go downstairs to eat breakfast?"

She wet her lips, studying him curiously. When he said, "I'm serious. Eat at the dinner table, not up here. Get you some real fresh air."

Now her smile beamed, and she said, "I'll get a covering for my face."

"Don't bother," he told her, and moved back to the open door. When he turned back, he said, "Come along, darlin'. I've got something to show you."

By the time Keegan had pulled McCulloch out of the spring, secured the raft, and soaked his blistered hands in the steaming but soothing water, McCulloch's clothes were practically dry. The desert sun did that all the time.

The river pirate had helped Keegan drag the raft into the weeds, lower the sail and the black flag, so that only a person looking for a raft in the middle of a desert would be able to find it. Well, that was their hope.

Keegan and the captain approached Matt as he tightened the rawhide thongs around his crutches, and finished wiping down and drying off his Colt.

"Captain," McCulloch said, as he began shoving fresh rounds into the revolver. "You trust us?"

"A pirate trust anyone?" Captain Long Juan Sacristán y Santo Seyjó laughed. "Now why should I trust you?"

McCulloch pushed the last cartridge into

449

the cylinder, closed the loading gate, pulled the hammer to full cock, and aimed the revolver at the pirate's chest.

"Aye," Captain Long Juan Sacristán y Santo Seyjó said. "I trust ye like I trust me dearly departed grandmother. She was a nun, ye know? Well, till she wasn't a nun no more."

McCulloch didn't lower the Colt. "We'd like to borrow some of your nitro."

"A pirate shares with 'is mates. It's the law of the seven seas."

"We'd like you to wait for us, too."

"Wait for us?" Keegan's roar almost made McCulloch grimace. "You think this —"

"How long?" the pirate asked.

McCulloch lowered the hammer, holstered the revolver, and looked at the canyon into which some of the frightened horses had disappeared. "Two days. If we're not back in three days, safe sailing."

"My time, mateys, is money."

McCulloch nodded. "How does twenty thousand dollars sound?"

The pirate grinned. "Aye. That, mateys, be more than what I was to be paid for a boat trip to Brownsville."

Chapter Forty-Two

McCulloch drove the wagon, pulling a string of fresh horses behind. Keegan rode a horse alongside the Studebaker.

"No one would blame you," McCulloch told the Irishman, "if you rode ahead or behind a couple hundred yards."

The former horse soldier chuckled and glanced back at the buckboard, noting the two strongboxes with the ransom money and the blanket-wrapped case of nitroglycerin.

"Nobody lives forever, Matt," he said after a minute. "Except us."

But he turned serious after they covered a few more yards. "Seeing that we just killed all those Holland men, how do you expect to find his headquarters?"

"Follow the trail," McCulloch answered.

"What trail?"

The former Texas Ranger nodded ahead. "Four, five of those horses got away. In this country, a horse is like a dog or a cat. Since they galloped away from the river, and since water isn't easy to find in this country, they'll head for home. Holland's boys were smart enough, good enough to cover their tracks coming out of that stronghold. But those horses are leaving a trail that a blind man could follow. Unless it rains." He lifted his head and saw only a pale, ugly sky. "And it's not looking like we'll be getting a soaking here."

McCulloch was right. Once they were out of the river area, moving northeast, the country turned sandy. Keegan had never considered himself much of a tracker, but the hoofprints and horse apples were easy enough for even a drunken Irishman to follow.

"How many men do you reckon we took care of back at the hot springs?" Keegan asked.

"Twelve. Fifteen."

"Aye. That's how I figured it. So that means he must have . . . ?"

"More."

Keegan drew in a deep breath and exhaled. "Odds aren't good."

"Nope." McCulloch flicked the reins. "But we do have nitro."

"Yes, we do, but I wish we had Jed Breen."

A long frown stretched across the old Ranger's face. "Me, too, Sean. Me, too."

"Chief," Breen said. "I'd like to ride ahead. My job should be with my . . . brothers . . ." He couldn't believe he had called Mc-Culloch and Keegan that. "I'd like to protect them."

Rojo just stared straight ahead as he rode on the ridge. "You protect them," he said, "by riding with me. By keeping an eye on those white eyes." He nodded at Newton Bainbridge and his men.

"Oh, my God."

Virginia Bainbridge gasped at the sight inside the cantina. The men . . . she couldn't count how many . . . they were . . .

"They're dead." The words felt strange on her tongue, and she looked away from the ghastly sight of men who had died in utter agony and saw Harry Holland beaming with content.

"Strychnine," he said. "Ranchers use it on wolves."

He took her arm, and pulled her out of the building, closing the door behind him. "Hungry?" he asked.

She shook her head.

"I figured. I'll show you the others." He

led her to the stairs.

For the next hour, McCulloch and Keegan rode without a word. The silence gave Keegan plenty of time to think. So when McCulloch stopped to give the team of mules and the saddle mounts a breather, Keegan sipped water from his canteen, then poured some into his hat to let his horse drink. "There's one thing I can't quite figure out, Matt," he said, letting the horse drink out of his battered old campaign hat.

"What's that?"

"That twenty thousand that we're carrying?" The horse lapped up the last of the water, and Keegan pulled the hat away before that nag tried to eat the felt. "That's a tidy sum for a man like Harry Holland to trust to the kind of men who ride for him."

"You ever wonder why Holland has so many men with him? He's not Quantrill or the Army. He needs that many men to stay alive. Rojo would cut him to pieces. Those men aren't going anywhere with that money except back to their home."

"And," Keegan said, "we're hauling nitro instead to them. Nobody except the most hardened felon — or a damned fool — would want to be close to those boxes."

Keegan thought about his words. "Does

that make us hardened felons or damned fools?"

"Just jackals." McCulloch found his own canteen and drank.

Keegan grinned and busied himself adjusting the cinch on the saddle. After mounting the horse, he removed his hat, wiped sweat off his forehead with his sleeve, and asked, "What do you suppose that lunatic pirate meant when he said he was to get paid for a boat trip to Brownsville?"

"My thinking," McCulloch said, "is that Harry Holland's quitting the territory. Get his twenty thousand bucks, make his way down the river to Brownsville. Once he's on the Gulf coast, he can catch a ship to . . . wherever he wants."

"Aye." Keegan nodded. "Once the colonel got Ginnie back, he'd never rest till he tracked down that scoundrel and killed him."

"And who in his right mind would think that Harry Holland would be floating down the Rio Grande on a raft with a crazy pirate?"

"Holland's smart."

"He's devious," McCulloch said. "To quit his men, to keep that ransom money, he'd also have to figure out how to get away from his men. Don't you reckon?"

■ ■ ■ ■

"Here's what will happen," Holland told Virginia after he shoved the dead sentry over the side. The body fell silently and landed inside the compound with a dull thud that spread dust. He pointed to the slot where the trail led from the canyon to the compound.

"The boys will be coming in." Holland patted the Gatling gun. "And I cut them down like dogs."

"There are fifteen of them," Virginia pointed out.

"Not after I hit the wagon with the nitro they're bringing."

"What about the money?" she snapped. "You going to blow it up, too?"

"The money will be back, far back, safe," Holland explained. "While I'm gunning down the boys hauling the explosives, you'll pick off the driver of the wagon filled with your daddy's money with a Remington Rolling Block. That's one thing I admire about your pa, darling. He taught you how to shoot."

Picturing the carnage, she seemed to wet her lips. The gleam in her eyes died, though, and she said, "But what about . . . those . . .

Apaches." Her Adam's apple swallowed.

"Rojo just wants me gone. I'll be gone. And I'll pay him five thousand for the trouble. He gets all the livestock here, the horses, the ammunition. He lets me and you ride out of here."

"Can you trust him?"

"Apaches have one thing folks like me and you don't have. Honor. But if he and his boys look like they want to lift our hair, we'll drink on it. Just like the boys had their champagne."

He didn't know how she would react, but her laugh soothed him. Virginia was as bad as he was . . . down to the core.

"Come on, darling," Holland said. "We need to move the dead bodies into the root cellar. So the buzzards don't give us away."

CHAPTER FORTY-THREE

Chief Rojo raised his hand and pulled his pony to a stop, so Breen did the same. The Apaches behind him stopped their horses, too, and the leader nodded at a small deer trail that appeared to lead from the ridgeline to the canyon below.

Without a word, most of the warriors turned their horses and began moving single file toward the path. It was not a ride that Jed Breen wanted to make, but he neck-reined the gelding and moved toward the line, stopping only when Rojo said, "No."

Looking at the fierce leader, Breen saw one other Apache move toward his chief. Breen thought Rojo must have been speaking to that brave, but the leader beckoned Breen forward with his finger.

"You and me . . . we ride farther."

Breen nudged his horse toward the two Indians. He hoped the next trail down the slope would be a mite easier than the one

Rojo's men were descending.

"Harry!" Virginia Bainbridge screamed.

Swearing, he tossed off the blankets, climbed out of bed, pulled on his britches, found a revolver, slid his bare feet into sandals, and left the bedroom for the rooftop where Virginia had stepped out to enjoy the fresh air with her morning coffee.

She stood near the Gatling gun, pointing at the trail below.

Thinking Fatty and the boys had made good time, he hurried to the Gatling. Virginia wasn't ducking, wasn't hurrying to get that Remington Rolling Block, and she called out, "Something happened."

When he reached the edge, he saw the lathered horses, below, worn out. A saddle was hanging on the pinto's side. The chestnut and the sorrel both had lost their saddles. One of them looked as though its heart would burst right then and die.

Something happened. That was damned sure.

He studied the trail, found the binoculars the sentries used, and looked even closer. When he was finally convinced there was no one where the trail began, he said, "You remember how this baby works." He patted the Gatling.

"Yes," she said.

"All right. We might have to change our plans. Instead of you shooting that Rolling Block. I'm going down to bring in the horses. If someone shows up out there, kill 'em."

"What if it's Fatty and the boys?"

"Kill 'em. Shoot them down like dogs."

"But the money . . . If that nitro blows up . . ."

"Just kill 'em. We'll worry about the money later."

It was cool here, but Harry Holland had started to sweat.

The Reverend Fletcher, the best scout remaining, said the wagon was a half-mile ahead. Two men. The crippled one and the soldier.

"No Jed Breen?" Newton Bainbridge asked.

"Just 'em two. Gimp's drivin' the wagon, the drunk's on a saddle mount. Pullin' out now."

"Is my money with 'em?"

"Three boxes in the back of the wagon."

"Three?" Bainbridge frowned. "There should be just two strongboxes."

"There's three, Brother Newton." Fletcher grinned. "The two you give 'em. Which I'm sure would be a fine tithe to any collection plate. The other, it's wooden, best I could tell. And that crazy-arse sergeant, he was wrapping one of 'em carefully with thick blankets."

The bourbon in Bainbridge's belly soured. He knew what that meant. He knew what those jackals had used back at the hot springs to kill all those men. Nitro. Damned nitroglycerin. But he damn well wasn't going to mention that to his men. They'd turn tail and run, the yellow dogs. Even the preacher. And Bainbridge was too close to revenge to fail now, so he forced a grin, shook his head and said. "Keegan. That drunk. He'll do anything to protect his whiskey."

"Amen." But Fletcher's eyes told Bainbridge that the preacher/killer knew what had been used at the hot springs.

Lying on his belly, Breen peered at the adobe and stone fort below through the brass telescopic sight on his Sharps. He hadn't been able to see anything with only moonlight, but now that dawn was breaking over the rugged, ugly mountains, he had a better view.

Yet he still saw . . . nothing.

Horses — some of them looking like they

were played out and half dead — wandered about the compound. Other animals — horses, mules, goats, oxen, cattle — were corralled. There were cannons and a Gatling gun.

"Holland should have men here," he said, whispering for he did not know how far his voice might carry in the cool breeze in this remote country. "I don't see . . ."

His voice trailed off and he swung the rifle around. He stared intently, finally lowering the rifle, and looking at Chief Rojo.

"Son of a —" Breen said. "She's kissing him."

McCulloch found a way to get from the back of the wagon into the driver's box. He set his crutches beside him and looked over at Keegan.

"Two six-shooters won't do you much good," he said. "Why don't you leave me that Schofield you stole?"

"Didn't steal it." Keegan smiled, drew the big .45 from his waistband, and handed it, butt-forward, to his pard. "Spoils of war. That's what the colonel called it."

"While you were burning Georgia?"

Keegan unfastened the flat of the holster. "You want my Remington, too?"

The Ranger shook his head. "No. You

might need it. That .45 and my Colt should be all I'd get to use anyway. And I've got the Winchester, too."

Nodding, Keegan took the key to one of the strongboxes, opened it, found a jingling pouch, and tossed it onto the bench beside McCulloch. He left the key in the padlock and climbed down from the back of the wagon, took his horse, and led it to the side. The other horses they had hobbled in the shade in the crook of the canyon, which spread out before them with about a hundred yards of open land before a beige and brown fortress surrounded by mountain rock.

Now McCulloch knew how the Apaches had never been able to drive Harry Holland's bunch out of this country. Short of laying siege, there wasn't much of a way for an Indian to get inside that impenetrable fort. But a couple of jackals?

"You think this is a good idea?" Keegan asked.

McCulloch shook his head. "It's the only idea I got."

The former horse soldier looked at the path that led up the ridge on the south. "Figure it'll take me an hour to get a good spot."

McCulloch found the sun. "All right."

"Want to switch places?" the Irishman asked.

Laughing without humor, McCulloch said, "I can't do much climbing. Hell, I barely got on this bench. I'll drive the wagon up to the gate. I tell them if they want the money, then send out the girl. When they do that, I get down and walk away with her. When they get near the wagon . . ."

"I shoot the crate of nitro." Keegan shook his head.

"That should blow most of them to bits and knock that gate down. I knock the girl to the ground, and with you up high, and me with two six-guns, my Winchester and that Spencer, we should be able to wipe them out."

"I'd feel better if we had Breen shooting that crate."

"Hell," McCulloch said, "so would I."

"When you have Ginnie," Keegan said, "move as fast as you can, pard."

"I'll run like a Thoroughbred, pal. Don't worry about me."

Keegan took a canteen from the back of the wagon, nodded, stuck the Springfield under his shoulder and held out his hand.

"Luck," he said.

They shook and Keegan made for the trail.

"Sean." The Irishman turned and looked at the Ranger. "Shoot that crate. Even if I ain't far enough away from it. That's our only chance to save Virginia."

"Halloooooo!"
Holland spun away from Virginia, and both dropped to the hard-packed adobe roof.
"We got your money! Send out the girl!"
They eyed each other, wet their lips, and then crept the few yards to the edge of the rooftop. Holland moved to the rifle port, keeping his head down, and looked outside. Virginia picked up the heavy Remington rifle.
"It's . . ." Holland paused, finding this impossible to comprehend. "It's just one man. In a buckboard."
Virginia cocked the rifle.
"It's . . ." Holland pulled away from the gunport and looked at Virginia. "That rock-hard Ranger. McCulloch." He looked again through the opening, scanning the land beyond the wagon. Again, he turned to face his lover. "Grab the binoculars." He peered at the Ranger. "That sorry-ass snake killed my kid brother."
"If you don't send her out, Holland, I'm keeping this money for myself." Again, Hol-

land looked through the gun port. Now he saw the Ranger tossing up a brown leather pouch, catching it in his hand, and sending it a few feet high again. He could hear the jingling inside.

"Holland!" the Ranger called.

Harry Holland took a chance and rose.

"Hell."

Keegan had managed to make his way about a hundred yards above a balcony of granite, but he was still about four hundred feet from the top. And looking down, he saw the wagon. He could even hear McCulloch's voice calling out.

Turning, Keegan unlimbered the Springfield and braced himself. He might make his way back down to the flat stones, but he might not. This was as good a place as any, he figured. He had a clear view of McCulloch and the gate.

He wiped sweat from his brow and waited.

"I still don't see anyone but one man and that girl," Breen said.

Rojo did nothing but provide a noncommittal grunt.

Newton Bainbridge grabbed his binoculars.

"Gate's open," Finbar Flinders Fletcher,

466

that evil parson, said, "and paradise is on the other side."

"Someone's stepping out," another replied.

Bainbridge looked through the binoculars, finding McCulloch first, at least his back, and then the figure walking through the fort's gate. He went past that person and swept a soldier's look over the walls. He could see a man looking through one of the portholes. But no one stood by the Gatling gun. No one manned the cannons. No fires came from the chimneys or the firepits in the compound.

A Mexican curse whispered to Bainbridge's left, followed by, *"La puta."*

That's when Bainbridge brought the binoculars down. He focused on the figure heading toward McCulloch and the wagon . . . the gold money and the explosives . . . He saw her face. The face stopped moving, and the binoculars lowered for just a moment. He could see the figures, the woman about twenty yards in front of the wagon. He peered through the binoculars again and saw her . . . The face of his daughter . . . the tramp who had betrayed him for a two-bit outlaw.

"There's no one in the fort," he said, "but Holland." He shoved the binoculars into his case, drew his revolver, and bellowed, "Charge!"

CHAPTER FORTY-FOUR

Holland dared not raise his head. Instead he yelled through the gun port. "How do I know you've got the money?"

The big man in the wagon found the crutches and pushed himself to his feet. He raised the pouch and tossed it up, caught it.

"I can bring this one for you to look at." He tossed the pouch again, balancing on the crutches, looking at the parapet, but now began speaking to Virginia Bainbridge.

"Keep walking. This'll be over soon. Just keep walking as far from this wagon as you can. There are horses hobbled just beyond where the canyon begins. How many men are inside?"

The girl whispered. "Just one."

"One?" McCulloch looked away from the fort and at the lovely girl.

"He . . ." She sobbed. "He . . . poisoned the others . . . It . . . It was . . . a terrible thing."

McCulloch had to make himself look away. He tossed the pouch again. "Holland." When the pouch landed beyond the girl, he yelled. "Come out and see for yourself." Then to the girl. "Just keep walking. Hurry."

He watched her come toward him, before turning to focus on the parapet. "Holland!" No answer. The girl stopped. He wanted to tell her to keep moving. No, she was moving, just not walking. She was pulling a double-action revolver from the small of her back — and aiming it right at McCulloch's midsection.

"Charge!"

The word sounded ghostly, far away, but it had to echo across the canyon.

Keegan turned, blinked, and almost dropped the Springfield to the rocks below. A soldier galloped out of the opening to the canyon, sending a trail of dust rising. And a few moments later, more horsemen thundered.

"Follow me, boys!" The echo bounced across the foreboding landscaped. *Boys . . . boys . . . boys . . . boys . . .*

"Give them hell!" *Hell . . . hell . . . hell . . . hell . . .*

"And give us glory!"

The riders behind the colonel — for the man leading this charge was none other than Colonel Newton S. Bainbridge — followed him. You serve with a man like that for all those years, Keegan knew, and you can spot him from a quarter mile away. How he sat in the saddle. How he handled a horse. How he rode like the fanciful image plastered on the cover of a dime novel.

Breen had been watching the man on the roof, but now swung his Sharps toward the woman. If that man stretched out near the Gatling gun and staring out of what appeared to be a gun port was Harry Holland, then that woman might be Virginia Bainbridge. But if she had been kissing Holland . . . ?

He found her through his telescopic sight. She seemed to be walking past McCulloch. Maybe she was all right. Maybe she was going to the canyon. But where was Sean Keegan? That Irishman couldn't be dead.

He thought, and asked, still peering through the telescopic sight: "Chief, that trail you pointed out, the one you said leads to the floor. Not the one where your braves went down . . . Where does that lead to?"

"Just before the canyon ends."

"Easy to find?"

"Even a white eye could find it."

Breen started to laugh, but the woman he saw was palming something, bringing it up, aiming it at McCulloch.

McCulloch was turning around, seeing the gun in the woman's hand, then hearing someone behind him yell: "Charge!"

The woman heard it, too, looked away, and McCulloch took that moment to dive on the far side of the wagon. He moved like a man with a badly busted leg, a man who hadn't slept worth a damn in days, and a man who was bone tired from a series of violent events. He hit the brake lever as he fell off the wagon, heard a pistol roar, drowned out by the thunder of hooves.

When he slammed into the dirt, pain sliced from his bad leg, and now his shoulder, head, and neck hurt, and he spit out dirt as he rolled over on hard rocks. Somehow, though, he heard a faraway gunshot, and a bullet hit near him. Through the spokes of the wagon's front wheels, he saw Virginia Bainbridge sitting on her arse, the pistol smoking in her right hand, then turning to look up the ridge, and back toward the sound of thundering hooves.

"Noooooo!" he thought he heard her scream. "It . . . It's . . . Father!"

The spokes of the wheels moved, and Mc-Culloch saw the rear wheels, then nothing but the woman, who sprang to her feet and yelled up at the fort's flat roof.

"It's . . . him!"

"Oh . . ." Keegan said.

Breen said: "Hell." And he hurriedly reloaded the Sharps.

Holland stood. He watched the panicked team pull the wagon toward the gate, only to turn, the wagon lurching, then moving toward the charging raiders, carrying with it the thousands of dollars he was supposed to have for himself . . . and with Virginia . . . at least for a while. His eyes found the pouch the Ranger McCulloch had thrown. Virginia started running toward the treacherous mountain, and the leader of those charging fools turned his horse, bearing down on Virginia.

"This is not how this is supposed to happen," he heard himself say. Reason took hold again. Sanity. He saw the Gatling gun, and knew if he wanted to get out of this alive, he had to act . . . now. He still had a chance. To get the money, and kill that damned brother-murdering Texas Ranger.

Hearing the hooves of the wagon's team, the screeching wheels, the rattle of the strongboxes, Matt McCulloch covered his head, and tried to bury himself deep in the earth — which was like trying to dig an inch out of bedrock.

Bainbridge was bearing down on the woman. Keegan couldn't figure out what his commanding officer was doing, why he was even here. He cringed when the wagon shot past the woman. He tried to find Mc-Culloch, but he couldn't see through the dust. But he saw some of the men — the men riding for Colonel Bainbridge loping toward where the wagon had been. Then he saw good old Matt, doing the sensible thing, trying to keep himself safe . . . for if that wagon blew up.

"Glory be to God," the Reverend Finbar Flinders Fletcher said. That wagon . . . that beautiful runaway wagon, filled with more gold than he'd ever find on the proverbial streets of gold, was riding straight to him.
He saw it coming. Coming right for him.
"Thank you, God!" he cried out.

■ ■ ■ ■

A bullet kicked up dirt against Matt's boot heel, and he rolled over. That shot had to come from behind. From whoever was riding out of that canyon.

Dust then swept across the flat.

The man who had to be Harry Holland was sprinting for the Gatling gun. He reached the lethal weapon and spun it in the direction of Matt McCulloch.

Breen swore and pulled back the heavy hammer of the Sharps.

"Aye. Judas Iscariot and Benedict Arnold all rolled into one." Keegan aimed the Springfield. He couldn't understand why that wagonload of thunder hadn't blown up by now, fast as that wagon was moving.

He lost sight of the woman and the colonel. Two riders were closing in on Matt, but Keegan knew he'd never hit them. The wagon, though, that was a much bigger target. And he figured his bullet didn't have to hit the wooden crate. This was like horseshoes. Just get close.

He also wanted to time this right.

He waited, following the wagon, looking

down the sights of his carbine but making sure he saw the main body of Bainbridge's wagon, led by a man on a fine horse. And when the riders were bisecting the runaway wagon . . . Keegan touched the trigger.

Harry Holland swung the Gatling gun around. He could kill McCulloch and those two riders easily. Then mow down the rest. And if the girl got shot by accident, well, there was always another girl waiting for him . . . in France.

For one brief moment, the Reverend Finbar Flinders Fletcher felt like he was Elijah, riding a chariot of fire in a whirlwind, bound for heaven. Yet the brief agony of pain told him he was headed in the other direction.

Heat blasted over him, singeing his hair, burning his neck. Matt McCulloch thought to himself: *God, don't let me look as badly burned as Jed Breen.*

Small rocks pelted McCulloch's back and pounded his arms and hands that covered his head. His ears rang. He tasted dirt and sweat and unnatural smoke. He counted ten, and back down to zero, just to make sure he could think. Still unable to hear anything, he rolled onto his back. Hell, he couldn't even feel how badly that must have hurt his busted leg. He saw dust and flames. He blinked.

The woman was nowhere to be seen. But it wasn't like McCulloch could see anything.

One man staggered out of the dirt, and vaguely, McCulloch figured that had to be one of the two men riding toward him. His left arm was busted. His right ear appeared to have been burned off. His clothes were smoking. Another man — the second rider, perhaps — appeared behind him.

The first man stopped. In his good hand, he held a pistol. He brought that up and aimed it straight at McCulloch.

McCulloch didn't remember cocking the Schofield. But he saw it in his right hand, and he felt the pistol buck, saw the man fall flat on his back, and then turned to shoot the second man if he gave him cause. He did. But the Schofield refused to cooperate.

"You killed my pard."

At least I'm not deaf, McCulloch thought. *I might be dead. But I can still hear.*

Keegan landed on the platform, those hundreds of feet from where he had perched himself to make that killing shot, having slid all the way down. He saw the Springfield bounce across the flat stone, stop at the edge, twist like a ballerina, then fall over the side.

His butt hurt. The heels had been torn off both of his boots. His left earlobe was bleeding, all the fingers on his right hand were jammed. He coughed, spit out a molar, and wondered if he would ever be able to walk.

Spitting out blood, he coughed again, and said, "Maybe that wasn't such a brilliant battle plan, me lad."

Pushing himself to his feet, Newton Bainbridge staggered, looked for his pistol, his saber. "Sergeant Major Reinhart!" he called, shook his head, spit, and leaned against a wall of cold granite. No, something told him, Reinhart had died at Antietam. "Sergeant . . . Keegan."

He cursed, blinked, and saw the flames, the sickening sight, some of his men staggering back toward the canyon, toward the horses they had found hobbled. Suddenly, other riders poured out of the mouth of the canyon.

Bainbridge felt sick when he realized who these new riders were.

"Apaches," he whispered. "God. It's . . . Rojo's savages."

He spun, saw the trail, a small trail for mountain goats or deer, but that was his only way out of this death trap. He didn't care about the money. About Virginia or Harry Holland. The Apaches would deliver Bainbridge's revenge to those two miserable pieces of swine. All Bainbridge wanted to do was live.

So he began to climb.

My God, he thought . . . I have to climb . . . climb . . . climb really high.

Harry Holland caught a glimpse of Virginia running along the edge of the mountain, heading toward the canyon. He figured he was the only one who could see her. He considered turning the crank, but decided to let her live. The Indians charging to pick off the Bainbridge men who hadn't been blown to bits didn't see her. Her damned fool father hadn't seen her. She might make it, but Holland doubted it. He figured he wouldn't make it out of here, either — all his great plans ruined. Somehow. He didn't know how everything had gone to hell. And he would soon be going to hell. But he would take the man who killed his brother with him.

Holland swung the barrel of his Gatling gun toward that miserable Ranger, that Jackal, Matt McCulloch himself, sitting in the dirt, holding a smoking pistol, turning his head and looking straight up at Holland.

"Raise your pistol!" Holland jeered. "I'm not in your range. But you're in mine, Ranger."

He bent forward. Laughed. Started turning the crank, but stopped because a spray of blood was splattering across the brass of the gun. Holland turned around, looked at the ridge above him. Something was running down the back of his head, messing up his thick hair. His fingers came away from his forehead, sticky with something, but Harry Holland couldn't see anything.

But he could remember, for just a second. He could remember when he had first met Chief Rojo and welcomed him to his fort.

"You could be trapped here," Rojo said. "Pinned down. Starved out. One man on that ridge could take potshots at you. Drive you crazy till the thirst drove you into our hands."

"Yeah," Holland had said. "You could. But Apaches don't fight that way. And no white man has the guts to come into this country and try it."

The man on the parapet pushed away from the Gatling gun, looking up, moving like a puppet controlled by a five-year-old. For a second, through the telescopic sight of the

Sharps rifle, Jed Breen thought that man, Harry Holland or whoever it was, might be staring straight at Breen himself. Still standing. After a bullet had gone into the back of his head out of the forehead.

The human body, Breen realized, was an amazing thing.

A moment later, Holland's body fell off the rooftop and landed in front of the open gate.

Newton S. Bainbridge reached up, found the handhold, and pulled himself to the flat rock. He was out of breath, but he had made it. He was scared, feared he'd fall to his death, but so far, somehow, he was alive. He came to his knees, struggled for breath, and rose. He started to laugh, praised his resourcefulness, knowing he had outfoxed everyone. Until he saw more granite, and as he raised his head, he understood that he had a long, hard climb ahead of him.

He also saw something else . . . *someone* else . . . a white man staring at him.

"Keegan."

"Aye, Colonel." The sergeant major stepped toward him.

"Sergeant." His eyes saw the canteen hanging over Keegan's shoulder. "Sergeant, I need your help. Let me explain. I can —"

He swung his fist, a solid haymaker, but that drunken Irish lout ducked like he had been in a hundred barroom brawls. The momentum carried Bainbridge around. He felt like he was a wobbling spinning top, and he tripped, tried to kick out in Keegan's general direction, but then he felt nothing but air. Just the way those nightmares had awakened him as a boy.

He tried to pull himself back to the granite, felt his boot slip, and then he knew he was falling.

A hand grabbed his blouse.

Bainbridge felt as though he were suspended in midair.

He caught his breath, lifted his head, saw Keegan's right hand gripping his tunic, saw the Irishman's cold, hard eyes.

"Keegan!" he yelled. "Pull me up."

"What were ye doin', Colonel, sir?" Keegan demanded.

"Helping . . . Helping you."

"What were ye doin', ye maggot?"

Bainbridge tried to swallow. Couldn't. His left hand clawed at the slick rock for a handhold that wasn't there. His right reached up for Keegan's arm.

"I . . ." Bainbridge closed his yes. "That rebellious girl I brought up . . . she ran off with that killer. She ran off . . . I had . . .

I . . . couldn't."

"Ginnie?" Keegan demanded.

"She's rotten . . . like her ma . . . like those — the ones who kicked me out of the Army. Like . . ."

"Ye set us up. Me and me pards. Ain't that the way this was, Newton?"

Bainbridge wanted to beg. He wanted to claw the Irishman's eyes out.

Then he remembered. Keegan was Army to the boots. He couldn't do anything but obey orders.

"Sergeant," he tried. "I order you to pull me up."

He saw Keegan's eyes soften, maybe tear up. Then he saw the fist that clutched his tunic, the swollen misshapen knuckles, the blood and scars. He saw the hand open wide, as if waving at Colonel Newton S. Bainbridge, as he fell, screaming as he sped down to the rocks below, and the hell beneath the rocks.

CHAPTER FORTY-FIVE

They laid McCulloch in the back of one of the wagons from inside Harry Holland's fort, his leg and other injuries treated with the Apache holy man's herbs and mud packs, and the smoke blown into Mc-Culloch's face. It wasn't much of a wagon, more oxcart than anything else, but Breen figured that since they had the cart and three horses, that would be enough to get them to the Rio Grande.

"This is for you," Rojo said, and tossed Breen the pouch. It jingled, and Breen stuck it in McCulloch's left hand.

"You gonna live?" Breen whispered.

The pouch jingled. "If the whiskey this buys us don't kill me," McCulloch said.

"That's all of Bainbridge's reward that's left," Breen said. "Thanks to that damned Irishman. Unless you want to mine for bits in this country."

"Let's leave this country to Rojo's boys,"

McCulloch said.

Breen smiled. "I'll be back." He climbed out of the cart and nodded at Rojo.

"You will not remember how you found this place," the Apache said.

"No need," Breen said. "Since it won't be here after you're done with it."

Rojo smiled. Already his men were herding out the animals. The dead had been moved into the disturbing room that had been filled with many other dead men. Poisoned by the looks of them. Harry Holland must have gone mad, but this land could drive anyone mad. Like a riverboat pirate. Anyone . . . but an Apache.

"Thanks, Chief. I'd shake your hand but . . ."

"Go." Rojo kicked his pony into a walk.

And Breen walked to the edge of the ridge, where Sean Keegan stood over one body they had not moved.

"Wasn't your fault, Sean," Breen said. "You tried. But with that hand." He nodded at the hand wrapped in leather skins that stank something awful, but that the Apache medicine man said would mend quickly. "You just couldn't have saved his life." Besides, Breen figured, Keegan would have just been saving the colonel for the gallows.

"Nay." Keegan turned away. "His life," he whispered, "wasn't worth saving."

After Keegan climbed into the cart, Breen mounted his horse, and took the lead rope from a young warrior and began riding toward the canyon.

Suddenly, McCulloch asked, "What the hell happened to that woman?"

At the hot springs midafternoon of the next day, Keegan saw the river pirate's thunder gun. It was sticking out of the weeds, buried in the river bottom up to its trigger guard.

"Raft's gone!" he called out above the buzz of flies.

"Guess that damned fool got tired of waiting," McCulloch yelled.

"Yeah." Keegan reached into the widened barrel of the old weapon, and pulled out the piece of parchment. He used that to wave off the flies as he moved back to the horses, his pards, and the oxcart.

The paper he handed to Breen.

McCulloch leaned against the rough wooden wall of the wagon. "Well," he said.

Breen shook his head and handed it to McCulloch. "It's in Spanish."

After scanning it for a few minutes, McCulloch said, "My Spanish has its limits, boys, but the best I can make out is that the captain says: " 'Mateys, if you are not dead' . . . and there's stuff . . . here I don't think are even Spanish words, but this is *'puta'* . . .''

"That'd be Ginnie," Keegan said softly.

McCulloch frowned. "And this is *'oro.'* "

"Gold," Breen said. "Even I know that."

"You would," McCulloch said, and he shook his head. "My best ciphering says the captain is taking the *puta* instead of the *oro,* and if I'm reading it right, he says they are sailing for Port Royal."

He handed the paper to Breen. "That's the best I can do."

"Way the sign reads," Keegan said, "I don't think Ginnie fancied the idea."

"That's a pity," Breen said. "Well . . . maybe not."

"She was as rotten as her daddy," Keegan said.

"Then I guess I'll call it justice," McCulloch said. "Though I hope Captain Long Juan doesn't get careless."

"Well," Breen said, "I think we should head back to Purgatory City before Rojo changes his mind."

"I got a better idea." McCulloch tossed the pouch to Keegan.

"Aye?" the Irishman asked.

"We cross the river here. Head west about

six miles. There's a cantina there. Been there for fifteen years. We drink ourselves into a stupor until my leg heals, the money runs out, or the two of your brains finally form. What the hell was this plan?"

Breen smiled, took the pouch from Keegan, and mounted his horse. "I like that plan, Matt."

"What the hell!" Keegan snapped. "That last plan, that assault on Holland's fort, that wasn't mine, laddies." He jabbed his finger at McCulloch. "It be yourn."

"It worked," McCulloch said. "Didn't it?"

They were still laughing, all three of them, when they crossed the Rio Grande and into Mexico.

ABOUT THE AUTHORS

William W. Johnstone has written nearly three hundred novels of western adventure, military action, chilling suspense, and survival. His bestselling books include *The Family Jensen; The Mountain Man; Flintlock; MacCallister; Savage Texas; Luke Jensen, Bounty Hunter;* and the thrillers *Black Friday, The Doomsday Bunker,* and *Trigger Warning.*

J. A. Johnstone learned to write from the master himself, Uncle William W. Johnstone, with whom J. A. has co-written numerous bestselling series including The Mountain Man; Those Jensen Boys; and Preacher, The First Mountain Man.